I0727043

Also by
Brandon Rolfe

Countdown To Doomsday
The Analyst
The Dromyrk File
Checkpoint
Betrayal

GHOSTWATCH

Brandon Rolfe

Published by Dolman Scott Ltd in 2023

ISBN:

POD: 978-1-915351-13-5

eBook: 978-1-915351-14-2

Published by
DolmanScott
www.dolmanscott.co.uk

In most precious memory of:

Annita

1

The Israeli IAI Kfir Mirage 111 bomber-fighter thundered on, tearing through the sky at 600m.p.h., its great seabird 'plumage' bristling with 30mm Defa cannon and Rafael Shafrir-2 air-to-air missiles, its General Electric J79-GE-17 turbojet engines screaming out in fury with 21,500lb thrust, rippling the cold air with 0.7 Mach anger. Sunbeams tickled the great bird's belly and pounded its beak, with others exploding into diamonds of coloured light on the glass-fibre wing tips and around a Perspex canopy, where two helmets bobbed and turned. The pilot helmet's white arrow turned 90 degrees to starboard as trained eyes looked out, darting about behind the rubber mask in overall check along the wing to the glistening rods at the engine nacelles, where sun lingered, but dared not enter, avoiding churning by roaring turbine blades. Swinging its convoluted oxygen mask round like a wrinkled proboscis, the head turned to look to port.

Looking down from 300ft above sea level, the same expert eyes watched sand, sand, and more sand of the great Sinai Desert rushing past. At 08.28hrs precisely, the intelligence signal had come in first to Hatzerim Israeli Air Force Base, reporting that EL AL's civilian passenger Flight 231 had gone down south of the Zin Desert stretch, just off the northern tip of Sinai Desert's western plain. Passing the signal to Ovda Air Base, no precious moments had been lost in sending the Mirage, codename ALBATROSS, racing out on Amber Alert priority.

This was part of Israeli Air Force Strike Force Command and as such, patrolled in 'friendly' conjunction alongside NATO's Baltic/Greenland maritime air-arm. Presently patrolling the water far below was the 22,000tons HMS Coventry, equipped with conventional and nuclear missiles, along with three Sea King helicopters and three Harriers, to investigate, and intercept, any instances of 'hostile influence' by the Soviet Bloc's Baltic Fleet. The Mirage passed over it, the pilot checking the chronometer dial. Nearly there.

Sun-drenched white desert slid past rapidly, the sands glistening below, nearer and nearer. The pilot's head bent over the Lockheed Red Fox radar screen, checking the electronic land map, while relaying his position into the rubber mask: 'Passing Kadesh-Barnea, CONTROL. About four minutes more and we'll be bang on bullseye. Changing twenty-three degrees west.'

Tipping the wing ailerons with the electric-hydraulic actuators, he swung the plane round smoothly to follow the narrow spinal route on the silver screen. For an awkward, annoying, few seconds, flocks of birds that hadn't been there, suddenly *were* there, squawking and frapping in alarm at the great monster bird that was tearing through their midst.

Crackling radio static interrupted his tense concentration with the birds: 'CONTROL calling ALBATROSS. Do you read me, Albatross? Do you read me?'

'Loud and clear, CONTROL.'

'What is your position, ALBATROSS?'

The pilot looked down at the sands sparkling gleefully, then at the silver screen. 'Just passing over co-ordinates 36/57. Leaving Moab, east of Kadesh-Barnea, heading towards Zin Desert stretch. It should lie between Zin and Ezion-Geber. Can't see anything yet – must be further on, nearer to Gulf of Aquaba, maybe.'

But it was further west, just north east of the tip of the Paran Desert stretch.

'Can you see PIGEON yet, ALBATROSS?'

'Not yet, CONTROL. The angle's too sharp at this level. Don't want to fly any higher and smudge somebody's radar.'

'Very well, ALBATROSS. Report as soon as you sight PIGEON. Back-up on the way.'

'Will do, CONTROL.' He watched the co-ordinates slide past on the silver screen.

CONTROL's promised support appeared as two dots in the sky far behind the Mirage. Growing larger by the second, two F-15 Eagle jet-fighters, sent up from Palmahir Air Base, south of Tel Aviv, were catching up fast. Flanking the bomber-fighter right and left, they closed in on it. Giving a thumb-up to the other pilots, the Mirage pilot had his great 'seabird' swooping down for a scavenger's closer look at 100ft. The two fighters climbed up steeply into the sky, banking over and circling round as the Mirage went below. It screeched down and over the sun-drenched sands with thundering fury --- and there it was.

Bereft of its right wing, and very much its former dignity, the El AL Israel Airlines passenger airliner, in its bright, alas, torn, company logo 'plumage' of red, gold and green, lay like a giant prize game-bird that had indeed been felled by those illegally 'out of season' 12 bore Merkel shotgun pellets. Twisted wing pieces, gleaming and smooth, fitted the scene like discarded broken bones. One of the Boeing 707's huge Pratt & Whitney JT3D turbofan engines poked out from beneath the mangled wing, sounding its great banshee howl no more. 'Entrails' spilling out and scattered all around were not all fuselage pieces – the bodies having their own unique *dead* look.

From high up in the sky, tiny figures scrambling over the wreckage looked hardly more serious than romping children on a treasure hunt. But instead of carrying wooden pirate swords, they attacked the plane with oxy-acetylene torches and heavy-duty cutters, working away steadily and interrupted only for seconds to look up in fright as the 600m.p.h screech overhead shattered their eardrums.

The blue beacons flashed on the roofs of the rescue vehicles trundling off and replaced by others, like a herd of pukka elephants, in a hurrying shuttle line of mercy from the scene of the plane crash. Not that there was much mercy, other than the spiritual kind, that could be given to those inert bizarrely-postured lumps of ex-life.

A sudden isolated blink of light some distance off caught the pilot's attention. Binoculars!

Forgetting the commotion below, he banked the Mirage up steeply into the sky, going into a tight turn, blocking out the view the tiny rescue figures scrambling about below. The whole of the Sinai Desert below spun round in silent carousel.

'ALBATROSS calling CONTROL. Do you read me, CONTROL?'

'CONTROL receiving you. Go ahead, ALBATROSS.'

'Bandits sighted. Repeat, bandits sighted. Two armoured troop-carriers, judging by their shape. Rapidly approaching wreckage site.'

'From what you're saying, sounds like the Russian BTR-15 with 7.6mm machine guns, for Syrian anti-Zionist terrorist group led by Hien Yaffou. Last 'shadowed' to pick-up point to equip with ground-to-air missile unit. We suspected Flight 625, Ben Gurion to Munich's Riem Airport, to be the target, but we got that wrong--- terribly wrong. It was the Ben Gurion to Dusseldorf's Lohausen Airport flight they intended to bring down.'

'*Dusseldorf*? So, what the hell is it doing down here south-west in Asia, when it should be heading north-east to Germany?'

'Scant intelligence coming in at the moment is that it was hijacked.'

The radio pipped patiently during CONTROL's hesitant silence before coming alive again: 'Don't let the bastards get away, ALBATROSS. Repeat: don't let the bastards get away. You have full permission to intercept, ALBATROSS.'

'Understood, CONTROL Going in now.'

'Good luck, ALBATROSS.'

Swooping round for another dive, the Mirage pilot prepared to fire an air-to-ground missile. Distance was too short for visual guidance by the missile's aft end flares. Operating the Ferranti Airpass-11 computerised radio command-link lock-on, he watched the display screen and fired the missile. Rocketing away from the wing with fire-ball fury it homed in on its target, while the plane curved away. Tearing into the 9mm thick welded steel plating, the 300lb warhead exploded the first vehicle, showering the other one with body shrapnel.

This time the rescue workers stopped, to look around, their anxiety mounting as the plane came swooping in again. Everyone dived for cover just before a second missile was let loose. The rocket screamed past over their heads to shatter the remaining vehicle in massive explosion of flames and smoke, spewing up a second shower of bone and metal fragments.

A deafening silence hung heavily in the air with the plane now disappearing into the distance, its mission complete.

Suddenly a startling cry from one of the rescue team had all eyes shaded from the sun to look across the open desert. A few seconds focusing had two distant optical smudges hardening into real solid objects. Popping up and down like two wind-hopping dragonflies, the AH-64 Apache helicopters bearing the Star of David came on at them at 130m.p.h. Backup promised by CONTROL, sent out from Ovda Air Base. Armed with four CRV7 air-to-ground rockets, AGM 114 Hellfire missiles, AIM-92 Stinger air-to-air missiles, and Spike anti-tank missiles, they also each carried a M230 chain-gun.

Hovering over the two wrecked vehicles, in a whirl-wind commotion of thrown-up sand, the helicopters made careful inspection to ascertain that retribution, in its deathly measure of deliverance, had been fully rendered by the Mirage. Satisfied, they swivelled round with loudening 'puck-a-puck' juddering and accelerating spin of the rotor-blades, to make their ascent into the sky, and head back to base.

13.05hrs. Frank Falzoni looked at the commotion around him. The earlier hubbub of differing voices had now been replaced by the solitary monotonous drone of a giant long-necked 'dinosaur' of a massive crane engaged in lifting a large section of the Boeing's fuselage onto an even more massive haulage vehicle's trailer. He waited for the cables to snap in disastrous crash --- but, no, nothing like that happened, with the load being swung round on those shining steel 'threads', the load resting down with a satisfying loud clump on the long trailer.

Two uniformed figures were approaching. Bright polished buttons and belt buckle on black tunics, only marginally darker than the Egyptian tanned faces, said they were policemen. The tassels on their tarbush headpieces swung in time with the determined steady oncoming walk. One of them was speaking to what you could guess was the superior officer, while he was pointing at Falzoni. A third figure, in 'civvies', trailed after them at a slower pace. A medium-sized man in small-checked three-piece suit and Harris Tweed trilby, you saw him in that distinctive air peculiar to the diplomat, of being official without looking distinctively official – that, along with the gold-emblemed leather attache case he was carrying. Sworn to 'sacred' family tradition whilst still in diapers.

Stopping to let the man catch up with them, the two policemen let him pass and go ahead of them to go up to the 'foreigner'.

'Knowles. Call me Bart. It's easier than Bartholomew'. Holding out his hand to Falzoni.

But Frank felt like calling him something else less polite. 'You couldn't have done worse if you'd arranged to meet me in a Brooklyn bar still suffering the shakes of 'prohibition', could you?' Frank gripped the other's hand, where he'd have preferred it to have been the guy's neck. 'What the hell have I been called out here for?' He swept a hand round, indicating the ongoing salvage operation. 'This is not my ballgame, looking after bent tin cans. Sorry, pal, not interested.'

'Not even in what they *contained?*

'You're taking a hell of a long time to tell me something, *Mister* Knowles. Let's have it in short sentences to make it quick, so I can get away from this damned place before its damned sand chokes me.'

Opening his leather case, Knowles took out a fat wallet, holding it out to Frank. But a hand that wasn't Frank's unexpectedly darted in to snatch it away from the Embassy man. The police officer looked thoughtfully at Falzoni. He took the passport Frank handed him. 'You are American tourist, Mister Porter?'

'Yes.' Best keep personal details brief. Long lingering statements were apt to have more questions coming your way. The policeman nodded his head up and down slowly in his own quiet effort of weighing up the situation. Seeing that the American 'tourist' was not keen on saying anything else, he decided to say nothing else either -- for the moment. Turning around, he beckoned the other policeman to come closer and stand beside him. He handed him the wallet. The junior officer took it and opened it up. After a few seconds inspection of the passport it contained, he shrugged his shoulders, none the wiser, and handed it back to his superior.

Studying it again, the senior officer then looked up at Falzoni. 'Are you relation to this person on plane?'

'No.'

'Then perhaps you know him, maybe?'

'No.' Keep it short. Considering the chain of questions logic was liable to induce, he was keeping his mouth shut. He had questions of his own running through his mind.

'So, what are you doing here?'

'Just passing. Stopped to see what was what. Where the hell are those Pharaoh pyramids? My tourist guide owes me money for sending me on the wrong trail.'

' "*Just passing*"; I see.' But the man *didn't* see, not sure how to take the American's words and not sure if he was satisfied enough with the blunt answers, to not arrest him. He stared at Frank for a moment, then looking back down at the dead passenger's passport, he read out the name in his heavy accentuation of the syllables: F-a-alzonee Fra-a-nsiss.' He put both the dead man's and Frank's passport in his pocket. 'You shall report to my office tomorrow at nine o'clock, Mr Porter. Good day.' Turning around abruptly, and accompanied by his junior colleague, he walked away as briskly as the soft sand beneath him would allow him to.

'And just exactly where the damn hell would that happen to b --- ?'

'Hebron – just a few kilometres south west of Jericho,' said Knowles quietly, catching a tone of irritation rising in Falzoni's voice.

Waiting for the two policemen to get out of earshot, Frank swung round to face a slightly nervous Knowles, who was uneasy at his charge's somewhat 'heated' response to area authority. 'Damn hell.'

'Don't worry, Frank, I'll hand in my signed official immunity endorsement warrant to keep them off your back and get your passport back. '

'You'd better, pal. I don't quite fancy sneaking around in second-hand Bedouin garb, with fleas feasting on prime Italian beef. What's this about some crazy mark using my name?'

'I can't provide an answer for the "*what*" part, but I can give you one for the "*why*" part. To answer your original query -- it's *why* you are here.'

'I'm listening --- don't make me hold my breath too long.'

Knowles flashed a quick reproving glance at Falzoni's impatience. 'Our Embassy crash investigators discreetly coming across evidence of someone masquerading as you to secure a seat in a plane that is hijacked, and later goes down in a horrific crash is surprise enough; but letting that surprise reach the wrong ears would be an even greater disaster of political flapping seeing no end.'

'And that fake name mirrors the one picked out of the hat to look into this?'

Knowles nodded slowly in confirmation.

Taking a deep breath, then letting it out, Frank turned to look around, shifting his feet in a restless shuffle. 'This damn sand is the only thing I've so far had a chance of getting anything in my mouth since that crap called a meal on the plane. You know the layout of land around here, Knowles. Lead the way to the nearest 'watering hole' where I can tickle the old tonsils with some Kentucky mouthwash.'

2

The silver Chevrolet swept along the graceful curve of the road winding through the russet forest of confers. 'Should be round the next bend, I think, sir.' The round white cap bobbed on the marine corporal's head as he said this into the rear-view mirror for the benefit of the passenger in the back seat. As it was, he hadn't the faintest idea if they were nearly there or not. But he had to say something to keep the man happy, seeing as how he kept checking his watch.

Eventually the trees around them fell away, giving sight of a small coppice of stone 'trees' ahead of them in the distance. These gradually became 'corkscrew'-style false Tudor chimney turrets giving off lazy twirls of smoke to the sky. Vertical streaks glinting in the sun were the tall windows that broke up the grey surface of the stone mansion. Nestling in the privacy of its remoteness from Washington, it served as an 'innocent' quiet country nook in old rural England where hushed discussion rose no higher than the soft rustle of the leafy surrounds. An improvement on the American presidential retreat, Camp David where, in spite of stringent security vetting, the Press, on too many instances, managed to sneak in a nose where it was forbidden to sniff. Away to one side, across a great open expanse of green field, two tiny figures mounted on their machines, were systematically moving back and forth on opposite ends of the field, diligently cutting the grass. Their real duty being to watch, warn, and guard against 'uninvited' intruders.

A gateway in the high iron wall of spiked railings allowed for entrance to the forecourt, where the building duplicated itself in countless grey chips crunching under the car wheels, spreading out everywhere and surrounding the grove of silver-bole larches. Some adventurous chips had even had a mind to enter the building, scattering up the stairs under the stone portico, but left behind by feet that had trodden there and gone in through the dark entrance hallway.

They parked beside the muddy-wheeled matt grey Plymouth P12. The white star on its side marked it as strictly U.S. Army property. Major Falzoni followed his driver into the house. Entering the hall, they brushed under the much-torn banner held up in the grip of an old long-forgotten medieval peasant-cum-soldier in dusty rustic smock that had suffered more rips than the banner. Second glance said it was a halberd, the brutal axe-head mounted on the end of the long shaft. The guy must have been a damn poor bugger, since he could only afford one iron-studded leather gauntlet – or was that the crazy fashion of his day? Broad tired carpet of faded red took up most of the polished oak flooring in front of them. Heavily worn-down wooden steps wound up and round in spiral ascent to a balcony, where dark grimaces glowered out at you from their framed canvases.

Somewhat incongruous in this period setting was the modern metal table, where a figure dressed in appropriate country-style Norfolk jacket and cavalry twill trousers, sat gulping down a mug of tea. And equally out of place was that modern master-control radio unit, with its winking red light and bright yellow flex, twisting like an umbilical cord over the back of the Tudor pale oaken high-backed chair, to dangle beside the head of the security officer sitting on it. Putting down his mug hastily, he got up to approach them, asking politely for their passes. They complied with the polite 'request', handing over their security passes for 'polite' inspection. He carefully checked these, one at a time, running a finger slowly down the list on the table. Satisfied, he handed the passes back with a polite 'Thank you.'

Watching all this, was the man standing over at the French window, quietly sipping his mug of tea.

No, no, it couldn't be tea. Falzoni let out a faint smile at this thought. You didn't get Goodblood imbibing a non-alcoholic concoction, especially one as weak as the camomile lot you could smell issuing from that mug on the table.

But he was. This contradiction was verified when Marley Goodblood casually ambled over to Falzoni. He held up his mug to what he saw as comically frowning query on Frank's face. 'The President asked for it. He's a little upset with something of a minor tummy-ache, it seems --- if only it was for that alone --- that we should be that lucky.'

'The *President?*'

Goodblood jerked his head, with his eyes indicating in the same direction, towards the balcony. 'Along with Kissinger, English Minister of Defence, Worley and Golda Meir with her 'right hand man', Colonel Moshe Dayan.'

Frank didn't hide his surprise. 'Jeez!'

'Well, you don't think you're '*invited*' down here to the country to just simply enjoy yourself picking wild daisies, Frank.'

'"*That'll* be the day", as Mister Wayne would say.'

Goodblood turned to the marine. 'Go grab yourself something to drink, soldier. There's tea and coffee in the kitchen, way back there, somewhere. At least it's what the Brits call coffee. It's the one that tastes worse than the tea. Tastes more like burnt-out Detroit engine oil.' He watched the corporal walk away, then turned back to face Frank. Sparing a few moments for an openly humorous up and down, head to foot, inspection of Frank's somewhat dishevelled presentation in tired suit, wrinkled and rumpled from hours of air travel, he then looked up, grinning, to meet Frank's eyes. 'Glad you could make it, Frank. I hope you've shaken the sand out of your shoes. We don't want to cause embarrassment to our President with you soiling the host's carpets.'

'No, we certainly don't want to do that. And for goodness-sake, keep your voices down. Your conversation can be heard all over the house from this hall, with these ancient stone wall acoustics giving out their reverberant echoes along its quaint passages.'

They looked round to see who the new speaker was, coming down the stairs.

Falzoni couldn't help smiling inwardly at the new guy rolling out his words smoothly like he did --like a railway marshalling yard, with all those wagons manoeuvred in from different lines, to position them finally in their correct places, in one single correct line – just like he did with those hordes from the Press bustling for place around him, anxious for 'only a couple of minutes' with the President.

Laurence Brubaker, private secretary to the President, nipped nimbly down the steps with the same smooth-flowing agility that he'd managed with his words. A smooth operator, for sure. That was why the President needed him close at hand, when bloodthirsty journalists caused him to retreat to the privacy of the Oval Room. He took Goodblood's hand. 'Colonel.'

'Mister Brubaker.'

Brubaker looked blankly at Colonel Goodblood's companion, waiting for an introduction, before holding out a greeting hand.

'A colleague -- Major Falzoni.'

'Major.'

'Hi.'

Barely able to hold his curiosity down any longer, Goodblood leaned a conspirator's head in closer to Brubaker. 'Right, so what the hell is going on? What are we doing here in this ruddy mausoleum of a place reeking of ghosts, if not on a ruddy ghost hunt?'

Brubaker caught the not too subtle teasing note in the Colonel's 'friendly' words. If Goodblood was one to hold down his rising vexations behind an officer's self-control, this one, in contrast, would be batting his sore points sky-high right out of the stadium --- officer's self-control be damned! That called for him to be careful – to measure out how the military mind before him functioned. Shrewdly, was a fair presumption. 'The concept is not entirely without premise, I grant you, Colonel.' A polite laugh. 'But like I was saying, we most assuredly appreciate your valuable presence here.'

'I think I've got that so far, as has my colleague. *And ----?*' Waiting for an answer, Goodblood saw a serious look cut through the otherwise casual expression on Brubaker's face, as he seemingly grappled with that in his mind. Frank also caught the trouble the diplomat was having, virtually choking, he could imagine, spilling out words that would blemish his clean, politically-correct, tongue. He'd worked with these 'Big Town D C' white-collar marionettes before and was familiar with their shirking from associating, let alone *working,* with the shadier side of Intelligence. With the President, himself, waving the starter flag for this operation, codename, GHOST, you could expect the White House mandarins' automatic denial of its very existence, their safer preferred practice being total abidance with diplomacy protocol.

'Frankly, Colonel, a situation has arisen in Washington from dissatisfaction with intangible mere gossamer threads of conjecture overriding solid substantial evidential fact. This in itself is giving rise to growing dissent and nervous agitation among varying opinions vying on Capitol Hill, not least of all in the President's own cabinet.' A small pause, before getting it out. 'We require your department to pursue the issue and provide a veritable report on its credence level.'

'You want us to prick the balloon to see if it bursts or remains there solid to annoy the President?'

Brubaker and Goodblood looked round, surprised at Frank's interruption stating the point so bluntly that it didn't fall short of the truth – just short of offence.

'As the Major says, Mister Brubaker, you want us to look into the matter – *covertly* – right? From what you're saying, I'm assuming the situation to be somewhat more acute than what I had understood from the brief communique I received from Washington. Its operational details were a little sparse, and no better explained by your people in the White House when I called them yesterday.' Whether this was from a soldier's form of getting plans out on the table, or because Brubaker was not yet sure if he could fully trust him, was not yet clear to Goodblood. But you expected this sort of doddering uncertainty between the white-collar brigade and field agents when setting up the skittles for an operation at their discretion. *Then* you throw the ball. And with the President, himself, no less, upstairs?

Brubaker saw Goodblood looking up in that direction, and nodded, moving towards the stairs. 'Follow me.' Turning into the first corridor on the balcony, they halted, almost colliding on Brubaker's heels, when he stopped abruptly and pushed on a gold-threaded tapestry bearing the face of an elderly Cavalier, whose gnarled expression suggested he wasn't finding things so 'laughable', unlike his 'Dutch cousin'. The thin black sliver of darkness widened with the wall panel swinging silently inwards. 'Through here,' said Brubaker softly, disappearing into the black void. Goodblood and Frank trooped in blindly after him, wherever he damn well was.

'Smart guys, those old Royalist country lords, building all these bolt-holes and tunnels to hide from Old Cromwell's Roundheads only too eager to run you through with three feet of cold steel,' muttered Frank. 'Not only could they dodge Ollie's heavy man when he came to collect tax and fill his loot-bag with gold sovereigns, they could also dodge the nagging wife and slip off for a sly one with the buxom maid milking cows in the byre, I'll bet.' He couldn't see the politically-correct man's face in the dark, but he could imagine it wincing in discomfort at the lewd inference of his cheeky remark.

It was little wonder that Brubaker hadn't thought of using even less words, tapping out instructions in Morse code with his finger. But then this wasn't yet 'official' Langley, so perhaps this was to be expected. Langley had not yet given the 'green light' for this mission, declaring, as they normally did, an essential need of clearance for 'dirty tricks' if they were to override the opposition. Thus, rendering President and Prime Minister somewhat unhappy, looking down on this shared mission's 'off-the-board' tactics, disapproving of its cloak-and- dagger skulduggery as being below that of good old professional intelligence gathering. But Langley was its own boss, running its operations totally independent of Washington bureaucrats' interfering mandates. It was virtually unanswerable to 'squeals' that did not emanate from the Oval Office, itself. Perhaps the President was feeling the shakes of uncertainty now?

As if he was mind-reading, Brubaker replied over his shoulder: 'Our laws of society do have their points of censure, I grant you, however well they may elude the blind eye; as for your fear of losing those frozen assets --- perhaps we have our way of eluding that also.' He didn't extend on his remark to enlighten on its point.

'Oh, yeah? ' Frank quipped back. 'You don't say a lot, do you, Brubaker? I tell you that for free. But I see your technique. You observe and absorb. Like a sponge. You're taking all this in, the rough with the smooth, politically speaking, making whatever it is you can of the total fudge with your analytical mind. And not giving out one word of a clue. Fair enough, that's what we're paid for --- to bend an ear to all you're braying.'

'And promptly forgetting it all thereafter, Major!'

'Yeah --- and "forgetting it all thereafter".'

'Patience, patience, gentlemen, and you'll see why we're here in just a moment.' Following Brubaker through the dark, they could tell, from the rough timber stanchions brushing against their shoulders on both sides, that it was a narrow passage between rooms they were in. Brubaker opened another door in front of them and they were in what felt like a small room, with a faint draught from somewhere bringing a mouldy smell to the nostrils that were already fighting with that from dust. Brubaker fumbled around for a few moments until there was a click. A screen lit up before them. 'As you most rightly remarked, Major,' said Brubaker, over his shoulder, 'the original owners were cunning, to the extent of spying on their guests. They had their very own peep show through a hole passing as the eye pupil in the oil painting on the other side of this wall. With the help of modern optical appliances, we now have improvement on the original peep hole's narrow field of vision, using *camera obscura* technique, to give a panoramic view of the whole room. Stepping aside, Brubaker let Goodblood have a look. 'What do you think, Colonel?'

The 16ᵗʰ century drawing room was spacious, with books taking up one entire wall. Morose faces looked down from the other walls, their stares forever suspended, along with polished blades that were too long to be cutlery, mounted between them. But your attention was drawn to the five live occupants in the room. At first glance, five *men* --- those heavy masculine facial features gave Israeli Prime Minister, Golda Meir, the mistaken semblance of a man, foretelling equally hard negotiating power behind the hard wrinkled folds of that face. 'With that large nose, those dark-shrouded eyes and hooded eyebrows, she's not too unlike late President Johnson.' Frank's little piece of 'brilliant' comparative deduction was non-too amazing. Sitting directly across from Meir, President Nixon may have possibly seen a shade of likeness to his immediate predecessor -------- possibly.

'But with the tougher banter flow coming from her, I'd reckon. What do you say?' Goodblood's prodding question to Brubaker.

'Ruefully, that there's a modicum of truth in what you say, Colonel.'

'Truth is only one card short of useless, if you don't know what game the dealer's playing. Like the Colonel said, what the hell are we doing here? What's with us having a spook peek at the Big Chief pow-wow through there, Brubaker?'

As if it would answer Frank's question, Goodblood leaned closer to the screen, his attention drawn to the five occupants, one at a time, seated there before them, in close-huddled conversation. Meir was giving ear to her distinctively one-eyed 'wingman', Defence Minister, Moshe Dayan, while Nixon waited for her reply. Hunched forward towards her waiting, his broad-mouthed smile belying the impatience behind his knuckles clenching and unclenching.

Stepping back from the screen, Goodblood looked round pointedly at Brubaker, waiting for the President's special spin-doctor PR man to fill in the empty spaces. And there were quite a few of those. Screen light reflected on the Colonel's face was enough to convey the message, with no need for words, to Brubaker. He inhaled deeply, preparing to give out one of his typical 'please everyone' White House Oval Room statements.

'Ah – it seems there is presently circulating an undercurrent of rumours – only *rumours*, mind you, of a degree of unrest and imminent violent agitation, not confined solely to the *civilian* populace, simmering just below the already, as yet, unstable surface in the Middle East.'

'Somewhere in the midst of all that semi-whitewashed diplomatic mouthful, I'm hearing '*War*'. Am I right? Are you saying that there's another of their crazy little 'Six Day Wars' about to break out again?'

'As I said, only rumours.'

'Yeah, as sure as I'm voting Independent Commie next time round.' Goodblood nodded at the screen. 'So how are *they* seeing it all meaning?'

'In the infinite, but not infallible, wisdom of Defence Secretary, Kissinger, armed conflict between Israel and a coalition of Arab states led by Egypt and Syria is looming up menacingly in foresight. As we all too well are aware, this Arab-Israeli territorial conflict has been an ongoing issue manifesting itself in many battles and wars since Israel, at last, in 1948 found itself to be a 'Founded' State. Needless to say, Israel's going further and securing the West Bank, Jordan's territory since 1948, as well as capturing Egypt's Golan Heights and approximately half of Egypt's Sinai Peninsula during that "crazy Six Day War" couldn't be said to have cooled this endless dispute to any degree.'

Frank had to say his piece. 'Yeah, I remember Israel re-running the reel of David clobbering Goliath in that mad six-day skirmish, sure enough. So, what now? How does Kissinger reckon things are going to develop?'

'With the support of concurrent opinion from his military advisors, he strongly believes that Egypt will initiate a primary objective of seizing a foothold on the eastern bank of the Suez Canal in order to subsequently exert these gains as leverage for negotiating return of those Sinai Peninsula territories presently occupied by Israel.'

'Hmm.' Frank tapped his chin, mulling over the strategic layout. 'I'd reckon that would place a lot of the fighting, aside of heavy armour, in the Sinai Peninsula and Golan Heights regions – with some combat in Africa Egypt and Northern Israel. *Colonel?*

'Yes, I think you could put the pins on the map like that --- until something more solid comes in.'

'*Precisely*, Colonel; bringing us back to the very point I was making at the beginning, regarding *substantial confirmation*.'

Goodblood ignored Brubaker's remark with its reproving tone, throwing it back in a different direction. 'So, do we have anyone else sharing Kissinger's views, in all this, apart from Moshe Dayan and Golda Meir?'

'One solitary analyst in the INR Bureau of Intelligence and Research for the State Department concurred with Kissinger's prediction, but failed to produce sufficient argument to persuade us not to ignore the report. Kissinger convened National Security Council's official crisis management group, the Washington Special Actions Group, which debated whether US should supply additional arms to Israel. High-ranking representatives of the Defence and State Department opposed this. Kissinger was the sole dissenter – saying that if US refused aid, Israel would have little incentive to conform to American views in positive diplomacy.' Brubaker paused for a moment, it not being clear if this was for breath, or irritation at having to regurgitate all these details. He continued. 'He argued further that US's sending aid might cause Israel to moderate its territorial claims, but this raised a further protracted critical debate of whether US aid would have the likelihood of making it more accommodating or more intransigent towards the Arab world.' Another short pause. 'All in all, our intelligence community,' Brubaker looked round pointedly at Goodblood, 'yes, including CIA, are so far not predicting an attack on Israel by Syrian-Egyptian forces. So, for the present, in spite of rumours stirring thoughts to the contrary, it is the official belief that hostilities arising between Israel and Syrian-Egyptian forces remains most unlikely for the immediate future.'

Frank threw up a hand to interrupt. 'Hold on, hold on! Where does this call for supplying US aid to Israel come from, if nobody is supporting Kissinger's crazy 'guru' ravings?'

Goodblood cut in: 'Would that, by any chance, be anything to do with the President's proposed Operation Nickel Glass, that we've had a faint whiff of only --- only -- *less* than ten hours ago?'

Brubaker took a moment for a preparatory cough, before proceeding through a *sticky patch*. 'Ah, yes; Operation Nickel Glass. This is, as yet, the *quietly* proposed plan of President Nixon for an airlift to replace all material loss incurred by Israel, should there be the unlikely occurrence of conflict.'

Goodblood wanted more clarity. So, how is Meir seeing all this --- I mean *really* seeing all this?'.

'Alarmed at foreseeing Israel's impending defeat, it seems that Dayan warned Meir that the "end of the Third Temple" was nigh.

'*Third Temple?*'

'*Israel*, Major, *Israel!* But in secondary coded format, also signifying Israel's nuclear weapons. With his having discussed this penultimate motion for using nuclear arms with the Cabinet, Meir has authorised standby preparation of twelve 20-kiloton tactical nuclear weapons for F-4 Phantom II aircraft at Tel Naf Airbase, and Jericho Missiles at Sdot Micka Airbase --- and these to be employed actively in what would be deemed in a last resort, as being absolutely necessary to stave off the apocalyptic finality of Israel 'dropping the Curtain'. Brubaker fell silent, looking into the distance, in apparent puzzlement. 'And yet ?'

'And yet?' Goodblood tried to edge Brubaker on.

Snapping out of his stalling conundrum, Brubaker looked again at the Colonel. 'Well, the way Israel's secret assembly of nuclear weapons was done *none too secretly* seems to suggest that -----'

Goodblood followed through with the other's thought: 'that this was a deliberate ploy on Israel's part to *accidentally* catch US attention. Yeah, I get it.'

'Good. An excellent point to end on mutual understanding.' Somehow managing to let the weak screen light catch a flicker of a smile on his face, Brubaker reached below the screen to take up and hold out a headphone to Goodblood. 'I have to go now; listen in to them for whatever else you think you need to know to assist you in your assignment.' He turned briskly to go. 'You know your way out.'

3

Falzoni fought his way through the crowd of people in the small relatively low-profile south-eastern Egypt location of Marsha Alam, on the western shore of the Red Sea, where he'd discreetly flown in by 'private flight', rather than risk the greater security of Cairo Airport. He was now engaged in a new struggle, against the tide of Egyptian camouflage battle fatigues pouring out of the train he needed to board to get to his intended destination, Cairo. Outnumbered in his civilian clothes, he edged his way with one elbow, through the contra-flowing river of soldiers, while holding on tightly to his leather-covered steel attaché case, lest it should be wrenched from his grasp in all the bustling. All around, the same battle was going on multifold. Shoulder-born army kit bags were swinging about, narrowly missing other bags and their bearers. Scattered about among the milling mass of uniforms, civilian garb in its drabness, reflected the sullen expression of weary faces. Here and there, dirty-faced street-wise children looked tiny, peddling their puny 'suckers' goods amidst the teeming crowd of grown-ups, their wailing sales-cries drowned to the ears of potential buyers, by the noise of the station's overall commotion.

A withered old man, wielding an angry fist at those getting in his way, anxiously sought a way through the equally angry crowd of human blockage, with his precious baby donkey that carried a crushing load of unripe bananas on its little back. In the midst of all that milling green and yellow camouflage, as well as duller clothes, hidden hands were snaking their sinuous ways to pockets that were not theirs. Yeah, if you couldn't trust your own alertness for beating these grease-fingered guys, you made sure you were wearing clean underpants and had padlocked them, rather than feeling yourself bare-assed from them having been whipped out from under you. Farewells between fighting men, about to depart for their assigned fronts, embraces with their crying women, welled up everywhere. All in all, a general air infused with the usual nervous preparatory excitement of moving out for 'weekend manoeuvres'. The public address system, with its unintelligible quacking announcements, would still have been unintelligible even if there had been no noise all around, and especially so if they had been in English, not Arabic. Overhead, pigeons fluttered and flapped freely from girder to girder, wondering what all the fuss was about down below.

Climbing aboard the battered coach, still defiantly retaining its gleam in the sunlight, Frank found himself engaged in yet a new battle trying to make his way along the narrow passage, searching for a seat. A million others, alas, had the same idea, so that carriage after carriage was full as he made his way along slowly, like a contortionist, squeezing, twisting, past others that had decided to stand, if not sit on the floor of the crowded passages.

Doors slammed closed along the vibrating rattle-can structure that posed as a train. With a sudden soft jolt, the long clanking thing shifted, seemingly causing the platform crowds to be sliding past, as it slowly accelerated along the platform, 'leaking' its steam rather than spouting it out proudly, as a better 'cousin' would have done. Frank wondered if maybe he should have hired that baby donkey to get himself to Cairo.

Flush against the metal side, and so unnoticed, it caught Frank's eye by miracle chance. He pulled the folding seat down, relieved to be able to sit down.

Chance was what he was going to rely on when he reached the city, so giving him mixed feelings. On this covert mission, he couldn't make immediate direct contact with Marley Goodblood's CIA lot just short of broadcasting the move by loudhailer. No, he couldn't afford to highlight his presence with even the littlest mistake.

Preoccupied with these thoughts addling his mind, Frank opened his leather-covered steel attache case to run through the classified dossiers. The way things were unfolding over the last few days, you couldn't dismiss the feeling, indeed the observation, that trains of thought were 'switching rails', so to speak, going off along entirely new tracks. And that wasn't on account of the clanking, clunking, commotion of the train's wheels negotiating a shift over the multi-rail juncture catching Major Falzoni's attention, as they headed slowly, ever so slowly, towards Cairo's railway terminal. No, it was Kissinger changing his tune.

Settling first for a 'soft' statement to Egypt's President Sadat that US's proposed airlift was a necessary precaution in the regrettable foresight that things were approaching a "nuclear culmination". Now he's saying that the nuclear aspect is not the prime reason for the United States's intended aid to Israel --- but rather, that it was the Soviet Union's continued programme of re-supplying Egypt, along with Sadat's blunt refusal to consider ceasefire that was responsible for President Nixon' decisive action.

Swaying with the old wagon's rocking motion over uneven rail-bedding, Frank let the recent classified report tumble about in his mind. According to Langley, European countries were not allowing US planes carrying supplies for Israel to refuel at their bases, lest it should bring about Arab oil embargoes. Portugal and Netherlands were more friendly. Portugal was consenting to lease out a base for our use in the Azores, while the Dutch Defence Minister was secretly authorising our use of his country's airfields.

A sudden lurching of the carriage to one side had two of the flimsy report sheets slide out of Frank's attache case, to float down onto the central passage floor. As Frank reached down for them, a dark-tanned hairy hand moved in to beat him to it. Matching in tan, the large dark mottled face opened in a wide smile revealing a black cavern of gold that could have caused a pharaoh to nervously check his tomb's treasure. He could have won a camel race easily by the length of that fleshy protuberant appendage of a nose.

'Yours, sir, I believe.' The hairy hand held out the paper sheets to Falzoni. No sooner had the sheets left that hand, transferring to Frank's, than a small bright card had materialised in those dark hairy fingers. 'My card. At your service, should the need ever arise.' A light, clean, English-educated voice, totally devoid of the coarseness you initially expected from that coarse Arab face hosting the words.

Frank looked at the card: **Dr Nafur-Nafiri, M D. (Oxon).** 'I'd rather not, Doc, but thanks all the same for the offer.'

'Oliver.'

'Yeah, sure, Oliver. I'll keep it in mind.'

A slight nod of the man's head, in dignified response. Looking as if he wanted to continue talking, he stalled, half turning, with a quick glance at the slim steel chain attaching the Englishman's wrist to the case handle, before decisively turning round fully and continuing on along the passage towards the inter-connecting glass doors. Frank watched him until he had gone all the way through the next carriage and was out of sight.

Cairo – at last they had arrived. Frank stood up, only to duck down again, just avoiding having his head struck by a heavy-looking steel tripod hoisted over the shoulder of a soldier who had come through the adjoining door behind him. For a machine-gun, of course, not a camera for taking those wedding snaps. He followed the young lad, along with the other passengers filing towards the exit door. Stepping down onto the crowded platform, Frank looked around. The long metal serpent of the train was flapping open its hinged 'scales', to disgorge more human parasites onto the platform. Standing outside the station exit, Frank scanned all around a full one-eighty degrees to take in his new surroundings.

There was a horse-drawn open carriage brougham-style taxi sitting there. Nothing else. He would have preferred an ordinary motor cab with its normal closed in cover for the sake of keeping low profile. Maybe those 'second-hand Bedouin togs with their feasting fleas' would have done him better. But there again, training school didn't teach its students how to 'drive' a dromedary camel. And there weren't even any of those around at the moment. Only people. Lots and lots of people.

Feeling his case being tugged in his hand, Frank looked round and down. 'Taxi, Herr Monsieur?' Tiny in stature, the cabbie tugged with two-handed persuasion without waiting for Frank's answer. The old man's wrinkled face, gaunt with prominent bones and sunken eyes like knots, was worthy of an old tree-trunk. Frank saw a work-battered life before him --- just like the horse; behind that that was inner worry having its toll on the old man.

Nodding with a soft smile, Frank climbed into the carriage. Swaying and hobbling along with a stiff-jointed gait not unlike a penguin, the cabbie got up into his seat, behind the horse, and took up his whip. They moved off.

Watching the myriad of glass and steel edifices replacing what had originally been of stone floating past them, Frank had to concede that it was some time since he'd last been here. What he thought he remembered of the place was proving to be deceptive. The more he looked out, the more he identified the odd street wrongly, the more his alertness was sharpened in dreading wariness of making a very bad mistake. No room for errors in this game, guys.

After several minutes, they stopped in a 'lowly' downtown marketing area swarming with a milling mass of 'lowlife' bartering for bargains, if not victims. Frank dismissed the cab, stepping down into a moving sea of people, animals and vehicles, all as ear-pounding as the other with their particular noises. Threatened with exposure to danger from honking motors, stamping dray-horses and gigantic wagons rushing in at him from all directions, his progress across this as yet unfamiliar square was slow. Animals and vehicles were united in common onslaught against him, it seemed. Virtually confirming this thought, the great white Italeri Rolls Royce Phantom roared past on its 100hp six-cylinder engine, sparing him only by inches, its resplendent polished silver accoutrements flashing life or death warning to other 'suicidal' pedestrians. The royal oil sheik playboy, or the likes of who could afford that damn machine, and therefore a better class of hooker than you'd find in this slum district, was looking for some kinky fun with the dirty dames you found here.

That subject in mind gave him his bearings, with him recognising the building. Its squat but massive bulk made it stand out from lesser structures, imperious without being palatial. Once a thriving hob of commercial transactions, but folding, alas, when legitimate funds had also 'folded', it was still, nevertheless, a business, this time with pimps looking after the funds and human 'stock'.

Waving away the car's exhaust fumes, Frank stepped thankfully between two fish stalls and up onto the haven of a pavement. The brothel also served as a 'good-as-any' impromptu safe house for the Agency. Inside, dark wood-panelled corridors reflected the bleak mood of wan-faced hookers standing about, listless and 'lost' in their misery at the doors of their shabby rooms that proffered half an hour of delight and ecstasy for 200 piastres. You wondered how the dupes could get their money's-worth from these puny things, some barely into their teens, that were mere 'sticks' of bone-racked skin. Looking at the poor creatures, you could be forgiven for thinking that you'd seen more beef on a fat fly.

The man's baffled expression dissolved soon enough when the American put down the dollars for a private room without the need for the beguiling beauty of a 'Nefertiti nymph' to enhance it. How long was the gentleman staying? 'Don't worry, pal --,' Frank tapped his wallet, '-- plenty, plenty'. To push home this message, and for re-assurance of getting 'no trouble', he opened his jacket just enough to show the heavy Colt automatic in its holster under his arm.

He sat down on the bed which, in spite of its sheets being folded neatly, couldn't escape its inevitably tired, if not, exhausted look. No more than did the lingering scent from doused joss-sticks manage to expel the pungent odour of sweaty sex. Frank ran his mind through the list of operational intelligence phone call codes, a different one for every twenty-four hours in the field, starting today. He had a lot to do, see, and hear, in this ancient city of a thousand mystical fables, its pedigree of dark tales plentiful, like the sand grains spirited by the desert Khamsin wind through its labyrinth of streets and dark alleyways.

4

Pulling open the fifteen feet high door of the great corrugated-iron building, Falzoni stepped inside. Bright warm sunlight was immediately replaced by a distinctively cooler darkness, pierced where holes permitted, by seemingly solid golden rods of sun filled with millions of dancing dust particles. Only a few tungsten lamps winked feebly from the warehouse roof that spanned 15,000 square feet. The eerie whine of an electric motor grew louder as a yellow Jungheinrich forklift truck ghosted up out of the distant gloom. The squat hulk hummed up closer, along the passage between mountains of wooden scaffolding all around him, holding carpets of varied Eastern design. Some crates also, stacked around him, so that nervous pigeons fluttered away to safer positions among the spider-work of steel roof beams. Coming up straight at him, the truck left Falzoni to do the sensible thing of stepping aside promptly to avoid collision and allow the damn thing to pass on its way. Cool as it was, the sound of wings flapping in the invisible dust inspired an even more chilly air to the place --- if that was all it was? With his eyes gradually becoming adjusted from bright sunlight outside to the dimmer light, he was able to discern what looked like a seated figure in the distance. As he walked closer, Falzoni saw that the woman was sitting on a folding chair beside a large wooden cable reel placed on its side to serve as a makeshift table. Strategically placed on the 'table' were two plastic cups and a bottle of golden liquid. Bourbon or brandy, he guessed. And what was posing

29

as a tourist's large 'look-at-me' camera, that was really a SCR 536 US Army field radio/walkie-talkie. Looking around for something to sit on, Falzoni dragged over a small wooden crate stencilled in black ink with its contents and destination: **KUNSTMUSEUM DEN HAAG**. Small red markings stamped elsewhere on the crate indicated the consignment was from the Far East. Good guess, China. Forged documents and an envelope bulging with money passed discreetly to a customs officer was enough to say that the crate contents were precious ceramics, and not military weapons. But this crazy box-load would not be going to that museum in Holland; no, the contents, like other similar consignments, would stay here, in Egypt, where President Anwar Sadat would have his loyal generals gainfully deploy them among their troops.

He sat down on the crate and stared at her for some seconds, searching for a sign of life, by way of a word or two, that is, if 'it' could speak, at all.

'And I guess we're not here for the combined effort of deciding which one of these fancy rugs you're considering buying as a present for your great Aunt Matilda?' said Frank, at last.

She ignored the remark, her attention buried in the dossier that she'd pulled from her bright-coloured tourist bag. 'That's another damn operation does a goddamn nose dive down the drain,' said Jocelyn Hogarth. Though perhaps just into her first quarter-century, the brooding expression and worried eyes weathered her beyond those years. Attired in a hirsute three-piece outfit of grey tweed, she took dignity from its dullness with a nonchalance that went with the family name. Just two simple golden ear rings making up her 'jewellery', in keeping with the deceptive plainness that she hid behind. But, hell, in no way was she plain. Far from it. She was an absolute beauty of a creature that embarrassed him in wondering if his eyes were popping out. For a moment he felt like that college kid pushing aside those 'sacred' fraternity house rules forever when setting eyes on his first 'serious'.

Hogarth. One of the oldest, much revered names in the hierarchy of New England's ancient 'aristocracy' that stretched back to that historic landing in Plymouth. You could virtually see the water dripping off her soft maiden's shoes after stepping off that plucky little vessel of Anglo-oaken spirit, *Mayflower*, along with those other original Pilgrim Fathers.

He dived in, just like that crazy college kid would have done, with a crazy remark to break the ice. 'I'm guessing it took a very clever tailor to see that you don't overcook in that outfit in this boiler climate.'

'Jermyn Street, London.'

'Of course. Manny, in lower Bronx does mine – mind you, if he's 'high' and feeling 'sunny', you can find yourself wondering what to do with the third sleeve.'

She poured some golden malt liquor into the brown-stained coffee carton and held it out to Major Falzoni. 'Here, this will help to dull it,' she said, with a wry smile and nodding knowingly to indicate the other's inner heated leap of emotion. She poured out a generous measure of the bourbon into another carton for herself.

'You can tell?' As if that was really what was the most important issue bothering either of them in their thoughts.

'We learn to recognise the signs. It's imperative in this game --- if we want to survive.' She took a long sip at her whisky while adjusting her direction of thought.

Frank held up his glass, looking at it pointedly, and then at her. 'And does your mom approve of her precious little girl imbibing the hard stuff?'

'Alas, my dearest mama can't get enough of it, I regret to say.'

'Say no more.'

'Don't worry, I won't.'

'We've damn well got to get better at this game, Major.'

'Call me Frank.'

'If we don't, they'll be hauling us back to DC, not, need I say, to welcome us as heroes with ticker-tape, but to have us cutting the ticker-tape in some lousy backroom.'

'And you're my handler in the field, and all.'

'Yes, but I'm not God.'

'Is that a confession off the record?' But you couldn't seriously imagine a Hogarth, let alone her, reduced to such a menial position when the family lineage guaranteed matching cuff-links and tiaras with society's brightest sparklers; no more than she was apt to use *Fiddlesticks!* as polite expletive to quell her frustration. Hell no, not with her old grandad, Vice Admiral Bergman, heading the Joint Chiefs of Staff Committee for the White House Strategic Defense Council.

Frank sipped his bourbon, giving a slow nod in rueful agreement. With critically too few agents in the field to make up a proper intelligence network, their choice of tactics was severely limited. With open battlefield aggression now gone with the ending of the war, they were now enmeshed in the aftermath that was still a relatively new 'cold war' game.

'So what of Hattan, with his failure to turn up?' said Hogarth. 'Do we still have high hopes – *any* hopes at all – for his coming over to us?'

'You're asking me? You guess is as good as mine.'

'You were assigned as his handler for the job. He's your pigeon.'

Frank wondered why it was that he had this faint feeling that she didn't want to handle this job by the way she was digressing to another mission still currently running over in Europe -- Germany, to be exact. If he was "reading the signs" correctly, that was what he read in those eyes staring at him. 'Let's re-phrase that as handler of a package of indefinite detail. I only saw him once briefly, in full view of a Potsdam market crowd that was more than likely peppered with inquisitive eyes of good loyal, law-abiding Stasi informants only too easy to pick out decadent capitalist subversives like us. If not actual official Stasi officers, monitoring our every move.'

Grimly repressive in its intelligence and secret police activities, Stasi, also known as Ministry for State Security, was the great beast of a bloodhound that constantly hunted them. With its extensive HQ complex situated in the Berlin-Lichenberg sector, as well as several other smaller units spread across the city, it made a formidable opponent to elude in their shadowy world of secrets, double secrets and betrayals. Since his taking over as the organisation's supreme head five years earlier, in '57, Erick Mielke was doing a damn good job snaring them. Understandable, considering that apart from his official agents, he had a vast army of suppressed, if not brain-washed, citizens to spy on the rest of the population, for him. Originally deputy to the Ministry's first Minister, Wilhelm Zaisser, who was later deposed by General Secretary, Walter Ulbricht, who in turn was replaced with Ernst Wollweber, Mielke had hung on through the mad-fangled internal card-tumbling, to eventually replace Wollweber and become chief headbanger. His iron rule application of psychologically destructive techniques to root out and destroy subterranean currents of dissidence was proving effective enough to be giving newly appointed mission handler, Jocely Hogarth, things to look out for, without getting too worried, which she was.

'*Schild und Schert der Partei*,' said Jocelyn, mouthing aloud the Stazi motto of: Shield and Sword of the Party. She held up and flapped the pamphlet in the air long enough for Frank to recognise the unmistakable official seal. Bright red, black and yellow flag with its familiar banner and callipers, and an arm wielding a bayonetted rifle --- the stern authoritarian badge of MfS. 'What do you make of that?' said Jocelyn, handing the sheet over.

Frank gave a fleeting glance over the words. 'Just another of their propaganda warning shots across the bow. Their usual crap to be used by the needy in the *can*, if you'll excuse the expression.' A small pause. 'So, what of it, that's old bird, already flown and gone elsewhere, over there.'

'*Is* it now? I wouldn't be so sure of that. Have another look, Major. Lower down in the second last paragraph. It's not your fault you missed it, but you did miss it, nevertheless. We can't have that. *I* won't have it. We can't afford to miss things.'

'Y-e-a-h, I see what you mean,' said Frank slowly, reading her need to get it right on her first field assignment as handler, and please old Grandpa.

'They now have their 'special envoys' of instructors in the field over here, fitting the cultural scene like scarab beetles, to root out 'tourists' who don't look like tourists.'

'Right.'

A thin sliver of reflection down the side of the bottle caught Frank's eye, signalling movement behind him to his right. He looked round, not expecting to see anything He didn't. The guy knew his job. He should, if he wanted to get paid. Hogarth's bodyguard, in the role of rich tourist girl's chauffeur. 'My driver,' said Jocelyn for clarity.

'Right,' replied Frank, nodding.

'So, before they do get caught, Frank,' continued Jocelyn, 'get to work on it. Make a connection.'

'On the other hand, it could be an equally clever ploy to snare us, making a connection dangerous.'

'*Sure,* it could. That's what we're paid for, Major. Work on it, and keep your head down.'

'I'll look into it,' said Frank, putting the sheet of paper away in his pocket.

'Good, with that done and out of the way, let's get back to Hattan. On the phone earlier you mentioned the Dreilinden location. So, you think there's a chance that he'll surface there?'

Putting the empty carton down on the ground by his foot, and feeling around in his pockets for his cigarettes, Frank lit himself a Camel and paused to peel away a tobacco flake from his lower lip before answering. 'It's the likeliest crossing point after Charlie. It's where I'd place my bet for his next attempt to make the cross-over to us.'

'That's if he's still free and able to. If our latest information is anything to go by, Generaloberst Gruber's been putting out extra field surveillance units as positive feelers --- not just as routine manoeuvres, but like he knows the target is specifically out and about. Has our 'package' been picked up and forcibly opened? Do we have a leak along the line, maybe?'

'That's as sure a possibility as anything. It's also negative, if not defeatist, thinking, if I'm to heed the old training manual.'

'Begging your pardon, Major, I virtually learned that book by heart, along with major studies in *Political Philosophical Cognition* at college and I feel like I'm still learning every day.' She coughed and choked on her drink for a moment as she chuckled at the folly of her own remark. Clearing her throat, she said, 'If only, Major, if only. But goodness me no, there's no quitting in this game.' Recovered, she took on a solemn expression as she looked across at the Major. 'You do realise this? *Seriously?*'

'It's the message constantly whispered in my ear.'

'So, with you knowing that and you still being here, does that mean that you're ready to come into the Company?'

The Company, was the unofficial name for the CIA. With war no longer fought out in the open, it contributed its vital active role in this new war, where open aggression was no longer considered suitable in relative 'peace time'. War hero, and former Director of OSS (CIA's immediate war time predecessor), William Donovan, now appointed as supreme head of CIA, was doing a good job running the 'Company'. But so was the Stazi's foreign intelligence branch (Hauptverwaltung Aufklarung) doing a good job, infiltrating its envoy instructor 'beetles' into this foreign soil of Egypt in preparation for the looming conflict. That was giving Hogarth something to worry about. Hence her question.

'I'm thinking about it.' Hell, wasn't Marley Goodblood's going on about it all the time with him enough? 'But understand, -- only *thinking* about it'

Seeing the uncertainty in the other's mind, Jocelyn took her approach down a different avenue. A more *personal* one. So why are you still here in Military Intelligence – much the same game, in a way, after all? What, with your Harvard degr---'

'*Yale.*'

' --- your *Yale* degree, you could be pouring vital legal advice into Nixon's ear, and sharing coffee with him in the Oval Office this very minute.'

'I'm thinking about that one as well --- maybe it's just the allure of bright Army buttons that's seducing me. Anyway, now that you mention it, why are *you* in this murky game, when instead, you could be at the helm of the Hogarth Empire flagship, reaping in the multi-millions?'

'Yes, seen that way, I suppose it also has its 'allure' of those millions coming in as a result of hard work. But I'm thinking that sitting back seeing the family millions, *billions*, pour in, on and on, without any real effort from me, could be very boring.' She breathed in deeply and exhaled with what seemed relief from the thought. 'Let's just say I went for something that I thought – *think* -- is more exciting.'

'That has got to be a minority viewpoint, if it can be believed,' said Frank.

'Take it, or leave it; suit yourself. By the way, we're having a dinner-do on Friday next. You're invited.' A little quiet pause. 'I'd like you to come, Frank.'

'Ah,' said Frank, caught off guard, with her actually calling him by his first name. 'Am I expected to come in a penguin-suit, cummerbund, and all the regalia?'

'You can come in your birthday suit, if you want,' she couldn't hold back a choking chortle at the thought, ' --- I wouldn't mind, but perhaps some members of family sitting at that ever so long table might, to some degree, feel somewhat affronted at that mode of 'costume'.

'Right.'

'Is that, yes?'

'Yes.'

'So that's settled. Right?'

'Right.'

Crumpling up the empty carton in her hand, Jocelyn cast it down on the makeshift table. Leaning over to pick up the field radio piece, she stopped, to look at Frank with a hesitant expression in her face that signalled dismissal. 'Don't let me keep you back from your work. Until Friday, we've both got a lot to do on our hands.'

5

Emblazoned by golden sunrays, a brass sign-piece in the shape of the legendary mystical 'magic lamp', suspended above the doorway, heralded the old bazaar's tourist souvenir business. This seemed to be the place, all right, concluded Frank Falzoni, putting the scribbled address away in his pocket. Pushing into the heavy-beaded curtain, and shouldering his way through the 'tentacles' still trying to hold on to him, caused a shrill tingling of tiny suspended bells to shatter the inner dark serenity of this little 'cavern of eastern wonders and curio antiquities' nestling in this quiet Cairo backstreet of dilapidated dwellings. But nothing else moved in the languid hot air of the summer morning, except convection currents twisting around the bright yellow lever-pump water tap growing out of the sun-parched ground like a septic polyp. This was a safe distance down the street and so anyone coming to quench his donkey's thirst or his own, was hardly likely to spare him a glance. Up on the sun-baked roofs, wary lizards spasmodically jerked their heads, darting among the forest of broken chimney tiles, disturbing no-one but the beetles peering fearfully from stone cracks and gutter sludge reeking with not only that of camel and goat dung, but possibly a fair contribution from humans as well.

Frank paused in the doorway, looking back, to take all this in with a sweeping scrutiny. Satisfied, he turned and pushed on in, into the dark interior. There wasn't much to stop the eye in its search of a 'rare piece', except a handsome bronze-gold Saracen scimitar half drawn from its leather scabbard inlaid with brass serpents. The 17th century Ottoman lantern clock had its own elegance to hold your attention. He gazed at its lovely silver dial, suspended there in doleful silence, and appreciated his own taste for metals, over that of ceramics. Likewise, woods and glass he invariably left to others. Glancing outside, through the swaying dangling beads, he half expected to see a uniformed figure wielding its standard issue rifle descending on the shop with its authoritative air of pounding boots. Nerves, of course. Working on a covert assignment like this made you feel edgy. The feeling never went away, no matter how many 'miles' you'd covered.

Just as he was about to cough to signal his presence, a high-pitched whine suddenly cut the heavy silence, as a lathe cut away on another 'ancient treasure' being readied to fall into the excited grasp of another duped tourist. Frank looked about to locate the source of the noise, judging it to be from a backroom. He coughed loudly. The whining ceased and an inner heavy curtain flapped open to let out a bent shape as ancient and scarred by the years as the leather apron wrapped around it that wasn't its face. Before either of them could speak, a faint new sound caught Frank's ear, from low down, in the darker shadows of the dark interior.

What his eyes picked out in the obscure light made his inside jump. Roughly 100lbs, easily, in that massive coiled form, with threatening forked tongue darting forward between curved fangs, the huge Anaconda python began slowly uncurling itself, hissing with increasing menace as it swayed closer to him.

'Jeez! What the hell! What do you feed that bloody thing on --- *mother-in-laws*? No, it would probably spit those out again, for good reason.' Frank had never ever liked snakes, for no particular reason, save a Freudian one, perhaps. Now he had a reason. He didn't dare move, lest it should signal his untimely demise.

A snapping of fingers by the old man, and a low guttural signal that was a mixture of growl and whistle, had the great reptile moving back, seemingly with some reluctance, still hissing, to disappear into its enormous basket. Where the hell was the bloody great chain and ten- ton steel vault door to keep that bloody thing in its place, Frank wondered. In the ensuing silence, both men looked each other over, their loaded curiosity not fully answered. Plainly neither of them was seeing what he anticipated. Thinking that he had made a ghastly mistake and come to the wrong address, Frank turned to go. Before going, he held up a street map, flapping it to show that he needed help.

'Perhaps I can help the good traveller; if he sees not what he seeks among my humble host of precious artifacts of time past, then may my wisdom foretell of the well whence his thirst be fully quenched.'

Frank held out his map to the man, making a point of shifting a finger to reveal a missing segment of the map. Seeing the triangular piece neatly cut out of one of its sides, the man's tourist-welcoming smile faded for a second. Turning to open a small ebony casket, the man took out a small triangular piece of paper. It fitted exactly into the cut-out space on the guide. Frank's good cheer at not having made a gaffe made him sigh with mild relief. He looked the guy straight in the eye. 'Right, got it, pal. If you like, I'm Sinbad, so to speak, and you're the mystical Grand Wazir of Wisdom. Great stuff for Broadway, I'm sure, but in the meantime, can we get on with it, a little more low-key. Those beads don't stop the wind from blowing in sand'

The man nodded, and signalled that they go into the backroom.

Frank followed him, his nerves brittle, like the cracked tiling beneath the carpet under his feet, unsteady as they were in his uneasiness.

In the backroom, the old man was getting ready to leave, removing the leather apron, to replace it with an old tattered striped kaftan you could imagine having once adorned Moses or his likes. Frank's inside jumped as a figure suddenly appeared out of a dark corner where only carpets had hung a moment ago. Round-faced with flabby cheeks, and a wide mouth that put any ventriloquist dummy's broad grin in the shade. The new man looked at his watch. 'Come back in about an hour,' he said to the old man. 'We'll have finished and be gone by then.' Watching the old man go, the new man called out after him: 'And for God's sake, don't forget to secure that damn demon thing in its basket before you go. We don't want to have it eavesdropping on us. Right?' Another disharmony of 'tings' from the curtains, followed by the heavy clumping of an outer door being closed.

Sinking back into a wicker chair piled high with cushions, Frank studied the new guy standing there, in all his anonymous presence, fiddling with the lathe. The guy looked round at Frank. 'Lavery.' He held out a hand to stop Frank speaking. 'No, don't tell me your name – not even your field code name. It's enough that you've identified yourself as the guy I was assigned by GHOST to meet.' Satisfied at having established that scant connection, he spared a second to set about putting a light to a small gas-ring to heat up a pot of black coffee. 'Sugar?' he asked, without looking round at Frank.

'Yeah – one.' Frank thought for a moment over what his hastily summoned mental dossier could rustle on this guy, Lavery. 'You've only worked for us once before, on this kind of mission, right?'

'Yeah, that's about right.'

'*About* right? Let's be definite, pal, – is it right or not right? One or the other --yes or no.?

'Cyprus --- Akrotiri, to be precise – '61'

'You did, in fact, turn down an assignment, did you not? Am I correct?' Frank was putting aside his usual friendly air to come on more pressing.

'Correct. Dispatching someone with a needle of strychnine in a mosque of all places, is not exactly within my field of expertise. My training didn't include that category of work.' Lavery paused to lift the pot of coffee off the gas-ring. 'I was given the choice of accepting or declining the assignment.' He glanced at Frank to see how his statement was being taken.

Frank reflected how that declined assignment had come from a source of Russian security, where choice of accepting or declining a mission was allowed – *within reason*. This had come about with Lavery, different codename then, having worked as a double agent for Russian security. 'This was the *only* reason? There was no *other*?'

'I wasn't aware that another reason was needed.'

'No, but your being dropped thereafter by Russian security meant our losing you as our convenient ear to Moscow whisperings.'

Lavery paused, to pull back on his nervous defiance of what he felt was a subtle attack by Frank. 'So, what is it this time? A message or a 'package'?

'Information, in general, on the whole.'

'Of what, exactly?'

'Don't be so bloody naïve, Lavery! Or perhaps you're playing obstinately dumb to demonstrate that the mouse, in its own territory, *your* territory, is not afraid of the cat. Well let me reassure you that between us, only the cat gets to eat his dinner. You know very well what nature of material I need you to get for me. We didn't to go to all the bother of manoeuvring you into your position here so that you could have access to camel rides as a tourist guide at a cut rate. You're an important unit, in an important, position more importantly, within convenient proximity of an extremely important source – the Egyptian Strategic Strike Force Air Base – albeit not the one we're ultimately interested in --- but it will do for starters. You are in that very important position so that you can pass on invaluable information to us. That's all you need to know for now.'

Shaking his head, with a clear expression of admonishment on his face, Frank leaned in towards Lavery: 'If you're thinking that after your awkward spell in Cyprus, it's going to be an easy 'walk-over' situation for you here in sunny 'tourist-town' Cairo – forget it! My money's on things heating up pretty soon, to an escalation point that spells trouble --- and trouble means that in a martial arena like this, spooks like us are shot by trigger-happy lots on the spot in the street, without a moment spared for trial or questions.' Frank sat back again. 'Am I getting through to you?'

'I see. Will I be working alone? Can I expect to have some form of assistance, at all?'

'You'll receive specific details of procedure along with implements necessary for the operation in due course.'

'I see

'Yeah, well I hope you do, and appreciate what we're really asking, and what it involves on your part, Lavery. I hope you really do.'

Lavery poured out the coffee and handed Frank his cup. 'Cheers,' he said and sat down himself.

While they both sipped their coffee, Frank looked round the room, idly inspecting the amateurly jumbled range of mixed Asian culture artifacts that made the old man vendor's existence a carefree one. He wondered if he saw a similarity between this and Lavery's character trait as a loner. 'You pretty well lead your own solitary life style, don't you?' he said.

'Yes, more or less. I suppose life is like a blank canvas, really. You have to dab on your own colours to make anything of it at all.'

'And that's how you see it, is it? Hmmm,' sounded Frank, not quite sure if he was happy with Lavery's philosophy. He'd read various reports on the dangers that always had to be born in mind with sleepers in potentially 'undecided' territories. How they could be tempted by the relatively inactive nature of their role and become so integrated in an ordinary habitat, so as to adapt to the softness of the mainly passive lifestyle that they led, as to be firmly rooted there. A waste of the money and effort put into their training, in fact.

Frank took out of his pocket a shoddy pamphlet printed in Islamic characters, with English translation. Inducement for Western infidel tourists to find cleansing redemption in a holy mosque of Allah. 'You're not getting interested in this rabbling lot, are you? Because we are hearing disturbing rumours, if not official reports, of you doing just that.' Frank's fearful suspicions were hardening into a dark frown.

'They try to give a truthful picture of what they believe is the Ultimate Way of Allah. Or at least, so I'm told.'

'Meaning that others don't? Is that what you're saying?'

'Now that you put it that way, it does sound a bit like that, doesn't it? Fancy that.' Lavery's eyes sparkled with mocking fun against Frank's stiff questioning.

'You know, you want to be careful what you say around here. Words like that can be dangerous outside these walls. I'll pretend I didn't hear them. In fact, I'd strongly recommend that you forget any ideas you have of attending any mosque meetings.

'I didn't say the words, and I've no intention of going to any mosque meeting. I'm only repeating what my housekeeper says about her teachings from the mosque. I merely let her prattle on and let her leave the odd leaflet or two in the hall when she finishes her cleaning and lets herself out. It comes under the heading of *integration* in the training manual. If I'm to blend in successfully with my immediate social surroundings without raising suspicion of any sort, I mustn't show any rough edges, must I? I shouldn't have to tell you that, should I? Or perhaps you'd rather that I sang a daily *Ave Maria*, and finished with a rousing rendition of the *Halleluja Chorus*.'

'You have a housekeeper? I wasn't told you have a housekeeper? Frank was suddenly alert and looking around. He felt that he had been let down by those compiling Lavery's dossier; what mess had they possibly made of other dossiers in the sleeper field section? You couldn't be blamed for feeling you were on unsure ground, with information like that newly hitting you.

'Relax; she's not in this morning. This is Thursday – Market Day, so I ask her to get me fresh vegetables and meat. She won't be back until late this afternoon.'

'I think it's about time we got on with some work,' said Frank brusquely, clinking down his cup, with its coffee unfinished. 'Never mind finishing your coffee. Let's go.' Pausing, he looked across at Lavery. 'Do you have 'wheels' – a car? Perhaps it would be less conspicuous if we went by your familiar transport.'

'A-h-h, that could be awkward. My jalopy's out of action, I'm afraid – broken axle.'

Frank threw his keys over to Lavery. 'We'll go in mine. You drive. I want you to take me on a guided tour of the place to point out some interesting points. I'll tell you where and when, as we go along. And we don't want to waste time with you going out of the way to show me where 'El Laurence' got off his camel to have a piss. Or any other such tourist money-grabbing spots. Are we understood?'

Understood'

They had barely had time to move off out of the adjacent street, in Frank's hired Renault, when brakes had to be rammed on abruptly at the shrieking from an angry face beneath a steel helmet looking out from the hatch of a 'rhino'-bodied 3-ton steel-plated Daimler Dingo scout car. This was leading a convoy of three 7-ton Daimler MK1 armoured cars. 'Leftover' gear ditched by the Brits in the aftermath of their somewhat ignominious withdrawal from the fiasco that had been their Suez Campaign. Frank watched the heavy vehicles negotiate their twisting way round a camel that had decided at that moment to deposit its shit there and then.

Minutes later, peaceful stillness and silence restored to the street was once again disturbed by a black Volga saloon coming into the street, crawling along slowly, to finally pull up several feet from the water tap. From there the occupants could view the whole street, including those who entered and left the antiques curio bazaar. The man in the passenger seat opened his travel bag to take out and seemingly consult a street map. When he had finished with the map, he put it down, still opened, over the still open travel bag. That allowed him to get at the 200mm zoom lens Nikon camera that was in the bag. That they had missed the quarry by mere minutes would certainly annoy some general; but you couldn't help reflecting, purely for the sake of conjecture, on the philosophical possibility that maybe generals' strategies on the whole were not strategies at all, but mere playthings in the hands of chance, so that both sides ran around in futile effort, missing their objectives completely. Makes you think of looking over your shoulder twice.

6

Captain Izhar Zilberman came out of Tel Aviv's Military H.Q. in the Hakirya district, a little ahead of Mossad officer, Shahar Biran, who had stalled in the doorway, scribbling in his folder. Worry was written on both their faces, like the official order of the day, after what they had been through upstairs. He scanned the clear blue sky, looking every bit like the symbolic little piece of that sky in his flashing bright beige uniform. Two winking specs returned the greeting, as they etched their way across the blue canvas, at the tips of the fluffy vapour condensation trails. To Biran they were all-weather Dassault Nesher fighters, but to everyone else they were just specs. Biran put away his pen and came out to join Zilberman in his skywards gaze.

'Nesher fighters,' said Zilberman.

'Really?' said Biran despondently, feeling that he didn't care what the heck the two dots were, at that distance. Like everything else in this wretched mess, they were too distant to reach or to matter. Just like those maddening dreams, Biran felt that he was frantically chasing something about without moving a bloody inch.

'Yes. They're damn good formidable numbers to have around when you need them,' said Zilberman.

'Let's hope the number doesn't come up and we don't need them, or we may well be "damned".' Biran didn't mean to be as pessimistic

as he sounded, but it annoyed Zilberman just the same. This pleased
Biran for a second, then darkened his mind, as he realised it was a sign
of his frustration needling him. Even with every man active in the field,
doing all that could be done, he was nervous at not being there to see
for himself, instead of filling in files with inert figures. He pulled himself
together.

They left the planes in their silent flight and started out briskly,
thinking of more mundane elements that lay ahead of them. 'I've arranged
for an emergency interim meeting to see if we can sensibly amend what
was disagreed upon upstairs,' Biran suddenly remarked. 'Tomorrow
afternoon should be time enough to get our minds concentrated on
things. It'll get them away from all else --- for the time being, at least.'
There was no need to say more.

'Good,' said Zilberman. 'I'm sure that was the decent thing to do.'
No more words were necessary and they walked on, silent in their private
thoughts. Biran pondered over the wisdom of what he had just said,
considering that he had another matter gnawing at his mind.

With just over thirty-eight hours before the 'mushrooms', as Moshe
Dayan had put it, the countdown was gathering momentum. On top
of that, the Blue Steel crisis was still a sore thumb, and it was on that
subject that Dayan had stressed his points. It was exactly where a show
of strength was needed, to challenge, face-to-face, the Egyptian-Syrian
build-up of its strength along the border, at the Quneitra Crossing, in
the Golan Heights.

Like a latter-day Sword of Damocles. Zilberman had disagreed.
Almost by intuition, he spoke on his thoughts. 'I still disagree, of course.
Look, I'm not one to be called a warmonger, but what he is suggesting
is hardly going to make a rabbi blush.'

'Can you be so sure that your plan would be any more sensible?'
said Biran. 'Would you not say that your plan for direct harassment is
applicable only when aggression from them is imminent?'

'Imminent aggression?' fumed Zilberman. 'When they discover it's
a glove with frozen fingers inside?'

'I think we should know the answer to that pretty soon,' said Biran, sobering up the two of them. 'I would say that they should have caught a whiff of the rumour by now. I'll bet on it.'

'Even money,' said Zilberman.

Biran looked at his watch. The next meeting was at twelve thirty, and he still had to go to the Hatzerim Air Base. Time was pressing. While half listening to what Zilberman was saying, Biran scanned the car park for his contact, who should have been there. They walked on through the cluster of official cars to see the great Yankee monster US Army staff car parked on its own. It was the only way it could be parked. With that acreage of tin, you could make a Mini out of one of its wing mirrors. A man was leaning against it. He watched them openly as he spoke through the open widow to the brown smudge of a US officer inside. The officer's cap, with its half-acre of badge, bobbed out of the window as he spoke, but the man outside didn't move at all. He just kept staring their way and smiling mechanically from behind the twin-mirrored sunspecs as they got nearer.

'Unless I'm mistaken, that looks awfully like your American acquaintance behind those weird glasses,' said Zilberman. 'I hope he's not going to weigh us down with bad news; it always turns out to be the case, as if we don't have enough to worry about already.'

Biran wished he could have corrected Zilberman on his gloomy presumption, but he let it go. He stepped away from Zilberman to go over to his contact. 'You go on ahead. I'll catch up.'

Major Falzoni straightened up, to step away from the car, and walked slowly up to Zilberman. This relaxed manner was slightly off-putting to Biran, where he was used to bearing the brunt of hard talk from the American. Not wasting his time to give anything resembling a smile, Falzoni simply came out with a non-committal 'Biran.' With that, he waited for the Captain to pass on by, out of earshot, turning his head to watch him like a silver-eyed robot. Biran looked at the Major, watching the two tiny reflections of Zilberman prance across the convex lenses to recede into the distance.

Falzoni turned round and they both assessed each other's state of affairs in silence for a few seconds. Just as Frank suddenly broke out his wry smile and looked as if he was going to follow up with some cynical idle remark, Biran beat him to it and came straight to the point. 'Have you got it?'

'Sure thing, pal, sure thing.' Frank put his hand against his inside breast pocket, tapping it, and whistled Beethoven's sinister four bars to mark the shady undertones. He opened the car door and looked around outside before getting in. 'I get shy standing about in these open places. Too many 'tourists' about with their Walkman radios tuned in --- and not to Elvis.'

Biran got in beside him in the spacious back seat. He could almost have parked his own car in here. He closed the door. Frank peered over his sunglasses to meet the driver's eyes in the rear-view mirror. The airman switched on the cassette player's deafening loud blast of pop music. That would put the fear of Babel into any bugging device that had the misfortune to listen in. Frank opened up a black leather wallet and peeled off a thin sliver of telex paper and another of 16mm microfilm. He handed them to Biran, along with a small folding lens to examine the film. 'Now feast your eyes on that, pal. Sure as hell, you should have your eyes insured, along with precious Torah Scroll and Redeemer Tabernacle, seeing as none but a nickel worth of people outside the Pentagon have seen that memorandum.' Biran was mainly impressed, with only a little doubt nagging at the back of his mind. In this business, a little doubt could go a long way, with massive backlash. Falzoni went on. 'And that's just the photocopy. The real thing's back in the Embassy with the internal affairs people.'

Biran was immediately alarmed. 'You mean to say you've told others about this? About what's going on?' The thought of such knowledge spreading out of proportion to the wrong ears and to disaster was scaring.

'Relax, pal,' said Falzoni, tapping the paper. 'You worry too much. Like I said, our Embassy people have the original copy, but that doesn't mean that they know what it is they have. What those dude diplomat college boys see and what they understand are two different things. When you've got your hands on the hooker's lovely ass, what is in the right hand and what is in the left hand is only *half* the story. Right? Understand, this only came in a few hours ago. I'm lucky to have this copy here.' He pointed to the telex paper. 'That O.K. is from our Moscow station. They're getting ready for a fix-up as soon as we can return the okey doke without making the place look like a buzzing beehive.'

Biran re-examined the film, trying to convince himself that he had no reservations over going along with the plan and its chances of succeeding. The film was a copy of the official statement specifying that the blueprints to the American ground-to-air missile, Skyhawk, were to be leaked to the Russians, in exchange for one of their agents; with the secondary ulterior motive of diverting attention from plans to root out the leak in the intelligence communication system. Skyhawk was top priority in the US Home Missile Defence Programme, being second only to Cruiser, the number one missile. To surrender these secrets to the Russians was no mean feat. This was what worried Biran. Would the Americans go through with it, in spite of what was stated and signed here, when it came to the final moment? 'But are your people going to go through with it, when it comes to the crunch?' said Biran, voicing his fears. 'After all, this is nothing short of colossal. Why would you give up your Skyhawk defence programme in exchange for our man? Tell me that?'

'Hell, like I said, man, you worry too much.' Falzoni studied the other man's expression, trying to measure the degree of worry coming out across it. Biran, in turn, couldn't see his opposite number's eyes behind those twin silver screens, having only the American's mouth to watch for any giveaway tension. Falzoni pushed the specs up to the bridge of his nose with a forefinger. 'So what if we do help our Hebrew cousins step out of the great quagmire mess they've created with your agent sweating away in Moscow's glory hole, Lubyanka? In any case, nobody knows.' He paused and smiled to emphasise the cheeky secret. 'Not even we two know that Skyhawk is next to obsolete and is due to be taken off the active priority list, and replaced by a superior model within twenty-four months. So what's with speeding things up a bit, to straighten things out a bit on the UK side of the big pond? So okay, Skyhawk goes a bit earlier, but you get your loony agent back, you update your armament schedule and the imbalance is resolved.' He motioned his hands up and down to signify the see-saw defence situation between NATO and 'contending' powers. 'The truth is, Biran, that whereas once upon a time your holy land was all yours, it's now one of our back gates.'

'We'll have to tread warily, that's certain,' said Biran pensively, handing back the film and telex paper to Falzoni.

'Sure, sure.' But Falzoni was more concerned at that moment with setting the film and paper light with his Manhattan Bendix lighter. They both watched the flames lick up from the gaping dragon's mouth that was the enormous chromium ash tray.

Biran was still worried, but now with a different problem. 'We can't make it too obvious that we want our agent back. If we profit too openly, they'll snap their teeth shut on their own fish to keep him in Lubyanka indefinitely, to find out what his value really is that makes us want him returned so urgently.'

'Yeah, well, we sure as hell won't be handing out secrets like cookies on a tray at an inaugural party at the White House.' Falzoni paused to light two cigarettes, giving one to the driver in the front driving seat. 'But see here, the final okey dokey has got to come from your people, rather than from me, to set the wheels in motion for the exchange. That's official policy, although I'm quoting off record.'

Biran saw why the Major was so unbelievingly freely handing out his help; or one of the reasons, anyway. 'That way you get no axle grease on your fingers.'

'That's about it, pal. Jeez, what more do you guys want in your Uncle Sam jamboree burger! At least we have the hardware to match Brezhnev's lot; you guys still don't seem to realise that it takes more than serving out chicken soup and bagels at the Wailing Wall, to outwit the enemy.'

'Fair enough, Major. Leave it with me, and I'll let you know. That will give you time to get things to 'just happen' at the right time, in the right places, about the right rumours of a secret leak.'

Falzoni turned away from Biran and fell back on the seat to blow out his smoke with relief. Biran saw the tightness that had been around the Major's cheekbone relax, and knew that the man had switched off his verbal onslaught. Biran turned his attention to the 'ordinary' soldier in front who, in spite of the noise from the cassette, had surely heard most of what they had said. The man had sat impassively through their entire discussion, showing no more signs of life than a tailor's dummy. He wore only a captain's sparkly bits of insignia on his uniform, but there was too much authority about shoulders, too much skull, too much austerity about the crags and cuttings in the veteran profile, to hold the man down to such a meagre rank. No, the man's real uniform, if he wore one at all, would have a canon's weight of brass, and his office more grandiose than this Pontiac's great interior. Biran couldn't bring to mind any particular person on his Mossad files dealing with US Forces European files. So the man must have just flown in, probably from the Pentagon. Biran wasn't sure if he was pleased or edgy with this idea. Falzoni watched Biran watching the soldier and a wry smile cut slowly across his half-hidden face. He rolled back his head and blew the cloud of smoke up to the roof, chuckling softly until he choked on smoke. Biran, in his irritation, cocked an eyebrow at the Major to question the private joke, then looked at his watch. 'I've got to go.'

'Sure, pal.' Falzoni sat up and leaned across to open the door for Biran. Stepping out after Biran, he closed the half-ton door.

As they stood there beside the Pontiac, a car came cruising along slowly. Drawing near to them, a dark bearded man looked out through the open front passenger seat window. He pointed his Beretta machine-pistol first at Major Falzoni's unsuspecting back, then moving the aim at the Mossad officer's back. Before he could pull the trigger, the bearded mullah leaned forward from the back seat to push the gun arm down. 'Later my son, later. There will come a better time later. The *proper* time, as Allah so sees it, and so decrees. The one thing we must not do is let our anger overrun our wisdom. Wisdom is a divine gift from Allah; wisdom belongs to Allah, just as anger belongs to Allah. Anger shall be used by us, but must be used wisely, in accordance with the will of Allah. It is so written.'

'So why can't we take action now? An action not taken, is an action lost – *lost*!'

A heavy hand from behind gripped the man's shoulder, its old fingers hard like steel, digging into flesh and bone. 'Better the fingers we lose on the hand that we keep, than to keep the fingers on the hand that we lose.'

7

From what he'd heard earlier of Jocelyn Hogarth's tales of wild partying, Frank hadn't exactly expected the host's residence to be standing out in traditional Arabian Ottoman style. And he was right. It wasn't standing, it was '*floating*'. *Salamander*. A great 70metres long, 11.5 metre beam, 1622-ton mass of super streamlined steel luxury yacht, powered by twin Caterpillar 1875h.p. diesel engines, to take it across any of the seven seas in a moment's notice, it rested there in quiet indolence on idle waters tinged a blazing golden yellow by a giant disc of setting sun casting forth its last rays of the day as it sliced down into the glowing red horizon of Cairo's Giza Port. Contrasting with the ultra-modern exterior, the yacht's interior captured an earlier Moorish theme in gleaming carved cherry-wood columns and arches, Oriental paintings, jade ceramics, jewels and weapons, spread across the walls of the spacious drawing room/dining salon. Mystical Asian expressions stared out in endless suspension from the walls, along with twisted blades that were a little too large to be cutlery, all reflected obliquely on the Venetian coloured glass topping the long pink Sienna marble dining table.

But Frank's attention was drawn to the occupants of the long dining salon. Well-manicured, well-pomaded, Western men in penguin suits and sheikhs resplendent in their gold-woven kaftans and turbans, covered in enough diamonds to put the Kimberly mines in a flurry of worry --- and that was the *men*. Business men, politicians, and the usual medley of socialite 'bright-lights'. Women, with lesser 'sparkle' of tiaras, were a minority. Most of the men were in earnest conversation, leaning in to speak in low tones. Each of the pairs seemed barely aware of those around them. Even at this distance, you could see the subtle signs of inner nervous tension belying the smiles on the outside. Agitation in preparation of business proposals and hopeful political procurement. Others, their minds in-drawn, elsewhere, were seated back in their heavily carved dark 19th century oak wainscot chairs. Yeah, you could say that was a bit heavy on the baroque with the chairs, considering, but then if you're the playboy, wild-partying, spendthrift, son of a 'royal' multibillionaire oil sheikh, then however crazy and ill-fitting your whim, the 'mould' would always bend to the 'clay'. And the host was just that. 'Prince' Faisal Nayef, sixth son of Sheikh Khalud bin Abdulaziz, and fun-friend of another rich kid, Jocelyn Hogarth.

9

The established setting on the whole was an ancient one that had the oddity, among establishments of its kind, of favouring the richly powerful ruler over the reclusive philosophy scholar. In a former age you were likely to have encountered servile mute females darkly shrouded in their dark bourkas matching the austere dark interiors of dark desert tents, where only the warrior was as much at home as his magnificent Arabian stallion. Only the blood from repeatedly retold battles would have flowed as freely as the jellah, with its refreshing taste of grape molasses, rose water, pine nuts and raisins, and bestowed only by Allah, to quench the thirst. But in tonight's select gathering of '*most select*' personage, when your diamond-studded silver goblet happened to run dry, you were sure it would be replenished with fresh pouring of wine and liquor.

This was definitely Jocelyn's sort of thing, from what he'd gathered. Apparently, she wasn't too bothered about giving herself away freely in parties like this, it seemed. But she wasn't around at the moment for him to see her doing it.

From over in a forgotten corner, beyond the throbbing hubbub of voices that had built up over the evening, there came the twinkling strains of someone's inebriated second-rate rendering of 'Play it Again, Sam' on the piano. So where was 'Ric', alias, Humphry B, himself? Poor in their harmonious accomplishment, the notes kept a balance in the room's noise, stopping the discordant snatches of conversation from pushing everything else out of the way. Frank had not expected to have been the only guest invited to the dinner party, but neither had he expected the guests to have included these classy numbers. You'd have expected their kind to be above such things as 'parties' – or at least the kind that Jocelyn had gone on about.

Seated seven places away and too far away to speak to, but constantly looking his way, at him, wanting to make contact, was a face he'd only recently noticed drift into their exclusive hush-hush clique. British, he recalled, or at least that was the affected impression he'd been given. The young eager to please 'apprentice' seated on the far side of the Brit was a second lieutenant 'business' attache who worked in conjunction with Knowles, the Embassy's CIA man whose acquaintance he'd met earlier, in that desert crash site in Syria. And he also wore a zig-zag pattern Royal Artillery tie. Yeah, as Colonialists, we chased them off our land all those years ago, but those good old Brits still liked to get a foot in wherever they could.

And where the hell was Jocelyn? She certainly wasn't the drunk plink-plonking the ivories over in the corner. Frank scanned along the double line of bobbing heads around the great marble table. On cue, a section of the far wall bookcase slid aside on silent wheels, and what stepped out of the black space thrilled Frank more than Botocelli's naked, new-born, Venus stepping out of that giant oyster shell, ever could. Jocelyn clutched the bottle of liqueur tightly, like the pearlescent pale grey silk cocktail dress, matching her eyes, and hugging her body tightly, bringing out all the rounded contours ---- there was really no need for that thin sparkling halter snaking round her neck – the dress was not going to release its hold of that voluptuous shape – no way! Jocelyn's matching pale blue eyes gazed into Frank's dark Latin eyes. Clearly, she'd had some before making her surprise entrance into the salon, judging by the happy expression on that beautiful face that hadn't shown such emotion the last time he'd set eyes on it. Not drunk, but 'liberal in movement' as she swayed and awkwardly navigated her way round the far end of the table, she walked up, stopping halfway along the great length. With a mischievous smile and nod of the head, she signalled to Frank to get up from his chair so that they could go talk outside on the deck, or rather, *one* of the great ocean-cruiser's decks.

Standing under the third deck's striped awning, in the balmy night's privacy, Frank looked long at her, his inside burning. 'The temperature plunges at night time here; you could do with something over those shoulders. Let me give you this.' Frank started taking off his blazer jacket. That, with white shirt and paisley cravat, had been the best he could rustle up at short notice, instead of a *proper* 'penguin' outfit.

'Well, goodness me! Rather than cover the damsel in distress, I would have expected Frank Falzoni to remove her of what she still had on. What's happened – are you slowing down?' She took a step back, folding her arms, to study him for a moment. 'Besides, why are you not married now, at your age?'

'I don't see a ring on that pretty finger, either.'

'You're older than me.'

'Well do pardon me, young lady --- mea culpa, mea culpa, mea maxima culpa.' Frank tapped his chest repeatedly along with his mock penitential craving.

'With that mouthful of words, I'm guessing that mama's still unbridled stallion son can only be brought in to paddock with a mare *latino* that can stir the pasta sauce with one hand, while holding a rosary in the other one.'

'Forget that idea, kid. Believe me, this old horse will gallop into the paddock, tail wagging, if the filly is ---' Frank raised his chin up slightly, to push home his point, staring hard at her alluring grey eyes, '--- if *she's* the one I can at last put all my money and shirt on in absolute certainty.'

She stared back, her inside, much to her surprise, warm – and *uneasy*.

Jocelyn suddenly lost her 'whoopee' look, her soft face taking on a more familiar serious expression. 'I think I'm missing out on something here, Frank. Why did Koravoski's lot contact us if they didn't want our help in the first place? Tell me that?'

'They didn't,' said Frank.

'*Didn't*? What do you mean, "They didn't"?' Jocelyn looked at the bottle of French liqueur in her hand. 'I know I've had a good mouthful of this stuff, but I'm not that far gone. Are you trying to tell me that some goddam magic genie popped out of a bottle to have the teleprinter speaking for itself with its own message? Is that what you're telling me, Frank? Because if it is, I don't like it. I don't like it at all!'

'Koravoski was given a message to contact us. They didn't send the teleprinter message. They don't know who it was that sent them the message. That's it in a nutshell.' Frank didn't expect that to please Jocelyn. He was right. It didn't.

'Holy Mother of --!' cried Jocelyn, almost tempted to put the bottle to her mouth and guzzle down the three-quarter litre remains of the dark liqueur to drown her fright. 'God Almighty! Major, it could have been Moscow's trap to lure you out into the open and grab you; a bold operation for them to carry out here in the West, but not beyond their gall.' Jocelyn took a tiny measured sip from the bottle.

'They nearly did,' said Frank. 'But I suspected as much and escaped their pincers.'

'Yes, well tell me that when we're one man down, with you lavishing the cordial hospitality of their Lubyanka torture cells.'

'On the other hand,' said Frank, pausing to tap Jocelyn's precious bottle, 'maybe we have something to drink to.'

'Oh, yes, meaning *what* exactly?'

'If the message sender was, *is*, genuine 'friendly', and was forced to keep the source anonymous, it must have come from over there.'

Jocelyn's beautiful eyes lit up. 'You mean there's a fruitcake over there who secretly reads Lone Ranger comics to his parrot and has a big yellow MacDonald's 'M' on the back of his Party badge, no less?'

Frank's reply was simple. 'Me, Tonto – you, Kemosabi. You got it in one.' He tapped the bottle again. 'Let's go find ourselves two glasses.'

'Could we possibly make it three glasses?' said a new voice from behind them.

They both looked round.

'Oliver!' said Frank, openly surprised. Sure enough, it was that crazy doctor guy again, Doctor Nafur-Nafiri.

10

Vice-Admiral Bergman was just closing his statement to the Committee: 'All in all, gentlemen, what we possibly --- *possibly* --- have is a holocaust imminent in our very laps. So, there it is. Any comments forthcoming?' He took his hands away from the table's edge and rested them over the white blotter. He peered, like a wise warlock, over his heavy steel-framed reading spectacles for a second, before taking them off to look down the long table. Seated beside him, Secretary for defence, Dr Henry Kissinger, agreed with what the Vice Admiral had said so far. Laurence Brubaker, seated beside Kissinger, quietly held back his opinion, trying to imagine how best to put the situation to keep President Nixon purring happily. The three of them quietly surveyed the others, lined there before them like two rows of legless chessmen. Once was not enough, with them doubling their splendour in dimmer, inverted, reflections along the table's sides. Even ignoring the colours, the linear primness of straight backs, expressions and ribbons, fitted the straight table and the high-backed chairs like only the military could. Their chests together boasted enough fruit cocktails of campaign ribbons and medals to knock the bottom out of the dealers' market.

Down the Vice-Admiral's side of the table sat Brigadier General Manning, Major General Wainright (Air Force), General Harcow, Major Brownly, Captain Mallison (Navy), Facing them on Kissinger's side were Admiral Smillsoe, Maj-General Greeley (Marines) General Hopeson,

Colonel Frewnhurst (Air Force), Lt-General Grovensby (Air Force) and Colonel Goddfrey. Facing Vice-Admiral Bergman head-on from the opposite far end of the table was Colonel Marley Goodblood (CIA).

It was an impressive assembly of distinguished services. More acutely, it was all the contacts ungently summoned from Air Intelligence, Naval Intelligence, Army Intelligence and Counter Intelligence for the 11.00hrs Strategic Defense Committee Meeting.

Standing out from all this splendour were Kissinger, Goodblood and Brubaker, in their civilian attire. The nearest Brubaker had come to soldiering was the lead dragoon miniatures on his study desk.

Several eyelids blinked and the odd finger twisted a blotter's ear as they considered the Vice-Admiral's words and all that they had discussed over the last thirty odd minutes. Goodblood especially considered the scathing looks Bergman had given him, like a Gothic gargoyle, with his foreboding of the looming disaster, stinging him no less than would a serpent's fiery tongue of flame. Between the two of them, there was no question of whose lap this great ruddy mess was being thrown.

The Vice-Admiral looked along the table, examining the faces for response – *something – anything*, that was more than a wrinkled service despatch. He looked at Goodblood, who was studying his watch more than his notes and who seemed more distant from the meeting than the rest of them. Whilst the others seemed content with the written reports and pieces of paper in front of them, Goodblood appeared to be preoccupied with activities elsewhere. His mood swing between restlessness and a studied boredom, shifting from elbow to elbow, making him conspicuous among the rest in Brubaker's eyes. When he looked up and caught Brubaker's eye, his face offered no expression or signal of communication beyond the long defiant stare. He fingered his blotter all the while, haughtily holding back what he was thinking and then looked back down at his notes. Brubaker returned his attention to the meeting, and again, more importantly, how he was going to put it to the President.

Maj-General Wainright glanced at Kissinger, and a moment longer, at Brubaker, before turning to the Vice Admiral. 'We have, in fact, as you know, had Operation SHELL in operation since fourteen hundred hours yesterday. With this new development, I think we are all agreed to go ahead with a Section One stand-by on Operation FLAME.'

All heads nodded and the Vice Admiral continued with the counterpart. 'It is, in fact, the best foreseeable measure to be taken. The crux of the matter is that this latest development only narrows the political margin in which we can be allowed to fail. And we mustn't fail, lest we should lose our heads --- the pun fully intended there. To meet the current crisis, we must supposedly cut a few tight corners, but otherwise, the best plan is already in operation. We must now wait and observe carefully.'

The Vice Admiral having heeded Wainright's wise words, and already a force behind Operation SHELL, now turned to Brubaker to be handed the new file on SHELL. He rolled his eyes up at Brubaker, the momentary brooding fire burning through the Vice Admiral's bloodshot eyes, where 'fish nets' of dilated blood vessels pulsed away over the yellowing white scleral surface. The old man's mood had worsened to this, following this new development of the Amber Alert Emergency Brubaker had set up in accordance with Nixon's orders – *'horse-brained' orders* -- of Operation NICKEL GLASS. The file was like a slab of lead to Brubaker as he handed it over. The Vice Admiral took the folder and turned away, resuming once more his air of being in charge, whilst wondering over the certainty of that, with Nixon's interference hovering in his mind. He could well see that Oval Room decision being interpreted as pre-emptive enough to have them smiling in Moscow. Donning his glasses once more, he ran his eyes over the sheets with their bright red CLASSIFIED stampings.

Even as simple words typed on simple paper, the details of strategies to countermand possible nuclear devastation razing hundreds of square miles with multi-megaton fury, were scathing, even in mere thought. The Vice Admiral's eyes twinkled with quiet wonder and he shook his head in private disdain. He looked up at the others with a benign smile. 'I must be getting nearer retirement than I realised, gentlemen, but I suddenly feel the need for water at the table, which I see has once again been neglected. Perhaps something stronger, when we adjourn.'

Polite strained smiles broke out all down the table and everyone took the message to shift the topic to another stage. Admiral Smillsoe looked up to the top of the table. What do we have on this Doctor Nafur-Nafiri situation?'

'Up until now, from what we have here, is that he could only be classified as ideal for the situation,' said Brubaker, sliding his file about pensively with his finger. He wasn't happy with the scant details it gave. Like an out-of-date Superbowl ticket, it may have had its use in the past, but it didn't fully answer the million and one questions currently hovering about, bringing on mild headaches. There had to be more. Something that would give some rational explanation as to why an otherwise settled individual would suddenly do the oddest thing of absconding from his post of head of an important classified government department and the serious responsible duties it entailed. But had it been suddenly? Brubaker pondered over this. He continued with a delivery on Nafur-Nafiri's dossier: 'Elite upper-class background, with ancestral family-tree tracing back, on *wrong side of blanket*, alas, to Saud bin Abdulaziz, son of Abdulaziz ibn Saud, original King of Saudi Royal Family; private school education; first class honours at Oxford in nineteen-sixty-one; went over to Cambridge, Massachusetts, to take medical bio-engineering research doctorate in MIT's Koch Integrated Cancer Research Laboratory; took up lectureship in Blood Plasma Physics and Nuclear Fission Mechanics, still at Cambridge, in nineteen-sixty-seven; returned to England, screened and appointed to full scale salary by the British Ministry of Defence in nineteen-seventy; thereafter access to the British Ministry of Defence Armaments establishments, with notable interest in chemical warfare developments at the Porton Down Laboratory.' Brubaker flipped the file's cover shut. Its job was done. It had simply put a name to the man. Now they wanted to get on with the real gritty stuff of peeling away layers to understand why the man had done that for which he was under the spotlight.

'Are we to understand that he's been allowed personal access to everything?' said Smillsoe.

'No,' said Brubaker, 'he worked all this time in conjunction with his superior, Doctor Martindale. And, of course, other members of staff. However, Doctor Martindale was taken ill some eleven months or so ago and is now in New York's Langone Hospital with lung cancer. That situation, in all probability, has obviously afforded Doctor Nafur-Nafiri the opportunity to take over as Head Scientist with a total freehand in exclusive access to Top Secret material.'

Someone muttered and tapped a pen.

'As far as motives are concerned,' Brubaker went on, 'it would appear to be personal so. From what material we could gather, it seems that Doctor Nafur-Nafiri was discreetly promised an MBE in nineteen-sixty-nine. That, alas, didn't materialise. He was also turned down in his application for a professorship at his Alma Mater two years ago.' Brubaker paused, stroking his chin, not fully persuaded by what he'd just read out. 'Still seems a bit curious as to why he's offering to help us in this bother we're having with the Middle East.' His continued chin-stroking spoke as much as his mind's searching thoughts. Could the guy be missing the royal connection he felt he was denied? Good old-fashioned revenge?

'Personal?' A query from the forgotten far end echoed Brubaker's very thoughts.

Heads swivelled round atop of their bright uniforms, looking towards the figure in mid-grey hounds' tooth worsted three-piece. Goodblood didn't bother to look up from his folder, toying with its flap.

'You have something further to say on that for us, Colonel?' Brubaker's chin-stroking ceased, with him suspended in anticipation.

'A possibility – widening the scope.'

'And ---?' But Brubaker didn't expect anything else from the Colonel. You knew he didn't waste time promising what he didn't want to give. If that was all he gave, then that was all you got. Goodblood simply looked up with an expression of restless impatience as an answer to Brubaker's question. He then looked pointedly at his watch. Brubaker got the message. He tidied his papers into his folder, picking it up, giving a curt glance to Vice Admiral Bergman. As chairman of many such meetings,

Bergman was accustomed to closing them with a slower mode of casual conversation. He didn't much like being hurried—pushed – especially by a civilian – even if he was the President' lackey. But he appreciated Brubaker's haste in getting on with things.

The Vice Admiral stood up. 'Same time again tomorrow, everyone? Unless, that is, unless something else gets in your way.' The icy intonation in the words were for Brubaker's benefit. Ignoring the Vice Admiral's loaded remark, Brubaker affected to look down the long room for any further comments. As everyone rose slowly and put things away in their cases, it was apparent that most were not satisfied, wanting to go off with something more substantial to chew over.

'Have we direct contact with Nafur-Nafiri, then?' said Brigadier General Manning.

Brubaker looked to Colonel Goodblood.

With a little reluctance only Brubaker recognised, Goodblood took his cue. 'We haven't managed to pin him down to his exact location at the moment just yet, but an all-out vigil has been mounted on all airports and seaports since the alert over his disappearance went out yesterday. A single flight ticket in his name, by British Airways to Munich was confiscated by officers at Gatwick Airport last night. Enquiries, with casual contacts, into his whereabouts, have revealed his latent urge to leave the country --- to head east, in fact, -- possibly to his second 'homeland'. We're not sure why. The chances of him rendering any measure of impediment to our plans, or those of the other side, are equally balanced, fifty-fifty. We just don't know yet.

'So, you're saying that we can't be so sure that he won't resort in the end to 'spiking our guns', Colonel?' asked Manning.

'Yes, well, we have kept this in mind and have taken the precautionary measure of ----'

Speech halted and all attention went to the bright red scrambler phone perched on the elegant Sheraton side-table, flashing its light and 'peep-peep-peeping' beneath the quiet Turner water colour. Goodblood stopped sidling towards the door. Brubaker stepped over promptly and picked up the phone. He listened. 'Yes, one moment.' He turned and held out the phone to Goodblood. 'Colonel, it's for you.'

Goodblood came away from the door, to take up the phone. 'Yes, Frank, I'm listening --- yes --- all right.' The click of the phone being replaced on its rest cut the room's electric silence. Goodblood took a few moments pinching his nose with finger and thumb as he thought. 'That was one of our field operatives. It seems that Nafur-Nafiri has made a brief appearance ---only to go to ground, immediately thereafter. Vanished completely. Possibly with an Egyptian, maybe Russian, cell. To Goodblood, the news, with its untimely interruption, was like a power-cut, fluxing on-and-off in his report. To Brubaker, it was more like a complete disconnection, his cable and plug being yanked out rudely beneath him.

Colonel Frewnhurst broke the silence. ' Nafiri or no goddamn Nafiri, the task's not yet lost. I wouldn't put it down entirely as bad decorum to pressurise their Embassy, to release Nafiri. In the meantime, I suggest that we all get out of here and get on with it.'

Murmurs of approval went out all around and Vice Admiral Berman took over. 'Very well, gentlemen, if we have no more to discuss, I once more declare this meeting closed. If we could have your attendances tomorrow, at the agreed time of eleven hundred hours. Thank you.' He shuffled up his papers and handed them to Brubaker.

Everyone started to leave and their informal talk bubbled out along with the general rustle of things being put away. Just as the door was opening, all the noise suddenly ebbed away to an expectant silence. The scrambler phone was once more calling for their attention. Brubaker calmly took up the phone and held everyone's attention on his back for an eternal few seconds. He then turned to face into the room, summoning everyone back with his pen held up in the air as he listened. 'Yes, -- Right – All right.'

They waited as he put the phone down.

'A letter from Doctor Nafur-Nafiri to his solicitor has just been confiscated and opened. It was to have been read by the solicitor sometime in the future. The message is grim. The Doctor was intending, firstly, to stem the Saudi oil-field power-control, and secondly, to blackmail Egypt to tone down its political stance of military aggression on Israel, or else have the country's entire population suffer the havoc of biochemical poisoning. Perhaps he's seeing himself in a Moses role, bringing down God's wrath on the 'Pharaohs' a second time. He doesn't say in the letter how such a disaster was to be brought about, but a separate intelligence report has just come in to say that a canister containing enough genetically engineered germs to wipe out an area roughly the size of Saudi Arabia and Egypt has been found to have gone missing from Porton Down.'

'All in all, that wouldn't help Israel much, with an ill-wind blowing those damn germs east,' said someone.

Goodblood paused to take in the dismayed expressions all around. 'Further to this, reports are coming in that a Jihadi terrorist operation is underway to take out airports and civil government establishments in Israel. He took a long breath to let the news sink in. 'There are also unconfirmed whispers going round of a sixty-hour countdown from noon today. We're not quite sure about that; needs some looking into.'

Maj-General Wainright blew into his handkerchief. Nobody was able to give a better answer than that.

11

Vice Admiral Bergman stood in the doorway of Laurence Brubaker's office of Presidential Secretary, in the long cool corridor of the not-so-cool White House, where current political temperatures were on the rise. 'The man's obviously a lunatic – a complete paranoid lunatic.'

'Probably.' Brubaker's perfunctory reply was an attempt to shrug the Vice Admiral off his back, so he could get on with his work. He didn't fully agree with the old guy's hasty diagnosis. Bergman could be short-sighted in his judgement as well as being time-consuming with his personal interference. There had to be something more to Nafur-Nafiri's behaviour than loose marbles. Okay, it was just a gut feeling, but you just knew that there was something else, something they were missing – something they were overlooking.

Giving a deaf ear to Bergman's words, he turned and walked back into the room, going over to the safe, to open it, and take out the folder with that day's classified telephone codes. There were a lot of calls to put out, lunatic or not. You were surround by lunatics in this job, with differential pay-grades, up or down, not mattering one solitary iota. Miles of dossiers on them being stored in computers and filing cabinets lining the walls of this great building, once a scorched, scorned, black, and later 'white-washed' to become its resplendent white embodiment of the Constitution's Declaration of Justice, Liberty and Freedom. And all the while they were classified as personnel belonging to a family of privileged powers, senators, whose actions may have been alien, but otherwise tolerated, if not fully accepted, by the voting populace.

Brubaker found the codes he wanted and prepared to dial, looking over at the Vice Admiral to show that he was busy. Bergman missed, or ignored, the message and went on: 'And you say there was nothing else in Nafur-Nafiri's letter? No ransom, no secondary ultimatum?'

'None whatsoever --- or at least, if there were, they haven't been put through to me, so far,' said Brubaker, wondering over this himself, at the same time to put the first two codes through to the classified desk switchboard. From there they would go to the officer in Special Communications, who would put out calls and have them returned at prescribed intervals, these themselves, in turn, being classified. 'Like you said, the man's probably experiencing some form of hysterical neurotic syndrome. All it needed was that little bit of something to jump-start him into motion – in whatever direction he intends heading. But what *is* that something?' Brubaker's last remark was a subdued muttering, more to himself, as he worked on, head down, through the list of contacts. 'It really doesn't change our position. We'll clear up that little conundrum when we get back in touch with him. We'll get him.'

'You've damn well lost the bloody man, damn you. How do you answer to that?'

'We have everyone we can manage working on it, as far as circumstances in the field will allow it. We can't tread too warily out there, lest we should put birds to flight, and so alert the opposition. If we move too openly with scarce mind to caution, we don't get a second chance,' Brubaker paused there and tapped the file in his hand, 'until it's too late.'

'You're slipping,' said Bergman.

'We're going out full stretch.'

'You're damn well slipping, and it's got to stop.' The insistent note was one of anger.

Brubaker didn't answer the remark, but went on putting the other three codes through to special Communications.

The Vice Admiral came up slowly to Brubaker and tapped the safe pontifically with his forefinger. 'You would do well to bear in mind that when others before you went 'out full stretch', they stretched until they broke and had no more to give. That's what the man in the street expects of you, for the tax he pays – that's what the President expects of you, if you want to keep your job, Brubaker!'

Brubaker put the file in the folder and back in the safe. The steel door closed with a heavier than usual clump. He turned round to face Vice Admiral Bergman. 'I'm trusting in Colonel Goodblood's judgement in assigning the agent most suitable for the mission. I wouldn't have assigned him, otherwise.'

'I'm having no question over the wisdom of your selection, but ---' Berman paused, in what seemed a moment's hesitance '--- but isn't there a secondary agent assigned to the task?'

Ah, so that's what was bothering him; the old bugger was feeling a thorn in the ass about his precious granddaughter's safety. Brubaker afforded a faint smile at the Vice Admiral. 'As far as I'm informed, she's attending her duties in absolute accordance with protocol.'

The Vice Admiral nodded, playing on his lip with his finger. 'So long as you think so, nobody is disputing your judgement on that aspect, Brubaker.' He paused a moment to think and then glanced sharply at Brubaker. 'Perhaps your trouble is that you have a Presidential whip, but you don't know how to crack it.'

Brubaker went over to his desk considering that there might possibly be a modicum of truth in the Vice Admiral's observation.

A knock on the open door broke the room's thoughtful silence, and Colonel Goodblood came in. He looked at each of them in turn, suspended in their aborted topic, waiting for them to finish their business. The Vice Admiral looked at the other two, knowing the tussle that went on between them. He went to the door and then turned round for a parting remark to Brubaker. 'A good dog can be told to sit down or else be plumped down on its rump. The end position is the same in either case, but the dignity is acutely different.'

Brubaker acknowledged the inference with some embarrassment, seeing as its subject, Goodblood, was standing there listening, with no inkling as to what the words meant. Brubaker had noted that of all the others at the Meeting, Goodblood had been the one least put off by the bad news they had just received. In fact, it seemed to have bucked him up with a new-charged surge for action. Perhaps their being on the virtual edge of a circumstantial precipice situation was the personal catalytic whistle-blast that the Colonel needed to prompt him up and over the top of his own individual trench.

Goodblood looked at the bulging folders fighting to stay in the wire baskets on the desk and decided to balance the folder he'd brought on top of the intercom. 'That's the report you wanted. It's all in there, the best we could rake up so far, on schedule to the hour.'

Brubaker stared deadpan at the green file, then turned away to walk aimlessly about the room with his hands in his pockets. 'It's what's not in there that concerns me, Colonel. The rules have changed, as we all now know, with that last call. We're now playing the game to his, or should I say, *their* rules, *their* deadline, and when the whistle goes, there'll be no extra time to play.' He suddenly stopped walking and leaned an elbow on the filing cabinet to turn and look at Goodblood.

Goodblood put a cigarette to his lips and lit it, closing his eyes slightly, to scrutinise his 'superior'. He leaned over to open a window, without taking his eyes off Brubaker. He was keen to see what this college boy, stuffed with his congruent triangles and Euclidean theorems, could suggest that could possibly improve his own methods of ferreting out terrorists.

'Your slipping, Colonel, and it's got to get better. We've got to get him now!' Brubaker wondered if Goodblood could detect the tinniness in his voice as he used the second-hand words borrowed from the Vice Admiral. Goodblood cocked an eyebrow and smoked on slowly, watching the other intently. Brubaker leaned his head down, to run his fingers through his hair. 'Have we no idea where he is, at all? Has Major Falzoni really lost him, like he says?'

'We can't afford to employ regular surveillance operations, scraping shadows off walls and streetlamps, on the chance that one of them turns out to be him, under the Egyptian's very noses; their security is tightening, with their countdown for mounting assault rapidly approaching. Precise spot checks on all the places he would go to, or could go to. He apparently knows this territory from early childhood memories. It takes endless diligent checking and back checking, with time in short supply. A few minutes can make all the difference. If we miss him, we can only hope to re-locate him again by more systematic back-checking, until we get him by elimination.'

'And if he's vanished, that simply means that you've missed him momentarily, and that you'll get him by simply back-checking? Is that what you're telling me, Colonel?'

'No, that's something different altogether. If he's vanished, it means, in all probability, that he's using a different bolt-hole. No, we allow for a certain period of back-checking to come up with positive results, before we apply the term 'vanished'. If we still come up with negative results after that period, then he's ---'

'--- vanished. I get the picture – or at least half of it. So, if he's gone to ground, using a new bolt-hole, as you say, and it's not in any of the regular suspected places – how do you *fucking* know where to look! – tell me that, Colonel.' Brubaker hardly realised that he'd swore, until he saw the broad smile break out on the Colonel's face, with Goodblood removing his cigarette for a moment's amused stare.

Goodblood evaded the direct question with its shaky ground, where there were uncertainties, and fell back on the secondary sense of past experience with its proven ground. 'It can be an advantage, in a way. If we know for certain that he's no longer in any of the regular places, we can remove our attention from these locations and concentrate our strength entirely on new ones.'

'Like groping in the dark, you mean? Sounds dangerously vague to me, Colonel.'

'It may seem vague to you, but there's a sound methodical system involved in it, I can tell you. It's not easy,' he paused, looking with innuendo, at Brubaker's empty chair, as you well know, or *not* know.' He blew out his smoke, examining the hopes and doubts switching on and off on Brubaker's face. 'You don't seem convinced. Maybe you'd like to make a field inspection? Be on the spot and see things for yourself?' The smile crept out on Goodblood's face.

Brubaker straightened up. 'You know what, Colonel, I think I'll take you up on that.' He went over to the intercom and jabbed the button. 'Have the call from Communications put through to Signals when they come in. Have Signals put them through to me via Colonel Goodblood's field code.' He looked round at the Colonel for his code.

'Seven one nine.'

'Seven one nine,' repeated Brubaker. 'Got that? I'm going out; don't know when I'll be back.

'Understood.'

Brubaker pressed another button and instructed the secretary to inform the President that he would be out indefinitely. He grabbed the files and virtually threw them into their cabinets, locking them away securely. 'All right, Colonel, let's go.'

As they went down the stairs, Goodblood gave Brubaker a sharp arm-prod. 'Your file on Nafur-Nafiri wasn't quite up to scratch back there. It seems he spent an unmentioned sabbatical in Massachusetts away from, and nothing to do with MIT research. And who knows, maybe a lot more time outside of that period. That would tie in with them having their knuckles bruised as well, and not just on this side of the water. Langley are looking into it. I'll put a sure bet that that's where the seed for this whole business was planted. Mark my word, Brubaker.' Absolute conviction on this was another hard prod to Brubaker's arm. You always knew Goodblood hadn't yet lost his rag when it was only one new sleeve that you needed refitting on your Saville Row jacket.

12

She had no sooner been shown to her table by the thin 'penguin' waiter clad in his chest-high to ankle-length immaculate white apron, than the man moved in with carrion crow speed, inviting himself to sit down opposite her at the table. Very close-cut hair gave his head the semblance of a stubbled billiard ball that split across its front with an ingratiating smile to the lady. But he saw from her eyes and slight stiffening of folded arms, that his attempt to win her favour had not succeeded, but instead, put her on her guard.

With them seated at the long row of wrought iron tables directly outside the brightly-lit window of the Café Bijou, the man had his back to the blazing illumination, putting his face in silhouette. He greeted her politely. The sudden alert reaction that had sprung up in her at his unexpectedly swooping in dissolved itself *almost* as quickly. She studied what she could of the man's shadowed features, sensing as she did, that he was making a similar soul-searching scrutiny of her own face in turn. His words came across as educated, without any need of an affected finesse to hide their rough edge. If his wallet was fat enough for him to frequent this exclusively 'up-town' district of Cairo's luxury casinos, bars and nightclubs, as his playground, it was money he'd earned, not inherited via a 'silver spoon'. She saw him as a self-made man street-wise, world-wise, with the hard determination that got him what he wanted, exactly how and when he wanted. All this coming through to her from that hard face, shadowed as it was, and his only just discernible tensed posture contrasting with the relaxed air he affected. Always heed and beware the false air. Definitely not custom-made, his canvas jacket and trousers fitted him as non-pretentious work-pieces. Although normally frowned upon in these affluent surroundings, this somewhat questionable mode of attire was readily accepted, in place of black tie and cummerbund, when a brazen front and money pushed the way through.

Her attention was drawn to his hands, with their wrinkled skin ridges shining like hard polished brown leather in the small circular pool of light from the low table lamp. Looking at them, she suddenly had the feeling that those hands had killed, or knew how to.

As if uncannily reading her mind in following her gaze to its focus point of attention, he leaned forward to playfully snatch her glass away just as she was about to pick it up. Holding it to the lamp light, he made a mock inspection of its contents. 'But, alas, the good lady eludes the evening's bountiful delights with this bodiless concoction of nut and gas bubbles.' Placing the glass of dark cola back down between her soft white hands, he shook his head dejectedly in mock sadness. Deep-down probing suddenly leaped forth for a moment's glint in his eyes as he looked at her sharply. 'But then perhaps an imam's strict catecheses tenets forbid you going beyond this adolescent's beverage – if not an 'all-possessing' mother?

'I'm not Muslim – I'm not religious. And as for that, mom would suffer a stroke at the thought of no alcohol coming in --- how she survived the Prohibition Years is a mystery in itself.' She looked at him with her own questioning smile. 'And *yourself?* You're without any glass at all. Perhaps *your* imam lays it heavy on you?

At this he let out a hard cutting laugh that was a strange mixture of icy humour and anger, as he sat back heavily in the metal seat. 'That I should be chastened by an imam would most certainly have dispirited my parents. They were so honoured for their beliefs that cost-free transport and accommodation was generously accorded them for life-long residence at Germany's most-welcoming Auschwitz establishment. Needless to say, that they spent the rest of their lives there.'

'I see.'

'Ah, yes, the spiritually non-seeing sees! So, *what* do you see? What do you Americans, in your free state of Constitutional Liberty, Freedom and Equality, ever see? What do you see in today's Egypt? What do you see here, in its capital, Cairo?' Despite his rising tones of bitterness, a smile, albeit cynical, managed to find a way into his face.

Seeing the situation escalating, she sought to quell it promptly. 'Beneath a deceptively cheerful tourist-welcoming surface, one can detect in the city's atmosphere a populace fraught with tension over its ideological conflict with the neighbouring terrain of Israel. This effect is strengthened by what appears to be a subtle excitement and anticipation over the build-up of civilian activities and military manoeuvres amounting to a latent cauldron of dangerously simmering belligerent upheaval.' She threw a challenging smile at him. 'Will *that* suffice?'

His smile broadened, to win its overall way over his now relaxing expression. 'Indeed, so --- for the moment.' He rose from his seat opposite her, to change for the seat adjacent to her, and sat down. She couldn't help feeling that this was the opportunity that he'd waited for since the moment she'd spied him studying her crossed legs from his previous position at the adjacent table. And he, in turn, hadn't failed to notice her acutely precise delivery of her assessment of the current social, political, barometer-reading. Or was that a deliberate ploy? A signal, perhaps, for their meeting halfway across the 'bridge'? 'But even as a non-believer, you surely do have a *Christian* name, do you not?'

'Jo – Joyce.'

'Ah, yes, after the saintly seventh-century Jodocus.'

'If you say so –I wouldn't have known otherwise. And *yours?*' But he ignored her query.

Instead, he held her glass of puny cola drink up high, beckoning the waiter to take it away and return with no less than the restaurant's best honourable vintage wine. Satisfied with the label held out proudly for him to inspect by the waiter on his return, he then ordered it to be poured into Jocelyn's glass, then his own. All this without seeking a single word or nod of approval from her. He clearly liked things done his way.

Holding up his glass in salutation, he asked her, not a moment too soon: 'You would care to try some wine?' The joke's irony was washed clean with both palates savouring the rich taste. He watched her lips taking on a richer red tinge with the thin rivulet of wine trickling over the glass rim into her mouth. She was liking it. Brandishing the bottle up at eye level before her, he let her read the label for verity of the vintage sweat of the soil she was taking in with every drop she drank.

She felt the glow of the wine warming her inside, and that made her appreciate at the same time, the chill of the evening's temperature plummeting. She'd been warned about that. A quick glance of her reflection in the Bijou's window caught her unawares pulling in her thin blue nylon cape tighter around her bare arms; her smooth milk-white flesh and freshness of face, lit by bright sparkling eyes, contrasting with the ruggedness seated beside her, gave the window's reflected double 'portrait' the semblance of the young charge chaperoned by the world-wise adult. She wasn't quite sure if she should be pleased with that or not. And cigarette smoke from surrounding tables said no-one else was concerned, apparently. He thought he saw what was unsettling her. 'Perhaps you would prefer it if we went inside? Discomfort from the evenings cooling so rapidly is perfectly understandable in those newly experiencing it. But you'll develop a tolerance for it with time; you just learn to grow a hard skin for ---' a soft laugh --- 'Well, perhaps not in your case, obviously. Just as the Nile travels its long winding course, so does one find that wearying route bearable through perseverance.'

'Is that what the Rabbi drills into your young mind at the Bar Mitzva?'

'It's the spiritual 'leather' that our people use to sole their bare feet in treading the long, seemingly endless, route through exile.'

With him being a Jew in this land swarming with rabid anti-Zionist Arabs in their millions, she wondered how he eluded the difference coming to the surface. Perhaps, in his dealings, he let money do the talking, with its guarantee of falling on ears turned deaf to all but the satisfactory transaction of business assets. This was the ready language, not solely of traders bartering in the bustling markets here in the city, but by all under all flags.

He managed a brief smile. 'Being here in Cairo, on the Nile that flows on as endlessly as ever, one is reminded that it is from this very land that our equally endless meandering trek through the ages first began. But as you have already said, you are not a Jew.' He gave her a look that said tired, if not disappointed, in this fact. 'Such a thought would not be expected to come so immediately into your mind.'

She wasn't quite sure what he was expecting from her. Was he wanting details of her personal lineage taking root and springing up fresh with her birth --- wanting her to go rambling on like him about the essence of family tradition carried through with tribal observance and obedience, and everything else implemented by ancient prophets that cemented religion and race together? If he was, he was so unlike her father.

'I suppose that makes sense, as much as it's fact,' she said. The halls of her family home, in her upbringing, had never echoed with religious mention. She'd grown up in a family gathering where religious scripture was never the spoken word. Whilst her father had never ever openly declared himself to be an atheist, neither had he ever laid down any strict stipulation that she should, or should not be, atheist herself. The impulse for her to believe in a supernatural state at the will of a supreme deity, had so far passed her by, it seemed. In the midst of all this dwelling in religion, the thought suddenly came to her, not without some humour, that if she were ever to marry, she would have no objection to the children being baptised as Christian, if the husband so wished it. She smiled to herself at that last thought.

'Ah, but you are far away,' he said, catching her private smile and reading distance in her eyes, glazed in long-focus. 'You dream, perhaps, of the romantic shifting sands and battling winds of the desert – of mystical Bedouin sheikhs, robbing the rich to feed the poor, if not of Rudolf Valentino, then of the ever so heroic Laurence, with his mounting of victory for the British Empire, where glory is law.' He paused to take breath after his long-winded mouthful. 'But, alas, you miss the rancid stench of that sun-scorched sand, with its rabid particles piercing the eyes, with all the howling fury of Force-Ten storm winds behind them. But those sands at this very moment are not being disturbed by legendary stallion hooves, but rather, by solid steel runner tracks driven by inch-thick amour-plated 44-ton tanks gearing up for war.'

'And all of their periscopes revolving three hundred and sixty degrees, scanning the horizon for tanks bearing the Star of David.'

'Precisely.'

'And are there?'

Rocking slightly in his chair, he tapped the table with his knuckles in an uncomfortable lack of certainty that was not enough for rendering a solid answer. 'Not yet. We are very much guilty of being critically slow in getting up off our 'haunches', I fear.'

'But surely, with President Nixon's Operation Nickel Glass airlift plan now actively launched, and your Golda Meir's authorising stand-by alert of tactical nuclear missiles, your lot are now at last fully awake to the situation?'

'Some people have runaway tongues! Didn't your mom warn you about speaking to strange men?' said a voice belonging to neither of them.

They both looked up to see Major Frank Falzoni standing there, hovering over their little secret discussion. 'And where's the neon sign?' Falzoni continued, looking pointedly at her.

She shook her head, not understanding his remark.

'Announcing to all around that you two are broadcasting!'

'You haven't forgotten that one about hiding the needle in a jar of needles, by any chance, Frank?'

'Yeah, well, one of those needles can give a mighty painful jab, if you're not careful.

'Unless I'm mistaken, I'm gathering from this *friendly* exchange of words that you two are intimately familiar with each other, Major?' said the man.

'I think *acquainted* would be a more appropriate term, Colonel.'

Equally surprised, she looked across at the man she'd been taking into her confidence with the intention of recruiting him. 'You *know* the Major?'

Falzoni dragged an unoccupied seat over from an adjacent table, placing it so he could sit down between them. He looked at her. 'This guy here is, Mossad spook, Colonel Biran.'

The Israeli Secret Intelligence officer leaned across the table stretching out his arm for a handshake with Jocelyn. '*Christian* name, Shahar --- if a little belated.' He accepted her smile and nod, when she didn't proffer *her* hand to him. So that was why he had been giving her the eye earlier – not because of her attractiveness, but because he had reckoned her to be a catch worth reeling in as a potential intelligence source. Well, at least, she had Frank's company again.

Frank gave her a broad beaming smile worthy of the Cheshire Cat. 'I seem to recall that as Field Case Officer, *you're* supposed to be looking after *me*. This is going to look good when I submit my report.'

'You wouldn't, would you, Frank?'

Biran affected a deliberately loud cough to bring 'order' back to the table. 'If we could return to matters of some greater importance.'

Frank's face switched its cheerful expression to a harder one as he looked at Biran. 'Your Moshe Dayan appears to be losing his former icon glow, with his power melting faster than snow in a furnace, with him fleeing yesterday's broadside surprise attack by Syrian and Egyptian forces, causing him to fly north after finding the Golan Heights defence line has collapsed. What's your initial sum-up on that?'

'He's gone north with specific instructions for our Air Force Commander, General Peled to have our planes cease attacking the Egyptian anti-aircraft batteries, and instead have them mount their attacks on the Syrian front closer to our own heartland.'

'Do you consider that a wise move? Dayan's normally been a cool decisive guy in the past, given to bold thinking and action, as far as I can see, in my opinion; but with this high-tailing it out of the way reaction, you can't help wondering if he's suddenly come to the somewhat late realisation that he and the General Staff have been building up Israel's strength for the wrong war and that the enemy is already inside the gates? Like I said, Colonel, it makes you wonder.'

'Our trucks are bringing loads of documents down from the Heights in preparation for a general all-out withdrawal.'

'And Egypt and Syria are still coming, like a host of scarab beetles newly surfaced in the desert, with their Soviet-built forty-four-ton T-34/100 tanks, with their 100mm main gun and 100mm BS-3 howitzer and 7-62mm bow-mounted machine-guns. Can we really turn a blind eye to ignore that, Colonel?'

'We can at least take solace in the fact that their tanks have barely improvised World War Two armour that is utterly no defence against the armour-piercing projectiles - sixty carried on board – sixteen ready to fire – with a twelve-point four miles range – launched from our Soltam L-33 forty-six-ton tank, with its seven-point six-two air defence machine-guns. And yes, we acknowledge with gratitude that the United States and Britain are responsible in their providing Israeli forces with these superior weapons. In comparison, the Soviet-built T-34 is defensive in its active field-strategy, opening fire, from relative concealment of virtual 'blind' spots, on unsuspecting Israel tanks. A somewhat *cowardly* act I'd say, but for the fact that battlefield tactics in war invariably have to be dirty'

'If you say so, Colonel – if you say so.'

'Believe me, I do, Major.'

Frank sat there looking at Biran for several long seconds, trying to measure how much was confidence, and how much was hope, in the man's words. Giving that up, he let out a loud sigh, and standing up, tapping his pockets, looked around for the waiter. 'Where the hell is he? I need some cigarettes and a book of matches. I'll get them in there,' he said, pointing with a thumb, at the noisy hubbub of voices issuing through the Bijou's open door.

'Don't tell me you've gone and lost that cute souvenir gold lighter of yours'? said Jocelyn.

Frank looked at her with a chiding shake of the head. 'An inconspicuous way of also getting round to using their phone. I've got to make a phone call to my old ailing 'uncle'. Shouldn't take more than a couple of minutes. Don't run away while I'm in there.'

13

The flame from Frank's gold Manhattan lighter fought fiercely with the wind to light the end of his Camel cigarette, and for a few seconds succeeded only in throwing his and Biran's shadows about the truck's interior, as the vehicle moved off at a slow crawl out of a sleeping Cairo's city centre. Biran leaned out of his window so that the night's invisible turbulence seized up his tie, to throw it back in a cautionary gesture. He moved back a little, tucking in the tie. 'It's a terribly rough night,' he said with a tone that suggested a foreboding of something more than the elements. But the wind had already snatched his words away too quickly for Frank to hear them. Biran repeated his remark and Frank muttered something about fresh air, between long nervous draws on his cigar. 'That would appear to be about the only thing that hasn't been fouled by some means or other in this den of cosmopolitan corruption,' said Biran, watching the city crack up, with side streets opening back into slum rookeries. There was a vague nod from Falzoni that did not confirm if he agreed or not.

Biran settled back into his corner, snuggling more deeply into his uncomfortable stiff standard Army-issue metal seat and clapping his arms despite the air being too chilling for this action to dispel his shivering. He smiled for a second when he saw Frank pulling in his own collar tighter. But the smile was dispelled and replaced by a frown, when he noticed the sweat running down Frank's brow. Frank was experiencing a chilling shudder running through his inside, that had nothing to do with the cold air around them. A legacy kindly bequeathed to him by mosquitoes in his bygone G.I. days with the 2nd Armoured Division in North Africa.

'Are you all right,' said Biran, a little worried at what he was seeing in Falzoni's face. 'Do you want *me* to drive?'

'I'm all right, pal, don't you worry yourself over me. You only have to worry if we're going to hit a tree – and since there's no damn trees in the damn dessert, where we're going, then, like I've said, you don't have to worry. The only thing you need concern yourself with is telling me which way to turn at the 'traffic-lights'. Right?'

'Right.'

Their two faces were continually slapped by the street lights, on and off, as they looked out at the shifting buildings steadily losing their grip on the truck. The crumbling continued until at last the city disintegrated into a random scattering of houses, decreasing to a roadside colony that held on as long as it could, before being snatched away with a contemptuous snuffle, as they gradually began to break clear of it– then indistinct shapes of crumbling abandoned dwellings – then nothing but solid blackness. Mischievous night air attached itself in a stifling joyride to the new night traveller, the current streaming round the truck to freeze their faces, ruffling the driver's hair but not affecting his smoking concentration. The engine seemingly took advantage of this, with wheels turning faster and pistons stepping-up their plunging and rising, giving free movement all round as the truck cast off its shackle and headed for the desert.

With nothing more outside to hold his attention, Biran fixed a momentary gaze on the red glow of Frank's cigarette reflected in the windscreen. Frank, steeped in thought, focused his mind on the distant star that peeped out from behind the ragged clouds racing across the silvered sky in great rips of Wagnerian fury, to the screaming horn and violin crescendos in his head. He wondered if perhaps, those Three Magi had heard more angelic strains when witnessing that stellar spec – so far away, yet so powerful.

What thoughts Biran had troubling him, he voiced aloud. 'They used a veritable weapon as old as the Pyramids --- *Surprise* --- They used *surprise!*

'What are you going on about?'

'That sixth day of October, when a great many of us, civilian and military, were on our knees, figuratively and literally, on that Sabbath of Sabbaths, Yom Kippur, Egypt and Syria launched their combined assault on us when we were least expecting it, and so caught us with our guard down. Spear-heading their two-pronged assault on the Suez Canal Crossing and the Golan Heights, their dastardly clever strategy cost us the heavy loss, over two days, of one hundred and eighty of our two hundred and fifty tanks deployed in Sinai. This from their heavy barrage of anti-tank guided missiles. But our Twenty-First Armoured Division managed to block off Egypt's divisional offensive on the nineth. More fool us – taking our alertness of them off as we did in our preoccupation with the Yom Kippur litany of holy concentrated observations on fasting and atonement.'

'And you, *yourself*, Colonel?'

'*Me?*'

'Did you flay your back, in repentance for your sins, with a good old cat-o'-nine tails?'

'Of course --- as would *you*, no less, in your own atonement season of Lent.'

'Touche!'

Conversation was limp after that, the topics bearing no relevance to the important concern ahead, and so dying off soon after their utterance. This was so for the entire journey but for one instance when, as if the distant star had dimmed in lustre, Frank suddenly pulled out his cigarette to look round at Biran. 'Have you let on, with anyone in your cell, where tonight's little sortie far into the desert is taking us?'

'Is it important?'

'Well, *have* you?'

'No. Is it important?

But Frank gave no answer, only looking back again at the bright point beckoning from the other side of the universe. The very remoteness of that pin-prick star was serving as a point of refuge on which to hang his attention, in faraway distraction from that tormented part of the universe inside his own mind. Biran's announcement that they would soon be there had Frank casting his cigar out the window, so that the red cinder flew backwards, to disappear with the track dissolving magically in the mass of sand behind them. As the way twisted and straightened ahead, great sand dunes shifted aside to let feeble lights spring up, approaching quickly to give rise to a tiny look-out post preceding the camp. With the spread of tents increasing, a twinkling effect arose from the spotted lights competing with black hulks moving across their path. Poles, or possibly puny palms, were there and gone in moonlit flashes, the tall indistinct shapes masquerading behind ghoulish nocturnal habits giving uneasiness to the unfamiliar. Something that was too large to be nurtured by soil was moving up towards them, but it was hard to see what it was with the track they were following twisting round in sharp angles. The track at last straightened out to let the military camp, almost within reach, come out of hiding to reveal itself openly to them.

An abrupt surprise outline of protruding gun turrets and menacing metal projections, mounted on a great thirty-foot hulk of steel, swung round on its steel-plate roller tracks from out of nowhere to block the truck's path. Even before the truck had braked to a halt, a host of figures wielding menacing FN-FAL 7.662mm rifles swarmed down and around them, like scarab beetles closing in on their prey, from the thirteen-ton Zelda M113 personal carrier bearing the proud Star of David.

'Shalom,' said Biran blindly, through the open window, to whoever it was shining the powerful torch-light in his face.

'Shalom. Papers!' The voice was reasonably polite, with no sign of aggression.

But when the young officer passed the torch to another young soldier, to take the Biran's ordinary civilian pass, not his Mossad pass, Biran saw that the officer held in his other hand an Uzi sub machine-gun primed ready to let loose a burst of its deadly 9mm lead venom.

'These seem to be in order,' said the officer, handing back the passes to Biran and Falzoni. 'But what are you doing out here in this active zone, and more so --- how do you two civilians come to be driving this military vehicle -- or more correctly, this *ex*-military vehicle? It's not showing its operational code letter plates, so that leaves the question unanswered.' He stepped back, lifting his Uzi to a more ready position. 'Step down, please. Both of you. Now!' Looking round, he ordered two of his men to clamber up and into the back of the truck to make an inspection. He cast a hard warning look at the two civilians. 'So, let's see what jolly black-market contraband you're carrying.'

Biran took out his Mossad pass with careful slowness in order not to temp the young man's trigger finger. He handed it to the officer that he judged to be about half his age, who was taking a long time staring at him before deciding to look down to examine the official secret intelligence credential.

'I need to have a word with your C.O,' said Biran taking the pass handed back to him.

'*Seren* (Battalion Company Commander) Ezcika. I'll take you to him. If you'll follow me.'

'And you are?'

'Captain Sheenas.

'Right, Captain, lead the way.'

The camp was quiet, with flapping canvas taking over from rough time-worn stone in providing shelter for resting soldiers, as they passed on through between indistinct shapes of what had been a military outpost in another age's war. Lights, though bleak, from tents all around had a warming effect, after their cold journey across the night-chilled desert. A dozing resting camaraderie atmosphere emanated from the tents, multiplying itself where the path opened out into a tiny square area. Over and beyond this space, ultimate grimness tapered off into the omnipotent infinity of some ancient stone pagan deity.

The black mass stood imperiously over them in its timeless watch. An awesome mass of jutting staunch buttresses and narrow stone piping ascending to a terminal profusion of barbed pinnacles and demonic arcs wrestling with the sky. The towering shape needed no lighting, unlike the lesser tents below it, being structurally and dogmatically firm in darkness as it was in daylight. The overbearing presence was sufficient testimonial of its godly formation. Frank looked, puzzled for a moment by a group of slim palm-tree boles, topless with no palms, until realising that they were what remained after being caught in the crossfire of a modern war's artillery barrage shrapnel. You could always bet on war leaving behind some oddball changes on the landscape as a reminder of its woes in the aftermath.

A running staccato sound of coded wireless transmission cut into the night's silence. 'Lior, our lifeline to H.Q,' said the captain, over his shoulder to the two following him, neither of them considering this piece of information to be of any importance.

The thin pulsing sound drifted after them, fading gradually, as they crossed the open square, treading now, not on sand, but cobble-stones of an earlier Mesopotamian age, heading for what looked like it could be the camp C.O.'s tent. Dark figures began to materialise around them out of the shadows, watching them, guns ready to fire on signal from Captain Sheenas. This was how Frank was interpreting the setting. The camp was particularly 'cagey' about visitors, so far out in its remoteness from base, that as the two civilians walked by, searching eyes charged with newly awakened alertness followed them. Safety was strictly guarded here and anything upsetting its indolent pulse was apt to be met with the appropriate measure of aggression. Satisfied with no call to arms, the onlookers dropped their guard and gradually ebbed away into the darkness whence they'd come.

Frank's eyes searched for an opening on the broad expanse of tautened ropes and canvas billowing out from the strong desert wind. But they turned off sharply to be faced with a long wall of sand bags piled three layers high, blocking their way. A dug-out, darker than the night's darkness, loomed up to lead the way down with wooden steps, to swallow them up and allow them to pass under and through an arch opening in a stone wall. An ancient civilisation's ceremonial presentation entrance, and an archaeologist's dream.

Frank felt the ground beginning to slope down before them as they entered into a tunnel. Moving along slowly between dry stone walls, they stopped suddenly at the captain's warning of steps falling away immediately at their feet. The stone slab walls gave way to a mixture of small stones, earth and wooden struts that led the tunnel eventually to another flight of steps, this time of newly cut fresh wood, that climbed upwards. Mounting the steps, they stopped before a large door-sized canvas flap. 'Keeps the biting draught out better than the door does,' said Sheenas, knocking on a wooden door behind the flap before opening it.

Seeing two strange faces behind his captain, the young guard, raising his Galil 5.5mm assault rifle, was about to ask for a password, but Sheenas waved him aside. Biran gave a smiling 'Shalom' to help put the young guard at ease. They were *all* young men, as far as Frank could see, on entering the isolated outpost's Strategy Room. Commander Ezeika's years on their own made up for the total ages of all his men in the room, it seemed. Being nothing particularly special to look at, he carried that heavily burdened look that characterised his race, with his very own half acre share of deep lines etched into his forehead and cheeks.

The man got up slowly from his folding camp-seat, his eyes making an open inspection of the two strangers for some long seconds. In contrast to his quiet appearance, the large hard hands, a soldier's hands, hung at his side with their fingers splayed out as they did in outlining manoeuvres on campaign operations charts. 'Shalom,' he said to Biran and Frank, in a heavy timbred voice that gave the strength and ease that enabled him to send young soldiers out onto the battlefield at the risk of their lives. Both Biran and Frank recognised the cold irony of this in the old man's eyes. They were all in the same game that pushed sentiment to the side. 'Shalom,' They quietly returned.

Introducing the two civilians, Captain Sheenas saluted and took his leave.

'Please, gentlemen, sit down --- that is, if you can find somewhere to sit in this crowded cubby-hole of an operations room.'

At that, a soldier promptly got up to surrender his seat to one of them. Frank took it and sat down. Biran sat down at Commander Ezeika's table.

Commander Ezeika insisted that, following their bone-chilling journey all the way from Cairo, to out here in Israeli-occupied Sinai, roughly 20 miles west of the Khatmia Pass, between General Sharon's 6th Armoured Brigade and General Bar-Levi's 3rd Armoured Division, south of their Bir Gifgafa forward-operating Airforce base, the next immediate course of action, before embarking on matters of a more serious nature, would be to partake of some body-warming beverage. The adjutant soon afterward brought in three metal cups of coffee. 'A little tepid, perhaps, needing some warm-up,' said Ezeika, with a wry smile, pouring the brandy from a tiny bottle into each cup. Leaning forward to give Frank his mug, he saw tiredness in the younger man's face. 'You look unwell.'

Frank was openly irritated by this close attention. Inwardly he felt he could scream if another person said he was not well. 'I'm all right.'

'I can't order you to, but I'm strongly suggesting that you drink your coffee and rest. I'm familiar with the latent malarial strain fever simmering before coming to surface, Mr Peters --- which I'm supposing isn't your real name, just as I'm supposing that you're the IDF's (Israeli Defence Force) pipeline for US aid.'

'You suppose correctly, Commander ---- *hopefully.*'

'*Hopefully?* Am I mistaken in believing that your President Nixon has already initiated this vital aid plan with his having giving the go-ahead for his Nickel Glass Operation?'

'No, you're not mistaken, Commander, but there are, alas, a critical multitude of senators of the 'Dove' persuasion on Capitol Hill who consider the President to be mistaken in what *he* believes.'

'For fear of your aiding Israel with your supplies airlift operation giving way to repercussion of the breaking-off of political and trading negotiations between the United States and the Soviet Union?'

'In a nutshell, Commander.'

'I see,' said Ezeika, nodding his head thoughtfully, before continuing to sip his 'toddy'. 'Like I've said, it will serve you well to rest a little while. I'll have Corporal Perelman here sort out a bed and some blankets for you. No use drinking the warm coffee if you can't keep the warmth inside you. Go with him.'

'Thank you, Commander.' As he got up, Frank pointed at Biran; 'He can fill me in later.'

With 'Peters' gone, Biran and Commander Ezeika got into their conversation with the usual slow circuitous build-up that went, as you expected, from this sort of meeting. As they did, Biran could sense that Ezeika's mind was only half there, only half listening, his deeper thoughts elsewhere. Not that he doubted Ezeika's willingness to give out details of the current strategic development in the field. Israel could hardly have less fervour in staving off this combined assault from Egypt and Syria, than countries that were experiencing the growing tongue of fire from political dissent's terrorism.

With these thoughts passing through his mind, Biran's attention was suddenly caught by an outbreak of dull thuds. He couldn't pin down the direction exactly, somewhat disorientated as he was, with his turning about in the tunnel. Somewhere to his right, uneven in their timing and still some distance away. Of course, missiles. Egypt's SAM (surface-to-air) missiles were being fired into Israeli military locations in occupied Syria, at the same time giving partial relief of pressure from Israel's blockade on the narrow coastal Gaza Strip settlement that closed checkpoints, so cutting off vital food supplies.

Seeing the direction of Biran's thoughts, Ezeika nodded slowly and smiled in wise justification. Another kind of sound filtered through, different from the distant dull soft thuds, to reach Biran's ear. Harder, sharper, tearing the air with menace, nearer – nearER – neARER – NEARER. The two F-4 Phantom II jet fighters bearing the proud Star of David on their fuselages thundered past overhead with ear-blasting resolve. A second later, two more roared past. Biran swung his head round to follow their path. All on their way to an enemy front-line to deliver their fury.

Ezeika watched Biran's face, with its split-second tension, surmising his train of thought. He nodded slowly in heavy thought, biting into the olive he'd put in his mouth, to separate and remove the stone from the flesh, before speaking. His heavy voice carried his words with the same solid conviction as those thundering engines. 'We do not retaliate *vengefully* – we deliver pain.' A pause, to chew on another olive and remove its stone. 'You will perhaps agree that pain is the universal guardian of health, yes? It is because of that pain that we know that something is wrong, that we are ill, that we have sustained injury. And so, we halt the action that we now realise will produce further injury.' Taking up another olive, he pushed the small open jar across the table to Biran. 'Have one.'

Biran declined, waving a hand. He didn't argue Ezeika's philosophy, but simply nodded. They were on the same side, fighting a common enemy. With all the olives reduced to stones, Biran manoeuvred the conversation so that what he was after began to come his way. Getting up from his seat, Commander Ezeika beckoned Biran to follow him over to the large wall map.

Giving a flat-handed slap to the map first, he then pointed to the area high-lighted by bright red-headed pins. 'We've sustained very serious loss of our heavy armour, from their initial attack, here, at Suez. About seventy-two per cent, in fact.' He looked around for confirmation of this figure, but everyone else was too busily engaged to have been heeding him. 'We have Bell Two-O-Five helicopters on standby at Gifgafa, ready to fly in our commandoes behind Egyptian enemy lines to pinpoint SAM missile batteries and warn our Air Force pilots when they attack. It doesn't help to ease the loss or the situation in general, with the heated squabbling between General Sharon and General Gonen. Even with Moshe Dayan throwing in his support for Gonen, the overall Chiefs-of-Staffs decision was to replace Gonen with Bir Levi.'

'Do you think that was a wrong decision?' said Biran.

'No, Gonen has definitely lost his sparkle, in my opinion ---- and Dayan, as well. But that last part is strictly off record.'

'Perhaps you should bear in mind, Commander, that in my line of work, nothing is ever off the record if there's a vestige of chance it can serve purposeful application.'

About to reply, Ezeika paused to look past Biran at someone appearing in the doorway.

'Sir,-------- H.Q.' was all the soldier needed to say to have Ezeika's full attention.

'You'll have to excuse me, Colonel Biran, I have to be elsewhere. I'm going to be occupied for some time, as far as I can say. Have someone show you where to go, to help yourself to some chicken soup and bread.'

'Right, I'll do that. Shalom.'

12

The evening fog pressed up against the **MIT Koch Institute Research Laboratory** window trying to join the gloom inside. The room's heavy atmosphere was cut by the doleful beat of a dripping tap. A faint tinkling came from the front bench. A solitary lamp showed a figure, with a shock of bright red hair, head and beard, in white coat and full-length plastic apron, working diligently before an array of test-tubes and beakers. Easily spotted among all of the Institute's white-coated figures, it also gave him his audience's attention, if only for the wrong reason, alas; but that constituted a start, at least, in their learning programme. Standing out aloof from the glassware was a gleaming brass binocular microscope perched up on its hind legs like a giant prey mantis with a triple turret proboscis.

Professor Selwyn Sefleck turned to the microscope. Snapping the lens turret round into its lowest power position, he then dropped staining solution onto the slide specimen. Placing the cover on the slide, he mounted the hair specimen under the lens. Turning the milled knob gently, Professor Sefleck raised the objective lens gradually, coaxing the bubble of blurred light to burst into a vivid circle of clarity. The hair held Sefleck's interest, outlined against the bright circle like a lunar landscape. Swivelling the turret round to high power, he adjusted the lens power once more. The 'moon' had now taken on a sinister darkness and the 'tree' had shot up close to touching distance, its rugged 'bark' revealing vile secrets.

Murder, in fact, was the applicable term. The poor wretch who had fallen mortally beneath the 'tree' had done so at the deliberate felling by another. In succinct tongue, the man had been poisoned. A quick scrutiny along the hair's axis past the sebaceous gland sufficed to show that the cortex and cuticle cells were blatantly ablaze with the fiery red pigment of murder. Plainly the guilty hand was that of the wife. Her rage dually vented on the husband's betrayal and the younger woman's beauty.

Sefleck lifted his head away slightly from the microscope, nodding in conclusion before straightening up. Nodding his head, he addressed his young students slowly, in a warm steady voice: 'Reflect on how the plight of the female poisoners has held itself up through the centuries. How they would have stained the pages of history with the darker shade of their fair nature, had closer examination been possible. The medical examiner had to go by the outward appearance of the body. A livid or mottled body indicated poison, though not acute poisoning. A rapid state of putrefaction was the supposed proof against this. But arsenic, alas, retards putrefaction so that considerable numbers must have perished by it. Diseases must have destroyed countless others with the false appearance of poisoning. But what hangman, given his pence, gnashed his teeth over a few wrong necks in the noose?'

A shy laugh here and there about the multi-tiered theatre.

'Little wonder then that arsenic's innocuous white oxide formed the murderer's favourite tool. Being both soluble and virtually tasteless, the powder could easily be mixed with food. An unsuspecting doctor could thus mistakenly diagnose the symptoms as gastroenteritis, and so prescribe the usual ten cents box of Dandelion and Quinine Liver pills.'

A single isolated laugh this time.

'A higher-minded consultant would perhaps deem cholera as the ailment more fitting to the grace and dignity of his professional fee. To the unwary eye, then, the effect of arsenic was its user's trump-card, arousing no undue attention. Unlike the vegetable alkaloid atropine of belladonna which strikes suspiciously swift. Or strychnine, which arouses horror from its victim's convulsions.' Sefleck broke off from his lecturing, to move over to the sink at the bench-end to wash the slide. Water cascaded off the slide, carrying the hair with it in a swirl down the sink hole. The clean slide was replaced in its rack.

'Observe!' he said, alerting his students, while looking round to spy out the pieces required for the next stage of his demonstration. He snatched up a jar of copper reagent and a bottle of concentrated hydrochloric acid. From amidst the glassware cluttering the bench, he drew forth a Bunsen burner. Pushing a tripod over this, he then topped the tripod with an empty beaker. Pouring out a measured volume of distilled water into the beaker, followed by an equal volume of concentrated hydrochloric acid. Sefleck then held a flaming match to the Bunsen's gaping mouth. The yellow sulphurous butterfly fluttered violently for a moment before the Bunsen burped and blew forth its white tongue to lick the beaker's bottom. Sefleck turned the Bunsen's brass collar and the mischievous flame disciplined itself into a hissing blue jet.

Plucking a piggy-tail twirl of copper from the jar, he burnished it with a file and dropped it into the beaker. After some minutes, the copper winked back brightly in unashamed purity.

'And so, we see, ladies and gentlemen, the copper retains its purity, so telling us *what*? '

Not even a timid murmur of an answer volunteered from the audience.

'So telling us that the apparatus is so far free of arsenic. Thus, any arsenic found in the analysis would have to come from the body.' A pause, to take in this negative finding. 'However, for further confirmation -----' Sefleck took up a small beaker containing filtrate of the victim's stomach and plopped several drops of it into the boiling liquid. The dark drops rapidly disappeared in the burbling mass.

After some minutes, the copper still winked back defiantly. Rescuing the copper from the boiling mass with a pair of forceps, he held it up for all to see its gleaming surface, showing that there was no precipitate. 'As before, we conclude no arsenic to be in the apparatus.'

The Professor next took up a flask that had a glass stopper with a thistle-funnel and a glass tap. Beneath this, another glass tube curved out of the stopper, to enter a long horizontal tube that contained calcium chloride for the purpose of drying gasses passing through it. This tube joined a finer tube toughened to withstand the Bunsen flame. Murmuring his approval, Sefleck stepped sharply over to the chemical balance, a jar of zinc and a spatula in hand. The glistening spatula snaked deftly to-and-fro, between jar and balance pan, in a swift flurry of precision. He paused to raise the balance. Watching the needle quiver to its central equilibrium point, Sefleck lowered the balance with a bump betraying his impatience. Seizing up the pan, he tipped the zinc into the flask. A pipette grew out of his hand, releasing a dribble of dilute sulphuric acid onto the zinc in the flask. Replacing the stopper with its funnel and tube arrangement, Sefleck paused to watch the mixture churn up its bubbles of hydrogen gas. He then poured some stomach filtrate in through the thistle funnel. The Bunsen was then placed under the fine end of the tube.

No deposit had formed in the tube just beyond the edge of the flame. Sliding the Bunsen away, Sefleck lit a wax taper from it and ignited the gas escaping from the end of the tube. It gave off a lavender tint. Splendid. Now a small piece of porcelain held to the jet grew a small patch of greyish 'skin'. He added a drop of nitric acid to the deposit and warmed it near the Bunsen flame. Holding a dropper just over the stain, he released a drop of silver nitrate onto it. The grey 'skin' blushed a definite brick red. *Positive.* One more test for certainty. With a fresh piece of porcelain, and this time touching the stain with mercuric bromide paper, the test was once more clearly positive. The stain had turned yellow this time from the halogen reagent. Arsenic was definitely present in the body.

'*Voila!*' With this conclusive cry of satisfaction, Sefleck looked up in expectation of a murmur, at least, of thanks for his demonstration, from his students.

Instead, a sudden draught and an outbreak of soft giggling from the student audience, caught the Professor's attention, so that he looked round.

With a soft knock announcing his intrusion, Marley Goodblood poked his head round the platform's side-door. Officially they were scheduled to be working together, but neither of them had much respect for the other. Their opinions were poles apert and their methods for tackling problems invariably clashed. They simply didn't like each other. Professor Sefleck's low opinion of Goodblood and his devious secretive dealings, was not particularly guarded. The FBI, for whom he gave lectures and clinical demonstration in forensic analysis to trainee .federal agents, was a government approved body operating legally 'above board', so to speak; whereas, the CIA---? So, that when he turned around, the disdain had not quite slipped from his face before it was caught by the CIA officer's sharp eye. Goodblood's square-faced expression gave off a cool message that went well with the job. The raglan overcoat was strictly 'regulation' with its dull iron-grey weave.

Deliberately ignoring the CIA man's impromptu presence for the moment, Sefleck continued with the lecture to his now distracted students. 'As I inferred earlier, before being interrupted,' he said, turning round to cast a cold reproving look at Goodblood, 'this man was poisoned by arsenic. We would have proceeded to go through the *Juris Prudence* protocol procedure of compiling your report on the analysis --- which would have been done to the full benefit of your studies, had our concentrated attention not been broken.' Another cold glance at the CIA man. He beamed back at his young college-fresh FBI trainee students. 'We'll complete this session tomorrow --- no, sorry --- Wednesday, three o'clock. Thank you.'

Goodblood had to put up with Sefleck's cynical attitude, having endured many of his kind along the long road that the job took him. His superiors back in Washington were finding the man's work in genetic engineering to be of vital importance in a vitally important situation. It didn't matter that the threat of an outbreak of widespread biochemical poisoning was *safely* far away in the Middle East; a dragnet operation was underway with all the security branches, with everyone, save those who couldn't get at least one foot out of the wheelchair, pitching in their effort. Desperately trawling for vital information – *any* information – from *anyone – anywhere*. With today's traders in terrorist intelligence being one big happy international family, nowhere was too far out to seek information if it helped save the day. An ear to the ground on the remotest outback on the globe was game if it picked up good vibrations. Where the hell was Dr Nafur-Nafiri?

In spite of this, Goodblood was instinctively wary of the man standing beside him. He watched his every action, down to the smallest mannerisms, with an experience instinct. There was something about the man – something he couldn't quite put words to – something that read low on his inner 'trust-meter'.

Turning away from each other, they looked in the direction of floorboards creaking out in agony as the dismissed audience stood up to turn and hurry up the narrow wooden stairway between the towering lecture theatre tiers, some of the fleeing students bounding up the deep steps two at a time. Goodblood smiled to say: 'They risk breaking their necks in their haste to get away from you, it seems, Professor.' With all the theatre tiers now empty, he turned his attention back to Sefleck. 'But I could have sworn that I heard you say arsenic was undetectable; that it looked like natural death from disease?' At Sefleck's frowning to question this remark, Goodblood pointed a thumb at the door: 'When I was waiting out there.' A tiny point Goodblood wasn't bothered with either way, but a simple way of starting their discussion.

'Your *second* observation is correct, Mr Goodblood. I did, indeed, quote the ravages of disease as often providing camouflage for the more sinister dealings of arsenic poisoning. But as to your *first* observation, *no*, I did not say that arsenic poisoning was *undetectable*.'

Goodblood made to speak, but Sefleck waved him to silence so that he could continue. 'Even the most circuitous of paths of poisons can be traced, where the pursuer is wary of his prey.'

'*Yeah?* Goodblood didn't quite get it.

Sefleck took a long, exasperated, sigh before going on. 'The one disadvantage of arsenic as a poison is that it is metallic, and so remains in the body after death. If it is there to be found, it can be found. One simply requires to know how and where to look. The murderer may flee, but the murder weapon remains embedded in the victim's body.'

'Like the proverbial dagger in the back, you mean?'

'Splendid, Mr Goodblood! Now you comprehend. Though perhaps a *chemical* dagger would be more appropriate.'

Goodblood raised an eyebrow in lingering doubt. 'And you think you know how to find this dagger, *do you*, Professor?'

Sefleck ignored the other's taunt, turning away to face the bench again. 'Observe!' He saw that Goodblood could no more appreciate the evidence than he could see specs of soot in the fog. A solid body of proof was needed that even the most myopic eye could focus on clearly.

This thought afforded Sefleck a quick glance at the Goodblood. The man's vacant expression was convincing enough. A positive demonstration was definitely required to dispel his lack of faith. Plainly nothing less would satisfy the CIA man.

Sefleck's eyes darted to-and-fro across the laboratory glassware and along the multiple rows of bottles and jars with their many hues of chemicals. Goodblood stepped promptly aside to let Sefleck pick up whatever it was he was looking for.

This puzzled expression prompted a smirk from Goodblood. Straightening up smartly, he stepped over to Sefleck's side. 'Not quite seeing what you want, Professor? Well, that makes two of us. All this so-called --- no, no, spare me, please!' He threw up a hand to cut off Sefleck's attempt to reply. 'No more long-winded explanations for these fangled theories and principles of yours, Professor. I've taken in more than enough of it over the phone from you, as well as going through your personal dossier, along with the official forensic report to us at Langley. As far as I'm concerned, this situation has to be solved through solid investigative intelligence channels and leg-work. It's no use shaking your head, Professor, it had to be said. I could say more, but I reckon that would be a waste of time --- yours and *mine*.'

Sefleck's lips twitched in annoyance at this remark but he refrained from commenting. It would, indeed, be a waste of time to mount his own argument against such a tirade of doubt, he agreed inwardly. As with that other doubting Thomas, Goodblood wanted his proof in the flesh. Well, with a little further endeavour, he would have his proof soon enough. Wasting no more words on the CIA man, Sefleck turned back to his work.

Feeling confident from the Professor's silent retreat, Goodblood took a different approach as he spoke to the other's back. 'Why don't you stick to what you do best, your research, that is. I'm not saying you won't come up with the solution eventually at some point, but we need something solid to sink our teeth into and work on *now*, not *later*.'

Taking these words in, and nodding in apparent understanding, Sefleck strode sharply over to a side rack, to pick up a retort half-filled with a dark fluid, ten millilitres of which he then extracted with a pipette. Dropping the fluid from the pipette onto what looked like a smear-line in a Petrie dish to Goodblood, the Professor then scraped the 'smear' with a long needle, next transferring what was on the needle's point to a clean microscope slide. Placing a cover plate over the small circular blotch on the slide, he mounted the slide on the microscope. Holding out an open-splayed hand to Goodblood, he beamed in smug invitation.

'What exactly am I supposed to be looking at, then, Professor?' Goodblood had a dithering moment of double-eyed winks of deciding which eye was the better one to continue looking down the microscope with. 'I can't see anything. Are you having me on?'

Sefleck tapped Goodblood's fingers with a spatula to guide them onto the microscope's milled racking knob. 'Perhaps just a small degree of adjustment to accommodate the minute distance that is the difference in focal powers of our eyes. Gently does it, now.'

'It seems worse, now. Gone all black.'

'Turn it the other way, then. *Slowly.* That's it.'

'Ah, that's better. I'm beginning to see something now. There, got it. So, what the hell is it, exactly? Looks like a squashed red Harlem Globe Trotters basket-ball lying on a great furry carpet.' Goodblood straightened up from the microscope, looking round, more than a little disappointed, at Sefleck. 'Is that it, then? The everything and nothing of an eye-boggling wonder that you consider to be something important for me to see?'

Sefleck tried to keep his patience at this barrage of ignorance over his scientific findings. 'That red basket-ball, Mr Goodblood, is, in fact, the remains of a brutally ruptured blood cell lying, not on a *carpet*, as you so quaintly put it in your layman's feeble ignorance, but vascular tissue hardened now to virtual 'concrete' stiffness --- that is, hard in compression, like that 'concrete', but violently fragmented on attempted extension. Thus, the vascular system throughout the body is disintegrated instantly. The overall full effect on the human system therefore, I'm sure even you can imagine.' Sefleck paused before letting out the important piece. 'This grotesque result I've only *just* managed to accomplish through long endeavour with the intervening appliance of metallic poisons, no less.' Sefleck tapped the desk in grim finality. 'The overall result being an outbreak of rapid dissemination of molecular breakdown of cell tissue in all the body's organs, rendering them non-functioning – or as you would say, in layman's tongue: *dead!*

'And unto dust we shall return,' murmured Goodblood quietly, to no one in particular.

'I beg your pardon?'

Goodblood shook his head, waving the question aside. 'Correct me If I'm wrong, Professor, but I'm getting the unholy feeling that you're saying that our Doctor Nafur-Nafiri is still dangerously a step ahead of anything you can so far hope to conjure up here with all your test-tubes, beakers and things. Am I right?'

'*Frighteningly* right.' Sefleck's voice betrayed fact that he was reluctant to concede to being that 'one step' behind his former assistant. But he could see that the CIA man, like the bulldog, having bitten, would not release his bite before getting what he wanted ----information.

'Very well, we're involved here with the somewhat convoluted, if not complex, process of *transduction*, which is the process by which foreign DNA is introduced into a cell by a virus or viral vector. The latter being typified by an organism, like a biting insect or tic, that transmits a disease or parasite from one animal to another. For instance, the viral transfer of DNA from one bacterium to another would be an example of horizontal gene transfer.' A short pause to look at Goodblood, who was nodding with understanding in a way that said he was *not* understanding. He went on. 'This transduction does not require physical contact between the cell donating the DNA and the cell receiving the DNA, that we have occurring in normal sexual conjugation. We use transduction as a common tool in the field of molecular biology to stably introduce a foreign gene into a host's genome.'

Pulling a blank page from a pad on the desk, Sefleck began quickly sketching, as he spoke. 'See here we have DNA from an infectious virus being integrated and replicating in the host bacterial DNA. Are you with me?' Another empty nod from Goodblood. 'Good, we can go on. So, this newly introduced DNA cuts the host chromosome line incorrectly and exchanges its DNA to that of the host DNA. This excised section we see here, removed from the host chromosomal line, comprises part host chromosome and part new DNA. This is transferred to a new cell where recombination occurs.' Another pause, and another 'knowing' nod from Goodblood. 'This recombination results in the cell DNA eventually having an entirely different genetic constitution from that of both the donor cell and recipient cell genetic constitution.'

Sefleck reached out to tear another page from the pad. But Goodblood held up a hand to wave it, signalling that they stop there. 'No, no, Professor, I think we can leave it there. I don't want you to waste good paper any more than you can waste my brain's effort trying to take in all that you've said. You could be right, Professor, you could well be right, as I'm sure you are, but you'll have to give me something more solid than this to satisfy my superiors in Washington --- and they can be a right pack of hungry wolves, when it comes to the point.' Goodblood gestured vaguely around at the jumbled arrangement of baffling scientific paraphernalia all around him. 'Something in writing is what I need, Professor.'

'You will find every necessary word entered up in my report of analysis of the progressive situation. And all duly signed at the bottom, as required.' Sefleck handed the CIA man the multi-paged report.

Goodblood perused the pages without comprehending as much as a single word of the technical material. 'That seems to be in order.'

'So good of *you* to say so, Mr Goodblood.'

Goodblood caught the sarcastic remark, casting a wary eye at Sefleck. There was definitely something bugging the Professor. He could see it, almost smell, it was that thick – and it wasn't the effect of all these chemicals around everywhere. Not the usual thing, not that there was anything much 'usual' about Sefleck. This was – what? Something *different*. Something about his whole manner just struck him as odd in phase from what he had seemed on their first meeting minutes ago. Sure, he was weathered by Sefleck's continual impudence and attempts to wind him up with sarcastic prodding. But that was not what this was. As always, when being 'brushed-off' by the superior-minded, Goodblood always managed to display the cautionary sense of holding back from going too far in response. He felt that caution seemingly evaporating. He could see that the bugger had changed. It was in his eyes. His expression, his body language, with his words coming out of that stiffening face with as much sincerity as they would have, if directed elsewhere. In fact, he didn't seem to be giving a damn about that notorious historical 'Black Plague' now making its entrance onto the 20th century stage.

Could it be that the Professor *wasn't* one step behind his former assistant, Nafur-Nafiri? Maybe he was that one step *ahead* of the doctor, or if not, had developed a biological key to securing control of that devilish virus. If so, he could sell to the highest of bidders kneeling before him offering perhaps not frankincense, or myrrh, but yes, the gold, its weight in US dollars, stacked up safely in the discrete subterranean privacy of a vault beneath the pavement of a small private Swiss family bank. That would make for a nice nest-egg to dip into on retirement.

Goodblood made it a point in his mind to check back with Langley, to see if there was anything that he, or *they*, had missed out on. 'But understand, Professor, if our technical team don't manage to come here to Massachusetts, you'll be expected to travel to Washington to give your personal statement to the President in the White House. And fill us all in with your usual brilliant scientific explanation of how to resolve the problem.'

'In that case, given the choice, I mustn't keep our President waiting. If you would care to follow me to my office, I have to pick up some things.'

'Right. But let's not be hanging about too long. We've only limited time to spare before that crazy 'Doctor Frankenstein' releases those bugs to let them come our way tickling our tonsils.'

13

The young man felt all the eyes staring – boring – into him, when he planted the large heavy-duty bolt cutters down on the counter in the builders supplies store. In his self-conscious mind, burning with guilt, the large tool seemed enormous. It was as if he had on a striped jumper, a mask, and was holding a bag marked 'swag', like in those crazy comics he used to read. And still did, sometimes, but didn't let on about that to the doctor. All these men, in the Christian district, watching his every move; and they were all infidels. Bastards! They weren't watching him, but that was how his paranoid mind made him feel. He could have shot them all, every single one of them, with his fantastic Beretta. But the doctor had taken the machine pistol from him before he had left the van. This had been careful insight by the doctor, who had foreseen the danger of his newly recruited young helper, Rasheed, having a tendency to overreact to a situation. Rasheed, orphan, simmering with his youth's blind anguish, couldn't wait to get out of the store.

The cutters were the last on the list of tools he had been buying on the doctor's specific instructions. All bought from different stores, so as not to draw attention to himself. He had also bought the boiler suits and caps they were wearing, so as to look like Muslims, and to blend in with the scenery of workers on a job. Again, on the doctor's instructions. The one commodity that the doctor had bothered to get out of the van, to get for himself, was in the back, in two metal cylinders. He had insisted on going to collect them on his own, disappearing into a deep metal canyon between mountains of dockside cargo containers. The cylinders looked just like ordinary gas cylinders like those that the stalls in the streets and suki used to cook food. But Rasheed had noticed the small yellow three-bladed propellor symbol denoting radio activity on the sides of them. Not knowing what that meant, he somehow didn't think that the two cylinders contained gas for roasting chickens on a revolving spit.

As they drove along the road, Rasheed was half expecting a great line of police cars to be racing after them. But there were no blue lights flashing in the rear mirror or wing mirror. 'No checkmate cars so far, it seems; how about that,' said Rasheed, with his boyish chirpiness.

The doctor, disturbed from his deep thoughts, looked around, puzzled at the other's remark. 'Checkmate? Sorry?'

'Yeah, you know – the black and white squares on the sides of police cars in American comics, like chessboards. Checkmate cars – get it?' But Hassani couldn't understand the boy with his strange ways of delusional thinking. Rasheed saw the doctor's puzzlement and gurgled with delight at his being one up on his 'boss'. He put his foot down on the accelerator and throttled faster along the road. The doctor at once put a restraining hand on the 'boy's arm to get him to slow down again. They could not afford to attract the attention of the authorities with minor traffic violation.

The reason for the bolt cutters became apparent to Rasheed when they drew up in front of the lock-up in the arch under the railway bridge. The large heavy-duty padlock glinted in the sunlight. The doctor, in his mind, saw a much greater flash coming soon. His KGB source had given him the location of the two unfinished bombs, along with the detonator mechanism trigger codes, and transmitter signal codes. This, along with the uranium-238 isotope fission material from the rare radio-active actinide series, also provided by the KGB, was all he needed to get the job done. Or almost. Ironically, out of all this specialisation, his KGB masters had forgotten to provide him with the simplest of things. A key to open the lock-up's padlock. Dr Nafur-Nafiri's need to flee was the cause of this oversight.

Rasheed cursed under his breath, at his lack of muscle-power, when he failed to cut the padlock the first time. With a concentrated effort on the long-levered handles a second time, the blades finally severed the steel. Rasheed couldn't understand why they had needed to buy the two replacement locks, one for this place, and one for the other place. After all, once they were in, they were in, surely? Couldn't they just set up the bombs and go? Doctor Nafur-Nafiri had to explain to the boy that the bombs, a last-minute addition to his original plan, forced on him by Russian 'persuasion', were to go off later, so that until then, the doors had to be relocked so as not to look suspicious, as they would, lying open with broken locks. A simple sensible caution against snoopers going inside and interfering with their set-up.

They went inside, Nafur-Nafiri in front, to make sure the boy didn't touch anything he shouldn't.

Dark as it was inside, they both saw it instantly, standing out from everything rusting and ancient around it, by its demonic sheen of glistening newness. A twenty-first century devil-child held in the dark womb of nineteenth-century brickwork around it. Rasheed was about to step forward to touch it, but the doctor stopped him. Having come this far, it would be a shame to be blown up now, on account of the boy's naïve carelessness. He walked round it slowly, making a very careful examination. He saw the work that had to be done to make it complement all his years of arduous research and planning, should his original operation somehow go wrong. But he had been briefed thoroughly by his Russian instructors for this side of the operation. It would be a worthy executive of justified repayment, considering the 'regal' heritage he had been denied so long ago.

They brought the material in from the van and Nafur-Nafiri got to work, while Rasheed stood watch inside the partially closed doors, making sure nobody walked in on them unexpectedly. Rasheed was a little disappointed at the need for this precautionary measure on the doctor's orders. Since the doctor had given him the gun back, Rasheed wanted a chance to shoot some Christian or Jewish bastard dead.

Tired of his servile role as lookout, especially when there was nothing to look at, Rasheed wandered in to bend down and look over the doctor's shoulder to see what he was doing. 'Get back to the door,' the doctor said sharply without taking his eyes off the delicate wiring in his fingers. Just as Rasheed was returning to the door, Nafur-Nafiri cried out again urgently. 'Come over here. *Quickly!*'

'Make up your bloody mind, will you!'

But Nafur-Nafiri had neither a second to spare for arguing, nor a millimetre's space to spare for movement. He was frozen, holding the vital components that could cause nuclear fission if he moved wrongly. 'Shut up and give me a hand! I need you to hold that little connector rod that's slipping out of that tube there. Can you see it?'

'Where?'

'There, beside the wire where the plate has come away. See it?'

'I see it now.' Rasheed reached out.

'No! Wait! You mustn't let it touch the filament that's beside it in the second compartment – the one on the right side. Move it slowly back into the tube and fasten it carefully with that clip inside the tube. Make sure it's fastened securely with the clip, or it will swing round and touch that filament.'

'And what happens if I don't?'

The thought of them going up in a flash, annihilating millions of infidel Christians, and so satisfying Allah, would have pleased a suicide bomber. But Nafur-Nafiri saw his scientific skill and knowledge as too valuable an asset to the cause, to be used up like that. His expertise would be needed many more times after this until his newly appointed contract with Soviet Russia's plans was fulfilled. 'Just do it! Quickly; we haven't all day!' Nafur-Nafiri watched the boy secure the rod safely. 'Good. Now just pass me those pliers. No, not those ones; the smaller ones – beside the callipers. Good.' The doctor worked on quietly, while the boy looked on, rapt in awe at the other's calm handling of the bomb as if it was nothing more dangerous than a faulty paraffin lamp.

The tense silence and the delicate finger-work ceased at last, and

Nafur-Nafiri sat back on his haunches to take an overall broad look at his handiwork. Rasheed judged that the job was done now. 'That's it, then, is it? So where are we taking it, then? The Ben Ezra Synagogue? That would be a good target.'

'It stays here.'

'You're kidding me! All this bother just to blow up a dump like this? Rasheed looked round at the dirty walls. 'Who's going to give a damn of a shit if a crap of a dump like this goes up in smoke at the back of nowhere, eh? People won't even know it's gone off.'

'Oh, believe me, young man, when this little creation sings, *everyone* will know of it.'

'*That* thing?' Rasheed looked around himself again. 'Do you really think so, with all these walls around us? I mean, those bridge supports are really massive. They'd take a lot of the blast and ---'

'A little help from Mr Fermi – it will be suffice.'

'*Fermi*? Who's *he*?'

'He was the very man who first split the atom and so gave us the atom bomb. And from that subsequently came – *voila!* – the nuclear bomb.'

'You mean --?' Amazement and fright registered on the boy's face. This changed into an inner 'whoopee' realisation of glory at the thought of this great beauty of a bomb roasting all those fucking Christian and Jewish shit-arsed bastards. Damn them all. Another realisation struck him and his mind came down to earth. There was a more sober tone to his voice. 'What about *us*? How do *we* escape the blast? Do we --?' Rasheed's unsettling thoughts of being a suicide bomber without first being asked, were cut off by the dark place suddenly going darker. Without turning around, they both knew that someone was standing behind them, in the doorway.

Rasheed opened his boiler suit to reach inside for the Beretta.

His ever-wise doctor boss stopped him.

'Too much noise,' whispered Nafur-Nafiri, standing up and turning round. A flashing blue beacon, on the roof of the car behind the man, caused Nafur-Nafiri's confidence to plunge with an electrifying jolt. Something metallic glinted in the police officer's hand.

CAIRO SECURITY POLICE

The bold words below the golden shield badge on the warrant card, held a few inches from Nafur-Nafiri's face, stood out to hold his attention, as they were meant to, with their brazen message. Further official endorsement was made more so by the smudged ink-ring of authority stamped over the Commissioner's name. At the bottom, holding command over all this was the chief, the Major General. A sharp tick in ballpoint, along with a small star embossed in plastic, sufficed here in place of a signature.

Affecting a fake surprised reaction at the card's sudden presentation in order to give himself time to think, Nafur-Nafiri made a deliberate point of stumbling as he jerked his head back from the warrant card. But he had already summed-up officialdom from his first glance of the stalwart stance of the figure in the doorway. He noted how the man, in open gesture, rested his hand for a moment on the polished leather open-style holster which held what looked like a Spanish version of a Smith & Wesson revolver. It probably used French Ordnance 8mm cartridges. All in all, not a man to be toyed with.

'Papers!' the officer said brusquely, deliberately leaving out 'sir' that would have made for a policeman's politeness. He obviously wanted to sound as hard as his power over public citizens allowed him to be. Holding his head back, he looked steadily at Nafur-Nafiri, watching him closely, as he slowly pocketed his warrant card.

Nafur-Nafiri sensed that the man actually wanted him to be difficult so that he could demonstrate his official power --- *physically*. And power he had. But Nafur-Nafiri had been experiencing this kind of situation for some time now, when his activities had caused suspicions to be thrown his way. His answers had so far been good enough for him to scrape through the looming entrapment those questions threatened. But would they suffice this time? Whilst considering this, he ran his mind over some old basic knowledge of 'body language', and what facial expressions to pose and where to focus the eyes for difficult situations. He hoped that he was doing it correctly.

Feeling the man's eyes digging in to him, Nafur-Nafiri wasted no time in handing over his ID documents. But he could see that the police officer was disappointed in not finding any fault in the papers as he gruffly handed them back – that he would very much like to have arrested him and taken him and the boy in for searching and interrogation. There was a brief lightened air of relief with the officer turning to go. Pausing just inside the door, he turned to look back for a long parting moment's scrutiny of the doctor and the boy, looking pointedly slowly from one to the other, to make his suspicions clear to them.

Nafur-Nafiri watched as it seemed that the damned policeman, with his hand still on the door, was having second thoughts and was going to come back in to question them further. He held his breath until the man let go of the door and made to step outside.

A sudden blurred flurry of movement caught the corner of Nafur-Nafiri's eye with the boy rushing past him. In a downward-sweeping violent arc of fury, the bolt-cutter struck deep into the policeman's brain, mashing its soft pink texture with hard sharp fragments of bright white skull bone. Even though the man didn't move on the ground, the boy struck him two more times just to make sure that he was dead. Satisfied, he threw the heavy tool aside.

'Very clever --- I think not,' said Nafur-Nafiri, slowly clapping his hands silently in disapproval of the boy's act.

'It's all right,' said the boy, very much caught up with excitement at his having killed someone. 'We can put him in here and lock up again. No one will know.'

'And tell me what, may I ask, of that 'large object' out there with the blue beacon flashing on its roof?'

The boy shook his head, lost for an answer.

'Precisely!' Nafur-Nafiri paused to look down at the corpse, then at the boy. 'Help me to carry him inside. Then you can go and switch the beacon off and lock the car.'

With that done, after taking a deep breath, Nafur-Nafiri looked around, making sure that all was well with their important work here completed, before setting about gathering their tools. 'Let's get all the equipment back in the van,' he said. 'We've another crucial task to carry out, about two hours from here. Come on, hurry up.'

When they had loaded all the equipment back into the van, Nafur-Nafiri shook his head slowly, sighing with quiet exasperation at the naïve stupidity of the boy. 'Most surely it can only have been through the will of Allah that you were chosen to help me. Otherwise, I would have chosen differently. *Most* differently. Have you not yet grasped the situation?' Nafur-Nafiri paused, to let his words, with their implied 'situation', sink into the other's dull brain. 'After tomorrow, there will be *no one left* to find anything, and *nothing left* to find.'

14

It wasn't that Frank had not cleaned his wing mirror --- in fact he'd given it a good wipe before getting in the car; but there it was, like a damn great bluebottle stuck on gum-paper, catching his eye every time he looked in the mirror. But this 'bluebottle' had four wheels and was sticking to him no matter what side-road he turned off into. And he'd turned several times. And it still hung on.

The car bowled along through the city's Islamic Muizz Street and on along through the Qalawun Complex, before Frank decided to turn off, towards the Qasr El-Nil junction. It was a necessary change. He had originally intended going on back the way he had come, via Bostan Street and Bostan Bridge. That way, he would have turned off before the bridge, to drop in at the prearranged dockside's cute little French tabac bar to meet the contact. But that was off now. Things had changed. Keyed up into this new developing situation, he frowned as he tried to think how much they had changed. The contact was high risk material, too sensitive to allow for phoning on a line that had an extra ear listening in. The man was familiar with the procedure, with the danger it entailed, and knew how to look after himself. Standard action was for contacts to disperse after an agreed time lapse, if the other side failed to turn up. That hadn't changed.

If only you could change the damned traffic lights! Falzoni thrummed the steering wheel, but the traffic in front paid no attention. It remained stock still. When the twisting snake of vehicles did move off again, it was at a snail's pace, bumper to bumper.

The junction spread out ahead of him, with its broad concrete, steel, and glass facades waving in its new commercial generation's farewell to an older city's 'moulting' stone front. It was awkward as well as sad. With its fresh labyrinth of concrete stairways and pedestrian underpasses spotted with colour-coded signs, you definitely needed an honours degree in geography to navigate your way around. Maybe his Yale law degree would have been better suited by a degree in water-divining to locate a public loo.

Frank drove along Saliba Road, before rumbling over the time-lingering cobblestones of Moez Street and then onwards along Talaat Harb Road. All the while he was tossing the new information about in his head. Deciding the best signals to put out from the embassy CIA station to other intelligence departments without dropping the egg. Somewhat tricky, considering it was an inside 'ghost' job that officially didn't exist. He needed to make a phone call. From an outside call box, if he was to play safe.

The traffic was slowing down again for the lunch-time period. He looked in the wing mirror. Damnit! His tail had moved along two cars nearer. Car wheel rubber screeched on the road's hard surface as Frank suddenly accelerated while spinning the steering wheel, to pull out of his vehicle column in a lightning decision to veer off course from where he was going – from where he *should* have been going on prime priority – to go somewhere else. A relative stranger to this old town, he had just realised, in a moment's escape from his muddled thoughts, that it was just nearby. From what he could recall in his shaky mental mapping of the streets, it wouldn't take long to get there.

Ignoring the blaring fanfare of angry car horns, he made a dangerous U-turn, mounting a pavement and off again, with an oncoming car missing his car by a hair's breadth. Cutting over the corner pavement with another hard bump, he was through a red light, round the corner, and down the side street, with another car only just sparing his own car's paintwork. Brakes rammed on everywhere as he sped off, leaving behind him a cacophony of screaming horns that only New York's Carnegie Hall could match in a pre-performance warm-up. You didn't bother about furious traffic cops grabbing your licence and passport when you were in a tight corner in this game.

Another check in the mirror. All clear. He had shaken off the damned 'bluebottle'.

Pulling up sharply in front of the house, he got out and bounded up the steps. He tried the handle. The door was not locked. For a CIA 'safe house', even an impromptu arranged one, to be unlocked before he had rung the bell or knocked on the door and been challenged from within, struck Frank as a little *unsafe*. Taking out his heavy Colt automatic, he pushed the door back slowly to step cautiously inside.

Darkness all around, where shutters blocked out the light, that tensed his mind for any oncoming danger. 'You can put that away, Frank. It's buddies only in this hideaway hole,' said a voice in the shadows.

'And you can put yours away as well,' replied Frank to a shape that was darker than the shadows.' 'With you toting that little pea-shooter of yours, I'm guessing it's your wing-man Broxley's day off.'

'Oh, he's around,' said Jocelyn, pulling a window shutter open slightly to let in some light. She was wielding, in fact, a hefty cannon of a .44 calibre Ruger Magnum revolver. 'He gave me this to try out for size. I think it would stand out too much under my silk chemise evening outfit. I'll just stick with my little 'pea-shooter'.' She patted her pocket where she stowed her small .38 calibre Sig/Saur automatic. Turning round, she handed the revolver back to her 'wing-man', Broxley, who had suddenly ghosted up out of nowhere. Putting the pistol back in his shoulder-holster, Broxley ghosted away again as quietly as he'd come.

'I'd expected you to have studied your street map of this place, Frank.'

'Meaning?'

'You took a hell of a long way round to get here. I was tempted to honk you on the horn to wake you up and make you put your foot down and pump in the gas.'

'Jeez! You mean to say that was *you* with the French wheels hanging on my tail, just short of kissing my car's ass?'

Jocelyn's confirmation of this was a beaming great brood-toothed effort befitting the Cheshire Cat. This newly realised fact gave reason for Frank to struggle over conflicting thoughts. 'Hell, but if that was you all the while *behind* me – how in hell did you get here *before* me?'

'Like I've just said – *maps*, Frank! – *maps*!' Although, to be honest, I did spend a good many sabbatical extra-mural months here, to consolidate my indoor college studies with some good solid outdoor foot-work.'

'Ah, so that's why the Admiral had Marley put his favourite granddaughter on her first assignment as Field Handler reeling out the line on me.'

'I'd like to think it was something more than that.' Her tone betrayed a mixture of annoyance and embarrassment at Frank's remark.

Amidst the mild amusement at these revelations, another puzzling point stabbed at Frank's mind that was trying to put all these surprising facts in their right order. 'So why all the sneaky business of tailing me when you could have let me in on the fact that you were coming here as well? Tell me that, Jocelyn. At least it would have saved us the cost for gas, with us using only the one car.'

As was her usual reticent mode, Jocelyn didn't answer the challenging direct question. She turned and walked away towards a door at the other end of the hallway. 'Come on, let's go talk over some coffee back here in the kitchen. There's an issue we have to straighten out before we send in our field report'

In the kitchen, 'wing-man' Broxley poured out the coffee.

The sky was darkening rapidly with brooding thunderclouds when the cream-coloured Renault van passed through the Nasser Junction, bowling along the Ramses Highway, towards Midan Abdel Monlem turn-off bend, and on into the capital. It was here that the olive-green Porsche took up the tail. At first only a small dot, it grew and gained quickly on the Renault, without the driver paying undue attention. As it nosed nearer, the Renault driver noticed it and smiled at the thought of what it could be. His passenger patted his pocket, where his Beretta machine-pistol was. The man's gesture didn't escape the driver's attention. '*No*,' he said quietly, to stem the man's excitement.

Jocelyn looked aside at Frank, who was driving the Porsche. 'I think he's on to us now.'

Frank's face twitched a muscle to show that he was listening above his concentration on the car in front. 'Yeah, I think so, too. That's pity. But we can't afford to lag behind too far in the city. That's all right for winding desert roads.'

'Do you think he could be leading us on? He could be a decoy. I've got a feeling he is.'

'Maybe. The thought had crossed my mind a dozen turns back. But we'll let him play out his lead, to tickle our onions a little longer, to see what he does.' The chase was part of Frank's cup and ball rattling game, in a clampdown on all Russian cells in Egypt. While some cell members were seized for interrogation, others were being allowed to run, so that they could be chased to bigger 'birds. It didn't matter which direction they ran, so long as information could be grabbed at the end. They had been chasing this Renault with its one passenger for some time now. Maybe it *had* been fooling them all this time as a decoy. 'On second thoughts, muttered Frank, 'I think we'll call their bluff and pull them in. Agreed?'

'Don't let me stop you, Major, just do it.'

'Oh, I see, it's Major, again, is it? What's happened to Frank – are we still moping?'

'Just *do it*!'

As the Porsche moved in closer, nosing up to the van's bumper, the van moved away; but not enough, and the Porsche gradually gained on it, beginning to slide slowly alongside. The passenger window in the van was now opening.

'Watch out!' cried Jocelyn, her instinct for trouble prickling. Frank tensed, half expecting the van to spit out its lead venom to pock their windscreen with a spider-web of bullet holes. That didn't happen. Instead, a gigantic white 'butterfly' flew out of the open window to attack them. The foam from the van's fire extinguisher stuck to their windscreen, flattened down by the slipstream, blocking their view. In a fleeting instant before the view was completely cut off, Frank caught a glance of two faces. With both being dark-skinned and shrouded in the van's darker interior, telling one from the other was impossible; but the profile of the driver, with its distinctly long nose, was recognisable as that of Dr Nafur-Nafiri.

'Hell!' yelled Frank, slamming on the brakes and upsetting the steering. Screaming tyres slid across hard dry tarmac and Frank fought for control, swinging the car round to a jarring screeching halt on the oncoming traffic lane. Jocelyn looked out her window, her mind spinning like those Vegas fruit-machine wheels. Only seconds away, the massive 44-ton Russian T-34 tank rumbled down on them, the great steel-plated roller-tracks not looking likely to avoid crushing the puny Porsche strewn across its path. With only inches to spare, the tank miraculously swerved adroitly past them off the road, demolishing a lamp-post and crushing a parked car. The great steel hulk's further impact brought a steel power-line pole down on a fuel-tanker, the pole's electric cables falling across it, causing a flurry of sparks that had the tanker belching out its inflammable vomit that exploded in orange tongues of dying fury.

The tank-driver sat trembling with a mixture of shock and anger. He was sure it wasn't his fault. That other bloody drunken driver in the Porsche had been on the wrong side of the road. He was sure of it. Looking around at all the damage he'd caused was enough to make him a little unsure of it.

Not staying to confirm or deny this, the 'road-hog' Porsche gave a heavy start-up gurgle and shot away in haste.

As they roared off, Frank wondered if he was the only one who could hear his nerves jangling like a calypso steel band. He glanced at Jocelyn and caught her eyes laughing at him. Foot down hard on the accelerator again, they sped away to take up the cat and mouse chase through the stony mass of the town sprawling out before them, beneath the darkening sky.

15

Mostly shrouded by cloud as it was, the moon gave off enough light to catch the gleaming steel of the railway line receding in a graceful curve into the distance beyond the trees. It was also enough light to catch the polished radiator grill of the Citroen car that was nosing cautiously out of the bushes in response to a moment's blink of torchlight from out of the darkness. The car returned the signal with a sharp flash of its headlights.

Suddenly it was not just trees that stirred softly in the breeze. Materialising out of nowhere, a host of figures ghosted up out of the night to form a double line alongside the steel track. Jocelyn reckoned their number to be about over a dozen, as far as she could see, as she got out of the passenger seat of the two-door cabriolet. Two of them that approached her preferred to keep a tight grip on their Heckler & Koch 5.56mm MP5 sub machine-guns, rather than offering smiling handshakes for greeting. One of them, who appeared to Jocelyn to be the leader, codename PLUTO, wore a Harris Tweed gentleman's country flat cap, along with a red and gold Paisley-pattern cravat, which was somewhat out of 'style' with the face of dirt and black painted camouflage streaks of the SAS officer. His second in command, standing beside him, was just plain dusty and dirty. Both easily identified as 'friend' not 'foe'.

In her briefing by intelligence, before flying out, Jocelyn had been made to understand that some contingencies of these British covert behind-enemy-lines fighters were lending their strength to Israel's counter-attack movement. Originally engaged in fighting against General Franco's Fascist army in bitter civil war, half a million Spanish Republicans, upon losing their struggle, had fled to France to evade imprisonment. But their effort to escape prison was not completely successful. Marshall Petain, in compliance with Nazi policy, had repatriated most of them, whilst retaining the remaining contingent of 120,000 to 150,000 as political prisoners for slave labour for Compagnies de Travailleurs (Companies of Foreign Workers). Roughly 60,000 or so of these had made their escape, so joining the Resistance Movement.

Jocelyn looked at the figures closing in around her – enigmatic shapes that revealed nothing but for the moonlight giving glints of steel in their hands. Whenever ground supplies ran out, weapons and sabotage equipment were supplied in great air-droppings that the poor pigeon couldn't manage – sub-machine guns, grenades, ugly but efficient B&T VP9 Welrod silencer pistols, plastic explosives and their pencil detonators. As if this wasn't enough, captured Mauser 98 rifles and MP40 sub-machine guns could also be used whenever they could be seized. Where need and opportunity presented itself, this would readily float down out of the overhead darkness.

The babble of unfamiliar foreign accents, especially in their rough provincial dialects, hit Jocelyn with a blast as the leader and one of his comrades, suddenly blurted out their words at the same time. A torrent of words in two different tongues together thrown at her and she couldn't understand either of them. So unexpected, it caught her off balance. She felt so embarrassed – so naïve and stupid – especially considering her college Ph.D. for studies in the Middle East's ancient culture. This wasn't how it had been at Princeton, where her lingual tutors had put everything across to her with properly accented vowels and consonants, giving her little thought for uncouth rustic vernacular that varied with the locality. And even less thought and readiness for a double-blasted barrage of the rapidly clipped English Oxford accent and the heavy guttural granite-rasping Glaswegian voice. It made her feel awkwardly out of step with those around her, so experienced as they were in this very real dangerous game. It made her feel even more 'not with it' when she had expected everyone to speak in low clandestine whispers. Instead, they gave a clamouring of voices so loud that she could virtually see hordes of gun-wielding enemy troops rushing out of the undergrowth to arrest them, if not cut them down in merciless fire. But the foliage around them stirred only with the breeze.

She pulled herself together at the sound of the car's driver-side door opening and clicking shut again.

Frank came over to stand by her side. Picking her up from the safe-house, he'd put his foot down, making the 6-cylinder engine's carburettor gurgle out its 'juice' to hold them at 84mph top speed along the empty desert roads, only slowing down whenever a vehicle that looked suspiciously 'official' came towards them. They'd had to stop twice at security checkpoints. That he was a freelance journalist war-correspondent seemed to carry some weight with the checkpoint guards since the car and its occupants were passed through both roadblock inspections with relatively little fuss. Egypt wanted to be hailed in the foreign press headlines when they claimed victory over a vanquished Israel.

Stepping over to the leader, Frank held up his Intelligence ID card. 'Major Falzoni,' he said.

'Captain Driscoll,' replied the Englishman. 'So, you hail originally from sunny Italy, then?'

'No, Captain, I hail originally from sunny San Fran', in good old US of A --- unless that baby, whose bare ass one those Sisters of Mercy slapped, was an imposter.'

'Right. I certainly got that wrong.' An apologetic nod.

'Let's make sure we don't get anything else wrong, Captain. So, fill me in on this operation.'

'The train is due soon along this line from the port city, Latakia, north west of here, carrying a consignment of heavy armour and ordnance. Downloaded at the docks from an Argentinian-registered ship, we believe the cargo is Chinese. Their 780h.p. ZTZ-88 tanks, armed with 105mm cannons, T-98 anti-tank missiles, PF-98 unguided anti-tank rockets, and heavy and light ammo'. I think the ZTZ is a relatively weak tank, matched against the formidable Israeli Centurion, or Sho't tank, that's rugged enough to carry on slugging it out, in spite of it having sustained heavy damage; but tanks are tanks enough, however weak, to cause mischief on the day, irrespective of statistical odds.'

Jocelyn suspected that Frank had brought her along not just because she wanted to see exactly how these dirty-tricks saboteurs used the new bomb detonators developed by back-room boffins, and how they carried out their general operation; but she suspected that he wanted to enjoy seeing how she reacted at being thrown in at the deep end in this operation with all its dangers.

'It's all right, give them time. They'll let you in when they get used to you. It's their way of sounding you out by being awkward.' Frank said this aside in a low voice to Jocelyn whilst listening to the others' words, mostly enquiring, if not complaining, directed at this new woman. He measured uncertainty, if not mistrust, in the faces of these hardened men who knew death through mere seconds of mistiming. He saw this especially in the eyes of the leader, Captain Driscoll. This was all Jocelyn had so far been told of him in briefing – nothing beyond that for the sake of security.

'Into the 'little boys' gang?' replied Jocelyn, 'Don't worry, when Grandma Bergman's pet goats are being awkward and not giving her milk, she promptly has them eating out of her hand, so to speak, so that the stubborn animals give her what she wants.'

Frank looked at the men clustered around them and then back at Jocelyn. 'Let's be sure of one thing, kid – these men are rough-trained, rough-living, hard-hitting killers – *not goats.*'

'At least goats have an excuse for not trimming their beards, and not having a bath,' replied Jocelyn. But she seriously realised that this was something more than a personal chauvinistic bias against her joining, if not interfering with the group's operation. Those political gurus back at Langley had warned her to possibly expect a lingering vein of Anti-Yank sentiment in some situations. This original resentment had arisen out of

Churchill's hard-line order to sink French naval vessels and their French crews at Mers el Kebir, rather than let them fall into the hands of the Germans.

With the liberated French general, De Gaule, broadcasting from England, the message for his people to fight the Germans occupying northern France was rabidly taken up. But in unoccupied southern France, where the wisdom of Petain was still respected, De Gaul's call to arms had not been so readily heeded. Only when Marshall Petain's Vichy Government collaborated openly with the Nazi forces was there a falling away of resentment against the English – perhaps more slowly in some remote instances. And Jocelyn reckoned that these guys didn't seem to be in a hurry.

She found her patience with Driscoll dwindling. She tuned in her ears sharp enough to the man's quick speech to sense a bickering attitude to everything she said. As she tried to continue questioning the tricky details for applying the XL-2 detonator to the TNT, he scoffed the need for all that explosive as being totally unnecessary. 'So, what do you propose we use in its place?' she asked, not caring if her irritation was beginning to slip out. She looked round at Frank for the help she thought she was going to need if Driscoll was going to hold things up by being obstinate.

Frank was liaison officer – 'messenger boy' – collecting and relaying important intelligence between field operations and Washington, and so knew next to nothing about the technicalities of field operations; what the hell did he know about handling ruddy TNT, or trinitrotoluene, as he believed the Brit guy had called it? But he saw that he was needed to step in for the Brit if things were to run smooth. He repeated Jocelyn's question to Driscoll.

'We simply remove the connector plates on the outside of the rails,' said Driscoll.

'Sorry, I'm not with you. How is that better than using explosives?'

'These Syrians,' replied Driscoll, shaking his head at her ignorance, 'they're not stupid. They expect their trains to be attacked so they take precautions. They will have a reserve engine at the back as well as materials to repair the damage to the track at the front. But if the outside connector plates are removed from the track on a mountainside stretch of the railway line, the whole train, repair materials and all, would be lost down the mountain. Paff? Like that.' He snapped his fingers and kicked a large stone down the line's sloping embankment to prove his point.

'I have to admit there is merit in what he says,' said Jocelyn, somewhat surprised at her own words. Her glance at the Englishman brought out the man's grim smile of satisfaction at her approval, with a wide white row of teeth cutting across his dusty heavily unshaven face.

'I suppose it does have its points,' said Frank thoughtfully, his mind painfully caught between the two ideas. 'Unfortunately, the nearest mountainside is over a mile back. The train will be here long before we could get to that point. It's too late. We stick to the original plan. So, let's get on with it.' Frank turned and walked off along the track, then stopped to scratch his forehead as a new thought struck him. 'There's something else. There's the town at the foot of that mountain slope.' Unlike the Israeli members in the group – Mossad operatives, in fact, -- he was not of a mind to sacrifice – *massacre* – innocent people, in spite of their being Syrians. 'We'll consider using your idea some other time, but we do it this way for now, Captain. Come on, time's running out.' He walked on.

Giving a resigned shrug, Driscoll shook his head, this time in great disagreement with the Major's ruling, beckoning his team to follow as he strode off after the 'interfering' American. Jocelyn stumbled over a sleeper beam, but regained her balance to hurry after those walking away fast ahead of her. She barely had time to get into the car before Frank was moving it off while she was still pulling her leg in and closing the door. His position as freelance 'observer' in town allowed him a privileged overlap of the curfew time, but that time was running out. He recalled his earlier wartime experience with the virtual forerunners of these SAS guys, the SOE (Special Operations Executives) --- Churchill's inspired creation of behind-the-enemy-lines-dirty-tricks saboteur agents, who had an average life expectancy of around six months since their radio transmissions of field reports were eventually picked up by enemy goniometer detection devices.

Jocelyn had come along solely as observer of operations on this, her first 'live' field mission. As they drove off, she pondered ruefully over this frightful statistic – another 'gem' handed out by her Langley experts. She couldn't deny that her feeling was one of relief at leaving before the fighting broke out. Perhaps she would feel braver next time. But would dying in a desert-skirmish shoot-out be easier than being stood before a firing squad, after brutal torture by the KGB? She thought back on the harrowed state of those agents needing medical – *mainly – psychological* debriefing at Langley following their return from assignments. Jocelyn smoothed the coat's creases on her lap to wipe this question from her mind.

Having planted the plastic explosives at their strategic points along the line, and connected the wires to the plunger-box terminals, Captain Driscoll and his team moved back, to hide as best they could among the shrubs and shadows alongside the track. They waited.

Nine minutes later than expected, they heard the rushing 62mph approach of the heavy SNCF 141.P Class steam locomotive. Two flat platform waggons with nothing on them were at the front. These were supposed to take the force of any contact mines on the track and so spare the rest of the train; these were followed by two armoured cars in their heavy steel plates. After this came waggons sprouting heads in steel helmets of troops looking out cautiously over the sides. Then came the waggon with rails and spare parts to repair any damage that may be done by any explosions occurring at the front. Finally at the rear, pushing all this, was the 144-ton engine. Since the explosives laid out on the track were connected by wires, to be detonated from afar, the two empty waggons at the front served no purpose.

Captain Driscoll nodded to his 'second' lying beside him. The man pressed the plunger down with enough fiery Scottish passion and swearing to send the 144-ton mass of steel bucking up off the rails, and toppling over on its side, while waggon-pieces, as well as bodies, hurtled into the air in great blazing blasts of fury. Several seconds of screaming and wailing elapsed before angry Arabic commands rang out – to be drowned in turn by steady concentrated automatic gunfire breaking out.

16

While Presidents and Prime Ministers talked over their 'hot lines' on the strategic build-up of their mighty warships in Atlantic waters, Vice Admiral Bergman and Laurence Brubaker looked on intently at the tiny tank being pushed across the large table map by Marley Goodblood. The Vice Admiral reflected that Goodblood bore a slight resemblance to his son, Harry, who would have been about the same age now, had he not been killed in the Midway conflict. But that was as ancient as it was morbid, and about as useful as a free duodenal ulcer in the medical clinic. He shook the thought from his mind and made an effort to concentrate on what the CIA man was saying about his little tank to those round the table. In rooms across the globe, men were bent likewise over their tables, studying their maps, as they pushed their tiny tanks. While the Kremlin pondered, then planned, the Pentagon planned then pondered, while Whitehall continued to whistle through its teeth.

Colonel Goodblood straightened up and stood back from the table, pointing at the tank as he spoke. 'That little piece of wood is two battalions of Soviet XVP paratroops in massive 'practise' airlift manoeuvres. And if that's not enough, we've also got a restless shuffling activity of Chinese units, with their commanders looking towards the west.'

'You have something to add to that, Lieutenant?' said Brubaker, seeing Flight-Lieutenant Ross wanting to speak.

'The latest intelligence coming in has bolder air-manoeuvres with their Albatross bomber casting aside its top-secret cloak and flying out from its Moscow military air base on flights *'accidentally straying'* further and further into Western air territory. Flying out also, in greater number, are the Tupolev TU bombers, scraping the sky with their ruddy great 164ft wings.'

'You could say, gentlemen, that it mirrors that host of biblical locusts gathering, yet again, for another colossal gorge, this time not over Egypt, but Israel,' remarked Goodblood pointedly.

All eyes in the room shot cold glances at Colonel Goodblood, not at all happy with his observation, considering its accuracy.

09.41hrs (GMT), Moscow. To meet world opinion, the Russian news agency, ITAR-TASS, was putting forth a staunch line supporting Russia's 'new' aggressive policy. Russia, it claimed, wanted war no more than anyone else. But it would not back down lest it should convey the false message that it believed its actions to be wrong. The Kremlin was resolutely unanimous in this, with a call for positive assertion in the face of American imperialism that would leave no one in doubt. It would not only ignore the United Nations Security Council in New York, but it would also step up the military programme by building up and sending out more troops and armoured divisions where necessary.

09.41hrs (GMT), Washington. The President was not at all satisfied with the Security Council's somewhat wrangled handling over his decision to comply with the UK's agreement for the United States to convey military support for Israel by way of Operation NICKEL GLASS. And as for that trigger-happy hash-up by the British deploying their SAS saboteur units on Syrian soil, it made a change for the critical finger not to be pointing at US servicemen for tactical blunder, but at the forever 'politically correct' British.

It was a wonder that the Oval Room's casual coffee table wasn't collapsing under the weight of damning reports that had come in – and were still coming in. Surrounded by seeming battalions of generals bellowing out their advice on how to advise the British Prime Minister, he was not looking forward to the call so much as an allied ear to level out troubles with, than as a landmine to avoid.

09.41hrs, London. In Downing Street, Prime Minister Heath was nervous over his intended report to the US President, especially over the Navy's botched handling of a missile flare-up with Iranian ships in the Gulf. With Iran' and Syria's now open support of an intended Hamas rocket onslaught on Israel, it was difficult to see on which side of the scale America's judgement would fall, over Britain's cajoling them into granting military aid to Israel. He looked in dismay at the papers on his desk. The report he'd just had from the Secret Intelligence Directorate did nothing to put him at ease. He waited, tensed, for the light on the red scrambler phone to flash its signal that the Us President's call was on the line. The heavy ticking of the clock in the otherwise silent room increased his tension.

Pigeons were having a quiet afternoon nap and didn't bother to hail Falzoni and Goodblood as they walked towards the brilliant white colonnaded front to the White House. The security guard nodded back as Goodblood nodded and Falzoni flashed his security pass. Several excited mothers standing outside the railings were certain that Falzoni was the handsome senator who had patted their babies' heads at the last mid-term election.

The President was already waiting for them when they entered the wooden-panelled antechamber. He made his point of looking down with a frown at his watch to demonstrate that he considered them to be late. Sloane's dairy-farming landscape oil on the wall may have possibly mirrored Nixon's private inner dreams for retirement, but nothing could have been further from his mind at that moment. That tempers were already fraught between Goodblood and the President was plain enough to Frank as he caught the expressions on their faces. But Frank guessed that Marley had somehow managed to ward off, if not completely blunt, most of the javelins of fury that the President had cast down from his privileged peak of superior rank. You needed more arms than an octopus to catch Marley out when throwing things at him. The voice on the tape recorder was that of Major General Greeley speaking on details of the alarming escalation of military confrontation between Soviet forces and our own, over the Middle East situation. They all looked up from the tape recorder.

Falzoni nodded to Nixon. 'Good afternoon, Mister President,' he said.

'Good afternoon, Major Falzoni; if only I knew what was remotely good about.' After a few exchanged glances, all three returned their attention back to the slow turning spools voicing out the unsettling details. Thet listened for another few turns before the President leaned down and switched it off. He was clearly not happy. Tapping on the recorder as he thought for a moment, he turned halfway round to speak to Falzoni. 'Colonel Goodblood has been giving me some details, which I can only describe as being not entirely pleasing, and the Major General, here, makes a very lucid point of assessing the cataclysmic consequences of our direct aggressive nuclear confrontation with Russia terminating with a ---' he struggled to find words to fit the horrific mental picture, '--- *nuclear holocaust*. I find it most frightful to say the least.' He afforded himself his usual 'toothy' transient smile and folded his arms. What a shrink would have classified as a defensive act. 'I suppose historians could only classify that remark as a gross understatement.' He straightened up and looked at Falzoni.

'I only wish that I could hope that you've come to tell me that it's all a mistake, but you *haven't, have you*, Major?'

'Not in so many words, Mister President, but we are endeavouring to make progress in the matter.' Frank felt that he couldn't have waxed the words more if he had been a candle-maker.

' "Endeavouring to make progress" – Jeez! What the bloody damn hell is that supposed to mean, Major? Tell me that. Give me something solid.'

'We're currently engaged in negotiations that so far are maintaining a stalemate stance between the two confronting forces. Both sides are earnestly seeking a way to averting a breakout of open hostility. With that, we're hopefully moving towards a more impassive settlement.'

'But I'm told that our generals are embarking on the broad operation of deploying a massive increase of military force, troops and weaponry, on Israeli and Syrian territory. Such a build-up can surely only be in anticipation of the need. Am I right? Tell me, how can this be a move towards a peaceful settlement?' The President would have liked to have shouted at them and said it wasn't good enough to be hoping for a peaceful settlement; but this latest report of the warring confrontation in the Middle East, between Egypt, Syria and Israel, had drained most of his bark, and what was left of it had been dulled by earlier heated discussion with Cabinet colleagues, as well as with Defence Secretary, Henry Kissinger. 'Perhaps I should have stuck with my old forte, law, and become a shining academic mentor to fledgling students in Duke University, in Durham, North Carolina; at least it's easier to highlight pupils' mistakes on their returned papers, than concede to my own errors.'

'We have to employ a wider strategy of force, infantry and armoured units, to put down and control outlying minor disturbances across a larger territory,' said Goodblood. 'And that calls for more men, sweat and --- '

'*Blood!*' cut in the President.

'---*metal*, as I was about to say,' said Goodblood, clearly annoyed by the interjection. He wondered if his military angle on the issue would be enough to quell the politician's anxiety.

'I'm not sure, in my ignorance of military matters, if that is to be interpreted as a sound military explanation or an apology, Colonel. I'm the last person to deny the fact that I'm only a figurehead in all that goes on in theses active field issues. I must be that last in line to hear all these snatches of information, like the news of this latest Syrian conflict that my secretary gave to me when I came in this morning. Only by popular vote of the people, and by courtesy of my chosen Cabinet members am I here. I fully appreciate the fact that there are professional heads, to whom a prompter delivery of this information is more meaningful in its implication. That's why I'm putting my full trust in you to save the day, gentlemen.' He looked searchingly at Goodblood. 'And do you, Colonel, in your active capacity in the field, see us resolving this situation before it worsens?'

'We're striving for that, even as we speak, Mister President,' said Frank, answering for Marley.

'Y-e-s,' said Nixon slowly, finding no real assurance in the Major's words to shift his hopes forward by one single iota. Changing his stance, to turn away and then turning to face them again, he paused to let an entirely different, but equally troubling, point come forward to the surface from the back of his problem-crowded mind. He looked at Goodblood. 'I'm told that we have, what's known in the field as, a leak. Have I understood it correctly, Colonel Goodblood?' The polite formality of names between the President and the Colonel was for the sake of the Major, for whom this was a first experience of the 'Big House's inner sanctum decorum.

'Alas, yes, that is correct.' Marley turned to Frank. 'Perhaps the Major would care to oblige us with some clarity on this point?' Frank thought he caught a gloating gleam in Marley's eye at passing the buck of blame onto him.

'There's solid indication of various operations falling through on account of the enemy being one step ahead of us.'

'Meaning, Major, that they know of your plans -- *yes*?'

'Meaning just that precisely, Mister President.'

'Can't the so-called 'leak' be plugged up to prevent further information falling into the hands of the opposition?'

Frank only just managed to suppress a laugh at the President's naïve concept of the situation. 'If we were dealing with a solid, finite object like a hole, yes, it could be plugged; but we're dealing with people.'

'Yes, I do gather that; I'm not that stupid, however little you may see my appreciation of your spying game, Major. I meant can't the culprit responsible be apprehended?'

'If only it were so easy, Mister President --- if only it were so easy.'

'So, precisely by that, I'm to take it that it's *not* so easy?'

Plainly the President needed more, so Frank went on. 'He, or she, is only one of a chain-line of units forming a cell. Each unit, or member, is known by codename only, and personal details and backgrounds are not allowed. This way, detection of a cell's activities is kept to a minimum and even if a member's cover is blown, the overall plan of the cell continues. The new 'carrier' taking over knows where the 'parcel' is going, so that the exchange goes on and on until the 'parcel' reaches its end point, the controller.'

'I see,' said the President, in spite of his *not* seeing, trying with difficulty to marshal his thoughts.

Frank and Goodblood stood watching this clean-shaven, professionally-pomaded, politician's face wrestle with some point that still escaped him. Enough said. Several moments of uneasy silence to allow all three to gather their reserves on what to say next.

'I see,' said the President again, to both free himself from his inner conflict, and to move on.

'All plucked and trussed like the Christmas goose,' quipped Goodblood, to add a touch of levity that hopefully would help them to move on out of the awkward discussion.

The President gave Goodblood a cold glance at this remark. 'I'm beginning to find that to be an apt description for myself. Perhaps I should have stayed on in the academic field' He was plainly feeling the strain of being involved above his own head in unfamiliar waters. It was all so unlike the comparatively docile duty of advising students on the basic rules for compiling their final degree theses. So unlike his now standing on the possible brink of World War Three.

On cue, to everyone's relief, the door began to open. They waited for the woman to lay down her sheaf of papers on the President's table and leave. But she didn't go out immediately. She stood for a moment to look pointedly at her watch, and then at the President. He nodded knowingly. He hadn't forgotten his next official appointment. 'Thank you, Mary.' His secretary, one of many, went out. The papers she had brought him were notes for his meeting later with the Israeli Prime Minister, Golda Meyer and the National Security Advisor, at three o'clock. He wasn't looking forward to it. Now that the door was once more firmly closed, the talk had to be resumed. 'And there's no chance at all,' said the President, leading the way into the inner room, 'of you resolving this problem, Major?'

Frank was hesitant in saying what he had to say next. 'There is the chance to see that the material stolen is '*doctored.*'

'I detect some hesitance in your saying that. There are critical factors to this ploy?'

Frank didn't answer this, giving only a slight nod.

'I fully understand; you can say no more on that issue. So be it. We'll end that matter there, then.'

They looked round as the door opened again and a different secretary poked his head round it. 'Downing Street has just been on to us. Prime Minister Heath wants you to call back as soon as you can find the time.'

'All right, thank you, David; no wait; have the car ready for me in twenty minutes.' Checking the time on the ormolu clock, he looked round at the others. 'As you can see, what little time we have, must be rationed. Apart from the Prime Minister, I've also got to decide which is my best foot to put forward, when I see Egypt's Anwar Sadat later today. So, we'll just make this remaining report brief.'

He switched the tape recorder on again. They listened to the Committee's concise statistics on 'collateral damage' as a result of encountering aggression from the Soviet build-up in Berlin and East Germany's Czechoslovakian Border, and Middle East borders. The President nervously adjusted his tie that didn't need adjusting. He pressed the switch on the intercom. 'Hills, cancel my four o'clock meeting with the Israeli Minister. No, wait; don't cancel it altogether, but have it put back to later this afternoon; I'll tell you exactly when later, when I know for sure myself. And keep everything else out of my way in the meantime.' He looked round at Goodblood and Falzoni. 'As you can see, gentlemen,

I am very much pressed for time. I think we can call this meeting to an end. Thank you for your time. Mary will see you both out.'

'Thank you, Mr President,' said Colonel Goodblood.

'Thank you, Mr President,' said Major Falzoni.

With the door shutting firmly behind them, what had seen the closure of a confrontational meeting with its awkward questions only succeeded in opening up another confrontational barrage of questions in Goodblood's already troubled mind. And the more they came at him, the more they multiplied in complexity.

Walking along the long narrow chequered-floor corridor from the Oval Room, Marley and Frank kept their eyes to the front, avoiding the searching scrutiny of those exquisitely attired, motionless, but live, 'busts' that were the President's personal Secret Service bodyguard of the White House.

With his attention still to the front, Marley gave Frank a secret tap on the arm. 'So, what the hell was all that mush you were feeding him back there? Cells? Coded ID's? Parcels? We know the crazy 'Doctor Frankenstein-Nafiri is working alone – so, what was all that about? –Give it to me straight, Frank?'

'He's no longer alone --- or perhaps I should say *they're* no longer working alone – Nafur-Nafiri, and Your Professor Sefleck, --- both of them now being assisted, whether they like it or not, by Moscow.'

'You're telling me that Sefleck and the Doctor are in this together?

'No, but their hold on this viral bomb is prize enough for Moscow to move in and seize control. I'm going to have to grab the next flight and get back over there.'

'I'll get onto Air Operations and have one of our Lockheed C-5's, scheduled to fly out with Nickel Glass supplies to the Palmahir Air Base outside Tel Aviv, stand by for you, Frank.'

17

20.31hrs. The Cairo Municipal Lights & Public Maintenance Dept van turned into the quiet street. It stopped behind a larger truck of the same department, and Frank Falzoni got out. Dressed in overalls, regulation yellow plastic jacket and white hard-hat, he looked the part. He climbed into the back of the larger truck. Colonel Biran looked round and then at his watch. 'So, you managed to get here? I thought with your mighty US back-up resources, you'd have borrowed the President's Air Force One plane to fly in over the traffic.'

Falzoni ignored the remark and went over to the spy-hole in the truck's side. 'Where are they, then? He said, looking through the small hole.

'Across the street, nine doors up. The one after the blue door ---- beside the mosque --- see it?'

'Yeah.'

'The third-floor window. The flat above is occupied, so are the two below, so, we couldn't get near them that way, to tap their conversation.'

'And the flat directly across from them, this side of the street? Same, I suppose?'

'Same. Otherwise, we could have used the normal sonic bowl to listen in on them. It could have looked too suspicious if we'd rigged up something on the truck roof and parked right across from them. We're better off parked down here at an angle.'

'Right, I get the picture, so, let's get on with it.' Frank looked round, searching for something --- saw the rifle and reached out for it. Biran stepped in to pick it up before him. 'I'll do it, he said, adjusting the telescopic sight.

'*Sure?*' teased Frank.

Biran looked Frank in the eye. 'Just tell him to switch on, and I'll take care of this end.'

Frank slid the hatch open and told the man in the cabin to go out and switch on the mobile generator that was standing further up the street. The man started the generator up and then played his part by fiddling about with the cables leading from the machine into the open manhole in the road. Biran took careful aim and fired. The tiny dart from the high-powered air-rifle thudded into the upper corner of the wooden frame of the window nine houses up the street. The noise of the dart striking the frame was drowned by the din from the generator. A listening bug inside the dart was now relaying all sounds from inside the room, back to the monitoring equipment in the truck.

Frank signalled the man up the street to turn off the generator. Biran switched on the receiver. The volume and clarity of the Arabic babble coming through was just what they needed, with it almost as if they were listening from outside the window itself. You almost expected the curtain to be suddenly pulled aside, as the room's occupants looked out at their eavesdroppers. But there was little likelihood of that, the curtain actually concealing the dart from the people inside.

'Sounds like two in the room with somebody in the background; probably the next room. Or is that a radio they've got playing?' said Frank.

'Sounds like prayers, with that extended lilting chanting tone,' said Biran, looking round for confirmation, from the small figure in the far corner of the truck. The woman, their Mossad translator, looked back at him, but said nothing, concentrating on the Islamic chanting.

'Prayers are not going to tell us much,' said Frank. How long do we have to wait before they tell us anything useful about their plan of operation?'

'If we rush them, they could kill themselves,' said Biran. 'If we take them alive, they could still hold back from us in interrogation over the limited deadline we have left. We have to catch them in their unguarded conversation.' Biran sat down on a folding canvas stool. 'We have to wait, Major.'

'No, you sit and wait,' said Frank moving towards the door. 'I'm going for a piss and a bite of something.' He held up his mobile phone for Biran to see. 'Let me know if I have to make it a quick splash.'

21.18hrs. Sounds as if they've fallen asleep,' said Biran to Frank, as they continued to listen in on the terrorist nest.

'Or gone into quiet meditation,' said the translator woman from her corner.

'Two of them, maybe, but not the third guy,' said Frank. 'He sure seems happy enough, the way he's rattling on. If he's Irish, I'd say he was seeing the sun setting down with the help of a bottle of the old blarney, and not Allah.'

'Sounds as if he's drank half of it already,' said Biran. 'He's certainly excited about something.'

'They do take their prayers with serious dedication, especially their Maghrib, their first prayer of the day, beginning at sunset,' said the translator, with another of her gems of ethnic information that were beginning to irritate the other two.

As they listened on, two of the three voices had got lower, as if in a relative background position, suggesting that they had, indeed, gone to rest in a backroom. With the background voices gradually petering out, to be replaced by an occasional cough, it was now a fair assumption that the two in the backroom were asleep, or trying to sleep. The muttering and humming in the foreground, accompanied by the occasional clink of crockery and the rustling of paper, suggested that the third member of the team was staying awake on guard duty.

From amidst the rabble of fanatical talk that Frank and Biran had listened to earlier, only the general outline of an operation --- "The Mother of all Retributions – Allah akbar" – could be picked up. Nothing more specific could be gleaned beyond that. There was little chance of learning more now.

Biran stood up. 'It's time we moved. We won't learn any more now, and we won't get them in a better position than this. Time for soldier boys to take over. Time for some real action; *right*, Major?' You could tell when Biran was digging you, as sure as when the mother-in-law *accidentally* reverses her golf buggy over your new set of clubs.

Leaving Frank in the truck, Biran walked down the street to meet the black van that was coming along at his calling. The four SAS men wore one-piece tunics with body armour designed to withstand armour-piercing bullets. Checking their 9mm Browning automatics and putting them in their holsters, they attached extra magazines and stun grenades to their belts. Rather than explode into fragments, these grenades were designed to go off with blinding flashes and ear-splitting bangs that would confuse the enemy. They picked up the holdalls containing, along with other gear, their 9mm Heckler and Koch submachine guns that had a firepower of 15 rounds a second. Finally, they put on the bright yellow municipal jackets for temporary cover in crossing the street. Checking that all was clear, Biran led the way, stepping out into the street.

'From what you've been saying, Colonel,' said Captain Driscoll, as they crossed the street, 'if we go in by their street door, by the time we reach the second floor, they'll be on their toes like ballet dancers, waiting for us. So, we'll do it our way. Where is the entrance point, again?'

'Over there, number eighteen just beside the small apothek with its pulsing green cross light. The first-floor flat is empty. If you force the street door, go up the first floor, break into the empty flat, you can jump down from the back window into the back garden. From there you can make your way along to their house, to mount your assault. Would've been better in complete darkness, but time is not on our side. We can't wait. All right?'

'All right, Colonel. Thanks for the layout. I don't think you'll be needing that,' said Driscoll, referring to Biran's checking his pistol inside his jacket. 'We'll handle it from here.' He looked round at his three colleagues. 'Ready? Okay, let's go.'

Following Biran's instructions, the SAS team was in the back-garden in minutes. Here they removed their council worker jackets and took their submachine guns out if their bags, slinging them under arm, their top straps over the head, so as not to fall off. They then donned their heavy rubber gas-masks, and fastened onto their belts radio units that were tuned into the receiver in the truck, attaching the head-pieces to one ear. This way they could keep a 'picture' of the inside of the flat.

Ascending to the roof of the four-storey building, they made their way along the roof's apex, until they were directly over the target house. Anchoring the grapnel hooks to the apex, they moved down their ropes, to hang out in space at the eaves point, their bodies propped out by feet against the gutter pipe. Two would go down the front, and two would go down the back.

Checking in his ear-piece that positions had not changed in the flat, Driscoll tensed himself, gave a sharp whistle signal, and all four abseiled down, pushing themselves out like hopping kangaroos, down the wall faces. Passing the top windows, each gave himself an extra hard push out abreast of the third-floor target window, swinging out and across, so as to go crashing in through the windows, back and front. The terrorists never knew what hit them, and it was over in seconds and two short bursts of automatic fire dropping the man in his fatal attempt to snatch up his weapon.

The door was opened to let Biran and Falzoni into the flat. Frank exploded in coughs as the cordite fumes attacked his nostrils and made his eyes smart. Biran's grin widened at Frank waving the acrid fumes away. The SAS team wasted no time. Their task completed, they left as promptly as they'd come. With curious neighbours' curtains shifting in their windows all around, the four black figures kept their masks on as they sprinted down the street to their van. The dead man was taken away in a body bag by Mossad agents.

The argument over who should take 'possession' of the two remaining terrorists was settled when it was agreed, at Frank's suggestion, that that Mossad should have them for interrogation, so long as a CIA officer accompanied them to keep a watchful on things. Biran was clearly not happy with what he interpreted as the Major's purely weak-kneed pragmatic surrendering to White House diplomatic protocol stipulations, but he said nothing. He didn't reckon that their two prisoners were going to be telling any more than they had already learned. And that hadn't been much. He saw them as members of a cell that knew no more than Mossad, or CIA, did about where the next cell in the line for this mission was, who was in it, and what its specific plans were.

18

The landing strip lights prickled the cold night air and danced on the spectacle lenses of the woman in a sheepskin jacket standing by the Buik, waiting on, and listening to the gradually loudening 'puka-pucka' juddering commotion of the approaching 10-ton 'tadpole' twinkling with lights, that was the US Army UH-60 Black Hawk helicopter's General Electric 1700 twin turboshaft engines, as it came in to land. With the slowly spinning four blade propellor finally jerking to a halt, the curved flap opened out on the broad fuselage and the figures began to climb down. Two of them were not crew; Selwyn Sefleck wearing a dark blue raincoat, the other one, his 'escort', CIA officer, Colonel Goodblood, wearing his Raglan overcoat. Sefleck stepped down onto the ground and Goodblood jumped down after him, beside the pilot.

The back door of the car opened behind the woman with the spectacles, and a tall thin thing, called a tired old woman, got out, blowing into her bony cupped cold hands and shivering in the cold night air. 'With only one year to go before retirement, I'm becoming a little too old for this sort of clandestine caper at this time of night,' she said. Pulling the long woollen scarf closer round her scrawny neck, she walked slowly, with a seemingly awkward lurching gait, aided by a stout walking stick, towards Professor Sefleck and Colonel Goodblood. Unsubstantial rumours had it that the stick's contents, whatever they may have been, but never disclosed, had enabled her, as an OSS operative, to curtail the plans of a Nazi VIP, and possibly the length of WW11, on the whole.

No handshakes; no smiles breaking out; just a straight-faced: 'Good morning, Professor Sefleck, --- and Colonel Goodblood. I trust that your journey down was not too rough. The weather up there hasn't been too agreeable, I gather.' She looked up at the sky, not that there was anything to see in the thick darkness, with heavy clouds blocking out the stars.

'Yes, it's a fine morning,' said Sefleck. 'And *you are* – if I may ask --?'

'You *may*.' But the woman didn't oblige and surrender the answer. 'It's awfully good of you to come all this way to see us, Professor.'

Whoever the old woman was, she probably had a higher I.Q. than that of the rest of them here put together. But Sefleck was more concerned with, and wondered, what to expect from that intellectual mind, behind all those polite words.

'I don't believe the choice was wholly mine.' Sefleck looked round at his 'escort' and then back at the old woman. 'Sorry if I've deprived you of your early hours of slumber,'

A smile managed to crack the weathered face for a fleeting second at Sefleck's sarcasm. 'Not at all, Professor, not at all.' Lies flowed out easily from the old woman, always a lady of professional manners and saying what sounded polite, rather than what was felt. 'It's not often at my age that I get the chance to breathe in the fresh air at this early hour. It's quite medicinal, my physician tells me. Moreover, I'm told that the kitchen staff have been so good as to prepare an early breakfast for us, so I'm told.' She looked round at the woman with the heavy steel-framed spectacles. 'Am I correct, Parker?'

'Quite correct, ma'am,' replied Parker.

Everything short, sharp and secretive, Sefleck noted. To be expected of course, no less than not expecting a rubber chicken to lay rubber eggs. It was automatically understood that this CIA crew would wield their power to their judgement in running this operation in the interest of national security. Facial expressions on those around Sefleck showed a shared urge to get things moving. But not so on the old woman's face.

Her annoying foible was to delay things for personal interest. She looked at Parker and the 'escort', Colonel Goodblood. 'If I could have a few minutes with Professor Sefleck?' She made to move away, without waiting for their permission. Sefleck followed after her.

'Certainly,' said Parker, watching Sefleck go off with his 'confessor'. While those two were wasting everyone's time, Parker used what time they had to put through operational instructions on the car radio.

Sefleck and the old woman walked slowly, shoulder to shoulder, towards the landing field perimeter, leaning forward over synchronised strides, one talking, one listening. Even in the dark, Sefleck could sense a grey mood sliding over the old woman's face, pushing civil manners aside.

'You're a prisoner here, Sefleck, only in so far as how you agree to comply with our wishes. If you choose not to ---,' silence spoke great volumes, 'your stay could be a long one. But that aside, let's speak of other things. Quite frankly, my being rushed here, at this un-Godly hour, with scarcely decent warning, to this ghastly God-forsaken-forest wilderness, God knows where, in Virginia, is as much an inconvenience to me, as I assume it is for you.'

'Monogahela Forest,' said Sefleck.

'I beg your pardon?'

'This is Red Creek Trail, south west of Parsons, in Monogahela Forest, West Virginia, or so I'm told by the Colonel.'

'I see. Right, right. As I was saying, intelligence reports reaching me only a few hours ago, out of the blue, did nothing to help my ulcers—no more than my arthritis. Even assuming that you are fortunate in not having experienced the discomfort of that gastric ailment, you can, nevertheless, imagine the malign temperament it induces in an elderly mind like mine. Thus, you will have gathered that I have been sent to this back-of-nowhere camp to oversee operations, for all the good that will do if things get out of hand. I'm hoping to high heaven, for all our sakes, that they don't, Professor.'

'I'm rather hoping something like that myself.'

The old woman glanced back, with a moment's longing, for the comparative shelter of the Buick's interior. 'But do go on, Professor Sefleck. Tell me more. Tell me something that, in your judgement, would dispel an old woman's chagrin.'

They had reached the lamp beside the long 'hump-backed' corrugated-iron Nissen hut, camouflaged in varying green shades merging with the surrounding foliage, so Sefleck handed the thick buff folder over. 'Perhaps you'd like to read through this. My written report, as promised to Colonel Goodblood; my research on the original genetic structure of the virus, with a precise extrapolation of what I see to be the final structure as reached by Doctor Nafur-Nafiri.'

The old crinkling grey eyes scanned the first two paragraphs of the thick report, and no further. 'No, no, you'd better keep this, Professor. *Words, words* on paper. Are we not all of us, in our professional craft, masters of deceit by word of mouth and paper? Spewing out our lies, as our duty requires, with no more qualms of conscience that those infernal machines, with all their paper, in our offices. Am I really to believe that you, in spite of all your academic integrity, are an exception, Professor?'

With the old woman, if she wasn't a witch on a federal salary, caught up like that in her already-formed self-persuasion, Sefleck didn't bother answering, just staring back.

'I thought not. Just tell me in your spoken words, if you will, in your own way. I'm sure you can make it sound that more interesting, however ineffectual it may prove to be.'

They walked on through, between more Nissen structures, so that the wind whipped out snatches of their classified conversation. The guards carrying telescopic *gamekeepers'* rifles, patrolling the perimeter of the long rectangular clearing, with its electrified fence bordering, were too far away for even their German shepherd dogs to hear.

The more Sefleck spoke, pouring out his version of the situation, the more he began to wonder if his effort was in vain, seeing as the old face simply continued to nod up and down, showing no sign of credence at the intake of related material in her stone-cold watery eyes.

'That's really quite a bellyful you've said so far, Professor. I'm told that you've already endeavoured to convince our people that what you're saying is the truth.' She paused to drop both arms down to slap her sides in a gesture of hopelessness. 'All to no avail, I gather.'

'You, yourself, don't seem at all too happy with my rendering of the situation, as far as I've told you,' said Sefleck. 'Don't you think that there's an element, a *not too remote element*, of truth in what I'm saying?'

A surprising smile, alas, a despairing smile, broke out on the wrinkled face as the old woman looked around them at the dark mass of foliage surrounding them. 'And just how exactly, Professor, does one measure remoteness? In solving that, perhaps we would move an infinitesimally small step towards understanding some of God's mysteries. If I, in my remaining few years of a wretchedly meagre mortal state, can be allowed to speculate, I would say any chance of approving your theory to snare what you insist is the real prey, depends on our concentrating on unearthing some solid supporting evidence. More than that, I am unable to say at this stage.'

Sefleck was becoming increasingly uneasy with the other's longwinded delivery, all the more with showing no sign of leaning his way. 'That's what I want to discuss; that's what we definitely *need* to discuss.'

'I'm afraid, Professor, that discussions here, in their majority, will be mainly one-sided. *We* shall be asking the questions; *you* will be answering those questions. Perhaps then, God, in His infinite wisdom, will decide which side hails His truth.'

'So, I can rely on God having a look-in, can I?'

'God *always* has a look-in --- at the *end*.'

Sefleck wondered if he should be taking that as a non-too subtle warning. He watched the old woman fumbling with a handkerchief, dabbing at a chronically wet nose for a few moments, before looking up to stare long and hard at him. 'Yes, I can appreciate your plight, with its perilous negative slide, Professor; all too clearly.' Putting her handkerchief away, the old woman turned and walked away. Sefleck stepped quickly after her to catch up, and they walked back together through the group of wooden buildings, towards the centre. As they emerged from among the buildings, out into the clearing, the driver in the Buick saw them and turned the car round in their direction. Chilly pellets came down out of the dark, and the old woman tugged at her collar in a futile effort to shelter from the rain. 'Another of God's Divine idiosyncratic gestures,' she muttered to the night, if not to Sefleck.

'No chance of my being released for a short break to speak in His ear, I suppose?' quipped Sefleck, in keeping with the old man's spiritual flights of thought.

'Rain, ma'am?' said Parker, holding out an up-turned palm in the darkness.

'Perhaps He's crying at an injustice befalling someone.' The old woman's face managed, for a second time, a smile, this time a forlorn smile, at the Professor.

'*Sorry?*' The confusion was Parker's alone.

'I honestly think that it's time that we had that breakfast --- a cup of tea, at least – that we've promised the good Professor. Will you be joining us, Parker? Of course, you will.'

'Of course, ma'am. Thank you, ma'am.' You could guess that Parker's CIA duties wouldn't range far beyond pushing a pen across classified documents.

The old woman turned to Professor Sefleck. 'And perhaps on the way, you can find it in your strength to try and forward me a little more of what we need to hear, Professor. *Yes?*' They drove off, with the landing-strip's wind-sock pointing the way, and the heavy raindrops copying out the yellow landing lights a hundred-fold on the windscreen. The soft seats and warmth of the car interior were relaxing, and when Sefleck stole a quick glance, he imagined he caught the old face surrendering its hard strength to open up and concede to an enormous yawn.

Parker reached out to retrieve the folder from the Professor, only to have it, in turn, taken from her by Colonel Goodblood.

As the building came through the trees at last, Sefleck was surprised to see that it was of a medieval design. Well, the stone tower *was*, with its crenelated rampart. But *here*, in the *American west*? Probably the whim of some old retired cattle-baron. With the tower top bristling with antennae, it appeared that the CIA had taken over as overlord of the fiefdom. The lower square building had massive corner buttresses that, supposedly, in historical times, had defied many an enemy. Sefleck was now feeling how that enemy had felt.

The limousine pulled in at the base of the tubular tower-house. As they walked towards the entrance at the foot of the tower, Sefleck caught the glint of something in an arrow-slit on the battlements. Where once that glint would have been caused by an iron siege helmet peering out over a crossbow, this one came from a high-powered rifle's telescopic lens catching the light from the searchlight mounted there. The overhead guard popped back in and spoke into a small hand radio, when he saw the 'groundsman' handing Goodblood back his credentials. A metal flap opened in on the iron-studded door and eyes peered out, before bolts being pulled back sounded on the inside.

Rough cast walls, with dowsed flambeau set in iron sconces, opened back to reflect the mood of the grey hall. Sefleck walked in before a guard of honour of generals' busts pensioned off quietly on their pedestals. Bronze skulls glistened peacefully through the patina where martial headdresses had been hung up long ago, like the breast-plates on the walls. Two fifteenth -century howitzers yawned by the next archway, bored from the day of their demob.

Out of place in all this was the modern radio unit, with its blinking red light and long green flex, twisting like an umbilical cord over the back of a sixteenth-century chair, to dangle beside the blonde head of the security officer sitting on it. As the blonde woman got up, Parker approached her, to draw her aside and speak in a low voice, inaudible to Sefleck. It was only then that Sefleck came to realise that he was standing by himself; the old woman and Colonel Goodblood were no longer there behind him, supposedly having taken leave of them through another door that had escaped his notice.

With the woman sitting down again at her post, Parker turned round to look at Professor Sefleck. 'Through here, Professor.' A quick jerk of a thumb, indicating the archway. They went through into an armoury that displayed its pageant of arms and battles. 'Wait here,' said Parker.

'I would imagine that breakfast to be getting a little cold by now,' said Sefleck.

'Don't worry, Professor, you'll get your breakfast. First, a few little preliminaries need to be seen to.'

'*Preliminaries?*'

'Just wait here!' With no more time to waste over more silly exchanges, Parker hurried off.

Sefleck took his stand by the wide-open fireplace, where a large coat of arms above it was partly obscured by two torn regimental flags draped around it. He followed rows of firearms fanning out diagonally along the walls from the fireplace. Matchlocks, wheel-locks, flintlocks, and snaphaunces, all rallying to the command of wigged generals, in silent skirmishes depicted in dark oil paintings. Swivelling the naval musketoon's heavy brass cannon aside, he looked at the dull photographs. Air reconnaissance shots carried the message clearer than oils or written reports could. The group sets were nostalgic of the camaraderie formed by the action of those days. Eisenhower and Montgomery were allowed to stand out for recognition among the faded smudge of uniforms. Patton was unmistakable, in his proud stance, speaking to a dust-faced commander leaning out the top of his battle-scarred M26 Pershing tank.

Sefleck snapped his mind out of the aura that was floating in the military past. That was then; this was now. He looked at his watch, shifting his feet restlessly, and waited. And waited.

Three figures seated at the long wooden table in the long dining room that was otherwise empty but for them and the spasmodic clinking of cutlery on plates. Knives and forks clinked and grated, cutting the room's silence, as well as two golden kippers on the old woman's plate, and a thick wedge of Texas T-bone steak on Goodblood's plate. Grilled with a generous knob of butter, the fish looked delicious, infusing the blade and prongs with heavy gusto, to thrust and parry, flashing the blades like proud sabre. Now and then the fork stabbed at the plate of steaming mussels, fresh from Maine's Atlantic waters, garnished with chopped onions and white prawn sauce. Switching his observation to Colonel Goodblood's plate, Sefleck took in another miniature martial arts display where 'samurai' strokes of the blade were rapidly reducing the meat around the bone. Sefleck had settled for a simple omelette and mushrooms, where 'something' had somehow dulled his appetite.

Parker sat alone at her table in the corner of the room.

With breakfast at an end, and plates being cleared away, a hand suddenly fell with a strong grip on Sefleck's shoulder. 'If you would care to surrender your 'hardware' before we go, Professor.'

Sefleck was about to say that he was unarmed, having never carried, let alone, needed a weapon, when looking up, saw the man looking down at his, somewhat over-sized for his thin wrist, gold chronometer. 'Of course. Presumably time stands still here?'

'You got it right, Professor.'

Initial confrontation with the interrogation panel, which included a shrink as well as a regular doctor, carried a casual air of exchanged 'friendly' greetings, where hostile differences were temporarily held back in truce by the row of coffee cups and cookies laid out between the two 'sides. Surprisingly, or maybe not so surprisingly, old Lady Methuselah wasn't there to throw in one of her intellectual mind-stallers. But you knew they were there watching, her and Goodblood, remaining in the background, perhaps to their advantage, monitoring how the minds ticked on both sides of this mind contest that was getting underway. That camera up there in the corner, after all, was not there to count how many rare butterflies had sneaked in through the window. And that window didn't look easy for even a butterfly to get through, considering the alarm wire leading from it.

As the questions and hours passed, Sefleck's view of time and its grip of the situation became a mishmash of garbled confusion batted through his tiring mind from a hundred and one voices from different directions. Hours passed into days; light of day and dark of night was determined not by natural order of the sun, but by the cruel action of the bugger pressing the switch on and off in irregular sequence to trip up the clock levers in Sefleck's mind. Interviews were followed by intelligence tests that developed into child's play. *Child's play?* Or so it seemed stupidly to Sefleck, fuddled in his mind as he was, when he was asked to carry out those nursery tasks you do when you are kids, balancing block, fitting round pieces into round holes and square pieces into square holes. Somewhere in the midst of the young and old howling together in contention in Sefleck's brain, a tiny midget voice was trying to say that all these silly kids' games were being dotted down in that shrink's clipboard as being something decidedly important. Not only was the shrink assessing how fit Sefleck was, how sane his mind was, but most importantly, where exactly in that convoluted recess of a mind the coveted truth was hiding. To help in this mental search, cold showers and blaring lights continually switched places in combined effort to break down the mind's resistance.

When the man coming into the room was wearing a white coat, Sefleck's confused mind didn't need to be told what this entailed. The kidney-shaped enamel tray, containing cotton wool, ether, and a hypodermic syringe magnified in its ominous purpose by its steely shine, made that clear enough. First a little ether dabbed on the skin, then the half-mile long needle eased into the exposed flesh.

All the distorted figures in the room grew smaller and smaller, now standing yards and yards away against the walls that had drawn away back, but with their shouting mouths up against his face; a remarkable, if not impossible feat, only made possible by a fuddled brain. Sefleck rubbed his forehead as he felt himself swirling round and round while going down and down on a floor that wouldn't stop sinking beneath his feet. The burning boiler that was his head, threatened to explode from overheating, causing great rivers of sweat, in great burst-dam torrents, to pour down his face. He felt he was drowning. His head was now swelling up, a gigantic balloon, pushing out against the walls and ceiling. Was this him escaping – out into the night? Out into the dark sky of the night that was black? Was that the sky going more black, or his mind going back – bl-a-ck – b-l-a-a-a-c-k---?

Sefleck was eating by himself in the empty dining room, a heavy quiet stillness about the place; or had it been like that all along, with all the bustle and activity occurring before having been solely in his mind, geared up in nervous anticipation? A mute-faced expression was his only answer, when asking the table server where everyone was, when he came to replenish his coffee. Giving up wanting to ask, he continued passing food down to a non-too receptive stomach, unsettled as it was, with unsettled curiosity.

Sefleck's thoughts in his solitary silent 'retreat', were suddenly interrupted when a hand noisily planted the large chronometer, glistening in the fresh morning sunlight, beside him on the table. He nodded his head slowly at their touch of dry humour, seeing that the watch had been stopped at the time it had been 49.25 hrs ago.

'Sorry, Professor; they neglected to return this to you.'

'*They?*'

The man, stepping away, in his busy mood, stopped and smiled at Sefleck. 'Gone.'

That was all he was going to get, it seemed --- like everything else he got, or never got, in this place. Sefleck held out his hand to stop the man before he moved off again. Just a moment; as a matter of curiosity, what the hell is that old woman's name?'

'*Old woman?*'

'Yeah, old 'Methuselah' with the faithful pet poodle called Parker, ready to lick her master's shoes whenever she asked.'

Still that set smile, with nothing revealing coming out from behind it. 'Eat up and enjoy your breakfast, at the taxpayer's expense, Professor; you've a long trip ahead.' The man paused for an afterthought, before rushing off; 'And try sprucing yourself up a bit. You're looking tired. You'll want to look presentable before the Big Chief in Big Town DC ---- if not before those inquisitive people in Moscow's Lublanka'

19

Tucked away discreetly in a quiet corner, a stone throw from the Qalawun Mosque beside the Qasr El Nile Bridge, in the affluent Heliopolis district, the intellectuals' and artists' bistro served its exquisite cuisine to a clientele of creative brave-minded free-thinkers revelling in 19th century period atmosphere. This was provided by waiters with pencil-thin moustaches, clad in red waistcoats over their long white gowns, with the blue tassels on their red Turkish tarboosh fezzes swinging about, as they darted about fussily, table to table, like those clockwork monkeys that clapped their hands when you turned the handle.

'*Sahissel ola jarrad al-bahr*,' said Jocelyn, disguising her nervous Arabic pronunciation by giving a disarming smile up at the handsome young waiter. The cracking of crustacean shells at nearby tables, with all the hubbub of happy conversation, suggested that Jocelyn's choice of lobster from the menu was a popular one. '*What?*' she said, looking over, with a questioning expression at Frank. 'You're *surprised?* Did you really expect me to mumble out the old weak: *Hal tatathadath alanjlyzia* line? --- the stereotyped English xenophobic for: *Do you speak English?*'

Throwing up his open hands in mock plea of innocence, Frank blurted out: 'Hey, whoa, there, honey; don't fire those poison darts at me with those beautiful eyes! Heaven forbid that I should so judge our much haloed cousins across the 'Pond'.'

159

A non-too sure 'Hmmm,' was all Jocelyn could give in response, looking down to give her attention to her rich maritime dish. Frank picked up his knife and fork, ready to tackle his choice of a select dish of roast gazelle and falcon, enriched in a sauce of goat's blood, paprika, cheese, dragon-flower root and wine. They started their meal quietly, or at least they *started*, until Frank looked up and stopped suddenly, laying down his knife and fork with a dismayed under-the-breath utterance of: 'Hell!'

Frank's face and inside spirit fell at the sight of Bart Knowles, the embassy man, approaching from across the crowded room, zig-zagging his way between tables towards them. He now regretted letting the damn guy know where he would be should he be needed back in their embassy's CIA 'safe' room. What Knowles had in tow was not in uniform, but Frank was familiar enough with the confident stride and sway to recognise a military gait. He also knew the man as one of Marley's drinking cronies --- and not someone he saw eye-to-eye with --- Colonel Paul Schroder.

'Things are sliding, Frank; we need to get up off our butts pronto,' said Knowles, standing at the table. Seeing Frank's forlorn look at having to abandon his meal, Knowles quickly cut in to correct his statement. 'No, no, Frank, not right away. Carry on and eat your ---' Knowles leaned in over Frank's plate to inspect it '--- what is that? Is that goulash?'

'Bedouin bird and beef concoction.'

That was enough for Knowles to step back disinterested. His interest was quickly rekindled when his eyes homed in on Jocelyn's glass of wine. 'Is there any more of this to spare?' he said at the same time as reaching out to take up the bottle to scan the label. 'Fifty-nine? I suppose that'll do,' he said beckoning a waiter to bring another two chairs and two more glasses so that he and Schroder could join in the drinking. 'Hogarth,' he said, nodding his greeting to Jocelyn. Half-turning to Schroder, while looking at Frank, Knowles said: 'I don't know if you know this is ---'

Introduction was unnecessary. 'Colonel,' said Frank, in stiff greeting to Schroder.

'Major,' replied Schroder. Curt exchanges between the two sufficed, with the less said, the better. Knowles caught the coldness between the two. Sitting down at the table with Schroder, he ordered another bottle of wine.

Schroder had that kind of long hard-lined face that weathered well in the prairie winds of the old 'Wild West'. But his richly accented vocabulary, totally devoid of 'Yups' and 'Nopes', placed him far back to the civilised east. An educated West Point man. 'As we've heard, the situation is continuing to deteriorate,' he said, with a foreboding nodding of the head at everyone around the table. He went on: 'Soviet and East German soldiers are building up their harassment of our vehicles and troop trains trying to enter the city, and Soviet authorities periodically renewing attempts to conduct unauthorised inspections of Allied vehicles as we cross checkpoints into and out of Berlin.'

Knowles had to get his piece in: 'And the Ruskies are damn well also now trying to establish new restrictions on our flights approaching the city, while allowing their fighters to buzz our Allied aircraft flying through approved access corridors. *Approved* corridors, mind. Jeez!'

All this was old news to Frank, so he waited for the punch-line.

Schroder saw this in the Major's face and rewarded his patience by continuing: 'It's just come through that one of our C-47 transports has been forced down by Russian aircraft when it strayed off course on its flight from Helsinki to Hamburg.'

'Hell,' said Frank quietly, tapping the 'innocent' white tablecloth with menacing metal fingers. Jocelyn's contribution to the tensed atmosphere was a subtle biting of her lower lip.

'We're already in there insisting that the crew be released,' said Schroder, 'maybe in a few days, hopefully.' He paused to take a deep breath and a portion of the unease that the others were feeling. 'Even following their release, with no harm done, the incident is heightening the tension for our pilots flying the Berlin routes. Not making anything better, their border officials are slowing down barge traffic, by implementing new inspection controls.'

'So how heavy a boot are we proposing to put on the other foot in response, Colonel?' asked Frank.

' "In response", Major, we're increasing the training tempo of the two battle groups of our 6th Infantry that makes up the bulk of the Army garrison in West Berlin, and placing additional emphasis on riot control drills and operations in the city. Grunwald Park is the only open space in the city with expanse enough for units to train, and host a series of exercises where the troops can test their readiness to attack and defend. We've got platoons donning civilian clothing and acting as rioters to test the ability of our soldiers to maintain order in the face of Communist-inspired civil disturbances. We're even going out of our way to ensure that the Soviets know exactly what we, the US Army, are doing. It's an essential element in the Army's effort to convince the Soviets that the United States will fight for West Berlin and that, while US forces might not be able to hold the city, we will, nevertheless, inflict unacceptable losses on the attacker. In response to our resolve, the East Germans are building an observation tower to get a better view of our training as it develops. Which is exactly what we want --- let them see that we are not bluffing.'

Knowles thumped the table with a clenched fist. 'I'm all for that --- letting them look over the wall, so to speak, at what we're doing in detail. We have to let them know that we won't be shifted --- that we're here to stay.'

'Amen to that,' said Frank quietly, with another slow thoughtful tap on the table.

Nestling quietly in a little street on the edge of the bustling El-Hira district's rendezvous point for guides starting their naughty tours of the city's 'red light' joints, the tiny bar was conveniently off the beaten track from '*Staatspolizei*' snoopers, sniffing around for someone to arrest. Just so, it served as a watering hole for those travelling through, to make a brief stop at, before moving on quickly. The bar's wooden façade, heavily run-down by the years, like its three sad wooden tables and chairs outside on the narrow pavement, reduced it to uninteresting and forgotten as soon as seen.

Thick soft russet carpeting surprisingly padded Major Falzoni's feet as he walked into the deceptively outwardly-weathered tavern. Refurbishment, in a bold phoenix-style effort, had the décor now twentieth-century, in sharp contrast to its 'dying' nineteenth-century exterior. Electric lights, replacing candles, had the curved pink walls throwing out a romantic pink shade onto the room's occupants. These were only three. The mission rookie, Lavery -- and his contact, presumably, a dark leather-faced man, – and the bartender, his back to them, *soigne* in his blood-red Cossack shirt and metal-studded leather armlets. Catching the man's enquiring look through the mirror behind the bar, the Major pointed to the Brandvein bottle on the bar. He couldn't see his preferred 'mouthwash', Kentucky bourbon, anywhere on the limited display, so that would have to do. The barman was quick to pour out the drink and then duck away and busy himself cleaning glasses in the corner's tiny stainless-steel sink. Whatever it was that brought these serious-looking people into his place, he wanted no part of it.

Taking up his glass, Frank ambled slowly over to Lavery and his contact, and stood there for a moment to observe while taking a sip of his Bavarian brandy. He saw a closeness between them that wasn't due to the wine they'd been sharing from the almost empty bottle on their table. 'Fieseen Bajali, I gather; Is this a private party,' he said to Lavery's 'pal' at last in greeting, 'or can anyone join in?'

'Ma-*yor*,' said Bajali, stressing the j as a heavily accented y, like those Afrika Korp soldiers had said it when he had been a mere boy, long ago, in the desert.

'Major,' added Lavery for his part, getting a quick amused glance in return from the Major as he sat down. There was no room to sit between Lavery and Bajali, so Frank had taken the seat on Lavery's other side.

Although only seeing him for the second time, Lavery saw that the Major's face had gone a shade darker since coming his coming in, and he recognised the anger that was simmering beneath his otherwise controlled surface. The Major was plainly sore about something and he didn't want to get on the wrong side of him. He could imagine that when he was in that mood, you could get swatted like a fly by his glare alone.

To cut the cold silence that had suddenly descended on them, Lavery offered a cigarette to the Major. Waving it aside, Frank took out one of his Camel instead. After he had carelessly singed its tip in delayed chastisement, Frank looked at Lavery through his exhaled smoke. 'So, have you got something for me that doesn't waste my time?' he asked curtly, through his hard frowning scrutiny.

Lavery felt the question split him like a butcher's cleaver, so that neither a yes nor a no would allow him to escape fully without blemish. 'We haven't really had time to work things out yet, Major. We're not long in here, ourselves.'

'And it didn't occur to you to let me know sooner?' Frank rasped, his anger now out in the open. 'You're expected to report back in prompt schedule to me, however small a snippet of information you've picked up – not disappear off the radar on a *romantic sojourn for two*', damnit! It's a wonder Colonel Goodblood has any hair left to pull out; and as you can gather, I'm not too happy either, with the interdepartmental upset at Langley, over you going AWOL for a casual stroll in the park at your own discretion. I've had to put my own plans aside in order to come and look for you – never mind your cosy pal – and pull you out of your mess.' Having let his piece out, the Major's anger suddenly appeared to subside, his mood seemingly taking on humour at the rookie Lavery's inept performance. He sat back, smiling as he looked at both of them in token wrist-slapping. Change colour, like the chameleon, to confuse the observer.

Lavery couldn't quite see his actions as having constituted a 'mess', but he didn't contest the Major's judgement. 'I did try to get back to you on schedule, but we – *I* – was hampered by the *Mabahith Amn ad-Dawla* (State Security Police) operations, assisting the military – tighter than usual, as you'd expect, in the situation, that have been suddenly thrown up. They've only just not long set up their high-pressure crackdown in smoking out and arresting suspected sources of Israeli influence. All the while we had to keep our heads down and hold our breath, so to speak.' He looked round at Feiseen Bajali for support. Bajali nodded back.

The Major appreciated the sense in Lavery and Bajali keeping their heads down to elude the stepped-up security dragnet, but he guessed that this was not the only reason for them hiding away. Their kind of 'togetherness' automatically carried the penalty of immediate execution in this Muslim land.

'From what I can see of the situation, it's in keeping with the developing pattern that we've been getting until now,' said Bajali.

'And what's that, exactly?' said Falzoni, playing the schoolmaster with him, to see if he had been doing his sums. True, he was Lavery's 'property', with Lavery his case officer in the field, but weren't they all supposed to be working towards the same end? He smiled aside at Lavery, wondering if he was feeling annoyed at his dallying with what he considered to be his 'property'.

'Pretty much a skin-hardened by doctrinal propaganda to look passive in resistance to capitalist attempts to find cracks in its surface. Cracks we are determined to prise open wider in a crusade that mustn't cease until that cracked skin of Communism is finally disintegrated.' Bajali tilted his head back slightly with an ease of confidence.

Hallelujah! That was one heck of a mouthful. Frank had to smile at his 'we', considering his age and experience; Mata Hari mode spying jobs among the cloisters of filing cabinets clerk that Bajali was, had not quite the dangers of working in the field; out there in the field, when odds turned against you and you're in a tight corner, back against the wall, you're a goldfish in a piranha pool.

Bajali understood all that without needing to be told, but said nothing. Seeing *Ma-yor* and Lavery had some things to discuss, preferably on their own, he indicated, with a nod at the little wooden carved man and woman on the door across the room. Excusing himself, he got up and went off to the toilet, leaving them to their low-talking cabal of professional tactics.

Watching him until the door closed behind him, Frank turned to look at Lavery. 'He doesn't talk much,' he said, as an 'opener', to see how Lavery reacted.

'You've got to get to know him better.'

'And you've managed that, have you?' said Frank, pushing away his empty glass; he didn't want a refill, and his cigarette would suffice to sustain his patience with Lavery. 'So have you made any progress, beyond 'getting to know him', with the *real* business we're interested in?' Frank assumed that Lavery had enough wits about him to catch the dual implication of his question.

Lavery gave a little nervous rocking motion from side to side, so that the Major read the embarrassment. 'I'm getting there. We're getting along great.'

'You're "getting along great". Is that the best you can give me? I was hoping to hear something more substantial than that little whine. Do I have to remind you that we're running a serious game here. If you're going to play our game, we'd appreciate it more if you would let us know when and where you're playing, and more so, see and play it *our* way. We haven't the time for any points grabbers chasing the ball alone and fouling up the teamwork. As a final reminder, let me emphasise that special word, team ---**T—E—A—M**.'

Sure, okay, I get the message, Major; you're right, I flopped, so I'm sorry. It won't happen again. We're on the same side, *right?*'

'Now how did I forget that?' said Frank, in final mocking rebuff, to let his anger peter out. He watched Lavery trying to rub a spot from his tie, without much success.

'I'll have to take this to the drycleaners,' said Lavery.

'You have to watch out when it comes to drycleaners,' said Frank. 'They're a law unto themselves. You don't want to find that when you send that off, that it's only the *spot* that comes back.'

Lavery looked at the Major's empty glass. 'That was German brandy, wasn't it? What's happened to the bourbon, then? I thought you were partial to bourbon, Major?'

'Don't ask me what happened to the bourbon. I find it a pain in the ass, when Americans are always labelled as bourbon drinkers. I guess it's like the English stereotyped for wearing bowler hats. Do you wear a green bowler hat on the St Patrick's Day Parade, Lavery?'

'I prefer the Sinatra pork-pie style, myself. But yes, I've had occasion to wear a hat, if you must know, Major.'

Oh yeah, and when's that then? Down in the jazz-joint cellar, with good cannabis reefer smokes to help straighten out those twisted clarinet notes piercing your eardrums?

Feeling his confidence coming back, Lavery 'spoke back' to his superior: 'If I'd known that I'd been called here to discuss American customs of dress and drink, I'd have brought along my protocol manual to study its officially stipulated rules.'

About to give Lavery another lecture on those very stipulations of protocol, which he virtually knew, page for page, Frank stopped himself at the sight of the little wooden man swing back with the door opening and Bajali coming out. Instead, in a low voice, for Lavery's sole benefit, he said: 'I'll leave you as better suited to get what we need from him' Raising his voice now for the benefit of everyone, he said: 'Right. So, we'll get to work on that. In the meantime, don't let protocol worry you over any little hunches you may have buzzing in those heads of yours. Don't be shy about sharing them with me. Just spit them out so that I can see them. *Right?*'

'So, who's worried? Not me, Major.' Lavery grinned at Bajali. 'We're not worried, are we?' He said to him. He looked at the Major again. 'If that's everything tied up, are we ready to go, then?'

Frank tossed car keys to Lavery. 'Volkswagen; parked outside the last house on the left. Wait there, both of you. I've got to put through a call to a 'sick uncle', like *some of us neglect to do.*'

'*Here*, on a public phone?' said Lavery.

'In *code*, buddy, in *code*. You'd better get down to seriously reading that protocol manual of yours.'

20

October16. The gigantic 180 metres long lizard made its progress in a slow methodical crawl across the sun-scorched desert sands in the manner of some magical salamander straight out of a mystical Arabian fable. But this great monster's skin and body, through and through, were made of solid steel. This was no ordinary lizard, being of solid steel, and comprising over 100 steel rollers, each 2 metres in diameter, and capable of floating and reaching the Suez Canal's far bank, as a single stable unit, and weighing a total 400 tons. It was an articulated roller-bridge. Codenamed Operation Gazelle, this was Israeli's plan calling for its forces to mount its attack on the Egyptian forces across the Canal. Urgent construction of pontoon bridges had been needed. But with conventionally constructed pontoon bridges being deemed to be unreliable, an improvement design replacement had been needed. This 'monster lizard' was it.

Taking the Israeli Engineering Corps four days to construct it, and having to be to be moved over the flat of terrain of specially selected well routes, it was taking sixteen M-48 Magash tanks to move it. Twelve at the front towing the colossal load, and four acting as brakes. Protection was provided by a column of Sho't tanks and M1113 Zelda tanks riding on either side.

In order for the roller bridge to reach the Deversoir area point for crossing the Canal, special roads, 'Akavish' and 'Tirtur' had been constructed. Heavy fighting, in the in the early hours of 16 October, around the 'Japanese Farm', along the 'Tirtur' road, delayed the roller-bridge's arrival, for just over three days. By way of the paved 'Akavish' road across Hammadia's southern slopes, it reached 'Tirtur' in the early hours of 19 October.

In spite of the IDF being equipped with four hundred and forty-eight M113 tanks, nevertheless infantry men chose to 'hitch a ride', perching on top of the vehicles, so deriving the heavy armoured vehicles' protection from land mines. Alas, with thick desert dust from rolling sand dunes on the steep slopes of Hammadia clogging up their engines, the four M-48 Magash braking tanks struggled unsuccessfully against the gradient's pull, so allowing the massive load to run out of control, resulting with one of the roller connections being broken. Combat engineers, riding alongside in an M-3 halftrack and an M-74 recovery vehicle, provided the necessary repair to damages that cost the mission four hours of delay.

An 'Ambutank' armoured ambulance equipped with and old M-50 self-propelled howitzer stood by in readiness for enemy attack during this crucial stalling period.

00.00hrs, 21 October, Syria, 'somewhere' south of Deir-az-Zur, and east of Damascus (co-ordinates classified), some three hours after leaving the Euphrates River behind. Frank lay flat and motionless, concealed beneath a web of camouflage netting, the thick black blanket of soundless desert night trying to smother him from above and everywhere around him. Or so it seemed to be doing, ever since he'd taken up this surveillance stake-out operation, from his hidden position inside this wadi (dried-up river bed), on Egyptian heavy armour divisions advancing with intent to cross the Suez Canal.

Surprisingly, and you had to admit, devilishly clever, they had commenced their initial onslaught of the war, on that crucial day, October 6, using high-pressure water pumps to spray and blast our Bar-Levi Line ramparts consisting of 1.5 billion cubic metres of rubble and sand, and hitherto considered to be impregnable to normal explosives. Using conventional earth-moving machines to make a way through the barrier would have taken days --- they'd got through in roughly four hours. With steel net- bedding laid down in the now bulldozer-flattened breach, their tanks and troops had poured through virtually unhindered, with their heavy artillery fire on our defence points along the Bar-Lev Line stopping us from blocking their crucial break-through.

It hadn't helped us any, with their M1-8 helicopters bringing in Al Saaqa Commandos behind our defence line to upset our inflow of reinforcements to the area. In devilish contrast, the Egyptians were assisted further by 720 assault boats landing 4000 troops on the Canal's east bank. And that had just been their first wave. Where the attacking infantry-men, laden with weapons and equipment, found it difficult to climb the rampart's steep slopes, ATGW and Strela missiles proved to be their urgently needed back-up by countering defensive attacks from Israeli's Armoured Corps and Air Force.

So far things weren't looking too good for us with the odds leaning the wrong way, the IDF (Israeli Defence Force) having to match its 570 artillery pieces against the enemy's 2055 pieces. And in the four hours or so it had taken to get the halted monster roller-pontoon on the move again in Operation Gazelle earlier, a 100 of our combat engineers, openly exposed to enemy fire, while repairing the pontoon, were killed. We were being increasingly forced to use our artillery, along with M109 155mm self-propelled howitzers, against the enemy's Russian 'Saggers' (line-of-sight wire-guided anti-tank missiles) and RPGs (shoulder-launched anti-tank rocket-propelled grenade), to rebalance the heavy losses of our tank units, and cover engineering units dangerously exposed in their tasks. At least we'd learned the trick of neutralising the Saggers, using heavy concentration of our artillery fire to distract or kill their crews. But our heavily armoured military vehicles are still at peril from their ATGW armour piercing missiles.

It was helping to compensate for our low artillery assets whenever we could capture their Soviet Katyusha BM23 mobile rocket launchers. Otherwise, for any realistic hope of having, *and holding on to*, a superiority in armoured warfare tactics that would win us this war, we were having to rely on our equipment being better, along with a command structure that was flexible from superior training. Attacking Egyptian airfields was proving to be dangerously difficult, their being protected by SAM-2 and SAM-3 anti-aircraft units controlled by Soviet specialists, to give their 'sting' range of 300ft to 15000ft altitude over a range of 20 miles.

In this quiet empty expanse of the desert, your senses were heightened, tuning your hearing in to the eerie vacuous measurement your mind made of the total absence of anything out there. But the threat of danger leaped immediately into your brain at the faintest whisper of sound which told you that something, or someone was out there. Sure, there was the occasional fleeting movement that caught the corner of your eye of the small Jerboa desert rodent sneaking out from his burrow, where he sheltered from the scorching sun during the day. What that poor little bastard expected to forage for to eat in this wretched land, seemingly totally devoid of life, animal or vegetable, you couldn't imagine. But listen as he did, the darkness so far wasn't willing to relinquish one single iota of its deafeningly heavy silence of the night. Only the moon and a sprinkling of stars above him, along with the dark barely outlined form of Colonel Biran lying two feet to his right, reminded Frank that he was not stranded in solitary isolation on this remote landscape. But with the low-hanging moon wanting to dip down further below the horizon, the desert night's blackness thickened so that everything all around dissolved into a featureless void.

Then suddenly there it was --- after two hours, or so, of patiently waiting, listening, he was hearing with his ears, not his imagination --- the only just audible sound of *something out there*. Frank reached out to tap the Colonel's arm. Biran lifted up a thumb to signal that he was also alerted to it.

Vague unidentifiable sound took on form, with the poor light giving an alarmingly demonic shine to the two massive rounded double horns appearing out of nowhere. A bloody ram! Those bloody damn Bedouins and their bloody weird sheep getting in the bloody way! A peculiar breed of sheep they were, with their long uniquely fat-filled tails that enabled them to function as the hump did for the camel. This gave them the necessary means of surviving the harshness of this dry barren desert environment. Get out of the way, you great ugly bearded brute! Bugger off!

As if reading Frank's mind, the animal turned to go back to its 'harem' of ewes, disappearing into nowhere as magically as it had appeared. But a new noise said different. Low at first, the growl became angry enough to become threatening. Out of nowhere, the scrawny-bodied form appeared. The sheepdog. Another bloody nuisance to block his view and possibly blow the mission if its growling and barking reached the wrong ears. The high-pitched yelping cut an alarmingly alien sharpness in the thick darkness, contrasting eerily with the bare stillness of the night.

A new sound, a human voice giving a command, caused the dog to drop its howling but continue with its persistent threatening low growl. The shepherd cast a young Moses image, with the long staff to guide the flock, and a long ankle-length striped robe, and leather sandals. But Moses had been a man. This was a girl. A very young girl – barely reaching her teens, from what he could make of her features in this darkness. And turning on his flashlight was out of the question. Whilst being taller than the dog, she seemed no better bestowed in flesh, her prominent bone lines speaking of meagre diet, like the dog, in this forsaken wilderness. The Bedouin father, sheikh 'Ali Babba', whoever he is, must be short of sons to spare, sending out this puny female urchin to guard his precious flock in this forbidding dark wilderness.

Frank took a firmer grip on his weapon. With Biran not being happy at the Major being armed with only a Colt automatic pistol for this mission, he'd lumbered him with an extra 10lbs weight of Thompson submachine-gun, with its flat magazine of 40 rounds of .45 calibre bullets. Biran, himself, had his 9lbs of 9mm calibre UZI, Israel's very own home-made answer to swatting 'troublesome insects', with its magazine of 30 rounds. Frank could barely feel movement in his hands. With temperature in the desert falling drastically at night, his hands were like blocks of ice. His limbs stiff with the cold, it felt like ice had taken over his body, leaving him only just able to manage gripping the cold steel of the Thompson, and 'finding' the trigger with his all but frozen fingers.

God forbid his having to open fire on the target if it moved forward and inadvertently stumbled upon their hiding place. The barrage line of searing lead bullets would puncture that soft body in neat entrance holes, whilst ripping the back open in gaping great canyons of blood, torn flesh and shattered bone. Again, God forbid that devastating horror occurring, lest he be trapped in the excruciating dilemma of indecision over whether or not to open fire. If it did, with him brutally cancelling out the life of that innocent child, it would violate all the rules, if ever they could be measured, whatever they were, of moral decency, let alone the military manual's so-called rules of engagement. But for the Presidentially classified secrecy of the mission, he would have been facing a tribunal for war crimes. A desperate prayer scraped through his brain that this circumstance would never transpire. Please, please, little girl, get away from here – shoo! shoo!

Yet, in spite of the chastising thoughts going through his mind, Frank found his hands reflexively adjusting the Thompson's sights to target the young girl. If the girl saw them, and raised the alarm, they were going to be in a whole lot of trouble.

Clearly consequences would be grave with the girl discovering them and him not opening fire on the wretched little mite. Their mission would be well and truly blown, bringing on them a massive onslaught of great strength from the enemy on them. Israeli forces were already suffering heavy loss of their armoured units, heavy and light, from this devilishly surprise broadside attack from Syrians on Israel's otherwise unexpecting, hence unprepared, military outposts across the otherwise 'quiet' desert plains —- resulting in heavy confrontational exchange fire of obliterating tank shells and rockets that spared few lives. The vanguard division of General Laneer's 7th Heavy Brigade Battalion had been totally wiped out, leaving few survivors in the aftermath

Although still a good few metres away from their concealment, the bleating sheep, milling and turning at the dog's guidance, were shifting dangerously closer. With the camouflage netting covering Frank, and his face marked with black camouflage streaks and general dirt, the girl would have to be virtually 'standing on their doorstep', so to speak, before she noticed something 'unusual'. A long hard peer into the black depth of the wadi would be necessary before confusing 'strange shapes' changed their form into something that made sense in that young brain. By that time, Little Miss Moses would be just yards away from the Thompson's muzzle. He'd be opening fire, if he did, at point blank range.

Frank wished to the high heavens for the little girl to damn well get out of here, pronto.

Turning away from the threat that was growing nearer moment by moment, Frank looked round to pick out of the wadi's darkness, the humped silhouette of their Land Rover. Selectively removed of roof and windscreen, with a combined four fuel tank capacity of 100 gallons, and provided with heavy duty chassis, heavy duty suspension, sand tyres, shovels, jerry cans and sand-ladders, differential guards front and back, with spare wheel mounted in front, it was a formidable beast to bring along on their 'picnic ride', considering its mounted GIAT 20mm cannon and highly effective 7.62mm gatling gun, general purpose machine guns, anti-tank gun, grenades with grenade launchers, rifles, smoke canisters, navigation gear and spotlights at the front and back.

Would the girl be able to make them out enough to comprehend what they were? Why the damn hell did those blasted sheep have to be there in the first place? They were spoiling everything by blocking his line of fire as they moved across the otherwise empty stretch of desert in their quest to find, gobble up and chew -- *what* exactly? Considering the absolute absence of anything other than sun-dried sand and rock that they'd encountered as they'd pushed on through this wilderness, you could be forgiven for thinking that nothing offering even a meagre nibble could grow in this God-forsaken sun-baked soil. But they were wrong, it seemed, and the sheep, in their innate wisdom, were right.

Frank dismissed the idea of grabbing the little imp without harming her. By the time he'd climbed out from under the camouflage netting and crab-crawled his way up the sheer-faced side of the wadi, no doubt dislodging loose rocks that would alert the kid, she would have scarpered --- and not without shattering the night's silence with her frightened shrieks --- and alerting the enemy bivouacked over there in their camp.

Back in those long-gone G.I. days in that other war, you had a platoon commander to issue orders according to his decisions. But here, running your own game, decisions were yours alone, drawn on operational experience. Going by the many missions he'd been on, Frank's experience report sheet could somewhat resemble the surrealist artist's effort, considering the scratches and blood-marks it showed. But there was nothing on that sheet about killing kids.

Timing was vital to their mission schedule, but Frank didn't dare move his arm to consult his watch. This movement could catch the young shepherdess's attention, and the luminous dial glinting for a fraction of a second in the pitch black, wouldn't help. With his weary eyes barely able to stop the eyelids from dropping, Frank scrutinised the restless shifting mass that was the flock. But was he right in now thinking that the girl had, in fact, meant all along to guide her flock to the wadi? It was becoming increasingly clear to him that this was her intention, leading her precious animals to greenery where they could feed. If there was any damn place in this wretchedly sun-scorched plain that could provide vegetation for hungry, thirsty sheep, the wadi was it. Given that rain fell occasionally, then conceivably a hardy shrub might cling tenaciously to life, its roots reaching down deep into the soil in the otherwise 'dry' wadi. Transformation would see an angry torrent of water rushing along the riverbed with its moisture soaking down into the much needy undersoil.

So, she was going to be ruining everything by coming upon their 'perfect' den, which they'd slid into just after darkness had fallen, hoping that this hollow, with its darkness, would conceal them sufficiently from enemy eyes. Frank's hands slid cautiously along the Thompson's cold stock, his freezing finger hovering over the trigger, at the same time adjusting his aim. With his keeping perfectly still, he hoped the girl had little chance of spotting him, swathed as he was, in his shroud of dankness.A rill of sweat found its way down along the cracks of hardened sun-baked camouflage cream on Frank's face.

But you learned that patience was a vital commodity that, alas, too few possessed in this life and death stage of the game. Thirsting for action left no room for a calm nerve waiting in long freezing hours to see if some unfortunate kid blundered into your hiding place. On covert stealthy operations like this, a calm controlled nerve was imperative if you didn't want your plans to fall through.

He was wanting the little girl and her damn bleating sheep to push off in any direction that wasn't to the east, so as not to block his line of fire on the Syrian soldiers they intended to attack. His bullets fired from this close would silence and remove her as an unwanted obstacle, sure enough, but their noise would ruin their surprise attack on the enemy. His only fret was whether he had the sang-froid to kill the child in cold blood.

Almost as if reading Frank's mind, she tilted her little head, puzzled, searching, staring, in his direction. He tensed at her little unsure steps bringing her closer. With electrifying reaction, Frank's reflexes geared him up to immediately remove the oncoming threat. A rush of adrenalin brought a pre-action burning feeling to his face. Pulsing blood thundered away in his ears, loud enough to shake the desert night out of its slumber. A voice was screaming inside his head: Fuck off! Damn well bugger off!

Looking about for a tantalising moment in her uncertainty, the girl nevertheless kept coming in short faltering steps, stopping at the edge of the wadi, with only feet between her and the death-delivering Thompson muzzle. Held in her puzzlement, her tiny eyes scraped the darkness, with her concentrated staring seemingly pulling him out of his concealment. For agonising long seconds, those two young frightened eyes stared in his direction.

Something had spooked her. For a second or so the girl seemed rooted to the spot, before shifting a nervous step forward towards them. From across the barely twenty feet or so between them, Frank could almost feel the girl's eyes connecting with his own. He could sense the girl's eyes peering right at him in spite of his camouflage covering. He sensed that by some uncanny means she knew that he, or something malicious, was there. He imagined he could just make out the girl's lips in their low nervous muttering of prayers her mama had taught her. Undecided in stepping back or coming nearer down into the wadi, she stood there, swaying precariously on the black cleft's edge. Frank's mind swayed between firing and holding back.

Frank's finger reflexively tightened on the cold trigger. As much as the thought of 'wasting' the innocent child with a horrific blast of bullets tearing into her young body reviled him, it would also waste their mission, raising the alarm with the roar from unnecessary gunfire.

A sudden glint of moonlight beside him caught his eye at the steel commando knife blade sprouting out of Biran's hand.

Frank's hand shot out to clamp on the blade. 'She'd see you and scream, before you can get out from under your camouflage net and at her. Our cover would be blown, Colonel.' The thought of that sounding as if this was his *only* reason for stopping Biran killing the girl, gave Frank's stomach a sickening turn of shame --- if it wasn't delayed guilt.

Yet long-learned reflex still kept his finger on the trigger. One single press on that cold steel would be all that was needed to release the cruel blast to reduce that young life to nothing -- as well as reducing that space allowing him to squeeze through those closing Pearly Gates when his time came. Ironic, perhaps, that he was here in the very land of camels, where maybe he could find himself one to help him get through the proverbial eye of that needle.

A moment's tension dropped suddenly with the small figure turning and hurrying away, throwing a frightened glance more than once over its tiny shoulder in their direction. Clearly the child had felt the danger of something that could kill hiding in the darkness of the wadi. But had it been just 'something' -- or *them* that she'd sensed? That she could raise the alarm at her discovering their presence caused Frank's moments of relief being replaced by his own alarm of the mission being blown rising up inside him.

As if uncannily sensing from afar Frank's eyes following her, the tiny figure diminishing in the distance began to scream out aloud with a shrieking piercing of the night's heavy silence. Apart from Frank's understanding of Arabic being next to nothing, it was impossible to make out anything intelligible from the shrill cries at that distance. At least the girl was no longer a threat that required 'cancelling'.

With their hands now taking serious grip on their weapons, Frank and Biron primed their action reflexes in readiness for imminent onslaught from the enemy. Their hearing acutely cocked to picking up the smallest whisper from the night, they waited. But the thick blanket of smothering blackness around them refused to relinquish a single morsel of its heavy silence.

Was the enemy not alerted by not heeding the girl's cries, or were they employing the deceptive defensive tactic of feigning unawareness of a surprise attack, in order to neutralise that attack's surprise?

Frank and Biran waited. Biran looked at the Major with query in his expression. 'I can't imagine Sun Tzu, in all his roughly two thousand years of wisdom, considering it to be a sound stratagem for us to move in on the enemy, having lost our vital advantage of surprise attack.'

'It's your precious land, even if only after you won it over from Syria in your Six Days War wrangling-match---so, I'll leave that decision to you, Colonel.'

21

'Nearly there, Captain. Not far to go now,' said the navigator, into his oxygen-mask's microphone, his words overriding the din of the Avro Vulcan's four Bristol Siddeley Olympus 301 turbo-jet engines, to reach the pilot controlling the great 37.7ton triangular mass of bomber plane.

'Maybe we should have put him in the bomb bay; that way we could have dropped him and saved ourselves the bother of having to land,' said the co-pilot, with his grin hidden behind his mask.

The pilot looked round, puzzled, at his colleague.

'Our mysterious passenger.' A finger pointing down, answered the puzzle. The figure was seated, a short ladder distance below them, in the passenger seat reserved for a Crew Chief engineer, close to the exit/ entrance hatch just behind the plane's huge nose-wheel.

The pilot's head nodded in smiling jocular agreement hidden behind his mask. 'Yeah, maybe.'

On and on the plane raced at its comfortable 400mph cruising speed, tearing through the golden sky, the engines giving out their mind-holding roar all the while, the mammoth shape of 111ft wing-span rocking and dipping in battle with the buffeting wind currents.

With the deep drone of its four engines reverberating in the sunny afternoon sky, the massive frame of the Vulcan gradually began moderating its velocity, in order to circle round in preparation for landing down on the Israeli Air Force Bir Gifgafa forward-operating airbase. Weighed down by the body-load of a gigantic bat, but moving with the graceful lightness of a gadfly, it came in round from the sky in a declining arc, screeching its fury to announce its arrival from England. Its enormous delta wings bounced the roar back down, drowning the striped commotion of military policemen and barrier rails at the airbase entrance. Straightening out gradually, it finally touched down on the landing strip.

Frank Falzoni, standing there beside Colonel Biran, looked on with mixed feelings as the plane rolled past heavily on its huge wheels. He felt thrilling pride at the potential punch it could deliver, vying with pangs of guilt over the searing memory of that disaster so long ago that he had been near enough to see, but too far away to prevent. If only the Hurricane had not strayed away from its flight escort position. If only. Himself a passenger aboard a Lancaster, he'd watched helplessly from his distance, seeing the plane 'snap' in two halfway along the fuselage, exploding under the impact of a 109 Messerschmitt's cannon bullets streaming into it like frenzied hornets. A tiny human figure had fallen from the spinning wreckage-pieces looking comically stupid with its tragically futile flailing of limbs in the merciless open sky. The falling figure's scream, muted by time's distance, wailed its horror silently in Frank's head.

The ceasing banshee howling of the Vulcan's four turbo-jet engines coming to a halt, jerked Frank's somewhat dismal reverie to a halt also.

The rectangular exit-hatch of a 'nostril' behind the Vulcan's nose opened down to begin drivelling out down the ladder, onto the tarmac runway, a 'mucous' of bright blue British RAF-uniformed figures. After a pausing gap of several long seconds taxing Frank's patience, the ladder once more showed activity; this time of a figure in much duller civilian hue of dark grey tweed three-piece clambering down with apparent awkwardness.

Stepping down onto safe terra firma, CIA Officer, Colonel Marley Goodblood, looked around in a panoramic sweep to take in his surroundings. In the distance, a built-up area bustled with activity where maintenance crews and criss-crossing lines of bomb trolleys, somehow managed to weave and wind their way, like hurrying ants under a hypnotic spell of urgency, across the bustling camp space without actually colliding and exploding. Over in the grass, three missile crews, topped in their white protection hoods, practised with MIM-14 Nike ground-to-air missile launchers. Each missile was armed with a T-45 nuclear warhead.

A small jeep raced out across the open tarmac, to be dwarfed by the huge silver mass it was moving alongside of, to pick up its passenger. Jumping smartly out of the jeep, the young airman stood to attention beside it. A silver metal oak leaf in a laurel wreath glinting low down on his left sleeve, told Goodblood this was a *Rav Samal,* or warrant officer. About to step up into the jeep, Goodblood's eye caught a distant movement over on the far side of the runway, beside the blunt stump of a control tower structure jutting up from the otherwise flat stretch of sun-glazed sand. One of the two figures was waving an arm to catch his attention.

'Hold on a second,' Goodblood said to the driver. 'Before taking me to your camp CO's office, take me over there, first.' He pointed at the two distant figures.

'Sir!'

At the runway's end, the Vulcan turned with the surprising lightness of a ballet dancer and taxied back up. It moved over into the service bay that was dominated by a large hanger and a hunchbacked goblin gathering of Nissen huts. The hanger's gaping mouth widened to let a long low-slung 'beetle' with lots of wheels speed out towards the Vulcan, to tow it inside. The massive bulk of the great silver bird receded slowly, inch by inch, into the hanger, to gradually disappear behind the deep shroud of the inner darkness.

'So how do you come to be riding in that great freight of a kite, Colonel?' said Falzoni. 'I thought we had enough of our own planes, to not go borrowing from our British cousins?

'A little side-issue, on Langley's request, for me to drop in at Britain's much-classified bug-breeding incubator, so to speak, Porton Down, to see if there's any trace of left-over 'dregs' of Nafur-Nafiri's work.'

'*And?*' queried Frank.

But Goodblood dismissed the subject with a curt wave of the hand. Biran's momentary frown said that he was not pleased with the non-too subtle hush-hush tactic.

Goodblood stepped down from the jeep to stand and give his usual admonishing smile to his sometimes cheekily insubordinate colleague, Major Falzoni, and his companion, whom he presumed to be Mossad officer, Colonel Biran. 'Shalom.' He said to Biran.

'Shalom,' returned Biran.

'Well, Frank, I hope you've got something for me that's worth the right rodeo bucking horse-ride I had flying over here.' He rubbed his back for a moment. 'I'm lucky if I haven't slipped a disc. So, what have you got?'

Biran took this as his opportunity to step in. 'If it becomes necessary, we're coming to the point, in agreement, of being prepared to employ *tactical* nuclear weapons.'

'*Tactical?* What's that implying exactly?' said Frank and Goodblood at the same time.

'Non-strategic weapons with a nuclear punch designed for open use on the battlefield, while still in the proximity of friendly forces and even on contested friendly territory. They'd have a smaller explosion power in contrast to normal strategic nuclear weapons to target enemy interior areas away from the front, against bases, cities, towns, munition and fuel depos, and other important large target areas, to damage the enemy's ability to wage war any further. There's a good, versatile, practical example with the small W48 TNW, that has the explosive power of 72 tons of TNT, whilst being only 14 inches long and looks somewhat like a fat bullet --- impressive for its size, you have to admit.'

'Yes, I'll have to give you that – impressive,' said Goodblood, nodding his head slowly.

Biran couldn't stop from going on: 'We also have gravity bombs, land mines, nuclear warhead torpedoes, depth charges, SAM surface-to-air, and air-to-air missiles, short range artillery missile shells --- all of these with nuclear punch. We can also demolish enemy blocking points, such as tunnels, narrow viaducts and mountain passes, using our new

Special Atomic Demolition Munition, fired from a special smooth bore recoilless rifle.'

'And you're thinking that this in itself will suffice in turning the tide? said Goodblood.

'If, alas, it should come to the point where we are having to accept that we have no alternative, then we would have to hope so.'

'Old Canute wasn't too lucky in his hopeful plight of trying to stop the oncoming waves. And I didn't even have to go to college to learn that,' remarked Falzoni.

Considering the Major's pessimistic quip, it wasn't too happy a look that Biran gave him. Letting out a long sigh of exasperation, Biran shifted, looking at the other two as he prepared to go. 'As you two have other things to discuss between yourselves, I'll take my leave. I also have pressing matters to see to.' Turning abruptly, he strode away.

'Come on, Frank, time we climbed aboard again,' said Goodblood, walking towards the jeep and its patient young driver.

As the jeep raced them on towards the camp's central area, white stripes and red and white notices on wire mesh fencing stood out in the glaring sunlight to stop all unwarranted entries: **WARNING: OFFICIAL PASSES MUST BE SHOWN; UNAUTHORISED ENTRY BEYOND THIS POINT IS AT OWN PERSONAL RISK: GUARD DOGS ON PATROL: [IDF Security Notice.]**

The jeep stopped before the red and white barrier. The MP, all resplendent in brilliant white helmet, brilliant white belt, holster with automatic, baton sheath and brilliant white anklets with stretch spats over the shining boots, stepped out of the gate's glass sentry box. He reached forward for the civilian's credentials. Goodblood eyed the automatic's butt poking from the holster's corner as they sat waiting. The MP's eyebrows moved up slightly as he inspected the pass. '*Major*. Sorry, sir, I didn't realise that ---'

'I won't let your CO know that you're carelessly lackadaisical in not reading the security roster --- *this* time,' said Goodblood, pointing at the MP's clipboard, and nodding to dismiss the error. He took back his pass. Anklets and boots bounced brilliantly in the sunlight with the guard stepping back smartly and saluting. The jeep rolled forward, under the rising barrier, while the other guard in the glass box spoke into the phone, watching Goodblood and the others all the while as they passed through. A patrolman from the background, watched them intently, holding his two fierce Rottweilers on steel chain-leads, by his side, while gripping the Uzi across his chest.

Tall, with a wiry slimness that came a lifetime's iron dedication to duty, the Camp Commandant, Brigadier Samuel Leevan, stood at the entrance to the Officers' Mess unit, waiting to greet the CIA Intelligence Officer, Colonel Goodblood, newly flown in from England. 'Shalom, Colonel,' he said, holding out his hand.

'Shalom,' Goodblood returned, with a curt nod. They shook hands.

'I hope your flight wasn't too bumpy, Colonel, in spite of the forecast our weather people gave us.'

At this, Goodblood cast a smiling glance at Falzoni, before looking back at Leevan. 'No, it was just fine, Brigadier, just fine.'

'The 'Huey' won't be ready for another thirty minutes or so, I'm told,' said Brigadier Leevan, looking over at the Bell UH-18 Iroquois helicopter, nicknamed 'Huey' because of its HU-1 designation, sitting there with its 1100hp engine purring away patiently whilst being attended to by its diligent ground maintenance crew. 'While it's being juiced up to take you to Tel Aviv, we can go inside and have ourselves some coffee and a slice of babka cake.' A hesitant pause, with Brigadier rubbing his two hands together in nervous thought. 'And some serious field issues we need to go over, that may well affect the overall proficiency of everything, and *everyone* here.' He took a long silent look at the camp all around him, and then a quick look up at the azure canvass of sky, with its thin trailing white threads of fighter jet streams drifting away, curling up and broken up, by the invisible fingers of the wind currents. 'If that's all right with you,' he said, looking round at Goodblood and Falzoni.

'That's definitely all right with me, Brigadier,' replied Goodblood.

'Anything to get out of this damned sand-ridden wind,' murmured Frank.

While they stepped through the doorway, following the Brigadier to his office, Frank whispered quietly to Goodblood: 'So what special lot have they laid on for you now, with a special chopper, no less, getting saddled up solely for yourself?'

'Not just me, Frank, but you as well, even if I have to spring it on you at the last moment.'

'*Me*, as well? I'm not so sure I like the sound of that word "spring". So, what the hell are you getting me in for this time?'

'Well, I've had you meeting President Nixon in the White House for a little chat; now we're going to meet and have a parley with Israeli Prime Minister, Golda Meir.'

'I wonder if, by any chance, her salver reserved for visitors will have a Pastrami sandwich or two on it.'

22

23.44hrs, Stanley Bay, Alexandria. The car seat creaked as its shadowy occupant shifted to look in the rear-view mirror, carefully watching the figure that had emerged from the lane. Scrutiny held for a few seconds and then the eyes relaxed, as the figure came nearer into the light. The brain registered friend, not foe. Leaning across the seat, the man opened the passenger door and his colleague got in with his paper-wrapped package.

'What kept you?' said the first man, more interested in the package than the answer. 'It's nearly gone midnight.'

'It's not that already, surely, Sergeant?' said the colleague over his shoulder, as he tried to close the door. He turned around and started to open the package. 'I couldn't jump the queue without risking attracting undue attention by causing a scene. Besides, I stopped off to have a piss in the scrap yard back there.' He handed over the sausage and carton of black coffee. 'That's yours, along with your change.' The ball of crumpled notes landed in the Sergeant's lap. Not bothering with words or money, the sergeant gingerly rescued his sausage and herb scroll from its tinfoil tray to sink his teeth into it savagely. Overcooked, it was harder than he preferred and the herbs around it flaked in abundance like chronic dandruff. 'Is this the best you could do?'

'That's what you asked for, isn't it? Sausage and herb, right? So, what's wrong with it, then?'

'What wrong with it? Well, I think I've seen a flea flex meaty biceps thicker than this lot.'

'Eat up, Sergeant, that was the last they had.' He paused to swallow a large mouthful of baba ghanoush eggplant sandwich. 'Anything been happening? He said, tapping the 15lb Nocta infra-red camera that was perched on the aluminium support rod bracketed to the dashboard. Not wasting any words, the Sergeant shook his head and gorged on into his sausage. His colleague leaned forward and looked into the camera's view-finder, switching on the battery power unit for the searchlight. The Nocta had a 35mm single reflex lens and a 300mm long focus lens, giving it a range of one hundred yards. Coupled on either side, like proud ram horns, were the searchlight and flashgun, both with special filters allowing only the infra-red rays to pass through. This made all the difference between night and day with the naked eye and the camera eye. Outside, the night was still dark and shapeless, but the man looking through the viewfinder has a brilliant daylight picture of the house they were watching sixty yards down the street. And could count the cracks in the brickwork.

'Anything?' said the Sergeant.

'Nothing,' answered his colleague, swivelling the camera a couple of degrees, before giving it up, to sit back in his seat again.

The Sergeant snapped on the radio. 'Hello, Rufus. Ferret Two here.'

Hello, Ferret Two. Have you anything to report?'

'No, but it's going on midnight and our relief is long overdue. I take it we're still going to be relieved, or has something gone wrong?'

'No, nothing's gone wrong. Don't worry, we'll send your relief out as soon as possible. Just wait a little bit longer. There's nothing else, is there?'

'No, there's nothing else, Rufus. We'll wait. That's it. Over and out.'

As they waited, a cat stalked along the wall and stopped to look at them. The Sergeant's colleague shot it between the eyes with his forefinger and a soft 'Sploof!' Not impressed, the cat twitched its ears and swung its tail back and forth, before moving on.

'Hello, who's this, then?' said the Sergeant's mate, looking in the rear-view mirror.

'Where?' said the Sergeant, seeing nobody in front of them.

'Behind us, Sergeant.'

Sure enough, the silver Audi rolled up out of the darkness and parked in at their rear bumper. Major Falzoni got out and came up to the driver's window, to give it a light tap. The widow slid down and the driver leaned out to look at the new arrival's face for a few seconds, before giving a longer scrutiny to his security credentials. He gave the pass back smartly to the American Major. 'Is something on, then, sir?'

'Yes,' replied the Major. We're going to move in and rush them. Back-up should be here in a few minutes.'

Just then, the radio came alive, and they all leaned in to listen. Hello, Ferret, are you there?'

'Yes, we're here, Rufus. What is it?'

'Stay put. We're sending back-up round now. New orders have come through from base. We're going raid the place. We should be with you in a few minutes, so stand by. Got that?'

'Got you, Rufus. Standing by. Okay. Out.'

The Major was about to go back to his car, when the driver's mate caught their attention, pointing in front. 'That's all we need.' He looked round at the other two, especially the Major. 'What do we do? We can't shift and upset scheduled operations.'

With no immediate answers coming from anyone, all three stared in suspended thought at the possible danger approaching them from along the quiet street. Straight-backed, with a deliberate threatening air of authority that was reinforced by their long rifles slung over their shoulders, the two Staatspolizei officers came on, nearer and nearer, their slow-stepped gait giving further assurance of their power.

'Maybe it'll be all right,' murmured the driver's pal hopefully.

'Get rid of them, before they blow the whole thing,' rasped the Major, in sharp under-breath, turning to move back to the cover of his own car.

The two officers swayed along up the street, and drawing abreast of the cars on the opposite pavement, they stopped and stood there, staring at the two vehicles with open suspicion. At last, they came across slowly to the front car, with one of the officer's radio cackling like a mina bird on his lapel. Speaking into it, the man bent low to knock on the car window. He waited for it to open, his right hand gripping the rifle's leather strap, ready to unsling the deadly weapon should it prove necessary. At the same time, the other officer made a point of noting, and writing down, the vehicle's licence plates, front and back.

The window slid down. Two sets of ID papers, accompanied with special extramural night passes, were passed out the window by the driver in one hand, while his other hand, held low between his leg and the car door, gripped a 9mm Beretta automatic, appropriately fitted with a silencer. Standard Mossad equipment.

Flashing his torch over the papers, and then over the two faces inside the car, the officer felt that he need proceed no further with inspection, when feeling the fat wad of EGP notes wedged between the papers in his hand. Putting the money in his jacket pocket, and handing the papers back, the man nodded. He then looked at the second car. 'He is with you, *yes*?'

'Yes, is uncle. Very rich.' The Sergeant held his hand out through the window, deliberately making an open show of rubbing his thumb and fingers together, to signify money, for the purpose of letting the Major know what to expect when the officer approached him in turn. The driver's gesture had its intended effect on the officer, so that he began walking towards the *'uncle's'* car.

Suddenly, the officer's partner's lapel-radio started blurting out what sounded like an urgent flow of messages. Answering back with an equal surge of urgency, he called out for his partner to forget about the second car, and come away from it. Their assistance was needed at headquarters. They hurried away, leaving the dark street, with its brooding shadows, once again under silent covert surveillance.

The two Mossad operatives and their 'uncle' waited, with the minutes seeming like hours. The Major checked the time on his watch and thrummed the steering wheel restlessly. Then suddenly, they were no longer alone. With ghostly subtlety, car doors and figures were growing out of the street's brickwork, where only the night had been, a few moments before. Clandestine shapes came out of the shadows from different directions and flitted down the street with a common motive in their stealth. Converging on the one point, they melted once more into the stonework, to await the zero signal.

Bored from hours of monotonous watch-duty, the two men in the front car were once again revitalised, like the mythical Phoenix itself. The raid was on.

A figure came along beside their car and rapped on the window as it passed by, on its way to the car behind it. 'It's the Operation Chief, himself,' said the driver, looking in his wing-mirror, 'and he's waiting on the American getting out of his car. Must be an important 'Big Knob'.' They got out of their car and went to join the main body of the Mossad team, while Colonel Biran stood talking with the American Intelligence man.

Major Falzoni finished briefing, and shook his car keys in the direction of the stake-out's target house. That's about the best we can sum it up so far, Colonel. So can we move in now, pronto?'

The statement was polite, but somewhere in there, Presidential Authority was pushing it through.

'Moving in now!' Colonel Biran was much older than the Major and didn't much like the way his operation was being directed by the lower-ranking officer. Nor would he have given a brass farthing for the scant information that Falzoni had dressed up in his sum-up, like icing to hide the dull cake. But then it was the American's, or his President's cake, so they could damn well choke on it. So long as the States abided by their pledge of providing Israel with vital supplies.

Normally Falzoni would have been concerned with this new cold attitude of Biran, since it was his urgent task to liaise between all parties concerned, but he was too ill at ease with other issues, those butterflies in his stomach now getting through to his brain as well. With time ticking by like a bomb in his mind, he was desperate to catch Nafur-Nafiri. That they had snatched out and caught nothing so many times so far, put him all the more on edge with the operation. It only occurred to him then, in his comparative nakedness in the empty street, that this make-or-break raid could end up doing just that --- break them. He had certainly put his signature to papers endorsed by Marley for many such operations in the past. But apart from that, his normal assignments always called him onto the scene after the pot had boiled over.

Just like that one earlier, when he had followed scheduled routine. It was the Navy SEALS who had done the last job. Not quite knowing what came next in the action routine was like facing the lion in the circus ring for the first time, holding the whip and chair in your hands. Do you hit old Leo over the head with the chair, or perhaps get him to sit down on the chair to talk things over sensibly? He suddenly felt himself wishing for a touch of Marley's big town Washington political protocol aplomb. The thought chilled him for a second with its implications.

'Do you think you could step in here out of the light, Major,' said Biran quietly, beckoning Falzoni to step along with him into the cover of the shadows between the two adjacent buildings.

23

00.09hrs. 'Everyone here? -- Gas-masks on?' whispered Colonel Biran looking around at those shapes crouched down around him, and those he couldn't see, assuming they were there. Heads nodded and shapes shifted in the obscure gloom of a garden, while the Colonel took the count.

'Alush and Hayoun in the back alley, *rasan*, (commander)' said a voice from the dark.

'Good,' said Biran. He turned to Falzoni. 'All briefed and ready to go, Major.'

'Right, Colonel. Let's not hang around. Let's get on with it.'

Figures shifted and moved carefully through the unkempt garden's rubbish, while not fully escaping the putrid smells that rankled the nostrils. Other odd shapes remained moulded in one great obscurity, except at the big incision cut by the alley, where some light had sneaked in between the buildings and scraped itself along the wall in a yellow smudge. Something they could well do without.

Stopping just short of the door, Biran turned round to issue last to his hidden team: 'Everyone know their strategic positions when we get inside?'

Not a word on this had been heard from the American standing at the back, so everyone looked in his direction, not sure if he would produce a bazooka or a box of popcorn from his raglan coat pocket. But it bulged out from the Colt Automatic he was gripping.

'Right, move in and go for them *NOW!*' Biran's command rang out barely a split second before they were drowned out by the loud crashing commotion of shattering wood, with the door being smashed back, and thunder-flash gas-grenades thrown in to clear the way for everyone to charge through into the hallway.

Rushing on into the house, they spread out into all its rooms, like fresh air rushing into starved lings. Every single bulb lit up, but the only living thing they found was the loaded electricity meter, turning away quietly beneath the stairs. Otherwise, no great revelations came from the small acreage of doors and drawers that were pulled open. The empty rooms became emptier and Falzoni felt his fears mount, so that the butterflies in his stomach were now using pneumatic drills. One man held up a half-full cup of dark liquid from the table: 'Coffee's still warm, *rasan*.'

'So is the pot,' said another man, lifting up the hinged lid of the tiny brass Moroccan percolator to look inside it. 'And there's still enough left for a second cupful.' All eyes went to the glistening white cup sitting empty beside the half full one.

'He's fled, -- we've missed him!' said Falzoni. 'Damn!' said Falzoni and Biran together.

Biran was annoyed and had to pick on someone. 'We didn't come here to collect cups and saucers for a suki bazaar stall. Keep on looking. If you've looked in a corner, then look again and count the shadows; one of them might not be your own!'

Maor Falzoni spoke matter-of-factly, ignoring Biran's barking at his team. 'I don't think we'll miss anything, working our way up from the ground floor to the roof.'

'Agreed, Major. Right, everyone, I want this place taken to pieces and every nook and cranny gone over with a toothpick, until we can count the maggots. God knows, the country's going to lose something more than sleep if we don't come up with something substantial!'

'Is that what he's saying, *rasan*?' said one of the men quietly to Biran, as they watched the American passing out into the hallway.

'Something like that, more or less,' replied Biran.

'Didn't he give any specific details?'

'To ask for more is to cry to the heavens for mana.'

'I get it.'

'No, you don't, but let's leave it at that, for the time being.' They both fell silent, looking round at the Major standing in the hallway. Falzoni pretended to not hear the Colonel's remark not intended for his ears, staying as he did in the background to let the team get on with the search in what was their 'patch'. A mountain of books and papers that could carry markings gathered rapidly on a central table, to be examined by the Major and Biran for hidden messages or codes. What the two of them could not manage to decipher there, on the spot, would be speedily transmitted by radio to Langley, via the Embassy's CIA room boys, for the experts to go through more thoroughly.

Suddenly there was a cry from the back garden, followed by the sound of scuffling. 'What the hell's that?' said Falzoni.

'I'll go and see,' said Biran. He returned with a satisfactory expression ahead of his good tidings by seconds. 'Our luck has taken a turn for the better. We've nailed one of them. Caught him leap-frogging over the wall halfway down the back lane.'

'Just the one? It had better be good, said Falzoni.'

Two of the team came in the back door, holding a man struggling between them. 'Says he hasn't done anything,' said a third man behind them, prodding the prisoner on the back with his Uzi. 'Says he demands his right to phone his embassy.'

'*Does* he, now?' said Falzoni. 'Oh, he'll get to his embassy, all right --- in a wooden box, when we've finished with him, if he's stupid enough to not play ball.' Biran pretended on the surface to not quite approve of the hostile implication in the Major's words, while being all the way with him inside.

Falzoni pushed his way to the front, to stand face to face with the prisoner. Everyone could sense the violence throbbing behind his angry expression, as he scrutinised the man from a few inches. Where there had been a degree of measured reserve up until now, everyone could now feel the pent-up destructive force building up in the American, where he could suddenly erupt and beat the man to a senseless pulp.

The man took in this message, clear enough, forgetting plea for exclusion by political protocol, and holding his smiling face back, stared with defiant silence into the furious eyes of the Capitalist American.

Falzoni jerked his head to the two escorts. 'Take him away!' The savage tone in his words plainly didn't fit the travel-poster image you saw typifying the ever so friendly, loquacious, American tourist.

'All right, get him back to base,' said Biran. He turned to the Major. 'You can rely on us having ways of loosening his tongue to get what we want out of him --- that is, if he *has* anything to give us. *Right*, Major?'

'Falzoni nodded his reluctant consent. 'But make it quick.'

'All right, move it,' said Biran to his team.

They had once more just missed landing the big fish, Nafur-Nafiri, instead, hauling in a mere tiddler, Falzoni feared would be the case. He was angry to the point of beating someone, *anyone,* to within an inch of meeting the Maker. Instead, he ended up shaking his car keys in great agitation and slamming the car door extra hard.

Their cars couldn't have cleared the area any quicker if a quarantine flag had been hoisted up the mast. Abandoning their low profile, they roared off round the block and away, cutting corners sharply and swerving widely round, to narrowly miss, a lad crossing the road. Two Staatspolitzei, seeing this, stepped promptly into the road, but the cars were gone, speeding away before their numbers, fake ones, could be taken down.

The young lad, Maneesh Hassani, Dr Nafur-Nafiri's one-time helper, muttered a silent prayer, thanking his God for sparing his life those precious few moments before.

While the Mossad team raced across the city, in its own private Le Mons bid to beat the traffic lights, other teams moved about the night with more clandestine stealth. Over in Cairo, the gates of the Russian Embassy swung to-and-fro every so often, like bat wings in the night, as 'cultural secretaries' flitted back and forth surreptitiously on discreet missions. With something obviously afoot in the air, all intelligences were feeling the vibrations, and were anxious to get an earful of its development.

00.27 hrs, US Embassy, Cairo. Up on the top floor, the CIA Station Chief, Melvin Reed, fretted his way coughing through another packet those weird-tasting Egyptian cigarettes, whilst pondering over the whereabouts of his agent, Bart Knowles. It was some hours since Knowles had cared to show his face, and his last report lying in forlorn abandon on the desk, had been brief and scattered like a sped-up reel of Tom and Jerry. What was worse, Melvin was being hounded by the Station's diplomatic advisor, who in turn was being pressed for a report in the morning by the Ambassador, himself. The US Secretary for Defense and the National Security Advisor would both be flying in from Washington later today for a tough parley with the Israeli Foreign Minister.

With Ambassador Greenfell as 'mother', passing the 'cheese and biscuits' between them, a bad report would leave that poor man with no more hair on his head to pull out. And as if that wasn't enough, Melvin would be paying for more than champagne and caviar when he hosted today's lunch for them at the no less than majestic five-star Luxor Hotel, with a sharp-eared Reuter journalist to sweet-talk him over the festering rumour of a naughty government laboratory bug-leak. But the damn guy was only one of a global network of like press snoopers that the CIA had in its pocket, who could be relied upon to give the 'true story' to the media. Provided, of course, they received their generous perks. And you sure as hell knew these guys developed sophisticated and *expensive* palates, when they learned they weren't paying for cordon bleu monkey balls. Melvin checked the money in his billfold. He opened the safe to take out some more. Safer to use cash. It was more discreet than the old plastic.

Going over to the window, Melvin peered down into the street at a figure walking along past their tall imposing marine-guarded gate. The man was too small to be Knowles. Melvin went back to his desk and slumped down into his chair. Opening another packet of 'poison fingers', he lit one, promising himself, yet again, that he'd stop smoking soon. He watched the smoke wafting up to the ceiling while he waited. The piercing shrill shriek of the phone, virtually leaping with urgency from its cradle, had him lurching forward for it, stubbing out the cigarette at the same time. 'Knowles, you fuckin' ----' he yelled into it, then broke off to heed the secretary's calmly delivered message. 'Major *who*? Oh, - right, - sure honey. Put him on, honey, put him on.'

00.30hrs, Sidi Barrani. (2 km north of Stanley Bay) The cold night breeze sent the beer can rattling along before it in an unsure meandering path, rolling in and out of the gutter. Stopping and starting again, its erratic clinking cut the night's silence to carry Maneesh Hassani's mind back to a happier time, when he was responsible for minding the family's tinkling goatherd. That was before the Americans had dropped their bombs. Only three of the goats had survived the bombings. That was three more than any of his family had survived. Not that he was unhappy now. He was simply devoid of feelings. Strict mujahadin discipline and personal resolve decreed that all his mental energy should be channelled into seeking out his revenge. Emotions had to be restrained in their lateral wanderings, to be directed forward as a sharpened dagger that would decidedly pierce the infidel enemy's armour.

Hassani was on foot, having just managed to escape arrest in that house-raid barely thirty minutes earlier, and wasn't risking hitching a lift from any passing car. Drivers had minds, especially at this late hour, for recalling their incidental passengers' faces and their specific drop-off points. But he enjoyed walking. He had walked many miles as a boy, simply to fetch the water for his mama to cook the family's meals. But walking kept his sinewy body fit for action. In compromise, he had 'borrowed' a bicycle, abandoning it shortly afterwards again, when he had judged himself to be still roughly several streets away from where he had been instructed to go, in the case of an emergency exit like this had been. This way, leaving nothing for the Staatspolizie to trace to himself or the rendezvous. The night air was cool after the heat of the day, but Hassani could barely suppress a cynical smile at the puniness of what tourists called warm, compared to the heat of those deserts, where Allah's chastisement had burned upon his Bedouin boyhood flesh.

Turning into the right street at last, he put the scrap of paper away in his pocket. It was a very long street. Counting down the house numbers, he was worried whenever a door, or several doors in succession, didn't show any. He didn't want to attract attention by knocking on the wrong door, even if only to ask for some directions, at this late hour. At last, the number he was seeking. Allah be praised.

Hassani could barely squeeze past the great bulk of the large vehicle that took up just about every square inch of what had been a front garden; and this was only because the low brick wall had been knocked down to facilitate a 'driveway'. His knowledge of cars was scant, but he could tell by its gleaming parts, that it was an expensive commodity and Russian. And this would not have been provided for luxury, but for fulfilment of a mission, by the Soviet State.

He didn't find it hard to imagine his coming across other signs of temptation winning over his control inside the house. He shook his head in sad disdain at lost opportunity. With some difficulty, he refrained from swearing under his breath to himself. That these people, who were pledging their loyalty to their motherland, could at the same time taint their souls by hoarding Western-style luxuries, contrary to their ideological Communist doctrine, was a lot to bear. But this was where he was supposed to come. He could not question the will of Allah.

A thin sliver of light sliced the darkness as the door opened a few cautious inches. Guarded suspicion passed between the two pairs of eyes. 'Salaam aleikum,' said Hassani.

'Aleikum salaam,' replied Fiseen Bijala.

'Who is it?' called a thick Russian voice from within.

'It's all right. It's the young Arab boy. Let him in,' said a soft polite English voice.

Hassani went in, and the door shut out the light, to let the night reclaim its dark shroud of secrecy.

24

Frank stood tapping his teeth thoughtfully with a pair of callipers, while watching Jocelyn's lovely ass fill out her trousers with their tight curved swelling, as she leaned low over the large map, beating the hell out of it for not lying flat on the desk. He pulled his thoughts away from that with Biran walking in to the room.

There was no time for dwelling on distractions in this work, especially in this present situation. Emotions had to be restrained in their lateral wanderings, to be directed forward as a sharpened point that would pinpoint a chink in the enemy's armour. You couldn't allow personal feelings to come between yourself and what was needed to see this assignment through successfully. Especially when Washington was pulling its hair out in its anxiety for him to send in a report of mission accomplished. Strict discipline decreed that all your mental energy should be channelled into fulfilment of his mission. Failure to bring home a nice fat 'bone' of completion would perhaps not see you being put before a firing squad, but you would certainly be in the 'doghouse', fair and square, which meant not being invited by Marley to any more of Edwina's cultural soirees. A last-minute blessing in disguise?

'Come in, Colonel, and grab yourself a chair,' said Frank, without looking up. 'Be with you in a second. I ordered coffee when I heard you were on your way up. I thought you would fancy a drink after your little escapade. I hope you've something useful to tell me.'

'Thanks,' replied Biran and sat down. After his fruitless search at Massri Straights, he didn't fancy another drink – well, not coffee or tea, anyway. Perhaps something stronger, but he kept that to himself. He lit a cigarette and blew out a thick stream of smoke towards Frank. One of his little ways he'd learned of annoying the American. But Frank burst the balloon on that one, ignoring the smoke and continuing to study the map. You countered Biran's occasional *deliberately* irritating mannerisms by offering no ball for him to bat when you saw he was ready to swing.

Biran studied the Major's haggard features through the curling grey haze. The tired face nearly matched the pale smoke, and Biran reckoned he'd no mind for pushing in even a half shekel's worth more to play that tired tune. In fact, he surprised himself by feeling sympathy for the Major by pushing his weight on the job, rather than notch up a point against the man. He let out a soft chuckle of surprised praise.

That got a split-second reaction from Frank, with his head half turning in a moment's reflex to see what new mischief Biran was hatching. To hide his alerted curiosity, he bent down close to the map to see what Jocelyn was marking on it. 'So, what's happening, Colonel?'

'Absolutely nothing. No-one turned up. No-one arrested.'

'So, like I was saying, Colonel, tell us about it.' Both figures straightened up from the map, dropping their preoccupation with their inner vision of waves of Egyptian armoured aggression flowing steadily eastwards across the sand, instead of just over this paper's surface. Frank looked at the dark-faced figure poised, with a latent throbbing energy, on the edge of the straight-backed chair, and somehow out of place with all the paperwork lying about. For all the dashing about on Mossad operations the man was doing, Biran looked no more put out than if he'd had to use an extra-hard tap to break a boiled egg. They waited while the cigarette glowed brightly once more and Biran blew out again one last time before saying his piece.

'So, what's to be said, except that we didn't pull it off? It's the same old inherent factor that goes with chasing a cell. With one individual, there's only one pair of eyes to watch our movements. But with a cell, there's more than one pair and obviously one of those pairs saw us and gave the alarm. So, it ends up with Nafur-Nafiri always being one step ahead of us.' A lingering pause. 'It that because we have a leak?'

Jocelyn stepped away from the table, towards Biran. 'You nearly grabbed the guy and then fudged it up at the last minute. A right cock-up, I'd say. It would have solved a lot if we'd managed to get our hands on the bastard.' Jocelyn's words were not intended to be the least critical of the Colonel's effort, but Biran didn't take it that way. His chest heaved up and the old chair creaked in its tired joints as he leaned forward in anger, short of bounding up at the woman.

'Now look here, it wasn't our fault! We didn't send out a damned social card saying we were coming! The entire operation was run in accordance with standard Mossad operational procedure.'

'All right, all right, all right,' cried Frank, stepping between them and shutting his eyes for a second, to stop flying off the handle *himself*. 'Calm down, Colonel, calm down,' he said, using the words to quell his own edginess. With it coming to that, he felt that he really must be needing the sleep that he'd lost over the last forty-eight hours. 'Nobody's blaming you. If we wanted to throw the book at you, we could say that it was your operation entirely, and let the buck stop there. God knows, if all we're looking for is a head to chop off, we wouldn't be playing around with these maps, trying to figure out how to divide the country up into neat slices of radioactive virus-flavoured human omelette.' Frank sat on the desk's corner and folded his arms. 'No, guys, our problems are much bigger than that.'

'It's as bad as that, is it? said Biran, going over to the desk to peer down, trying to make something of the mess of papers and maps.

Frank turned to stab the calliper's pointed ends down into the map, missing Biran's fingers by inches. 'That's us there, as far as we've got, damn it! Where the hell we move to next, is anyone' guess but ours.'

'Nevertheless, I still think we can guess *how* he'll be making his next move,' said Jocelyn.

'Oh, yeah? How's that then?' said Frank.

'I'm seriously thinking that he'll be deciding to do his travelling on foot, at night, in order to keep a low profile, rather than driving a car, or using public transport or any other means of getting about. It doesn't matter that travelling by bus offers some cover by way of their crowded capacity, now that he's been 'rumbled'; with the net closing tighter, he'll be reckoning public transport to be too much of a risk.' Jocelyn paused, to see how the other two were taking this in. 'Sure, moving from one safe house to the next may have easy before, but now, with our operations failing to snare him by just minutes, and security teams, ours, as well as *theirs*, alerted to the cataclysmic threat he poses, he'll be forced to lie low during daylight hours. What do you think?'

'Hmmm, maybe,' murmured Frank, pondering over the idea.

He stood up. 'I'd say we've just under fifty-two hours to go, Colonel, that is, counting on us not putting our money on a horse that needs a wheelchair to get it past the finishing line before sundown. But then, it's coffee time.'

Frank's interruptive remark had the other two looking round to follow his gaze towards the door. Sure enough, the girl walked in with her tray and they all stopped to watch her putting the three cups down on the map, careful not to spill a single drop on the bright white paper. Not that that would have mattered one iota, for all the damn bloody good the map was doing them! With the girl's pale arms and neck flesh standing out in alluring contrast from her black dress, the two men's eyes followed her every action across the room and going out the door, so that Jocelyn felt that she could have scratched the girl's eyes out.

'Thanks,' said Frank to the girl. She smiled back and went out, closing the door quietly behind her. Biran noticed that there were only two cups there. Frank was already picking one up. Jocelyn wasn't. Biran looked over at Jocelyn.

'It's all right, Colonel, said Jocelyn. 'I'm not having any. You can have mine. I've got to go.' She'd caught the faint discord that had grown between the other two. 'Never say stop in this business.' She turned to Frank while she zipped up the chrome drawing instruments in their leather case. 'Look, I'll take a run over there now and see what the hell they make of it -- see what *I, myself,* make of it, in fact, for that matter. I'll probably be back in about thirty, forty, minutes. So, I'll see you then. Okay?'

'Colonel.' Jocelyn nodded to Biran then was gone out the room.

'Won't we cope, then? said Biran as they sat down to drink their coffee.

Frank rolled his head back, looking across the ceiling and then out the window into the infinite beyond the sky. 'Let's say there will be a big change.'

'*Change?*'

'The Human Race has come this far only after many changes in the evolution game. In those days our ancestors weren't too fussy about what form they took up after mutation. Today, however, I think Man is too fond of his fine physique to want to grow another bunch of fingers, or an extra cluster of ears, following intense radiation dosage.'

'Do you think it will do that?'

'Hell, who really knows what it will do, Colonel? I think the Gurus have the right idea for it, when they see themselves as purely extensions of the cosmic media, all wrapped up neatly and manifesting themselves principally as energy forms common to all entities, so that the physical form amounts to nothing.'

Biran smiled at the former-lawyer American's long-winded philosophy. He was good at that sort of thing when he wanted to be on occasions, with his words like trains in a railway marshalling yard, coming out all organised along the right lines.

'And that will help us, will it – all that thinking?'

'Probably not, but it's food for thought. And talking of food ----' Frank got up to put on his jacket '--- is making me feel hungry. All that can be done here has been done --- for the moment, anyway. Time for a break, if only for the nerves. Come on, Colonel, and I'll buy you a last meal before the execution. There's a cute little Giza corner joint that does superb Javanese cuisine.'

'You give in too easily, to meet your doom, Major --- and incidentally, I don't care for Japanese food.'

'It's *Javanese*, not *Japanese*, by the way.'

'Javanese – Japanese – what's the differ ---'

'Jeez! Do I have to put it in writing, for you? I said Javanese!' Frank's words were icily sharp.

Anger flared up for a second in Biran's face, to be instantly replaced by a recovering smile and a steely laugh. The hostility backing down within the sound was barely detectable if you didn't know the man. 'Your nerves really are beginning to feel the raw edge, wouldn't you say, Major? I suggest we get going to this Javanese haunt of yours --- if that's all right with you?'

'Have we had anything further intelligence come in from your lot?' asked Biran as they went out the door.

'Nothing we don't already know. We know a lot of things, but they're all turning out to be applicable at the wrong place, at the wrong time.' Frank passed a hand over his tired face in weary acceptance of the cold fact that he'd just stated. It didn't help any, reflecting back on the last two frantic chases, both ending up with nothing in the bag.

'They're certainly 'passing the parcel', as I believe you Americans would say. Is there no way we can intercept the motion, Major?'

'It has to be just before they make the transfer. There's no knowing how many units are in a cell. Only one member of a cell knows of the link member of the next cell in the chain. That way, the units are isolated beyond detection by others. When a transfer has to be made, this is done by the one who knows the next cell's link member. That way, the other members don't know where the 'parcel's gone.'

'Sounds watertight, but we can cause leaks.'

'Yeah, how?'

'We keep three eyes open, and create pressure at the pipe-line's weak spots.'

Frank looked at the Colonel, trying to see the vicious side that lurked beneath the surface, kept in check by his aplomb for fending off the inquisitive with a beguiling facial charm that was forged by his bloodline's centuries of defiant endurance of persecution with its diabolical pogroms.

It had to be there to enable him to function in his job. 'I won't ask you how you do that, Colonel.' Frank checked to see his pager was switched on. 'I think we'd better make that a *quick* meal.'

Nafur-Nafiri moved as quietly as he could, navigating his way with difficulty in the darkness, among obscure shapes of the slum district's dilapidated old buildings, from one hiding place to another. Hours of hiding in the ruins, during the day, was worrying as he listened to the voices of men searching among rubble, their menacing presence forever coming closer. He couldn't tell if they were looking for him. Even if they were looking for someone else, how would they react if they came across him?

According to emergency plans, when darkness fell, he was required to go to an agreed point where he would be picked up on the hour, over three hours, and taken to the next safe house. He hadn't been able to be there on the hour, three consecutive hours, so his collector hadn't been able to hang around for fear of arousing suspicion. Instead, he was resorting to the secondary measure of getting there on his own effort.

Turning into what seemed to be the right place, from what he could recall of his briefing, he stopped to look around. An empty motionless place. Nothing notable that could really be put together as specific. That old Ford lorry over there with its back piled high with what looked like in the dark as over-spilling stacks of figs. Nothing else. Nothing. No flashing lights, as you would expect to see in that exciting movie. Hell, no such luck. His spirits began to fall.

As he swivelled round slowly, scanning the deep darkness, a movement caught his attention in the corner of his eye. Was he mistaken, or had he picked up a quick movement at the lorry's front? He stared at it. Again, a disappointing stillness.

And then the windscreen wipers jerked left to right, once, twice, and then stopped. A few seconds pause, and then the motion was repeated, once, twice, and then stopped.

He slowly moved cautiously, step by step, over to the vehicle. No longer having his firearm, he now held a piece of long sharp-pointed stick down by his side. If he was going to be put down by a cruel bullet, he would damn well try to be quick enough to take someone's eyeball along with him on that final single journey.

A shapeless black smudge behind glass was replaced by a thickly bearded mass that the darkness allowed to be called a face, as the window slid down slowly with a shrill squeak.

'Are you looking for a vehicle?' The words came out, with a 'tell-tale' awkward tone of caution, from the white patch of a mouth snatching a momentary place amidst the great black hirsute mass. 'Is this the vehicle you are perhaps looking for?'

It didn't sound like a Russian voice to Nafur-Nafiri. Arabic, maybe? 'Only if it is the vehicle I am *not* looking for,' replied the Doctor, nervously completing the coded exchange, with the forever present fear of walking into a cleverly sprung trap.

'All right, 'Doctor Frankenstein', jump in quick, so we can head off. It's a tight squeeze in here, but it's that, or a cold ride in the back with the figs, if you'd prefer that, instead.' Nafur-Nafiri recognised the voice, with its mocking lilt, coming from deeper inside the cabin, as that of Fiseen Bijala, Soviet-nurtured mole,

Nafur-Nafiri climbed up and got in. Before he'd even closed the door, the dense darkness of the place shifted, as a large section of it slid away on four wheels, leaving the rest of it behind with its thickly shrouded deep silence.

25

It was either remarkable coincidence, or simply that he liked the official air of doing it, that Colonel Radcliffe was always last to enter a committee room. He strode into the long austere Washington War Room in his usual hurried busy-on-the-move manner, letting the door close behind him with an appropriate loud bang, in place of bugles, to herald his arrival. Passing between four rows of military personnel seated in metal-framed chairs, he stopped at the front. He turned around to face his audience. Brown was roughly balanced by blue, with a darker tinge of blue taking in a small naval contingency. A fair haze of cigarette smoke had gathered near the ceiling from their waiting on his arrival. Discordant sounds of conversation petered out, replaced with an outbreak of polite coughs scattered around the room. Everyone waited.

'*Bengurian*, Gentlemen,' said Radcliffe at last. 'At least I think that's how you pronounce it – my mastery of the Dari or Pushtu tongue's rustic dialect for that specific region being not at all that good.'

A little smile, both on his face, and those of the audience, at this little joke of a personal admission. His face quickly went serious again. 'What once was a little dessert village lying some distance south east of Kabul. But now, according to incoming Intelligence reports, that hitherto virtual non-entity of a watering-hole stop-off point, back of beyond, has apparently taken on the important stature of a thriving encampment bustling with activity that speaks of an industrial – if not, *military* settlement.

'*B'y'gurchan*,' said someone.

'*Sorry?*' said Radcliffe, looking across the room to locate the speaker. He saw it was Bret Withers.

'I think it's pronounced B'y'gurchan -- with the ch stressed like the Scottish do with ach, but more abrupt,' said US Air Force Wing Commander Withers.

'Oh, I see. I beg your pardon. You're personally acquainted with the place, then, are you, Bret?'

'Well, no, not myself personally, John. But when Anthony Raffalini and I took our summer vacation from Princeton to do our Eastern Studies, Tony developed a keenness for digging up bones, artifacts, and the likes, and so headed that way, into the remote desert. I didn't share his love of wide empty spaces devoid of all but wind blowing sand and camel dung odours in your face, so I preferred staying where the 'grass was, indeed, greener' so to speak.'

'But a lot different I'll bet, from flying sorties across all that Viet' sand,' came the heavy Texan drawl from the silver-haired soldier decked in a chestful of campaign ribbons, seated behind Withers.

'I didn't like tracer shells strafing my plane's underside, inches from my ass either, but it didn't stop me doing my bit,' replied Withers.

'I think he's got you there, Hanny; 'bout evens,' quipped Colonel Marley Goodblood, from the front row.

'Anyway, that's how I know the name,' Withers continued. 'Can't give you any more gen on the place, though. Sorry.'

'I see. That's a pity. Thanks all the same, Bret.' Radcliffe breathed in deeply for a second to pull his mind away from friendly talk, and get back to the others on a more serious issue. 'As I was saying – B'y'ngur-*ach*-an --- which may at one time have served as a more idyllic venue for Tutankhamun enthusiasts – is now a devilish thorn in our side.' A creaking of seats, with attention all around now sharpened in readiness for heavier words than those they'd heard so far. 'A thorn sprung from a devious offshoot of the enemy that we must pull out promptly. If we fail to do this, we'll be in danger of falling back on our effort to assist Israel defeat her enemy's assault on her.' Radcliffe stood there, nodding his head at those before him, in deadly affirmation of his grim choice of words. He suddenly looked to the back of the room. 'Lights.' The room went pitch black. Low laughter broke out from different lumps of the darkness.

'Sorry, sir,' said a humble voice from the back of the room. The corporal had failed to turn on the projector before turning off the lights.

'For heaven's sake, do get on with it, Corporal,' said Radcliffe. He didn't like his display going wrong, and was irritated enough in his command to get the corporal flustered. 'What's your name, Corporal?'

'Corporal Miller, sir.'

'Well, get on with it, Corporal Miller.'

'Sir.'

A moment's whirring from the slide projector, then it lit up. The beam of light lit up the screen perched on the slim tripod, as well as half of Radcliffe, caught unawares standing in the way. He quickly stepped out of the way. Scratches and wiry blotches raced randomly across the screen while a large optic bubble danced to and fro, trying to find the right focus. Suddenly the screen went dark, focused on what looked like an ariel shot of a landscape, if it was anything, being so obscure.

'What exactly are we looking at?' said somcone in the dark.

'What we believe to be the site of secret experimental work on some new kind of weapon being tested out at B'y'ngur-*ach*-an. Our Intelligence people have suspected for some time that the Russians have been working on new weapons development. But we never could ascertain the location. Well, now we know – in fact, it's only recently we've discovered that they're working on some kind of hybrid flying bomb. A cross between rocket and engine-powered damn thing. Yes, a damned contraption that flies by itself. Absolutely demonic, from what I gather from reports that it may well carry, not explosives, but gas, if not deadly viral contagion. Nicknamed *Svetlyak* ––– if I can get my tongue round that correctly. Russian for Firefly, I gather.' Radcliffe looked across to roughly where he thought Withers was sitting in the darkness. 'Was *that* pronunciation all right with you, Bret?'

'Sorry, not my do. My guess is as good as yours on that one, John.'

'Right. Well, this flying-fire thing is what we're having to focus our attention on now,' said Radcliffe. 'And if that isn't enough to have on our plate, we believe they are also working alongside that on a more advanced development that promises double the load of vile deliverance in half the time. The slides clicked on and off in their turn on the screen, showing shots of what were very explicit beyond being mere tubular shapes, probably metallic, and rounded shapes that could possibly be concrete emplacements. Some 'things' seemed to poke out of the screen – probably the tubular 'things' standing vertical. One seemed to sit at an angle, as if lying on an inclined plane – on a launching ramp, perhaps? The screen suddenly went blank.

'If that's all there is, it wasn't very informative, I must say,' said someone, accompanied by mutterings of agreement from others.

'Lights,' said Radcliffe. The lights came on and the slide projector's hum cut off. An Air Force officer stood up from the front row and stepped over to join Radcliffe. Group Captain Tommy Hollings. He put a large illustrated board on a tripod. He looked round expectantly at Radcliffe, his cue for the Colonel to let him take over. Radcliffe, as if reluctant to relinquish his leader position, hesitated, before stepping away. Just before sitting against a table, facing the audience, he turned to hold out a hand towards the Group Captain. 'Group Captain Hollings, for those of you who don't know.' He sat against the edge of the table, folding his arms.

Hollings turned back to the board to point at its drawings. It featured what seemed like a large cigar-shaped structure pointed at one end. A tubular structure was attached a short space above it, at about halfway along its length. The artist had done the rough semblance of a short blunt-ended wing facing out this way; presumably there would be one on the other side, otherwise the 'thing' would be somewhat unbalanced. Hollings tapped the board with the back of his hand. 'The *Svetlyak*, or Firefly, gentlemen. Although we've suspected for some time – a long time in fact—we were put off the scent, so to speak, because of its rather misleading codename, *Flakzielgerat-76*, thanks to German ex-POW engineers lending their scientific genius to their new Russian masters. The term, I'm told, means flak-aiming apparatus.' He grinned over in Withers' direction for confirmation of his translation. Withers grinned and nodded back his approval. 'I think you'll agree, not quite the thing to spring up a picture in your mind of a great flying canister of plague and poison,' said Hollings. 'It's only within the last twelve months, with invaluable help from the Israeli Army Intelligence field units,' Hollings continued, nodding in appreciation to the Israeli Air Force officer, Captain Izhar Zilderman, seated on his own at the back, 'that we've been able to pin down our suspicions on what was going on – *is --* going on, and where it is. We lost a lot of damn time on the mistake.'

The Group Captain stood looking at the board with its deadly illustration as he went on speaking. 'The bomb uses a gasoline-powered pulse-jet engine that produces an eleven hundred pound thrust. We now think actual test flights began roughly twenty-four, perhaps thirty hours ago, over the remote Afghan range. And it has wings, which you can see here – well, one at least. It's plainly a rocket, with a long range, I gather.' Hollings paused for a breather. 'But its secrecy fell away when one of their planes on covert reconnaissance *'strayed'* over the area just nineteen hours ago.' Hollings searched for a face among the audience. He found it. 'Is that correct, Captain Zilderman?' he said.

'Yes, it was Flying Officer Perelman, along with Invar Yuval who took the aerial shots,' replied Captain Zilderman. 'Widened our scope on what we are having to deal with.'

'Thanks, Captain Zilderman. Anyway, photographs brought back from that airfield show evidence of construction activities with circular emplacements on the ground. Photo experts are not yet able to define anything technically specific; however, intelligence indicates that rockets have been fired.'

Colonel Radcliffe stood up suddenly to interrupt Hollings. 'As it happens, CIA interrogation analysts have been able to elicit, from two El Kalid terrorist prisoners, what may have been pure rumours, but now are perhaps confirmation of rockets of sorts. This information was given freely and boldly by the terrorists.'

'Pure bluff, surely? I can't imagine two committed zealots of their kind, fanatical as they always are, surrendering such vital information, face to face, on a silver plate, so to speak.' This sceptical outburst from a 'stuffy' old-guard Brigadier Roemont.

'That's precisely the point, Brigadier. Namely, that the prisoners were totally unaware that they had given their captors this information. Their threatening boasts were in what they had believed to be private secure conversation listened in on by way of concealed eavesdropping devices,' said Radcliffe.

'I see,' said Brigadier Roemont, ruefully rubbing his chin. It wasn't only that he had been corrected by the Colonel. He simply didn't hold with this kind of disagreement, if it wasn't squabbling, between officers, regardless of uniforms, regardless of circumstances.

Hollings took over again. 'We've since had the photo reconnaissance operations cover every square mile of the otherwise barren terrain. Further photo shots by our 13th Air Reconnaissance Squadron flights from our US Airforce Incirlik base in Turkey --- see here – and here.' He tapped the board with the projector's beam of light on the back of his hand blotting out the specific points indicated. 'We now have films readily identifying vehicles carrying what looks like long cylindrica objects. Latest material shows rockets lying on trailers near an emplacement. A shot of one of them partly erected gives us an estimate of about forty feet or so in length.'

Two silver stars glinted on the shoulders of the next person who felt the need to speak. US Army Air Force Major General Coolson Weelen. 'Hell, I don't mean to sound like some bellowin' longhorn steer, but like the Brigadier was sayin', can we be so sure that this whole Peen show isn't just *that* – a *show* – a damned put-up job, all along? Usin' dummy props an' all to create a distraction from what these damn Arabs don't want us to see somewhere else. Camouflage in reverse, if you want.' The Major General had gained his two stars on account of the influential Washington business contacts his family made as the country's number one provider of beef. So, you didn't need to dig deep beneath the uniform to find a cattle baron. And he treated his staff the same way that his family treated their cattle. He waved his hands to reinforce his point. 'Hell, we've all used dummy set-ups, some time or other, when we needed them – Jerry used them – so who's to say *they're* not usin' them *now*, over *there*. Hell, our reconnaissance flight guys have photographed enough dummy set-ups to put all the Hollywood studios together out of business.' Some polite controlled laughter from the others.

Colonel Marley Goodblood, seated in the front row, wasn't sure if he felt there was room for laughter, with the situation being so tight as it was. He kept his silence.

Group Captain Hollings was about to reply to Weelen's words, but seeing that Colonel Radcliffe wanted to say something, he stepped back. His mouth was getting dry, anyway. He poured himself some water from a carafe on the table.

Radcliffe paused for a moment, looking down at the floor, to consider his piece, then looked up. 'The idea of this whole Firefly situation being a hoax is not one exclusive to this meeting alone. Yes, admittedly there are some who think this is a hoax for the reasons we've just heard, namely, to distract us from important developments elsewhere. But also, on the grounds that such a large rocket is impractical. But consider this, if you will. If we believe it not to be a hoax, then we would bomb the site, certainly. It follows, in turn, the Arabs would only want us to bomb their installation if it was not a real operational site.' Radcliffe hesitated for a moment before giving his next 'reason' – given to him by Intelligence's Psychological-Warfare Strategy gurus. 'I'm thinking that President Sadat, in his country's state of superior omnipotence, would consider it to be below his station to consent to having his armed forces hiding behind a shield of deceit, rather than rely on their superior power to defeat Israeli forces.' He rubbed his cheek as an inner humour afforded him a faint smile. 'Take that as you may, we have another factor to help tip the scales of decision. We've just intercepted, somewhat by 'chance', an otherwise insignificant piece of evidence that decides the case. An official circular issued by the Soviet Air Ministry for fuel ration allowance to Soviet Air Force 'experimental stations' in fact. It shows the allowance for their Afghanistan venture to be above that of other stations that we know to be genuine. Thus, it suggests strongly that this threat from a puny desert watering-hole is not a hoax.'

'Unless *it also*, is a damned cleverly played dupe card,' muttered Weelen quietly in his lingering doubt.

Radcliffe glanced at Weelen before continuing. 'We also have air-photos of massive concrete structures at Kandahir and Haret, south of Kabul, both of them connected to newly-placed railway-lines, courtesy of Russian structural engineers. As far as can be judged, these give strong indication of stepped-up activity. This finalised report, codename LANDMINE, by the Special Operations Investigation Committee. As a result, the Joint Intelligence Committee, charged with coordinating information concerning secret weapons, has issued a strict official directive for the site to be effectively 'neutralised'. The operation will be codenamed: SANDSTORM, as agreed, under Joint Council.' Radcliffe paused to push forth his message with a stabbing forefinger. 'We must destroy these sites, before they can mount deadly attacks, and cripple, if not totally destroy, Israel's chance of retaliatory measure. Otherwise, their effect on Israel's public is apt to be one of terror since, if I've got it right from the experts – these bombs, unlike those dropped from planes, would seemingly suddenly come out of nowhere, to drop their death-loads silently down on innocent civilian masses.'

Radcliffe stopped there to look around and see what effect his last point was having on the others' faces. He consulted his notes on the table for a moment, and looked up again, to continue. 'SANDSTORM will be a joint counter-air and strategic attack operation by the US Army Air Force to delay Arab rocket attacks and limit their effectiveness before they can be launched. According to calculations, this will call for a small discreet number of sorties with a fair tonnage of ordnance'. He paused to take a deep breath, hesitating before his next gruesome statement. 'Primary objective is not only to destroy launching sites, but to ensure that they cannot be rebuilt, so engineering personnel must be killed. So, living quarters, civilian, as well as military, will be our primary target.'

Goodblood was urged to say his piece. 'Why do I feel this as tantamount to us openly inviting the Kremlin to accuse the United States of starting a war by way of its unwarranted open aggression on a peaceful country? And not forgetting their fury at our massacre of Russian nationals engaged in civil engineering construction.' All right, this was war, and killing was the inevitable part of it. As a soldier, you knew that, and did your share of killing. But this kind of killing – the killing you understood – killing *can* be understood – was man-to-man across a battlefield. Who died, and how one died, in that particular theatre of war was left for Fate or Luck to decree. But this sitting here, naming from afar, specific masses of individuals to be put to death, was moving him inside. He made to finish. 'Two lesser objectives: to destroy the potential threat of rocket attack installations and construction documentation – and to render the installations incapable of being replaced.'

Hollings sensed that Colonel Goodblood had said all he had wanted to say for the moment, and took over again. 'Strategic Air Command will be dropping approximately eighteen hundred tons of bombs on the site, codename OASIS, eighty-five percent of this tonnage being high explosive – the remaining load, incendiary.' He looked around to see the effect of these details on the others, before continuing. 'We've considered it to be best – *essential*, in fact, to employ the tactic of pinpoint bombing in this operation, where precision is vital, considering the smallness of the targets, in a night time raid. Strategic Air Command will be using one aircraft to control progress of the entire raid, orbiting above the target areas. With there being three aiming points, that is, living quarters, rocket factories and launching installations, pathfinder-scheduled planes will use crew shifters, moving from one aiming point to the next, as the raid develops.'

Whilst wondering what degree of success would come out of this operation, considering its massive effort and importance, Colonel Radcliffe couldn't help his thoughts brooding over Colonel Goodblood's interjectory remark.

'Why the hell can't we just shoot the damn things out of the sky, like we've done before?' said the Major General. 'Deal with them when they come. Seems like you Air Force lot handled enemy air attacks all right before. What's so special about these damn things that we can't just do the same again? Just use all that bombing effort you're proposing, to mount a proper job, instead, on Egypt, and not waste it on a couple of puny Arab dessert sand-pit spots.'

Hollings was momentarily at a loss, stalled by the interruption. Not just because he was put off what he was going to say, but by the technical nature of the question. His speciality was operational intelligence, so he was needing to refer to someone better qualified. He looked to the front row, at the Volunteer Reserve Air Force officer holding the long rolled-up paper tube across his knees. Pilot Officer Dennings, in spite of the uniform, could only look like the brilliant engineer, 'on loan from MIT's aeronautics laboratory, that he was. His specialised knowledge was an invaluable asset to Air Force Technical Training Command --- more so to Air Intelligence, as of now. His preference for books, rather than the sports field, at college had seen him labelled as the guy who was apt to stir his coffee with his slide-rule book-marker.

'Perhaps you would care to enlighten us, now that we're expecting the 'damn thing' to be on the attack,' said Hollings, with a wide grin at Dennings.

Dennings stepped up to the tripod. Taking spring clips from his pocket, he set about fastening the sheet to Hollings' sheet. It was a cut-away version of the one beneath it. Much like the anatomical drawings of an animal's inside, except that this animal had a venomous bite. He shifted himself from foot to foot for some seconds to ready himself. Alas, sir,' he said looking at the Major General, 'we cannot risk shooting the rockets down whilst in flight on account of our uncertainty of having fully destroyed the viruses ultimately, or left them lingering as a deadly contagion in the free atmosphere. Also, because this ingenious piece of engineering by far outclasses anything we have for velocity, except, perhaps, for our F-15E Strike Eagle. It will have a velocity of roughly

5 km per second. Our planes are too slow to catch it.' He scratched his chin. 'That is, unless they have a height advantage that would allow them gain speed through gravitational acceleration by diving down on it --- and even if they do dive down on it – 'it' will have moved on. No, they must be destroyed before they have a chance of becoming airborne.' He looked again at the Major General.

'Like I was saying,' continued Dennings, 'no plane we have can catch it, with it travelling at that velocity, at an altitude of two thousand kilometres, powered by a pulse-jet engine. Weighing around forty-seven hundred pounds, with a length of just over thirty feet, and carrying a contagious cargo that could wipe out a fair slice of humanity.' Dennings stopped to peer in close at the drawing. Turning round again, he touched the sheet to indicate a point, not that it really mattered to the others. 'This here, as I've said, is the pulse-jet assembly engine; an Argus-3 design, if I'm not very much mistaken – designed by Lussen, giving it an operational range of round about two, to and a half, thousand miles, more or less. I've seen his designs – quite clever, really, in their simplicity. Apparently, the engine pulses roughly fifty times per second, giving it --- if I've got my information right – thanks to Captain Zilderman,' a curt nod to the Israeli officer, '… what I'm told is a distinct buzzing sound resembling that of a host of insects.'

He judged it to be an apt moment for a small humoured piece to ease his listens' minds from the weight of all these technical details. Another nod and smile at Captain Zilderman. 'I'm further told the rumour that Sadat, on hearing the sound, trembled and wetted himself somewhat in mistaken thought of this being a second coming of Divine Wrath descending on Egypt in the form of a great host of vanquishing locusts.' Not a single flicker of amusement, or even interest, shown anywhere. Only impatience, with everyone waiting for him to get on with it. An awkward twiddling of his thumbs for a moment in the dead silence. 'Yes, well, I just thought I would mention it. No matter.'

Taking refuge from his gaffe by turning swiftly back to the drawing, he stabbed a finger at it. 'Fuelling is by gasoline octane seven-seven – a whole one hundred and fifty gallons of it. The engine is ignited by automatic spark plugs about two and a half feet behind the intake shutters – just about here.' He bent for a closer look. 'No, sorry, here.' He straightened up. 'The current for the plugs, of course, coming from a portable starter unit. Highly pressurised acetylene gas is issued from multiple nozzles, three, I should think, in front of the engine to start it.' Dennings turned around facing the others, rubbing his hands slowly together in reflex habit of removing the chalk-dust from his fingers as he normally did, standing before a class of students.

'I have to say that I think that the low static thrust of the pulse-jet engine, combined with the short wings causing a high stalling velocity, would make it virtually impractical for it to take off on its own power over a short distance. In which case I can only see it being launched either from a modified aircraft, or perhaps, from some form of aircraft catapult mechanism.'

But he had erred in his judgement. No aircraft was necessary. Even as Dennings spoke these words, one of those very rockets was being tested at a remote stretch of dessert. Positioned on an inclined ramp, the deadly carrier of death was launched by a steam-generator device, using stabilised hydrogen peroxide and potassium permanganate, to jettison it off with an initial velocity of 600mph into the sky that brooded with the dark gathering clouds of a gathering sandstorm.

Still rubbing his hands together, Dennings stood for a moment, looking around as if expecting questions, as he usually did with his students. But nobody so far questioned his obviously better knowledge. He went on, turning as he did, for a brief look at the drawing. 'It uses a simple 'autopilot' guidance system – made by the Hamburg firm, Azskardia, we think – to regulate altitude and airspeed. A weighted ----'

'If it doesn't have a pilot, it must surely need some form of radio-guidance to direct it to its target, otherwise how does it get there?' It was Brigadier Roemont this time throwing the question. 'All that's needed, surely – if I'm understanding this confounded contraption correctly – is to jam the bloody thing's radio frequency. So, what's the problem?'

When Dennings turned round, his expression was a mixture of wry amusement and scientist's irritation at the layman's tardy comprehension. He stooped slightly, nodding his head with patience, as in his lecturer's manner with students. He managed a smile as another train of thought came to mind. 'Ah, yes, well that is, perhaps, the simpler part of its setup. Namely, that it *doesn't*, in fact, actually *require* guiding, as such, along its primitive programmed flight passage. Instead, it needs only to be pointed in the right direction in its initial launching.' Another thought struck him, amazing him that it hadn't occurred to him before. Simplicity was, indeed, the key word. The thought of it being pointed in the right direction made his mind home in on the concept that should have occurred to him when he had said so. 'There is the further possibility that it is launched, not airborne, but from the ground – from an inclined ramp, perhaps. Such a method would eliminate the larger margin of error of the required direction, through unsteadiness, if launched from a moving plane.' The logic was better, but still niggled Dennings that he hadn't thought of it earlier.

He pushed his annoyance aside to continue. 'As I was saying, a weighted pendulum in the primitive guidance system stabilises a gyrocompass, whilst also controlling the fore and aft altitude measurements, so regulating the pitch.' He tipped a horizontal forearm up and down at each end. 'In other words – stopping it from nosing down or nosing up. As for reaching its target, I can only imagine that some form of digital countdown within is how the distance flown is determined. For instance – an anemometer – that is, a wind vane propeller – mounted on the nose would drive an odometer to give so many revolutions. So many revolutions, in turn, would represent one digit, which, in turn, means so many miles. The requisite number of digits, representing the target distance, is obviously set prior to the launching, with the counter set at zero. On reaching that number, I can only imagine detonating bolts firing, causing spoilers to jam the tail elevator gears, and cutting off the control hoses to the rudder gears, setting the rudder to neutral. The rocket, thence, going into a deep dive. With the cut off of fuel causing the engine to stop, the rocket thus descends in silence on its unsuspecting victims with its diabolical deliverance.'

Those last words gave the room its own extended moment of staring, thinking, thick, silence as the cold alarming message sunk in.

'Can't we just tip the goddamn thing's wings and send it spinning off into the wide blue yonder?' Goodblood, in his frustration, had intended the remark as a joke, to release the air's nervous tension.

But Dennings' scientific mind, as always in search a problem's solution, was at once caught up the fanciful idea, nodding his head, and muttering more to himself than others, saying: 'Yes – yes – if there was the chance of upsetting the gyroscope's control of flight stability ---'

Goodblood shook his head, looking at the 'mad' scientist, with his 'flighty' notions.

'What kind of percentage are we to expect?' said someone from what was becoming a rising collective outbreak of conversational murmurs.

'*Percentage? Sorry?*' said a puzzled Dennings.

'For our planes lost in the proposed SANDBLAST raid -- always assuming that those *civilian* engineers will have complemented their *civil* engineering with substantial *military* engineering air-defence batteries,' said Wing Commander Weelen. It wasn't him who'd thrown the query at Dennings, but he was just as keen as whoever had, to hear the answer.

Dennings didn't have that kind of data. Hollings had, but he wasn't sure how much he was allowed to say. He looked to Colonel Radcliffe.

Radcliffe pursed his lips for a moment. 'We're possibly looking at something in the region of about 3 point seven per cent.' That wasn't the figure that his advisors had given him; they had stated their losses to likely be nearer 5.1%., but Radcliffe saw no reason to let on about that figure this early, before the actual mission. He fidgeted with his fingers.

Goodblood juggled the figures in his head, as no doubt the others were doing. He reckoned that would make it a loss of about 5 planes. He didn't say anything. Neither did anybody else. He just lit another cigarette, to inhale deeply and blow out another tired stream of smoke

– tinged blue in the room's funny light, just like those guys in blue up there, in the blue sky, flying the mission.

The briefing didn't last much longer after that. Its expectant momentum was spent. All that could be said had been said. All those words now needed to be replaced by action. To convey this thinking to Radcliffe, Goodblood looked down pointedly at his watch to push the message home. Inasmuch as Radcliffe, as Chairman, didn't like his meeting being hurried to its end by another person's prompting, he nevertheless appreciated Goodblood's need to get back into the field. Tapping the table for everyone's attention, he announced the meeting's closure

With casual talk breaking out as everyone shifted in readiness to leave, a notable rustle of papers being thrust briskly into briefcases said that Goodblood was not alone in his urge to vacate the premises. As everyone began to leave, drifting in a crowd of small talk towards the door, Radcliffe signalled with an upheld forefinger to Colonel Goodblood. 'If I could have a word with you, Colonel Goodblood.'

'Sure'

'Incidentally, do you, by any chance, play bridge?'

Yeah, but I prefer to stick to poker, with the odd cigar and maybe a couple of shots of the old Tennessee bourbon thrown in while stacking up the hard bucks.'

'That's unfortunate,' said Radcliffe, with what seemed to Goodblood to be genuine regret, much to his surprise. 'Actually, Rear Admiral Beregen, Defense Secretary Kissinger, and myself, of course, are trying to make up a foursome, in foresight of what we're agreed are extremely urgent matters requiring discussing for final settlement.'

'I suppose I could maybe tag along,' said Goodblood, after a long moment's pause that caused Radcliffe's face to take on a hard frown of severity.

'We'll need a definite affirmative.'

'In that case, count me in, Colonel Radcliffe. Count me in.'

26

'All this damn waiting can go fuck itself!' Frank threw the strong suggestion, with its coarse wisdom, out the car window, along with his glowing cigarette-end.

'Oh, you can be ever so rude, Francesco,' said Jocely, looping her arm round Frank's arm, to pull him a little closer.

'Last time I heard it, my name was Frank, honey.'

She pulled him in closer to nuzzle her face playfully against his cheek. 'Oh, but Francesco is ever so much more romantic, so much more attractive.' She blew her soft warm breath against his cheek.

'You reckon so? Well, I guess that must be why my dear old padrina – *godmother* – Antonia, planted great slobbering wet kisses all over my face when I was making my First Holy Communion; half drowned me in her saliva.'

Seemingly unable to remove her face from Frank's, she caressed his cheek with hers. 'And did you go on to become a lovely angelic altar boy after that?' she whispered softly in his ear.

'And you figured out that last bit of holy truth all by yourself, honey? I reckon with your quick wits, you could put a lot of those Langley think-tank guys out of a job.'

'Oh, you are wicked,' she whispered slowly, while licking his ear. The light that had exploded on her first seeing him had made his dark points more acceptable, like the dark, yet homely, interior of a church. She had taken to him, perhaps not instantly, but soon enough to be totally captured by his bursting-with-life healthy American confidence, with its extrovert manner of projecting himself on you.

Frank turned to Jocelyn to give her his full attention. Freeing his arm from hers, he put it round her to pull her in close. She had predicted correctly that he would eventually thaw out, to lessen the distance between them, and warm to her. She tapped his gloved left hand. 'And this?'

Frank put his right hand over her hand, feeling it soft and smooth in his own broad hard fingers. 'Well, honey, that came long after a little friendly get-together with Jerry's Afrika Korps lot, near the little dung-fly infested village of Bir Jadid, on the Moroccan coast; where the passing bullets gave your face a better shave than your razor did, and you hoped that your guardian angel was watching over you, protecting you, instead of wandering off for a lunch break of bagels and bananas in the shade of a palm tree, among farting camels.'

Frank took his hand from hers to run it over his gloved hand, as he thought back over those distant battles, forgetting Jocelyn for a moment. 'Yeah, when I got this, Bret wasn't so lucky,' he muttered aloud to himself.

'You and he were buddies, right?'

'Right on the nail, honey. Yeah, you could say that we shared the mud on our boots over one heck of a trek.'

'But he wasn't a lawyer like you, was he?' said Jocelyn, wanting to get Frank's full attention back

'Bret was already established as a marshal, roping in crooks on the run across the States, when I was just swopping my Yale fraternity sweater for a collar and tie, to join the district attorney's team as a glorified junior, handing out case files to seniors, when I wasn't counting paper clips. You could well bet that the Jap Admiral Nagumo's Aichi E13A planes had barely returned from Pearl Harbor, when Bret would have been virtually collecting his bayonet and M-1 Garand carbine from Stores. Two months later, close on Bret's heels, you could bet that I was handing the paper clips over to some raw junior, so that I could enlist at the nearest recruiting office. Not that we'd yet crossed paths at that early stage.'

'So, when did the two of you meet, to forge your unbreakable comrades' bond?'

A broad smile broke out on Frank's face, just short of giving way to a chuckle. 'Do I see a stronger green tinge coming into those already green beautiful eyes of yours?'

'A green *what*?' Jocelyn drew back from him slightly. 'Don't be silly. Whatever gave you that idea?'

Frank let out a quiet laugh. 'If you must know, it was a chance meeting in a crater.'

'You don't mean that volcano in Italy, where you were fighting, do you?'

This time Frank allowed himself to sway back with laughter. 'No, honey, not that kind of crater; I mean a damn great hole in the ground created, seconds before, by an exploding thirty-pounder artillery shell. Some dumb recruit on the field-gun practise range was, for some God-only-knows reason, getting his co-ordinate points wrong and firing in our direction. At me and Bret, can you believe it? If Bret's lightning reflex hadn't had him diving into that crater, and pulling me with him, I wouldn't be sitting here with you now.'

'Oh, don't say that!' said Jocelyn, throwing her arms round Frank's neck, to yank his head in closer, and taking over from Padrina Antonia by showering his face with a deluge of exited kisses. As they clung together, it occurred to Frank that if she was tuned on so much by his battle experience details, by how much more was she likely to be turned on if he was to show her the abdominal scar he carried from his Palermo scrape? But indoors, in a comfy room, was the proper place to be doing that, not here in this damn stuffy vehicle, waiting on operations signals.

Pulling away slightly from Frank, her words came out in a hesitant note that was little sharper than a whisper: 'I'm atheist.'

'Yeah, I know.'

'I'm just telling you.'

'You've told me before. You're *always* telling me!' Frank sat up straight, away from her, to look into at her with serious concern. 'Hey, what's wrong? What's bugging you? I can see it --- something's bugging you.'

'*You.*'

'*Me*? What the heck's that supposed to mean – '*me*?'

'Your devout abidance to your faith's catechism rules and liturgy--- and I'm ----' She couldn't finish the sentence, the thought blocking her.

Frank managed to let a broad smile of relief break out on his face. He rocked back in his seat in relief. 'Is that all that's digging you, kid? Let me tell you, as a matter of fact, that He takes most kindly to your lot knocking on our door, wanting to come in. But if you want further reassurance, I can get my mom to have a word with old Monsignor O'Donnell, to put a good word in for you with the Boss.'

'You mean you'll go to all that bother of consulting the Pope --- for *me!*

'Not the *Pope --- his* Boss! A forefinger pointed upwards clarified it for Jocelyn.

Letting out a nervous giggle, she placed both hands on Frank's shoulders, to look him straight in the face, with her admonishing expression. 'Frank, sometimes you can be so -----'

She didn't get to complete her sentence, with Frank pulling her in close, and planting his lips fiercely on hers, and holding her in tightly.

Their long moments of passion were abruptly broken by the sudden outbreak of hard knocking on the car roof. The military policeman's face loomed up in blunt interruption, in the open window, waiting for Frank to hold out his ID card. 'Everything all right, sir? he said. 'Stuck out here, on your own. Engine trouble?' Switching his enquiring look from the driver to the woman, he knew full well what the score was; but he kept a straight face, where a broad knowing smile would have been inappropriate. He had to maintain his disciplined duty-face.

'Get rid of him,' whispered Jocelyn.

Frank patted her arm, to dispel her uneasiness. He looked at the MP. 'Everything's fine. Don't let us keep you back from your patrol duties,' he said in a voice that he thought would sufficiently hide his annoyance and his wish to be rid of the interfering bastard.

The MP stepped back smartly, to make room for someone else. 'Someone here to see you, sir.'

From the dark shape of a car that had drawn up and parked behind the MP's jeep, a figure was walking up to them. The man stooped down to look inside at them. Frank recognised him as one of Biran's men. 'Needed the Sergeant's help to track you down,' said the Mossad agent.

'Yeah?' said Frank, waiting for the important stuff to come out.

'Pigeon's flown.'

That was important enough for Frank. He turned to Jocelyn. 'Give me a minute to handle it, Frank,' she said, in her curt field officer's mode. Not waiting for any remarks from him, she got out and went over to the other car, and got in it. 'Pigeon', codename for Nafur-Nafiri, had been tag-marked by Russian agent, Fieseen Bijala, up until now. But now that the Doctor had flown, it seemed that Bijala's movements had been monitored somewhat carelessly, with the result that both had gone to ground. They'd goddamn lost Nafur-Nafiri!

When Jocelyn got back into the car, Frank felt that she had forgotten him, her showing only a hard smile, in place of her earlier affectionate advances that had now seemingly evaporated. The engine coughed into life and had them moving off to a new location, leaving no room for any more words of soft intimate affection.

'So, it's fun-time aborted,' said Frank in a preoccupied serious tone that Jocelyn was not happy with.

'Do you reckon on taking that thing with you, then,' said Jocelyn, referring to the paper bag, crushed into a ball, that Frank was squeezing and turning over and over again in his hands, in an action that was as monotonous as them sitting waiting in the car was.

'Don't suppose I'll be needing it,' replied Frank, pulling his arm back, ball in hand, in a silent practise throw. 'I played real swell in college. Had those girls squealing. Maybe I could have been something, if the old man hadn't continued to shout in my ear about what he never had, what my older brothers never had, but what I did have, which was the opportunity to study hard to become a hack lawyer. Which I did.' Frank slapped his own forehead, shaking his head in mock regret. 'The mad things we do to please others, eh, kid,' he said, looking round at Jocelyn.

'And you're still set on going in?'

'Well, you heard what Biran said, and we were all agreed, weren't we? With Nafur-Nafiri and Bijala both having gone AWOL, so to speak, we've got to find one of them, at least, under one of the stones we're turning over, in order to keep a finger on the intelligence pulse. Who knows, maybe I'll come across that belt of mine that I lost over there, in Palermo,' Frank joked, even although Palermo would be a far distance from where this mess was taking them. He handed the ball over to Jocelyn. 'You can have this. I'm not sure you'll have a hand to spare for it, with both of them occupied dealing with the kid, when it comes.' He noticed her reflexively caressing her midriff. 'Is that it kicking just like his handsome ballplayer daddy, with his shiny-haired, and finely sculptured Roman-nose?' Frank paused for a moment's long study of her form sitting there. 'Just like I can bet for sure that God, Himself, was standing right behind His angels, supervising them directly, when He had them sculp your beautiful shape out of the ethereal cosmos.'

Jocelyn's eyes took on a distant look while she rubbed her midriff slowly in faraway thought. 'Mother seems to have sunk into a gloomy sort of negative withdrawal situation. Perhaps not exactly what I would have expected of her, since she's no longer a normally a strong-minded person. And if that's not enough, *her* doctor --- whom she high-handedly appointed to handle *my* situation --- is seeing problems that are going to make it a difficult birth. He didn't quite make it quite clear what these were. I'm not sure if he knew himself; or perhaps that's just part of my subconscious excuse for not wanting to know the gruesome details of what I'm to expect as a mother.'

Frank patted her arm softly. 'You're being too hard on yourself, Jocelyn. I'll stick to staying alive dodging those goddamn Egyptian tank shells.'

A sudden pinpoint of light pierced the darkness ahead of them. 'There it is,' said Jocelyn, handing the 'ball' back to Frank, and shifting to get out of the car.

'Where?'

'*There*, eleven o' clock, in front of you, Bonehead. Let's go.' Getting out of the car, they walked quickly towards the figure flashing the torchlight signal. 'Have they got him?' Frank asked the Mossad man.

'No, not yet, Colonel, but it shouldn't be long. Dogs are being brought in to help sniff him out.'

'So, let's go get him, said Jocelyn, glancing round at Frank. 'Coming, Frank? You can practise your ball-shots later.' They worked their way down the heavily wooded slope, with dark figures on both sides of them helping scour the undergrowth, towards an abandoned wooden hut. As they approached a young Army officer, the man turned round. 'Help is on its way, Colonel. The van with the dogs should be here any minute now.'

'If we had some more damn decent light, we wouldn't need any damn dogs,' muttered Frank in a groaning voice, annoyed at the muddy soil and wet branches rubbing against, and ruining, his trousers.

Barely one hundred yards away, soft wind carried the sound of the search to Nafur-Nafiri's ears. Snapping twigs and voices trailing out through the air for several seconds and then cutting off again. And starting up again in recurrent cycle. The voices seemed to be coming in his direction from the left. But wait – a babble of voices rushing through the empty space said that they were also moving in from the right. And dogs, as well, from the sound of it, coming up at a fast pace from the rear. He had thought that he had been making fast progress through the woods; but they seemed to be moving faster. Change of tactics was called for. Nafur-Nafiri looked round for cover. He listened for his stalkers as their voicers and movement through the undergrowth became more audible. Footsteps slowed down and shifted around, dithering in the same spot, the seemingly unsure of what way to go next. 'Maybe it would be a better plan to split up into two lots; and get the job done quicker,' said Jocelyn's voice across the darkness. 'We'll work our way down on this side.'

'We'll work our way along this side and up towards the road,' said a soldier's voice. 'And for God's sake, somebody go and tell them to bring those dogs over this way, and be quick about it!'

Nafur-Nafiri listened as footsteps started up once more – only to stop again, as a close search hovered in its bit-by-bit progress nearby. Footsteps faltered and twigs snapped here and there, confusing Nafur-Nafiri's keeping track of exactly where his stalkers were. The sounds began to move away and then stopped. They moved up and down the slope a short distance, and then back to the opposite side of where he lay hidden. His nerves jolted him inside as a stick rasped along the top of a coarse stone ridge, in a sweeping stroke near his head. Otherwise, he didn't dare shift an inch. A sudden view of an inverted head moving warily, searching, over his covered hiding-place had Nafur-Nafiri holding his breath as the soldier looked to see if he had disturbed anything with his stick.

'Anything?' said an American voice – a man's, this time.

'Difficult to see. Nothing, by the look of it,' said the soldier.

'We've wasted enough time here. Let's try over that way,' said the female American voice.

Nafur-Nafiri listened to this, lying rock-still only feet away in a hollow, concealed as it was, by bushes. Breathing more freely, now that the sound of his pursuers was distancing itself down the hill, Nafur-Nafiri got up on his knees to look around cautiously, before moving off in the opposite direction. He had to find a way of getting himself out of this mess. Making good progress stumbling less and less through the undergrowth, his spirits began to rise.

They took a dip when he suddenly noticed that some of the trees in front of him were of a greenness that was man-made. *Uniforms!* Turning round to change his direction of escape, he was confronted by a great monster of a German Shepherd dog baring its teeth, snarling menacingly as it blocked his path. To add to his dismay, it was not being restrained by a leash.

Nafur-Nafiri braced himself as the fierce animal came closer and was about to leap up at him. A sharp cry rang out and the dog stopped, stepping back in obedience to its handler's command. A small copse of green 'trees' promptly closed in to form a tight cordon round him.

'Well, well, if it isn't Oliver, himself,' said Frank, stepping up to take Nafur-Nafuri by the arm. 'Taking a quiet solitary walk for meditation, are we, Oliver? Sorry to disappoint you, if we only had a tiny patch of woods to offer you.'

Nafur-Nafiri held his silence in defiance.

Frank, just about to say something else, possibly with the help of a fist, stalled to look past the doctor to see a shift in the cordon as it parted to let someone through.

Frank broke off from his intent to deliver what would have been classified as 'below the belt' treatment, at seeing the figure coming through the circle of soldiers, to look around, before stepping slowly over to him. The casual-footed gait, and the only just discernible red blot of anger on the face, in spite of the beguiling smile, was what you came to expect of Colonel Biran when you really knew him.

'All right, Sergeant, you can let us take care of him,' said Biran, stepping up to the soldier who was still holding Nafur-Nafiri by the arm. He saw that the Sergeant was a little unsure about the question over who had the jurisdiction for taking custody of the prisoner.

'It's okay, buddy. Don't let our different colour of uniforms bother you. Your boss will tell you that he's to be handed over to us so that we can put a boot up his ass to get him to play ball proper with us.' Frank looked round at Biran. 'Isn't that right, Colonel?'

'That's quite correct,' said Biran, not hiding his reluctance in conceding to this fact. Especially considering the American's cheeky jibes the last time that they'd met. 'Do as he says, Sergeant, and let the good Major have the prisoner, like he's requested, in keeping with protocol.'

Frank looked at Nafur-Nafiri, giving a head jerk to tell him to move. 'I don't know what the words are in your parents' tongue, so I'll just say it's '*goodnight*' for you, Oliver!' he said, drawing his forefinger across his throat to signify the man's ultimate '*goodbye*' through severe execution of justice.

27

They were there, sure enough, just as you would expect; they always had been there, or so you would think from their motionless, lifeless, atmosphere, standing apart away to the side, profiled against the gold-singed blue sky. Ancient guardians of time in time-worn stone, the pyramids, with their distinctly pointed angular shape, kept centuries of watch on all travellers, as with this one, sliding past in puny fleeting minutes. But the Egyptian tanks, with their sentries mounted atop, were guarding not time, but the long 147-mile stretch of land corridor that Falzoni needed to take him to Cairo, where he could catch a flight to Germany, and complete the final lap along the Autobahn 27 to Bremerhaven, in West Germany's state of Schleswig-Holstein, where his 'package', Nafur-Nafuri, would be put to the test by special shrinks.

As far as Frank could remember, there were three transit roads, Cherbourger Strabe, Grimsbystrabe and Poristrabe, branching off the Autobahn 27 into Bremerhaven. But he'd have to wait until he was on the plane, to check which one was the faster route.

In the meantime, both sides gave the monotonous view of flat empty nothing for mile after mile, where the landscape had been scraped clean to allow the sentries in their distant perches to watch without obstruction, the 'insects' rushing past. From time to time, a lookout was stationed closer to the side of the road, so that you could quite clearly make out the helmeted figure standing beside its machine-gun, watching you, watching him, without the need for binoculars, unlike its counterparts further back. More grim reminders of whose disputed land you were trespassing on, popped up periodically just off the roadside in the form of a 5.4-ton Sonder Kfz-1 armoured car with its MG-34 machine-gun, which you hoped would not get some crazy excuse to stop you and strafe your tyres with some of its 900 rounds of 7.2mm bullets; or if not that, then a 36ton Soviet T-55A tank, maybe.

All this in turn, was a cold reminder for Frank how the DDR was allowing the Allies two-way passage between West Germany and Berlin. This served as a useful release valve for anyone suffering from the claustrophobic atmosphere of Berlin's being an encapsulated colony far within Communist East Germany and only roughly twenty-seven miles from another Soviet-controlled puppet-state, Poland.

With 93 miles of the autobahn having no speed limit, only a recommended limit of just over 80mph, Frank Falzoni was able to cover more than half the distance with his foot pressed down hard on the pedal.

'We will be getting there soon?' Nafur-Nafiri's scraping voice almost had you ducking out of the way of a great gobbet of spittle as you wrongly thought he was clearing his throat. But he wasn't. The folded lines of tired dry skin on the scrawny neck didn't completely hide the long scar. A war wound, perhaps? Or maybe another scrawny-necked turkey had seen him as a rival and let loose its beak on him. With only a short time to question him since he'd conceded to us turning 'a blind eye' to his 'misdemeanour', provided he put his devious expertise to the benefit of our National Defence, we had so far been unable to pin-point exactly what squares he had occupied in that most nasty of nasty strategy board games --- early student politics, with their incumbent ideological leanings. Had he sported a loud banner high over skirmishing masses, or a short blade, a scalpel, in a lab – one of *those* labs? His background was, as yet, obscure. In the merry-go-round of espionage, true identity kept pace with that fifth ace in the pack that the card-sharp shuffled. Join the queue, pal.

'We'll get there, pal, don't you worry, we'll get there,' said Frank.

'You think that I am worried, Mr Porter?

'Well, aren't you?' said Frank, looking round to give his 'package' a quick 'once-over' inspection, especially the hands, which were engaged in a ceaseless fidgeting contest. 'Relax. Sit back and let me do the worrying while driving. We're getting there, pal, we're getting there.'

'But are we not going in the wrong direction? Should we not be going south? Tubingen is to the south. Unless the sun has made an impossible shift to the other side of the sky, we appear to be heading in a northerly direction.' Nafur-Nafiri's voice matched the nervous message of his fidgeting fingers.

'North west would be roughly more accurate, without me falling back on any Scout pack points I never got for navigation. We're heading for Bremerhaven, jolly old Bremerhaven,' said Frank with a touch of scorn in his reply. He threw a sharp questioning glance at the Doctor. What the hell was that anglicised Egyptian Oxfordian playing at? Who did he think he was fooling with his feigned ignorance? An educated man, with his travelling experience, and wanting to travel further afield, he surely knew which thumb to wet if he wanted to see which way the wind was blowing. And if he was as shrewd as they had to assume he was, he would have to guess, if not know exactly, which way this current game's wind was blowing.

'But then you're wanting to go to Tubingen, aren't you, Doctor? What's so special about Tubingen? What's pulling your fancy to that cute cosy corner?'

'You know perfectly well that I am scheduled to be going to Tubingen, Mr Porter. You are playing games, are you not? Why are you seeing the need to do this?'

'Well, for one thing, it helps to break the monotony in a long drive like this,' said Frank. 'You spent a short spell there, researching you said, didn't you? Maybe you're missing out on those rosy memories of boisterous drinking, bubbling, student days?' Frank paused for his next shot. 'Is that how you got the –' Frank pointed at the other's neck --- '---- *duelling*?'

'A foolish non-accordance in philosophical conjecture at Heidelberg.'

'Heidelberg – right,' said Frank. It was his turn to play dupe and so draw Nafur-Nafiri out.

'But, yes, I very much enjoyed my student days. And no, I was never ever foolish enough to have engaged myself in time-wasting frivolities of the so-called honourable sport of duelling. I put my precious time to the more important issues of my studies.

'But it's a pleasant enough place, all the same, is it --- Tubingen?' said Frank.

'With very much a marked mixture of old and academic flair; what one could only expect of a very historic university town, with students making up a large percentage of the town population. Regular farming markets to provide fresh vegetables and meat supplies for the town shops; pleasant people and pleasant countryside all around.'

'You make it sound just the thing for a short weekend break. Maybe I'll take the wife there,' said Frank.

'But you are not married, are you, Mr Porter?'

'No.'

'So, we are playing games again, are we not? Is that what you are paid for, Mr Porter --- to play games?'

'Isn't that what we're *all* paid for, *Oliver* --- to play games? Why don't you join us?'

Frank was now putting across his questions, with their open inference, in a serious tone that the Doctor couldn't mistake. But he didn't succumb to playing the game any further. Instead, he fell silent, staring hard at the roadside rushing past. The two minds thought quietly for a little while, with only the car's engine droning on and on to keep them company.

Frank decided to break the silence. 'So, you want to go to picturesque little Tubingen not only to sample fresh cows' milk, but also to bury yourself amongst test-tubes and beakers in this Nobel-awarded Werneir-Grunz Institute? Have I got it right?'

'That is correct.'

But Frank's mind was conjuring up an entirely contrasting scenario to that of the idyllic country town setting that Naffur-Nafiri was feeding him. Running his mind over the details in the file that secretary Rosalyn, on Goodblood's orders, had placed in his in-tray, he was assessing the situation to be something much more serious. Sure enough, Tubingen was a cute little place, as far as country towns went; but what was bothering Frank lay close by; too close by to be ignored as pure coincidence. He scraped his memory for those figures in the file: co-ordinates: 48"46'45N and 08"04'49E and 408ft above sea level, with asphalt runways of 10,800ft. Located near the farming community of Soellingen, in the municipality of Rein munster, in the state of Basen-Wurtemmberg, was the Canadian Forces air base: CFB Baden-Soellingen (*FLUGHAFEN KARLSRUHE/BADEN/BADEN*). This was the Canadian Air Force's contingency contribution to NATO' defence for Western Europe. Originally operational from 1953 with three Sabre fighter squadrons, 413 Squadron, 430 Squadron and 421 Squadron, the RCAF"s role was as fighter/interceptor. In '55 the Sabre squadrons were supplemented by four CF-100 squadrons. The Sabre squadrons had just recently been converted to F-104 Lancer tactical fighter units powered by superior Pratt & Whitney TF30-P-100 engines; in addition to their conventional armaments of 6-barrel M-61 Vulcan cannons and heat-seeking Sidewinder missiles, these were now equipped with 1700lb/2320lb free-falling parachute-retarded B28 thermonuclear bombs. This change meant that the RACF's mission was in the role of Nuclear Strike/Reconnaissance. However, strictly off the record, and definitely not in the file Goodblood had given him, circulating rumours were that NATO's French Cabinet wanted control of all nuclear weapons on French or NATO soil. Therefore, RCAF would be moving 421 Squadron at Grostenquin to Baden, and likewise, 430 Squadron at Grostenquin to Zweibrucken.

But that last piece of 'news' was for keeping under the hat, and best left for Marley to deal with, along with his CIA pals and Washington generals.

And Nafur-Nafiri had risked his neck --- *had he risked his neck* — coming in with us and wanting, if not *demanding*, to be positioned 'just along the road' from all that military hardware, with a nice panoramic view of it from his veranda? That called for some serious in-depth afterthought. Frank looked in the rear mirror at Nafur-Nafiri's suitcase on the back seat. 'I hope you're packing a toothbrush and pyjamas in your case. We're going to be spending a few days in Bremerhaven, before going to Tubingen. Some nice people for you to meet, who'll be wanting to ask you some nice questions.'

28

The gull screeched out and took off, startled by the head appearing above the stone wall. Coming up the final stone steps, Falzoni, with one end of the long dark Brockwurst smoked sausage between his teeth and the other end held in his right hand, and a carton of jet black kaffee held in the steel grip of his left hand, looked up with equal surprise, to follow the bird's flight. He hauled himself up to sit 'side saddle' on the concrete harbour wall. That way he could get a better picture of what was what in all directions of Bremerhaven's expansive sixteen square miles of harbour waterfront. A colossal tonnage of moored vessels, whether by their steel plating, or by water displacement, a massive lot for sure.

Aloft, sentinels wearing black and white livery circled round in long scrutiny of his being there. The gulls gave out hoarse warnings and then moved away. There was a confusion of shadows, and a sea bird landed on the wall beside him. Powerful wings collapsed and lost themselves in the streamlined body of feathers. Stout yellow-scaled legs reminded you of hidden strength.

Frank trained his eyes on the sea's distant horizon. A quick scan from left to right and back again, revealed nothing worth noting. According to his watch, he was ahead of schedule, with roughly an hour to wander around idly, dodging the bird droppings aimed at his ominous human

243

form. But for the fleecy cirrus cloud hurrying on its way to nowhere, there was nothing worth watching that far out at sea. His scanning dipped, drawing a panoramic view nearer, to catch the silent swarm of gulls that had a similar design of descending on the crates of fish laid out along the long grey narrow stone finger of a quay. Further out in the water, a clamorous swarm besieged a small trawler with its tanned deck covered in a paraphernalia of rope, seines and balls, the small wooden vessel bobbing about on the water like a spunky cork, the white flecks hovering around the fishing vessel like a cloud of midges. Their noisy attack was carried inland as an odd plaintive squeal on a cool breeze.

Standing out conspicuously as they ambled along the narrow stone walk were two small figures clad in black coats and hats, the austerity of which contrasted sharply with the bright yellow oilskins and brown leather gear of dockside workers around them. For all the modern advancements he was making, Stasi Foreign Intelligence boss, Markus Wolf, still hadn't learned to ditch the grim Gestapo 'men-in-black' image of field agents that could be sniffed out a mile away. Unless that was their game, that is, to let you know that they are forever there, forever watching you.

If this could possibly be something to fret over, Frank made no visible show of it, but simply leaned back to look up at the sky that was a faultless cerulean canvas spread out evenly on all sides of the golden disc. The sun blinked as the gulls criss-crossed before it, their shadows racing over land and water, their shrieks lifting the humans' attention upwards. Smooth leisurely flights carried the gulls up to haughty stalling positions overhead, so that rival fliers hastened to equal the elevation, their wings pumping furiously. All at once the beating stopped and the gulls soared up with an ease that was understood only by them.

If only man had wings, or wing-like contraptions, Frank mused, taking another sip from his carton of kaffee, as he watched the ariel display. How mad-cap Adolf had dreamed of sending out battalion upon battalion of such wing-equipped armed troops on ariel sorties. Well, these more recent birds, with their green/brown plumage and red star tails – MiG's -- were certainly doing their share of damage now, attacking Israeli bases.

Frank's thoughts were broken by the cries of more confounded birds. Despite their swoops and loops in aerobatic feats of grace calling for applause, the human below was no longer interested in them. He was watching the figure approaching from the distance.

Marley. Early, too. How about that!

Placing his kaffee carton on the wall, Frank changed his Brockfurst roll over into his left gloved hand, to take out a Camel, insert it in his mouth and light it with his right hand. He breathed smoke in and out slowly, while watching the other ambling casually along in his long free-flowing fawn gaberdine coat and tweed angler's hat festooned with fishing hooks, in spite of him barely knowing one end of a fishing rod from the other. But that casual holiday gear wasn't going to fool anybody. There again, letting the tracker think that you haven't fooled him is a good way of causing him to be careless in turn and drop his guard. In the same manner of ploy those two goons on the quay were playing.

'I gather from your expression that there is nothing to report yet, Frank,' said Goodblood.

Frank took another bite at his smoked sausage. 'It's only to be expected at this stage, having to wait around, like I've doing for the past hour, wondering how much longer it's going to take those goddamn shrinks to squeeze what they can out of the Doctor, before letting me go and collect him. Putting pre-selective schedules on things before they develop naturally can lead us down the wrong path, if we're not careful.'

'Jeez, I hope that this little jaunt to the seaside is going to reward us with something more substantial than wind-reddened cheeks and salt-laden lungs to take back to Berlin for relaying through to our Langley masters.' Goodblood cast a momentary envious look at Frank's sausage. 'Supposedly we must hold with lateness being the prerogative of the paranoid with double checking. It couldn't be an error in communication, could it?' said Goodblood, betraying a faint touch of inner anxiety.

'I double checked the cypher myself,' said Frank. 'There can be no question of error there. It's just as well. Lavery went out on field duty early and so reported back to us in time to make arrangements.'

'Lavery?'

Frank had to grin openly at Marley's feigned surprise, before taking another bite at his sausage. 'It's all right, we know you have a 'thumb' in Herr Wolf's files. Fieseen Bijala grade 2 sleeper, in DDR intelligence archives. Your over-the-wire contact for picking up and relaying field messages to Langley'

'Right, of course, I get it.' Goodblood frowned. But hold on, do you mean to say that you didn't make contact with Lavery before then?'

'Something of a last-minute alteration in plans to test the man's resourcefulness. To see how he would react to a sudden unexpected procedure.'

'And?' said Goodblood

'So far, so good. Fieseen Bijala acted as expected, by having written a coded version of Nafur-Nafiri's initial debriefing reserved as standard, which was passed on to his KGB field handlers.'

'Why the hell didn't you just tell me straight out, and save all this round about fuss with cyphers and things?'

'I don't have to remind a fully-fledged, sworn-in, all-badges scout like yourself how the good old handbook frowns on procedures judged to be in abeyance of standard protocol, or words to that effect, as far as I can remember, do I?'

'Yeah, the good old fucking handbook. So, we don't hang our bets on Lavery, then?'

'You're getting there, Colonel.'

'I'm only just a little peeved in your not conveying this information to me earlier, Major.'

'Yeah, well you know where to find me, if not in my office,' said Frank. 'And you can be sure of good coffee and blueberry muffins, whenever you can find time to drop in on me.'

'Let's hope this operation today is going to pull through as we want it to, and not as a damn empty fiasco. It will, *won't it*, Frank, since the arrangements are entirely of your choosing?'

'Sure thing.' An *unsure* tone, that neither of them missed, hung on those two words.

Marley cast another hungry look at Frank biting off another mouthful of his Brockwurst. 'Where did you get that sausage?'

'Over there at that stall.'

Marley dug deeply in his pocket for money. 'I think I'll get one myself.'

'You'd better make it lightning quick – they're rolling down the shutters.'

29

Doctor Nafur-Nafiri's knocking on the car window betrayed a degree of irritation behind the impatience. As well as a degree of hurt in the eyes that Falzoni saw, looking at him for a moment before pressing the catch to open the passenger door.

'Get in,' said Frank. Turning away to start the engine, he had the strong feeling of Nafur-Nafiri's eyes staring, burning into him. 'So, have you enjoyed your grilling by our mind analysts, here, in jolly old Bremerhaven, Doctor?'

'It did not meet my expectations,' replied Nafur-Nfiri with open bitterness in his words. His fleshy hand darted about, conducting its own invisible orchestra, in physical expression of grievance.

'Yeah, well things can tend to be quiet this time of year, I admit, and the weather hasn't been too good either' for tourist trade,' said Frank, enjoying his deliberately misreading the nature of the other's complaint.

Nafur-Nafiri grimaced hard, shaking his head in disapproval at Falzoni's light-minded view of the situation. 'I was referring to my most questionable manner of reception by your people, Mr Porter.'

'Yeah, how's that then? Did you do something to displease them? Misunderstood the party games, maybe, and stepped on someone's foot, so to speak? Easily done when playing turncoat to swap allegiances --- not forgetting leaving a bomb or two of nasty bugs lying around under a 'carpet', to be swept up, and out from under, don't you think? Good job we found out in time from you, which 'carpet' they were under.'

'In what aspect of manner did I displease them, you ask?' said Nafur-Nafiri, his annoyance verging on anger. 'I have most willingly come over to work for you. I am agreeing to contribute my scientific knowledge and experience to a most renowned institute for America's National Defence, and still you infer that *I* have displeased someone --- still you seek to uproot perfidy on my part!'

You couldn't help but fall back in amazement at this guy's effrontery of whinging over his dented dignity, after all he'd done, or intended to do. 'And you made that all perfectly clear to them, did you?' Frank gave a broad smile so as to upset and confuse with his message not taking the Doctor's high-falutin' plaintiff squeals seriously. 'These things can often be taken the wrong way round, if they're not put across the right way – know what I mean, Oliver?'

'I understand you perfectly, Mr Porter, and so should they have understood me perfectly. I told them everything they wanted to know.' Nafur-Nafiri was getting angry. 'I am feeling insulted that I, in my professional capacity, should have been submitted to such a degree of questioning. For hour after hour, to no seeming end, they saw fit to throw all manner of questions at me. And to what end, I am asking myself.' Looking at Frank, he threw up a limp hand in lamenting gesture.

But they hadn't used the polygraph on Nafur-Nafiri. Frank knew that. In the hands of the experienced interrogator, trained to watch body language, the human subject is in itself a ready lie-detector. The machine merely measures body responses and the interrogator interprets these. Whilst sodium thiopental or sodium amytal and sleep deprivation could increase the subject's suggestibility during questioning, there was always the underlying possibility that these methods could inhibit the subject's ability to give accurate and truthful information. Using the technique of emotional mechanics, if the subject is lying, this will generate a degree of guilt, so that he will avert the interrogator's eyes when questioned. In cognitive terms, lying demands more concentrated thought, so that in its relative neglect, speech is more open to errors. But if lies are based on half-truths, this could lessen the chance of verbal slip-ups. Frank had read the reports and watched the interrogation through one-way glass panels, so that he saw Nafur-Nafiri as a mixed half-and-half bag of what was what, and what was *not*.

'You must be tired.' Frank reached down and handed Nafur-Nafiri a small bottle of orange juice. 'This'll freshen you up a bit. Long drive ahead. Next stop – Tubingen.'

'I am indeed tired, but in the mind, not the body, Mr Porter.'

'If you say so -- you're the doctor, you know best.'

But the bottle was nevertheless virtually wrenched out of Frank's hand and the liquid gulped down to dispel tiredness, be it of the brain or body. 'Perhaps I am not wanted here in the West. Would you have it that I proffer my professional services to Soviet Russia? In aiding the West, my work will create substantial threat to the East, from whom my life will thereafter forever be under threat. You appreciate that, do you not, Mr Porter?'

'Just as a few lives are also risked in getting and giving you our safety, pal,' said Frank. 'I'm on your side. Get that clear in your head, aside of whatever else it is that's giving you the mental jingles.' The Doctor gave Frank a long cold look that could only be construed as nervous uncertainty. 'Listen, Doc, you either let me know what's bothering you, or you don't. The freedom of personal choice is yours; just one of the many tricks of democracy we have here on our side, in the good old 'decadent' Capitalist West, that you'll find hard to come face to face with in the good old Peoples' Republic of Soviet Russia. But it's a long drive south, and I don't want my concentration spoiled trying to figure out for myself whether or not it's possible the debriefing team took a dislike to you simply because you tie a double knot in your shoelaces.'

Nafur-Nafiri remained silent. Frank noted the time on his watch for how long this silence would last.

'I was graciously accepted for the important post of Research Associate at the Institute, by Head of Research, Professor Weirmann, in the Psycho-

Genetics Laboratory,' said Nafur-Nafiri, after a long pause. 'He is a good man to work with; I am honoured to be his assistant.' Nafur-Nafiri's hands came up, clasped together in a moment's nervousness. 'If your people do not trust me, will this be to the detriment of my being allowed to work at the Institute?'

'Whoa, there, pal; where do you get the idea that we don't trust you?' Frank tried to look as best he could, in sympathy with the man's pleas.

'But all those questions thrown at me in their piercing manner; what else could that imply?'

'That's just routine procedure. Everybody gets that. If the Pope was visiting, he'd probably be asked by the security team how many pieces of host bread for Holy Communion his bishop was carrying with him for the visit. Just crazy questions to keep the guys emptying their pens scribbling down crazy reports. Don't worry about it.' Frank's deliberate play of light words let him try a different angle. 'And this guy, Professor Weirmann, that you've worked with before, Oliver --- you're pally with him?'

'That is correct.'

'I take it that was before the war – or maybe *during* the war? said Frank, in an effort to prise open Nafur-Nafiri's clam-tight clamp of reticence, for something, *anything*, that had not come out at the interrogation.

The Doctor went on: 'We met and worked together on field hospital duties, wherever that abominable conflict happened to take us.'

'And apart from working in the field, you never had occasion to put your medical expertise to use elsewhere, perhaps?'

'No. But this "*elsewhere*" --- I do not understand?'

'Right, right, it's okay. Let's leave it there,' said Frank waving the issue aside and turning his attention back to driving. Enough said for the moment, and the time it would take them to reach Tubingen.

As they passed the airfield, they could see lines of Lancer planes standing in long lines ready for action. Looking at the cockpit covers cocked up in the air in open defiance, you could reckon that you were seeing that WW11 scene second time around. There was a sudden flash along the line of gleaming bodies, and Frank and Nafur-Nafiri looked round, expecting to see the fighters closing their cockpits and moving off down the runway. But the planes had not moved. It was a momentary blocking of sunlight down the line, as a USAF B-29 transport plane droned past overhead.

Frank spoke without looking round at Nafur-Nafiri. 'Here we are, Oliver, with Tubingen just down the road. No fear of boredom with plenty for you to see here.' He paused to steal a sharp glance at the Doctor. 'But then, of course, you'll not have any time, or interest, for that that; you'll be too deeply engrossed in your important work in the Institute.'

Nafur-Nafiri didn't reply.

30

But for the large curve formed by the boiler suit pulled tight round the stooped figure's rear end, you wouldn't have guessed that it was a woman. She had no face – only a black plastic panel fronting her leather-hooded welding mask through which she peered closely at the fussily fusing metal plates. Like a great spluttering fountain of light, giant menacing sparks arched out in all directions, causing Nafur-Nafiri to step back promptly as some came near to him, one just missing his face.

'Serves you right if you gets hurt, mister,' said a hard voice that belied the soft female form lurking beneath the welder's otherwise rough outer appearance. 'If you don't know where to step to keep out of the way, and out of trouble, it means you 'ave no business being here. 'Ow did you get through the Institute's guard-room gate without a bloomin' pass, anyway, eh? You lookin' to get arrested then, mister? The words, in spite of their being innocent, along an entirely different theme haunted him, with their echoing along a line parallel to his *real* situation.

The sparks suddenly cut out at the same time as the grim mask went up. Hardly any prettier than her grimy overalls, she at least had a friendly, if cheeky smile, in spite of the horrific scarring, inflicted by a stupid past war, on the left side of her face. Free now of the mask's protective visor, she saw the pass Nafur-Nafiri held out to her. 'Right, so what does I call you, then? An embarrassed pause. 'I can't read.'

'Doctor, will suffice.' Taking on what he considered to be an appropriately more friendly attitude to compliment this dedicated worker, Nafur-Nafiri looked down at what she had been doing, without having an inkling of what it actually was. 'Fine work, I see.' He coughed to hide his ignorance. 'What exactly is it you're doing?'

Laughing at the question, she cast an outstretched arm round in a great sweep to take in, with a running commentary, an imaginary panoramic view of a naval dockyard, with its tumultuous commotion, both on and off the quay, involving great mountains of steel that comprised part of Germany's fighting fleet moored to mighty bollards lined along the quay's edge. Giant cranes and tiny specs that were men—and women – earnestly going about their tasks of making these great grey rivetted monsters battle-worthy before sending them as the Fuhrer's Kriegsmarine menacing 'invincible' sea-power of warships and deadly U-boat wolfpacks to engage with, and hopefully, destroy the Allied Fleet.

'*Doing*? What does I not do's more like it. I does battle ships, submarines – the whole bloomin' lot an' all. That's what I bloomin' does.' Searching in her pocket, to bring out a cigarette, she reached down for the blowtorch, to light the cigarette from the fierce hissing blue jet flame. She took a drag, then blew out the long train of smoke before continuing. 'Used to work in a wool factory before that; easy work but boring, compared to what I does now; this job's great.' Stopping to peel of a tobacco flake from her 'good-side' lip, she went on. 'Cept now I can only see me 'old man, that is, what's left of 'im, every second day, because of the long shifts – ten hours nightshift,' Another deep drag and blowing out of smoke.

'Most commendable – most commendable,' said Nafur-Nafiri in a dismissive tone that said he had wasted enough time on idle banter and his attention was elsewhere, in a hurry to get away and about his more important business. But he needed directions. He had thought that his memory of the place from his last experience here in Tubingen would have seen him right—but it didn't. The more he looked about, trying to identify different buildings and their functions, from what he remembered, the more he felt lost. His vague concept of what had been —what he *imagined* had been – was proving to be deceptive. Of all the buildings before him, he should have recognised the medical block – imposing, without being imperiously palatial, standing out from the rest of the university's buildings. But, alas, he didn't.

Things seemed changed. More vehicles, some of them concerning security set up on behalf of his situation, he couldn't help thinking. There was that air about them – about the whole place's atmosphere, it seemed, if he wasn't just unduly nervous and over-imagining.

Nafur-Nafiri wondered where best to ask for information; the man in the guard-house hadn't been of much assistance. He didn't think that the welder would know either, but nevertheless, on turning to her and about to ask her, he spotted the security guard in white cap and white belt with holstered side-arm coming along. The man also had a fierce-looking Alsatian guard-dog on a steel chain walking beside him. Nafur-Nafiri wasn't sure how the animal would interpret his approaching its master directly, and so hesitated.

The problem was solved by a long shadow stretching out along the ground at Nafur-Nafiri's feet. He turned round to see a tall figure silhouetted against the morning sun. Plainly of official importance, the man, in rimless spectacles, stood there, tall, in a long white coat that had to be long in order to fit the wearer that was outgrowing it at both ends. An official smile squeezed its way into the pale long face, between the jet-black moustache and the neat goatee beard.

'Guten morgen,' said Nafur-Nafiri.

'Guten morgen. Can I be of assistance, Herr ---?' The frigid tone was far from helpful to those members of the public intimidated by hospitals' generally oppressive atmosphere.

'Doktor Nafur-Nafiri. I have an appointment at ten thirty, with the Clinical Director.' He slipped the letter out of its envelope, and handed it over.

The man reached out with a rigid official arm to take it. 'Ah, ja, with Die Professor Weirmann.'

'Ja. That's correct.'

'Danke.' With an official flurry of wrist and fingers, the man refolded the letter and handed it back to Nafur-Nafiri. He consulted his watch. 'Ja, there is still time. I will take you there. If you would care to follow me, Herr Doktor Nafur-Nafiri.'

With a stiff back and a brisk stride, the man led the way into the building and along its corridors. The corridors were bleak, with dark-tiled walls. Their mood was reflected in the wan faces of patients sitting about, listless and 'lost'. The two men's heavy foot-falls rang out resolutely on the stone floor, so that fuddled minds looked up, and 'out' from inner illusory worlds, expecting to see trolly-loads of horrible medicine to be forced down their throats. But the two gentlemen passing by weren't carrying any of that horrible stuff. Curious eyes lost their interest in the passing gentlemen and returned to their inward-focused glazed stares, where the mind saw only what it chose to see.

As they turned round a corner, Nafur-Nafiri almost collided with the over-developed bust of a *krankenschwester*. The nurse was carrying an empty newly rewashed enamel bed-pan, but a faint odour of its recent faecal contents still clung to her uniform. Passing the Neurosurgery Theatre and then the Electrotherapy Unit, they finally reached the relatively light atmosphere of Psychotherapy Wing B. Along the Wing was the sub-unit of Experimental Medicine Clinic. Here Nafur-Nafiri would be working on his specialised field of Psycho-Genetic Transfusion Transference.

Finally reaching a door as unrevealing by its being closed as all the other similar doors were, the man stopped. Telling Nafur-Nafiri to wait outside, the man went inside. After what seemed a very long 'several minutes', the door opened, and Nafur-Nafiri was bade to enter by the man who then took his leave.

The room was vaguely as Nafur-Nafiri remembered it. The one bookshelf had more space than books on it, and there was little in the way of academic papers, instruments, or otherwise between the four walls. Only a single folder on the plain pinewood table, along with two straight-backed chairs, made up the furnishing. It was like an over-furnished monk's cell. A 'thinking room', rather than the workplace of one of Germany's up and coming renowned specialists in experimental medicine, who had worked under a previous 'great', Wernicke, no less, assisting him with his monumental research on *Die Gehirinkrankheiten* – brain diseases – before eventually going on to mount his own recent pedestal of honour in the newly developing field of Viral-Genetic-Transfusion-Transduction.

With his back to Nafur-Nafiri, a man was standing at the table, having a brief perusal of the file's contents. 'Bitte nehmen sie platz,' said the man, still with his back to Nafur-Nafiri.

Nafur-Nafiri took the 'invitation', that carried a faint touch of 'command', to be seated, attentive of the deep blue eyes reading through him, when the man turned about to face him. That was not the face of the Weirmann he knew. A growing uneasiness was rising up in Nafur-Nafiri's mind.

'These are the reference codes for the files on their airbase that we need you to get for us, in the little time that you have.'

'In what little time *I* have! And *you* are, if I may ask?'

'You *may*.' An open mocking smile for a few moments to enjoy pushing home the taunting omission of the answer. 'There's no need for you to know who I am – only for me to be sure of who you are. But I'm given to understand that you come with *good referral*. If it makes you feel more relaxed, simply understand, and accept, that I'm a temporary locum replacement for the good Professor Weirmann, who, alas, has suddenly been taken ill.'

'Oh, very relaxed – I think not. But what about my passport and visa clearance I'm supposed to be getting? I understood that to be promised arrangement – the sole reason for me risking breaking cover – coming here to collect them?'

'You'll get those as soon as you bring those important files. Be assured of that'

So, that was the game being played now, Nafur-Nafiri thought, with a sinking feeling. The original promise made to him by Moscow had now been downgraded a degree to an *assurance*. 'But what if ---'

'Let's get on with it, shall we!' The words were commanding in their hard utterance. 'Concentrate on those numbers; they can't be written down. You've been trained to memorise things in a short period of time, I gather. I'll give you five minutes to do that – no more. We haven't the time.'

After the five minutes had elapsed, the man took the slip of paper the numbers were written on and burned them with a cigarette lighter over an ashtray. He then put something in Nafur-Nafiri's hand.

'What's this?' said Nafur-Nafiri.

'It's made to look like small plastic bottle, which it isn't, labelled: **Eserine Eye Drops**. You'll notice what looks like a puncture dot on the label in the middle of the letter **e** in **Eye**. That's the lens aperture for the micro camera that the 'bottle' really is. You'll take the shots by turning the false screw-top clockwise and then back. The camera takes fifteen shots. Let's go.' This final message was made clear by the man taking hold of Nafur-Nafiri's arm and urging him to get up out of the chair.

'How, and to whom, am I to pass these film shots onto, should I manage to take them successfully?'

Oh, *you'll* manage.' The threat was clear enough. 'Leave that to us. We'll handle that.'

'So, we're still playing that game, are we?'

'Yes, we're still playing that game.'

'It's a game I don't want to lose.'

'None of us do.'

On reaching the door, the man took Nafur-Nafiri's arm again. 'Good luck.'

'I think I'm going to be needing an abundance of that, for sure, if that's the only surety I can rely on, and granting that there's enough of it to go round.'

31

Major Falzoni got out of the car and hurried down the stone path to the house, with a mixture of feelings knocking inside his chest. This was mostly a mounting expectation coupled with a slight disbelief. He found it hard to believe that their hectic chasing around could lead to this tranquil patch, where supposedly, the only excitement was that of mad professors chasing butterflies across the meadows with their nets. The quiet little mock Tudor cottage with its oriel windows resting on corbels, was in keeping with the docile image of the street. And yet this was it. Or at least, this was one of the three places where the transmitters were installed, according to the latest reports.

The Major's contact in the Underground had only been one of a series of cat and mouse check-ups that had finally led him to this piece of information. During that time, he had had to shake off a KGB tail twice, and that was only after he'd made sure that the tail could be no use to him. The Russians here, it seemed were in the dark about what was really happening at this stage, and were anxious to follow on and find out. The agent who had initially set the operation in motion must be operating on direct instructions from Moscow. In total secrecy from the KGB guys stationed here, virtually scratching his back. Quite possibly had gone back east. Easier that way, leaving the 'comrades' here, in their ignorance, to fry in the 'mushroom omelette'

An Army Bomb Disposal man appeared in the doorway. 'Major Falzoni?'

'Yes.'

'It's downstairs, in the basement, sir.'

'Lead on, Lieutenant.'

They clambered noisily down the wooden steps that lead to the door with its large glass panel. The lieutenant reached out to open it. There was a sudden cry of alarm from beyond it within, and Falzoni's reflexes sent his hand to his pocket. Glass fragments stung their faces as the explosion blasted the door outwards, hurling them back against the stairway. For several seconds they lay dazed on their backs, surrounded by glass shards and splintered wooden panels. The light had survived, swinging nervously to-and-fro. Fingering his forehead, Falzoni felt the blood trickle down slowly from a small cut. He rose and made his way through the thick smoke billowing through from the ugly gap.

Inside was an uglier sight. The place was a heap of twisted metal and wooden strips, where a heavy wooden workbench and metal bracket shelves had stood. Little tongues of fire licked up hungrily in corners, where there was a remnant trace of workshop spirits to feed them. Just perceivable through the smoke issuing from the far corner was a pair of legs. A second form stirred in the smoking shambles and crawled over to its mate. Falzoni stepped round them to look at the weird dark rectangle of mangled metal that loomed up in the corner. He knew nothing about transmitters, but his knowledge of this one's significance was so holding that it was tightening his stomach into a hard billiard ball of a knot. The explosion, with its frenzied moments, had told his frightened brain that *the* bomb had gone off.

But he had recovered his senses enough to to realise that this was not so. What did scare him now was the thought that the explosion could still have upset the transmitter so as to trigger off its system for detonating the chain-line system of nuclear bombs those damn Russians had planted.

'What happened?' Falzoni put his stupid question to no-one in particular, but to anyone in the place who was live enough to hear him, while keeping his attention on the awesome thing in the corner.

'The fucking damn bench blew up,' said the man kneeling over his injured mate.

'The bench?'

'Yeah, over there.'

Falzoni was puzzled. He turned to look at where the bench had stood.

'Yeah, it was standing right there, sir. I reckon we were damn lucky it was so thick. It gave us a shield when it blew out the other way towards the door.'

'What were you doing, exactly?'

'We were nowhere near the bench. We had no reason to be. We were over there in the corner, going over the transmitter like we were ordered to ---' The man swallowed his nerves and broke off to reach in his pocket to pull out the paper chit. 'We got orders from HQ to ---'

'Never bloody mind that! What the damn hell happened, man?'

'We were examining the transmitter, going over the regular routine, when we came across the booby-trap wires leading to the bench behind us. It had to be the last place we expected to concentrate our attention. When we realised that we'd set the damn thing off, it was too damn late! It was lucky we had our backs to the bench.' The man looked at his colleague lying there. 'He looks quite bad, sir. I think we could do with a stretcher.'

Falzoni paid no more attention to the man's shocked ravings, and looked up at the transmitter and back to where the bench had been. So, the cunning bastards had booby-trapped the bench as a warning to them to keep their hands off the transmitter. The thickness of the bench had indeed been a deliberate means to shield the transmitter, *not* the meddlers. But how could they be so sure? Frank felt the dryness in his throat. How could they be so sure that the shock waves wouldn't upset the transmitter's programme, to set the other bombs –those *real* bombs --- off sooner than intended? He paused in the dazed stupor wondering if he could hear any big bangs outside.

A commotion of feet and voices sounded outside on the wooden stairs and someone rushed in with a fire extinguisher to dowse the mischievous flames still lingering. Two more shapes rushed in to help the injured soldier. The lieutenant came in, leaning against the door jamb, holding his eye, where blood was trickling down. He followed the Major's stare to the dark apparatus shrouded in the corner's shadows. 'In God's name, sir, what is that thing?'

Frank shook his head. 'I hope we never really find out.' He paused pensively in the doorway. 'I can see the danger of being 'switched off' by inexpert tampering; but how do you draw the line between expert and inexpert, except when it's too damn late?' He closed what remained of the door behind them. 'Let's get out of here and get some fresh air.' A nip of it to clear the lungs. He looked round at the lieutenant. 'You coming?'

'Yes, sir.'

'Right, so let's go.'

31

Snapping twigs in the wood froze Falzoni in a motionless position. He could tell the sound was coming from far off, but he still took no chances and dived for cover. It could be anything; a poacher or what? It wasn't being too fanciful with the odds for Nafur-Nafiri turning up here since this was one of the many hot surveillance areas under inspection. The noise stopped and he had no real idea of the direction it had come from. Either he played the fool wasting time searching in the wood, or he could continue on, more sensibly, as originally intended, to the next reconnaissance lookout post. Thumbing the safety catch back on the Colt in his pocket, he consulted his luminous compass and moved on.

Engrossed in this action, he didn't notice the two 'trees' in green and brown camouflage combat dress that were watching him. One of the 'trees' held a long walkie-talkie. The soldier spoke into the radio and the message raced out to a 'fox' hiding out across the wood. This Fox was steel-plated, with a 30mm Rarden cannon for a snout. Ex-British Army, the vehicle now proudly bore the Star of David on its sides. A beret with a Signal Unit badge bobbed in the armoured-car's chest, below the gun. It turned in as the message came through. 'Sir; message from BADGER. Reports presence in sector Z-Nine now. Coming this way. That's all, sir. Oh yes, and does anyone want a fine rabbit for breakfast?'

The commander, seated on top, with his head above the armour-plated shell, didn't bother to turn away from his toy. He spoke with his face buried in the knobs and pieces of the Mel Infra-Red periscope. 'All right, relay the message to HQ. While you're at it, better tell them we've seen no further signs of activity at HUB since our last report at 02.00hrs. That'll do.'

He busied himself with the rectangular periscope and focused it on HUB, that was a tiny hamlet mounted on the rolling landscape in front of them. It was the wheel-hub, or centre point towards which a selected troop unit was striving to drive away any possible prey, in their search of that specific area. The periscope functioned in total darkness over a range of 1000 metres, so he had a good view. He continued to fuss with the instrument's finer points until the new buzz of activity from the heat-seeking radar below attracted his attention.

'Something approaching fast, sir. Too small for a vehicle. Could be a motorcycle. Could be a moped.'

'It is a moped. I can hear it coming now,' said a second voice from below.

The commander rotated the turret so that the periscope faced the road leading to the hamlet. 'So, let's have a look, then,' he said adjusting the eyepiece power. 'Yes, you're right, it is a moped.'

A squat figure with only a dark line between its legs to support it, whizzed past and receded in the distance, like a wizard on a broomstick. With the rider turning off the road, into the homestead in the hamlet, the turret swivelled back to its original position.

Silence was broken by the sound of someone coming out of the darkness just beside them. Frank handed his pass to the soldier in the front hatch. 'Major Falzoni; Intelligence,' he said curtly. Normally he would have barked the soldier down for not making a thorough inspection of the pass, but he was in no mood for barrack-room games. There were more important things to be critical about. He put the pass away in his pocket and looked up at the commander. '*Nothing?*'

'Nothing so far, Major. Just a few locals. Nothing unusual from outside.'

Frank stood looking round about at nothing but darkness for a few minutes, before making up his mind to move on to the next observation point. He was about to knock on the steel hull to signal that he was moving on, when the periscope spun round suddenly to the side as a new subject came into the field of view.

The commander spoke sharply. 'Get on to HQ. Tell them, new subject approaching HUB from sector Z-Nine.' He remembered the Major behind him and moved his face a few inches to the side of the periscope to speak askant. 'Someone moving in towards the hamlet clearing from the wood, Major.'

The hazy figure danced side to side before settling in the centre of the infra-red viewer. It shed its fuzzy skins, as the focus changed, to become a clear figure stumbling through the brushwood. It didn't look like a poacher to the commander. He gave a sharp command. 'All right, get that camera out; sharply, now! About forty-five degrees right.'

Before the words were finished, the infra-red camera was nosing out from the steel hull. It moved right, wavered, then stopped, before proceeding to suck flat copies of its prey in out of the dark. Frozen forever, by the eye of the long optical snake.

''Could be one of them, Major,' said the commander. 'Seems to be in a bad way, by the way he's stumbling.'

That triggered off Frank's reflexes. 'Get them to move in a cordon immediately!'

'Right away, Major. I'll get this thing started, while we're at it.' The commander climbed down inside to start the engine, but Frank called out to stop him.

'Don't! That'll attract too much attention. We don't want to frighten him back into hiding. Give me one of your men to show me the way down.' He looked at the soldier in the front hatch and pointed at him 'You'll do. And step on it!'

The soldier clambered out and went off into the black void where the Major had vanished. He caught the air-cutting sound of the steel slide on Frank's automatic being pulled back to spring a cartridge from the magazine into the chamber, ready for firing.

32

A bright spot in the distance gradually grew into a headlamp flux of a car speeding along the road bordering the Ben Shemen Forest's edge. Banking round at the Nashan Junction, it momentarily disappeared as it entered the forest, reappearing as flashes between the trees as it travelled along the winding road. Flashes sharpened every so often into silver rapiers of light thrusting expertly between slender trunks, and then withdrawing again with equal adroitness. The car swept round into view like a regal chariot attended on both sides by legions of stalwart pines. A torchlight started waving from side to side some twenty yards down the road, and the Porsche slowed down and halted.

Biran looked out into the glaring torchlight. 'Colonel Biran,' he said curtly. The torchlight moved onto his passenger.

'And Agent Hogarth,' said Jocelyn holding out her credential card for inspection.

'Is this the place? said Biran, into the face he couldn't see behind blinding light.

'Yes, Colonel. Just down there, by the clearing.'

'Have they got him?'

'Not yet, Colonel, but it shouldn't be long, we hope, in spite of their clever turnabout tactics.' It was indeed, a most diverting ploy of Nafur-Nafiri's 'rescuers', to flee not out of the dragnet area, but in unexpected reverse, into the centre of it, in this largest of forests in central Israel.

'So, let's get on with it,' said Biran, glancing round at Jocelyn, before getting up out of the car. 'God knows, we have to get him. It's the last link between us and salvation.'

'Let's hope so, Colonel,' said Jocelyn. 'We've had so many links up until now, we could open a chain store.' Right as she was, Biran didn't say anything. He wasn't in a particularly joking mood.

They worked their way down the obscure pathway towards the small clearing, while dark figures skulked about to the right and left of them, scouring the foliage. As Biran and Jocelyn went on down the wooded slope, they saw the armoured car, where its commander on top, was speaking into its radio microphone. He turned round as the two new figures approached, putting the microphone back inside the steel hatch. 'Better light is what we need,' he said to the Colonel, looking up at the sifting clouds. 'That'll help us catch him.'

'We've got to get this man before the daylight comes. If we don't it'll be the darkest day this side of hell,' said Biran.

'I agree with you there, Colonel,' said a voice behind them. They turned to see the figure emerging from the darkness between the tress and become recognisable as Major Falzoni.

Jocelyn breath a quiet sigh of relief.

Silence reigned over the shore and in the village and in the rough countryside all around. It was suddenly shattered, one mile away, at the crossroads clearing, by roaring engines. The sleek Fox military armoured scout car raced out of the woods, chased by two troop trucks, and made a sharp U-turn before they all rammed on their brakes. Heavy doors opened and slammed, while the young lieutenant popped up and out silently from the scout car. The NCOs banged on the trucks' sides and the soldiers clambered out with the tailboards rumbling like a drunk hooker's piss in an empty drum. The sergeant was a bit puzzled and walked to the back of his truck to look in. 'Come on, Izhar, what's keeping you? Get a bloody move on, we haven't got all day to wait for you.'

'It's okay, Sarge,' replied a cheeky voice.

'Don't you bloody okay me, son. Get the bloody hell out of there, pronto!'

The man jumped down, grinning, from the back, with his SA-80 assault rifle in his right hand, whilst still clasping a crumpled cigarette in his left hand. Swinging his rifle over his shoulder, the sergeant spun round to face the lieutenant. 'All present and correct, sir.'

'All right, Sergeant, good. Now this is what we do next. Let's see now.' He hesitated, to look at his map, and then around at the surrounding trees. Right, Sergeant, get the men down off the road and move them into the wood silently, so that even a dormouse, or whatever it's called, doesn't hear you. You'll then move the men forward into position B and wait there. As soon as I give the signal, you'll advance the men slowly, but slowly, mind you, towards position A, and wait for further instructions. That'll put us at eight-eighty metres from the target. Is that understood?'

'Yes, sir.'

'All right, Sergeant, synchronise your watch. You have exactly two minutes and forty-six seconds to get the men into position B. Any questions?'

'No, sir.'

'Very well then, carry on.'

'Sir!' Staccato commands rang out, followed by staccato boot-crashing that had the men dashing off like well-ordered nags. The noise and commotion faded into the trees and the lieutenant looked satisfied at last. He climbed up onto the armoured car and spoke down into the hatch. 'All right, Fedan, get on to Field Command and tell them we're here. Confirm that Section Five is moving into position B as directed. Zero countdown for position B is now two minutes, thirty-one seconds. Got that?'

'Yes, sir.'

'All right then, Corporal, get on with it.'

Three-quarters of a mile off, in front of the advancing Section Five, a civilian contingent of the same operation waited silently in the bushes. Being civilians, they had no section number, but as such, they were the

Mossad vanguard of the operation. They were also appropriately armed. Six men to each of the two cars, with two Uzi's to each car. The four of these lay nuzzling the men's laps like happy pets. What weapons the others had, were hidden, like their thoughts, as they waited, tensed.

Biran made the only noise, turning the pages of his code book, when he wasn't checking the time on his watch. At last, he leaned over and gave the radio officer a coded message to put through to HQ. The answer came back and Biran set about deciphering it with what seemed an eternal slowness, while everyone got more anxious. Finishing the code, he looked up. 'That's it. We've intercepted their message to their submarine, *Yeltzva*. They're ready to go out to their UNCLE'S BOAT. So, we nail them now, as they break from cover and make for the open sea.' Biran got ready to move. 'The Army's standing by with six field sections, just in case anyone slips past us. They're throwing a cordon round the place at half a mile radius and less, and will move in when we give them the signal.' He looked round at everybody. 'Right. Everybody know what to do?' The heads all nodded.

'*Sure?*' Biran's eyes went to Falzoni, and lingered for a second on the spot where he knew the Major had his Colt.

Frank held the Colonel's scrutiny. 'We're all waiting for you to lead us on, Colonel. Don't worry about me holding things back.'

'Don't worry, we won't.'

Biran nodded to the man at the back, and the man knocked on the rear window to signal the others in the second car. Biran tapped the radio officer on the shoulder. 'Wait until we get halfway down that slope and then send out the zero signal. Right, let's go.' Everyone but the radio officer piled out of the cars and started moving down towards the village.

33

Jocelyn came away from the second car's group to walk beside Frank as they followed the others down the slope to where it made a sharp incision through the sprinkling of houses scattered around what looked like a quay. Bleak walls were grey and bleached to a blankness that told of endless marauding by Mediterranean Sea wind. This night was no exception, and the cold wind current blew in, cutting their faces. It also carried the sound of voices. But you didn't need to be an expert linguist to know that the words catching their ears were neither English nor Hebrew.

As they closed in on the boathouse, something moved behind its black window and everyone dived for cover, leaving Jocelyn standing alone, caught off guard. Frank pulled her down and they crouched beside what was a pile of fish boxes, going by the smell of them. Jocelyn fumbled for the safety catch on the long piece of cold steel growing out of her freezing hand. She managed to find the catch and slide it off.

Biran gave quiet orders and the four men armed with Uzi's moved off down to the water, to prepare a reception for any Russian sailors who dared step ashore. The others moved in on the boathouse. Biran raised the latch softly and eased the door open to peer inside. A great gust of wind suddenly rushed past and slammed something violently somewhere inside. Jocelyn jerked from reflex, and Frank got ready, close behind Biran, as they followed the others charging inside like a heard of buffalo.

273

Jocelyn followed and almost missed her footing on the narrow plank-walk.

The door which had slammed now shuddered open with a groan, to let Biran and the others out onto a shingle beach. Frank followed on, just stopping himself from blasting a lobster pot to shreds as it swung to-and-fro on a creaking rope. When a sudden single gunshot struck the boathouse door, two short automatic bursts responded, sounding like firecrackers to Jocelyn.

'Over their heads,' shouted Biran. 'We need him alive.'

Darkness made it difficult for you to see who was who in the commotion around the small dinghy, except that some figures were being pulled about and falling into the water more than others.

Someone fired a flare into the sky, and night turned into day, catching everyone out, including those on the deck of the Russian submarine. The *Yeltzva's* dinghies bobbed up and down on the waves, like the humps of a visiting sea-monster. But this monster wasn't welcome, and warning bullets from the shore chopped up the water around its 'humps'. The man standing up to his waist in the water beside the first dinghy barked out orders, and flames and bullets spat out from around him, sending stones jumping and skimming about along the beach, in a return warning spray.

'Watch out!' cried Biran to Jocelyn. But she needed no telling, crouching down for cover beside an upturned boat. She couldn't help wondering, for a very brief second, if Simon Bar-jona, aka St Peter, on a shore such as this, would have needed the cover, with him having been divinely made to have no fear of death.

That was when Frank saw the figure skulking among the prop beams beneath the boathouse. It seemed a strange shape, as if it was turning round. It suddenly exploded in a violent orange flash. The bullet ripped past Frank's ear with an air-tearing screech, almost taking the ear with it. Frank dropped forward onto his knees on the awkward stones and aimed his Colt stretched out at arm's length in a double-handed grip. He found that he could hardly see his own pistol, let alone the target, in the dark, with the two bright orange spots from the gun-flash, still dancing blindingly in his eyes. But he couldn't wait for his eyes to clear, pressing the trigger once, twice, three times, letting loose his fury into the dark. Something fell with a dull thud in the shadows beneath the boathouse. The wind blew the Colt's cordite fumes into Frank's face and he coughed. He got up slowly, with the cordite fumes smarting his eyes and nostrils.

'Are you okay, sir?' asked one of the men, running past Frank.

'Never mind me: have we got him?' replied Frank, poking fingers into the corners of his eyes, to try and rub away the two orange spots still dancing around.

But the man ran on, down to the water to join the others there. Frank went down among them and looked out into the darkness, where others were wading about in the water. The *Yeltzva* party had retreated back out to sea. The 'unfortunates' left behind would have to fend for themselves. Two prisoners were half dragged, half marched, back out of the water onto the crunching shingle. Somebody held up a torch to their faces, while Biran inspected them.

'That's not him. That's bloody well not him, either!' said Biran angrily. 'So, where the hell is he? Don't tell me that they managed to get him away, out onto that damn submarine, out there!' Biran held the man's jaw in a mad vice grip with one hand, while pushing the man's upper teeth back with his gun in the other hand. The man's eyes bulged with fear, but he couldn't speak properly with the grip Biran had on his jaw. '*Where*, damn you, *where?*' Biran asked again.

'Somewhere back there,' said the other prisoner, pointing vaguely in the direction of the boathouse.

Horrifying realisation jarred Frank's brain. He had just shot Nafur-Nafiri! Most likely killed the bastard! Frank ran back, stumbling frantically over the stones, with the others chasing after him.

The man was dead, sure enough. While two of Franks 'blind' shots had missed, a third fluke of a bullet had gone through the back of the man's head. He'd caught the fatal bullet when he'd turned to run off.

'What bastard did this?' shouted Biran. 'I'll strangle him.' They turned the body over.

It wasn't Nafur-Nafiri. The forehead had been blown away, with the bullet passing through at an angle, but there was enough face to show that it wasn't the Doctor.

'Look for him, for God's sake; he's here, somewhere, shouted Biran, angrily, and everyone scattered in a mad search. Frank could feel the minutes running out like sands in a glass.

'There's something over here,' cried Jocelyn. 'Let's have a torch over here, somebody.' Everyone crowded down into the small inlet hollow, where obscure boat shapes lay aground all around. One of the 'boats' was lying face downwards in the tiny streamlet. Nafur-Nafiri was silently slowly drowning.

'Get him out of there,' cried Frank, pushing his way to the front. 'Don't let the sod drown.' They all looked down at the figure on the ground, hoping grimly that something other than water would come out of its gaping mouth. Nafur-Nafiri lay inert, the face like stone, while a man worked over him, applying pressure to the chest, to pump the water out of the lungs. Pumping on until his arms flagged out, he let someone else kneel down to take over what was seeming to be a futile task. The brief pause permitted a passing of glances. Nobody's expression was hopeful. Eyes returned to the operation in hand.

'I don't believe this,' cursed Frank in anguish. 'How the hell did we let this happen?'

'The poor bastard's been abandoned by his Russian rescuers. So much for compatriots,' said Biran cynically. 'When they saw the 'tide was turning', if you'll excuse the pun, they dumped him and fled, to save their own skins. That Arab bastard, Bijala, must have got away with them, climbing on board for his Order of Lenin medal, I'll bet.'

Frank looked into the black sky for their last hope. 'Where's that damn bloody chopper? Damn, damn, damn,' he muttered as he fretted. 'He can't die out on us now, just when we had him. Damn!' He looked at the Colonel, but didn't bother casting abusive blame on him, over Nafur-Nafiri's precarious condition. No use blaming anyone in particular over a botched operation. Everyone would be paying the same penalty of the threat hanging over their heads if the wretch slipped out of their reach now.

The arduous pumping went on and another man bent down to examine the seepage of water issuing from the mouth. 'Try the mouth,' he said. The gawking face rolled over and the man applied his lips to the Doctor's. Two respiratory systems were joined together to become one, the warmer vitalising air rushing along to fill the other lungs' cold humid chambers. The new exercise gave fresh concern to the onlookers. Each breath was drawn in and blown out through in the same rhythm by all, in a mass subconscious attempt to aid recovery. The torpid body lying on the ground was less optimistic. Soaked in water, it lay there like a fish out of water; so close, yet so far away.

But he was slipping away, and so was the urgent information of where the Russian bomb had been placed, slipping away with him. The nearness of such a loss, defied by a slim thread of hope, was excruciating. Frank would have admitted that his non-concern for Nafur-Nafiri's life, but for the vital information it held, was downright callous. But that was the least of his worries at this crucial moment in time.

At last, like a true angel of mercy, the sea rescue helicopter from the Israeli naval base descended out of the night in a maelstrom of whirling propellor fury. A figure jumped down from the helicopter and cantered up to plunk down an oxygen cylinder. The rubber mask was clamped over the face and the gas hissed out. Leaning down closer, the naval rescue man took a look at the face hidden beneath the respirator. 'Touch and go, I'd say. It's a pity you couldn't have called sooner. Who is he, anyway? Someone important?'

Nobody wasted time giving names or stories. They all bustled to help load Nafur-Nafuri onto the helicopter. Frank also jumped on board, the rotor blades whirling them up and away in a swift banking swoop down and along Israel's Mediterranean coastline, heading for the Haifa Naval Base. Frank looked at his watch. Twenty-nine minutes was all they had to revive the Doctor and get his details of where the Russian bomb was, and stopping it from exploding. Just twenty-nine minutes to stop one explosion that could lead to a resultant chain reaction of retaliatory explosions in a colossal global nuclear holocaust.

37

As far as Washington, London, and Tel Aviv were concerned, it was an ordinary day, with ordinary weather, come rain or shine. Dark happenings of earlier nights had lifted like a natural morning mist. Folk moved about a new day, unaware that a bogey had cast evil perpetrations over the days and nights only recently, but like all nightmares, their gossamer fog cleared away with the morning. With the mightily resolved strength of Israeli forces finally pushing the combined Egyptian and Syrian assault back, into eventual defeat, the need for further war dissolved its menace like a child's fantasy in a bad dream.

Some, if not all, households would have seen it fit, and just allowable, to hold small family celebrations, whilst prematurely off the religious calendar, of Hanukkah, lighting their candles and singing, before handing out nuts and oil-based dishes of latkes and sufganiyot. *Hanukkah, everyone!*

When Frank came into the office, he was smoking a Camel in what seemed a suspiciously calm manner, Marley Goodblood was thinking. For all the hassle and pain Frank had gone through, Marley wondered what he could be hatching in his mind, to look relaxed – or was it *distracted* -- like that. They looked at each other for a few seconds, then Goodblood put his open palm under the report sheet and wafted it up into the air. 'So, what's this supposed to be, Frank?'

Frank watched the flimsy sheet float back down with a final flutter, while he took another slow drag on his cigarette. He leaned back against

279

the steel filing cabinet and rubbed his hard-lined brow with the back of his thumb. 'You could say that we had virtually counted every speck of dust in every nook and cranny, looking for him. But he was no longer there.'

Goodblood ran a hand over his face in anguish. 'What it amounts to is that you let him give you the slip; you damn well let him get clean away! Do correct me if I'm wrong, but did you tell me in your rushed report that he had vanished? ---*absconded* – was how you worded it in your report'

'Your CIA, along with a team of Mossad guys, ran the operation with what they considered to be enough men for surveillance and to mount a cordon round the main establishment and its outlying annexed units. By the time the cordon had been put into operation, the bastard was gone.' A pause to draw in and blow out the smoke. 'That kind of crowded scenario doesn't make it ideal condition for that sort of manoeuvre – at least, not for us – for *him*, yes.'

Sour humour crept out in a smile on Marley's face. 'Let me remind you, Frank, that we haven't got the choice of ideal conditions; not in this sort of fiasco, or anything else, since the whole nightmarish muddle began. What's more, things are going to allow even less leeway of a choice if we don't pull off something pretty smart in return, pretty soon. With all the catastrophic damage that this has brought about, exposing our security set-up to Moscow, our agents over there are in danger of being ruffled out of their diplomatic cover. Our system has to be overhauled, and scanning mounted all over. Not only do you have to watch you back, Frank, but watch your shadow as well --- it may not be yours.'

Frank took in the agitated words, connecting their acid bite with the little bottle of bright yellow pills with its lid off standing on Marley's desk. He shrugged his shoulders. 'I guess that figures.'

'Well, thank God, we're agreed on that little point.' Goodblood let out a little laugh as he stooped to pick up the report sheet on the floor. 'But tell me, what the hell is this you're asking – this last piece of Falzoni genius on the report? You want to set up and *head* a mission to hunt down those involved in spiriting Nafur-Nafiri out of our grasp, and so preventing us from employing his diabolical expertise to our own diabolical purpose as a weapon, and bring them in for interrogation.' Marley cast the paper aside, so that it settled once more on the floor. He threw his hands up in a pleading fashion. 'It's done, thank God, with Nafur-Nafiri disclosing the bomb's location, before he expired, Frank! Let it go! The damage that's been done can't be rubbed out by tax-payers' dollars sending a few thousand volts for a few seconds through prisoners' frames. Have no fear, they'll experience their own punishment of a kind over there, in Moscow, if not confined to indefinite 'residence' in Lubyanka, itself. The Politburo hierarchy forever refrain from publicising the fact that their field operatives can possibly be guilty of failing in their missions.' He looked at Frank to beam a broad smile of satisfaction.

Frank nodded a slow surrendered acceptance to all this, ambling slowly over to Marley's desk. He looked down at the pile of folders fighting for space in the wire **IN**-basket. 'What's this?'

'There's a lot needs going through. Do you think you can handle it, Frank? You look exhausted, which I can imagine you are. Take a few days off. Come back when you're ready.'

'Is that the best you can offer me?'

'If you mean is that an apology, it's the best you're going to get; so, take it or leave it, Frank. It's what the job entails. It's what every damn thing we do in this job is about. It's what we're paid for, thanks to public Joe taking dollars from his pocket and putting them into the Revenue guys' pockets – so we can serve our country, happily and gloriously for ever after, and all that baloney, amen.' Marley stood to attention to give a mocking military salute.

He sat back against the edge of his desk, passing a hand over a tired face. 'Alas, Moscow had somehow sensed our last-minute awareness of Nafur-Nafiri's devious intended plans, so giving him time to flee our clutches.' Marley put both hands to his face in exasperation. 'Which he has done, for *good,* all dead and gone!'

'Let's leave it there,' said Frank, looking down to focus his concern on the mountain of folders. 'Fill me in on these. What's been happening in my absence?'

'In your absence?' Marley sighed. 'Well, if we didn't know better, it's almost as if we're seeing double, with things reverting to almost what we had earlier. It seems we've got a repeated show of Soviet force, their aim being, as ever, to extend their control over German territory. So, as before, we have British, French, and of course, our own troops standing on alert, reinforcing our already established checkpoints at the border crossings, with extensive doubled patrolling along the constructed barriers. We've also put out additional infantry, taking in the French and British contingencies, at the checkpoints along the border.'

'What about reinforcement of armoured divisions?'

'Three more tank units. In addition, we're moving in two companies of the 3rd Battle Group, 5th Infantry as vanguard front, with three other companies standing by in reserve at Tempelhof Airport. Our patrols are running three times over twenty-four hours, with a mobile backup of two rifle platoons mounted in armoured personnel carriers, along with a light section of tanks surrounding the airport.'

'It would appear that the crazy flare-up that we witnessed on screens, here in Washinton, did have did have its good points, after all. It gives us fair warning and puts us on our guard; something we can never overdo. The point is, what's Nixon meaning to do about general developments in that field? Better still, what's Secretary Kissinger proposing to pull out of the magic hat? Whatever it is, I reckon it will be one to exhilarate the warmongering 'Hawks', and scare the pants off the faint-hearted 'Doves' on Capitol Hill.'

Goodblood paused to pinch his nose between finger and thumb in a moment's thought over what was clearly bugging him in its needing to be put forth as best in a mouthful. Old McNairan has, in fact, been colluding with his pal, the Supreme Allied Commander in Europe, General Nevell, to join him in lobbying the government for even greater US military in Europe. Never mind our Seventh Army in Europe being the best ever peacetime force our country has fielded in dedication and commitment with Allied NATO forces; the time has come for dropping the 'soft glove', with its guise as merely training exercises, and show ourselves as an aggressive force, when threatened, with a louder growl and fierce claw than any Russian bear dares muster. He's also calling for the joint Chiefs to send out further naval and air forces where they can contribute their readiness, along with the Seventh Army to position their exercises in appropriate locations that would enable units to move rapidly into alertness when necessary. In all, an increase in US military strength in the European field in order to maintain peace as a better alternative, the *only* alternative, to us having to engage in nuclear war.'

'He's not asking for much, is he?'

'His words, not mine.'

'Whoever's precise words originally, however translated, it still makes for a big bag, with more 'tricks' than 'treats' in it.'

Marley turned round to face the desk, patting the folders. 'And it's all in here. Do you think you can handle it, Frank?'

Sitting down in the seat, Frank lifted up and opened the top folder. 'This looks as good as any a place to start.'

'In that case, I'll leave you to it. See and work hard on those, Frank.'

Frank looked at his watch and suddenly stood up. 'In second thought, I'll take up your offer, and do them, starting either tomorrow, or the day after.' He turned towards the door. 'I've got something else important to see to.'

Marley's curiosity perked up. 'Oh, yeah? What importance is that, I don't know of?'

Frank gave a conspiratorial two-fingered tap to his nose: '*Ahah* – That would be telling.'

Pulling open the heavy oak, iron-studded door, Frank entered the soft stillness of the basilica, with its long hall and pillars, and stained-glass windows. He stood in the centre of the main aisle to look around for a moment at the church's peaceful dark interior. He felt the reassurance from the pew's hard wood, as he put a hand on it, genuflecting, before kneeling down on the well-worn wooden knee-rest. So different from kneeling down for cover from bullets.

A fluttering sound made him look up. No, it wasn't an angel come to collect him. Its wings beating the air feverishly, the little bird hovered to-and-fro, in desperate attempt to escape the curved stone entrapment of the ribbed vault roof. Trapped, just like him. The thought made his mind jump. Why on earth did he make that association? But he couldn't kid himself. He conceded to the fact that he had been having his own little 'flutterings' concerning the wedding. Most people would have said straight away that it was a plain case of the old 'cold feet' syndrome. But he didn't think it was that. True, he had been having uneasy emotional tremors of hesitance – even uncertainty – over the idea of tying the matrimonial knot with Jocelyn. That admission embarrassed him for a second. He wasn't sure what was bothering him.

Shifting off his knees, he sat back on the oaken seat to marshal his thoughts. A lot of guys married their dames. He rubbed his cheek slowly at the thought that he was only getting married because of the baby, as yet to join this crazy world. Was this what was niggling him?

Or was he just being stupid with nerves? Heck! He thumped a hand down on the pew in front to shake off his morbid mood. A small greying head, over by the pillar, turned round to see what the noise was. Frank tried to crack an apologetic smile at her, but the old lady turned away. His need to quell a rising frustration had him reaching into his pocket for a cigarette. On second thoughts, better not to – not here, under the Chief's roof. This had him looking over to the empty confessional, its dark red entrance curtain drawn back, in open invitation. That was another thing he would have to see to, before the big day.

He saw them just a moment before their voices reached him, loudened with the opening of the vestry door. Jocelyn and the priest in his flapping black cassock. It wasn't Father O'Reilly that he'd introduced her to. This one was smaller, with balding head and round bespectacled face befitting the Pickwickian image. And just as merrily loquacious, it seemed. He was doing all the talking, while she listened on in that 'obedient' mindful manner of hers that pleased generals and juniors alike. As they approached, Frank got up and went to meet them halfway up the aisle.

Smiles flashed from one to the other. Whilst Father O'Reilly would still be the celebrant for the Mass and wedding ceremony, urgent parochial matters were unavoidably demanding his presence elsewhere at this hour. So, this priest, Father Trelawney, had kindly consented to step in and help the loving couple through the rehearsal ceremony.

As they talked, Frank got the impression that Jocelyn was using the conversation to keep a distance from him, taking cover behind the semi-formal flow of words. She barely spared a glance to look him straight in the eye. But when she did, it wasn't *her* looking at him. Not the warm loving woman that he held deep feelings for. His growing uneasiness was not helped by the 'jingly' nerves state he was experiencing over the wedding virtually rushing in on them. He wondered if she was having similar cold mood changes in herself. Unfamiliar moments of awkwardness between them grew into minutes, until rescue came with the timely interruption of silence suddenly upon them. All that needed to be said, had been said.

Putting her hand in his, she put her other hand on his shoulder. 'Are you all right? You seem to have been a little –' she hesitated for a moment to find a way of saying it ' – a little bit far away out of the picture, the last few days.' She wondered if she should say what she wanted, or *didn't* want to say. But she went on. 'Are you perhaps thinking that maybe we're doing all this in too much of a rush, with all the arrangements getting you down?' There, she'd said it, and caution be damned. Oops, sorry, not in a church.

But she deeply wished that she had not said that last part. It confirmed her dreaded suspicions on how he had been behaving recently over their coming wedding. She couldn't help feeling that he was cooling over the idea of them getting married, and had sensed his slowing down, if not stepping back completely from it all. This had touched her coldly inside, just like it had been making her feel distanced from him over the last week. But whenever he put a firm hand on her, with his eyes and breath so close to her, it fired her inside with a great surge of determination. She wasn't going to let him slip away that easy.

Pulling on a great reserve of inner strength, she forced a warm smile into her face. 'Mummy couldn't possibly have imagined her daughter being married in a holy place like this.' Her short nervous laugh betrayed her uneasiness over the statement.

'Quite,' said Frank bluntly, not knowing how to follow on from that without risking contradicting something somewhere, in all that.

'Shall we proceed with it?' said Father Trelawney, smiling warmly at them, and turning to walk away down the aisle, towards the altar.

Jocelyn followed after him, then stopped, to look back at Frank who was still standing stock still. 'Frank, are you coming? We don't want to keep Father Trelawny waiting.'

But Frank didn't appear to be heeding her anxious words – his attention far away.

'Frank, are you coming? Please don't tell me you're getting 'cold feet'. Please don't tell me that you're having second thoughts about marrying me.'

But Frank's mind was deeply preoccupied, far away, elsewhere. His memory flashed back to that time earlier, in Syria's Sinai. Desert, where some guy had tried to steal his identity, passing himself off as a second Frank Falzoni. What cheating card from the bottom of the deck had the crazy guy been intending to deal, and to what end?

Two possibilities flipped up, over and over, like a coin tossed in Frank's mind:

On one side, he could be taking on the bitterness of a mother-in-law's viper tongue ---- on the other side, looking into this new crazy game that had just popped up for his attention, all things considered, you had to see it truly as being a real spikey monkey-puzzle of an *incubus extraordinaire*.